Praise fo

"Harbison's latest is a ca[...] charm.... An engaging n[...]"

—*Romantic Times*

"A fun, chick-lit romp about four women with the same shoe size and passion for footwear."

—*The Orange County Register*

"More fun than a pair of Manolos, more exciting than some Prada platforms!"

—Molly Jong-Fast, author of *Girl [Maladjusted]*

"Start to finish—or heel to toe, as the case may be—*Shoe Addicts Anonymous* is an entertaining read."

—*Memphis Flyer*

"I love women's friendship novels—especially ones where nobody dies! *Shoe Addicts Anonymous* is uplifting and funny. A real page-turner. I guarantee you'll be rooting for these four women."

—Susan Elizabeth Phillips, author of *Natural Born Charmer*

"A group of women with one common habit, spending a fortune on shoes...Great book!"

—*Wisconsin State Journal*

"Shoe lust brings four very different women together in this funny, poignant, and unforgettable novel. I'd love to come to the next meeting."

—Celia Rivenbark, author of *Stop Dressing Your Six-Year-Old Like a Skank*

"I was hooked from the first page and read it in one sitting—I couldn't put it down...*Shoe Addicts Anonymous* was a pleasure from start to finish."

—Marian Keyes, bestselling author of *Anybody Out There?*

Shoe Addicts Anonymous

Beth Harbison

 ST. MARTIN'S GRIFFIN ✖ NEW YORK

This is a work of fiction. All of the characters, organizations, and events portrayed in this novel are either products of the author's imagination or are used fictitiously.

www.stmartins.com

Design by Kathryn Parise

Library of Congress Cataloging-in-Publication Data

Harbison, Elizabeth M.
    Shoe addicts anonymous / Beth Harbison.
        p. cm.
    ISBN-13: 978-0-312-34823-6
    ISBN-10: 0-312-34823-1
    1. Female friendship—Fiction. 2. Shoes—Fiction. I. Title.

PS3558.A564 S56 2007
813'.54—dc22

                                                                2007010081

First St. Martin's Griffin Edition: May 2008

10 9 8 7 6 5 4 3 2 1

To my mother, Connie Atkins,
and her partner-in-shopping, Ginny Russell—
the original Shoe Addicts in my life.
They're probably in a shoe store right now!

*

And to Jen Enderlin, my editor and friend.

Acknowledgments

Writing is a solitary experience, but living, if you're lucky, is not. I'd like to thank some of the friends who have made me laugh, saved my sanity, and inspired the friendships in this book: my sisters, Jacquelyn and Elaine McShulskis; the friends who have been there almost as long as my sisters, Jordana Carmel and Nicki Singer; my neighbors and pals who saved me time and again, either by taking the kids or pouring the drinks (or both), Amy Sears and Carolyn Clemens; and the generous souls who have read, re-read, advised, and commiserated—often over snack food—through many years and many books, Elaine Fox, Annie Jones, Marsha Nuccio, Mary Blayney, Meg Ruley, and Annelise Robey.

Chapter 1

S ex in a box. That's what it was. Spine-tingling, heart-stopping, decadent sex in a box.

Lorna Rafferty pushed the tissue aside, and the heady smell of leather filled her nostrils, sending a familiar tingle straight through her core. The feeling—this *thrill*—never got old, no matter how many times she went through the ritual.

She touched the tightly stitched leather and smiled. She couldn't help it. This was wicked pleasure at its sensuous, tactile, hedonistic best. It made her skin prickle from head to toe.

She ran her fingertips along the smooth surface, skidding over the graceful arch, like a cat stretching under the midday sun; she smiled at the sharp but satisfying prick of the spike. Yes. Yesss.

This was hot.

She knew it was wrong, of course. Twelve years in Catholic school hadn't been for nothing: she'd pay the price for this indulgence later.

Well, hell, she'd been planning on that for *years*.

That debt was going to have to get in line with a lot of others.

In the meantime, Lorna had these peep-toe ankle-strap Delman platform sandals to comfort her. She could walk right into the fires of hell if she had to, in shoes to die for.

One of the only things she could remember about her mother was her shoes. Black-and-white spectators. Little pink sandals with kitten heels. And Lorna's favorites: long, slim satin shoes, with heels like narrow art deco commas, and tiny bows at the toe that were frayed slightly at the end from the years since her wedding.

If she closed her eyes, Lorna could still picture her own small feet shoved into the toes of those shoes, the heels clapping treacherously behind her as she traipsed across a faded Oriental carpet in her parents' bedroom toward the fading blur of golden hair and big smile and the waft of Caron's Fleurs de Rocaille perfume that was her memory of her mother.

Of all the things she knew or remembered about her mother, and all the things she *didn't* remember, Lorna knew one thing for sure: clearly the love of shoes was hereditary.

She took the Delmans out of the box slowly, mentally shoving away the memory of handing over her credit card and waiting—like a gambler who'd bet it all on red—for the yes or no from that faraway Credit Card Roulette Approval Commission.

This time it was yes.

She'd signed the slip, promising (to herself), *Yes, of course I'll pay for these shoes! No problem! My next paycheck will go to these shoes),* while assuming an expression of one who pays their entire balance with every statement and whose entire life couldn't be repossessed by Visa at a moment's notice.

Pfffft.

She'd ignored the other voice: *I shouldn't be doing this, and I will make a promise, here and now, to God or anyone else that if this charge goes through, I will never ever spend money I don't have again.*

Best not to think about the repercussions.

If pushing away uncomfortable thoughts about money burned calories, Lorna would have been a size 2.

She admired the shoes in her hands for a few minutes, then put them on.

Ahhh.

Magic.

Pleasure that, treated properly, would last a lifetime. Pleasure she'd *always* be ready and in the mood for.

So what if she'd had to charge them? By her next paycheck, she'd be able to throw some money at her debt. Within—what—a couple of years, maybe three, possibly four at the *most*—and that was assuming she wasn't all that strict with her spending—the debt would be gone completely.

And these Delmans would be as awesome then as they were right now. And probably worth twice as much. Maybe even more. They were classic. Timeless.

A good investment.

No sooner had Lorna had that thought, sitting in the living room–dining room of her small Bethesda, Maryland, apartment, than the lights went off.

Her first thought was that the electric company had turned off her power. But no . . . she'd paid the bill recently enough. Had she missed a thunderstorm somehow? Summers in the D.C. area were notoriously hot and muggy, and this early August day was no exception. Citizens like her paid monthly for electricity that occasionally—in the worst of summer—went off for *hours,* sometimes even more than a day.

She got up from the sofa and tottered in her Delmans over to the phone on the hall table. She called the power company, fully expecting to be told everyone had overtaxed the power grid by cranking their AC, and that the power would be back on soon. Maybe she'd go to the mall and kill an hour or two in the cool air there before work, she thought idly, dialing the number on the old pink princess phone she'd whispered secrets into since she was twelve years old.

Ten minutes and perhaps fourteen automated-system touch tones later, a power company representative—who had identified herself as Mrs. Sinclair, no first name—gave Lorna the response she had, deep down, been dreading.

"Ma'am, your power was shut off due to nonpayment."

Okay, first of all, that *ma'am* was totally condescending. And second—nonpayment? That wasn't possible. Wasn't it just a couple of weeks ago that she'd had a couple of really good tip nights and had come home and paid a bunch of bills? When *was* that? Like mid-July? Early July? It was definitely after the Fourth.

Or, wait, maybe it was just after Memorial Day. One of those cookout holidays. She'd worn those adorable pink Gucci sandals.

She looked dubiously at the pile of mail on the table by the door—it added up so quickly—and asked, archly, "What do you show as the last payment received?"

"April twenty-eighth."

Her mind ticked back like the calendar at the opening of a bad 1930s movie. Okay, she'd gotten that July windfall, but maybe she hadn't paid the electric bill that time. Maybe she'd paid it the time before, which was, what, maybe June? Could it *possibly* have been back as far as May?

Surely not *April*! No! No way. She was sure there was a mistake. "That's impossible! I—"

"We sent another notice on May fifteenth, and on June fifth," Mrs. Sinclair's voice rang with disapproval, "and on July ninth, we sent a cutoff notice, warning you that if we did not receive your payment by today, your power would be shut off."

Okay, she did vaguely remember at one point she was all ready to pay her bills when Nordstrom had sent a notice about their half-yearly sale.

That had been a great day. Those two pairs of Bruno Maglis were a *steal.* So comfortable, she could have run a mile in them.

But she'd definitely paid the bill the next month.

Definitely.

Hadn't she?

"Now, wait a minute, let me check my files." Lorna scrambled to her computer and pushed the button to turn it on, waiting a full five seconds or so before realizing that the computer, which held her payment records, ran on the very electricity the snarky woman on the other end of the line was withholding from her. "I'm sure I'd remember if you'd sent a cutoff notice."

"Mm-hm."

It was easy to picture Mrs. Sinclair as a nasty little troll sitting under a bridge, with a pinched face and curly hair. *You want electricity? You're gonna have to get past me first. So riddle me this: When was the last time you paid your utility bills?*

Lorna gave an exasperated sigh and reached for her wallet. She'd been here before. "Okay, forget it, just tell me what it will take to turn it back on. Can I pay over the phone?"

"Yes. It's eight hundred seventeen dollars and twenty-six cents. You can use Visa, MasterCard, or Discover."

It took Lorna a moment to digest that. Mistake. Mistake. It had to be a mistake. "*Eight hundred* dollars?" she echoed stupidly.

"Eight seventeen twenty-six."

"I wasn't even *here* for a week in June." Ocean City. A week of espadrilles and Grecian tie-ups that made her feel like she was vacationing on the Mediterranean. "How could I have used eight hundred dollars' worth of electricity? That can't be right." Something *had* to be wrong here. They had someone else's bill confused with her own. They had to.

Maybe that was the collective bill for her entire floor of the building.

"That includes a one-hundred-and-fifty-dollar reconnect fee, and a two-hundred-and-fifty-dollar deposit, on top of your three-hundred-and-ninety-eight-dollar-and-forty-three-cent bill and finance charges of eighteen dollars and—"

"What's a reconnect fee?" They'd never asked for *that* before.

"The fee for reconnecting your power after it's been turned off."

This was unbelievable. *"Why?"*

"Ms. Rafferty, we had to turn off your power and now turn it back on."

"And that's, what, like a switch or something you have to flip?" She could picture pinched-faced Mrs. Sinclair sitting next to a great big cartoon ON/OFF switch. "You want me to pay a hundred and fifty dollars for that?"

"Ma'am"—there it was again, that ugly condescending tone—"you can do whatever you choose. If you want your power back on, it's going to cost you eight hundred and eighteen dollars and three cents."

"Whoa, wait a minute," Lorna interrupted. "A second ago, you said it was eight seventeen something."

"Our computers just refreshed, and today's interest was just added to your account."

The apartment was getting hot. It was hard to say if it was because the air-conditioning had been turned off or because Lorna was getting so frustrated with Mrs. Sinclair—whom she'd now decided was probably not married and had taken this opportunity to tag *Mrs.* onto her identity despite the fact that she hadn't had sex in years, if ever.

In fact, her name probably wasn't even Sinclair. She probably just used that as a pseudonym so that people wouldn't hunt her down and kill her at home after talking to her on the phone.

"Can I speak with a supervisor?" Lorna asked.

"I can have someone call you back within twenty-four hours, ma'am, but it won't change your bill."

Except for the added interest by the time they got back to her, of course.

Lorna took her Visa out of her wallet. It was practically still warm from the Delman purchase. "Fine." The battle was over. Lorna had lost. Hell, she was losing the entire *war.* "I'm going to use my Visa." Assuming the charge went through.

A split second of satisfaction seemed to crackle over the line from Mrs. Sinclair to Lorna. "And the name, as it appears on the card? . . ."

*

After hanging up with Mrs. Sinclair, Lorna decided to look in the pile of mail by the door, to see if there really was a cutoff notice. Somehow, right up until that moment, she had remained half-convinced that there was a mistake.

There was a mistake, all right. In fact, by the time she'd opened all the envelopes, there was a large, ugly pile of mistakes, all of them hers.

To be honest, Lorna had known for some time that she needed to go through the stuff. The pile had sat there by the door, like a thing on fire, and she had tried to ignore it and the dull ache she felt in the pit of her stomach every time she passed it, or thought about it in the middle of the night when she couldn't sleep. She didn't have the

money to pay the bills, but she always felt like she'd have it soon.
Another paycheck, a good tip night. But her spending was out of control, and she knew it.

She just didn't know how completely out of control it was.

What on earth did she buy with all that money?

And why did she still feel so empty?

She wasn't extravagant. She hardly ever went out, and it wasn't as if
she was sitting around sipping Dom Pérignon all the time. The only
thing she bought that could, conceivably, be considered a *nonnecessity*
were a few shoes here and there. That is, if you could possibly consider
shoes unnecessary.

Sure, once in a while, when she found a really great pair, she'd get
an extra, just in case. Like with the Maglis last summer. But, seriously,
one pair cost a mere fraction of her rent. How did that add up to tens
of thousands of dollars?

Until that moment, she'd kept thinking she'd pay the debt down.
Money would come in, and she'd go through the bills and everything
would be fine. She'd had $250, even $300 tip nights at the restaurant
now and then. August was always slow in the restaurant business, but
as soon as September rolled around, she was sure she'd make a lot.

But looking at the bills, it hit her hard that she was never going to
be able to make enough to get this debt under control. There were late
fees, over-limit fees, finance charges . . . two of her five credit cards
had raised the interest rate to within spitting distance of 30 percent.
Of the $164 minimum payment on one, $162 was pure interest. Even
Lorna knew that paying down the capital at two dollars a month
would take decades.

And that was assuming she didn't *use* the card anymore.

She had a problem.

This was serious, serious debt.

It had begun simply enough, with a Sears charge card the department store had been gracious enough to send her in her first year of college. Having grown up very comfortably in the posh D.C. suburb of Potomac, Maryland, she always assumed that she would not only meet but would *exceed* that upper-middle-class suburban life. That was a *starting* point, not the *high* point of her life.

So when she got the credit card, it just felt *right* to go out and make a few small purchases that she would pay for herself.

Her first purchase had been a red pair of Keds. She'd seen them on the Lucite stand and immediately pictured herself dockside at the Chesapeake Bay with friends, her skin a deep bronze from the sun, her blond hair gleaming like the front of a box of Clairol Hydrience 02 Beach Blonde, her new boyfriend—the son of a wealthy family who owned car dealerships all across the D.C. Metro area—so enamored of her that he would propose and they'd live happily ever after.

At just eleven dollars and ninety-nine cents, plus 5 percent tax and a mere 16 percent interest on the Sears card, those Keds seemed like a good investment. She'd pay them off before the first statement was out.

On the way out of the store, though, she'd seen just a few more things that caught her eye; the new Sony Walkman was a *steal* at ninety-nine dollars, and who could begrudge her buying one little pair of silver earrings—seriously, come on, they were shaped like *flip-flops*. . . .

Unfortunately Lorna was a *little* bit short when it came to paying the bill, and the boyfriend had dumped her a few weeks later, after cheating on her rather spectacularly with her best friend at her own birthday party; she'd spent the summer working miscellaneous temp jobs indoors, so the tan had never materialized; and her hair had grown out to a light brown that was lank and flat from the artificial environment of office buildings, rather than the spun gold she'd pictured blowing fetchingly around her face as she stood on the bow of the boat, sailing comfortably toward happily ever after.

But come fall she met a new man—one who loved salsa dancing. The footwear was magnificent. Stilettos, strappies, the man was a dream come true. It wasn't cheap, but who could put a price on a dream?

Of course the dream ended, and Lorna woke up and finished her college education as a single girl. Which isn't to say there weren't great shoes along the way—she got credit for taking ballet (she didn't make it to toe shoes, but the slippers were fun), jazz (there were full-sole *and* split-sole jazz shoes as well as *boots*), and tap (noisy patent leather!). She was a terrible dancer, but the shoes—the shoes!

So Lorna had marched steadily on toward her future in one pair of appropriate footwear after another, hope springing eternal that she would finally find the Prince Charming that went with the shoe. In turn, Lorna would lead the easy upper-middle-class life she'd grown up with—two or three kids, a golden retriever, a walk-in closet in her bedroom, and no money troubles.

It hadn't worked out that way. Boyfriends came and went. And came and went. And came and went, long beyond the time when people stopped saying, "You're young, you should play the field!" and began saying, "So . . . when are you going to settle down?" When she'd dumped her most recent boyfriend—nice, but dull dull dull George Manning, who was an attorney—her coworker Bess had all but called her stupid, saying, "He may be boring, but he wears Brooks Brothers and pays the bills!"

But that wasn't enough for Lorna. She couldn't stay with the wrong guy just because he offered financial security, no matter how tempting that financial security was. So she'd lived as if some answer—some miracle that would wipe her slate clean—was going to turn up around the next corner. The solution was always coming right up, in her mind.

Therefore, Lorna hadn't done nearly so much as she should have to find her own solutions and stop her spending problems before they got out of control. Like the gambler who kept doubling the bet with the idea that the big payoff *had* to come, statistically, Lorna kept doubling her troubles until finally, now, she realized she was holding a losing hand no matter what she did.

She was in a very real crisis. If she didn't change something, and quick, she was going to go broke.

Not just *I can't buy these strappy sandals* broke, and not even *beans and rice for dinner for the next few months* broke, but honest to God, *corrugated cardboard is warmer in subzero temperatures than plywood, so hang out behind Sears and get a refrigerator box before all the good ones are gone* broke.

She had to do something.

Fast.

Chapter 2

"So you're taking birth control pills and letting him think you're trying to get pregnant?"

Helene Zaharis snapped to attention. The question wasn't directed at her, but it could just as well have been. In fact, it was so completely accurate that for a moment she wondered if someone had figured her out and sat down at her table to blackmail her.

But no, the conversation was between two twenty-somethings at the table next to hers at Café Rouge, where Helene was meeting Senator Cabot's wife, Nancy, for lunch.

Nancy was late, which was fortunate, since Helene found the conversation next to her far more interesting than the conversation Helene and Nancy would invariably have about who was going to the point-to-point races in Middleburg in October and what political figure was the latest to propose what preposterous tax cut.

Or tax hike.

Or whatever other hot button was lately of interest to those inside the Beltway.

None of it was of much interest to Helene.

"It's not exactly like suffering." The woman who was evidently on the pill giggled and sipped a pink drink. "He just has to try a little harder . . . and a little longer."

Her friend smiled, like she loved being in on this particularly delicious secret. "Then you're going to stop taking the pills?"

"Eventually. When I'm ready."

The second woman shook her head, smiling. "You've got some nerve, girl. You just better hope he doesn't find the pills in the meantime."

"Not a chance."

"Where do you hide them?"

Duct-taped to the back of the drawer of my bedside table, Helene thought.

"In my purse," Pink Drink woman answered with a shrug. "He'd never look there."

Bad move. Rookie mistake. Men respected that particular boundary only until they got a small inkling something was up. Then it was the first place they checked. Even the stupid ones.

If Helene hid anything in her purse, Jim would find it right away. He'd passed that point of courtesy a long time ago.

She shuddered to think what he'd do if he found out she was foiling his attempts at reproduction.

But Helene was firm on this. She didn't want a child. It would absolutely be unfair, primarily to the child, since the only reason Jim wanted a baby was so that he would have the perfect little family to trot around during campaigns.

Camelot 2008.

She'd had baby dreams once. The longing to hold a warm little body, to kiss fat little fingers and fat little toes. To make peanut butter–and–jelly sandwiches for lunch every day, and to slip a little *I love you* into the bag.

Oh, yes, Helene had had baby dreams once. And family dreams. And a whole lot of other dreams that had been churned up and spit out as waste in the Washington Political Machine.

She didn't ever want to bring an innocent child into this now.

"Can I get you something to drink, at least?" the young waitress asked. She had the nervous twitch of someone starting a job and wanting to do it right, yet having no idea what that meant. Helene recognized that. Fifteen years ago, that had been her.

"No, I'm fine, thanks. I'll just wait for my—"

"Miss!" a boozy businessman barked from a couple of tables over. He snapped his fingers, like he was summoning a dog. "How many times do I have to ask for an Irish coffee before you bring the god-damn thing to me?"

The waitress looked uncertainly from Helene to the man and back again, tears forming in her eyes.

"I'm sorry, sir, I've been checking, but it isn't done yet."

"Quality takes time," Helene said, with her most charming smile. The jerk didn't deserve any indulgence at all, but if someone didn't run interference, he was going to have this poor girl's job. "And a *lot* of us are putting in bar orders today. It's not her fault."

As predicted, the man laughed, revealing ugly yellow teeth. Helene would have bet her last dollar he was a cigar smoker. "You are one hot number. Let me buy you a round."

Helene smiled again, as if she were absolutely *delighted* to have this hunk of manhood's attention. "One more, and I won't be able to drive home," she lied. "This nice girl has run back and forth to the bar so many times, she must be getting dizzy." To the waitress she added, "I don't need anything now. Thanks."

The girl looked confused but profoundly grateful as she turned to go.

"Hey, how about you and me get together later," the man started to suggest, but he was interrupted by the arrival of Helene's lunch companion.

"Helene, dear, I'm so sorry I'm late. I had *such* a time getting through Georgetown this morning."

Helene stood, and Nancy Cabot kissed the air on either side of her cheeks, wafting the heavy old-fashioned scent of Shalimar as she moved. She glanced at the yellow-toothed man, who must have recognized Nancy because he grimaced and winked at Helene.

"It's not a problem at all," Helene said to Nancy. They both sat down. "I've just been sitting here, enjoying the atmosphere."

"It is a lovely spot, isn't it?" Nancy gazed out the window, where the Washington Monument was visible in the distance, under a pale blue sky.

For a moment, Helene thought Nancy might be on the verge of saying something philosophical about the majesty of the city, so fixed was her gaze into the distance.

Not the case. "I just wish we could clear out the dilapidated old buildings over there." She pointed south, indicating what was admittedly a slum, but one that the residents were working hard to improve.

"Give them time," Helene said, treading lightly so as not to show how deeply she cared, lest it clash with her husband's proposed policy this week. "The urban improvement program is going extremely well."

Nancy laughed, clearly thinking Helene was being sarcastic. And that it was amusing. "By the way, I've been meaning to tell you. I think we've *finally* found the right venue for the DAR fund-raiser."

"Oh?" Helene tried to arrange her features into a look of interest,

rather than the sleepy detachment she felt. She was no more interested in the DAR than Nancy was interested in urban renewal. The
difference was, Helene was obliged to feign interest, though she would
have loved to come out with a great, hearty laugh as Nancy just had.
"What do you have in mind?"

"The Hutchinson House in Georgetown. Do you know the place?
On the corner of Galway and M."

"Oh, yes, that's beautiful." She didn't know the house, but she knew
that if she confessed her ignorance, she was in for a long lecture on the
history of the Hutchinson House, the furniture in the Hutchinson
House, the people who had been to the Hutchinson House, and, of
course, the cost of the Hutchinson House. Frankly, Helene wasn't sure
how long she'd be able to keep the polite stillness in her expression.

"Now, about the silent auction," Nancy began, but they were interrupted by the arrival of the waitress.

"I'll have a Manhattan," Nancy said, then raised her eyebrows to
Helene in a way that indicated she did *not* plan to drink alone.

"Champagne cocktail," Helene said, thinking it was the last thing
in the world she wanted right now. "And a glass of water," she added,
with good intentions to concentrate on the water and not the champagne. "Thank you."

A busboy passed their table, and his wide-eyed gaze lingered on
Helene for just a moment.

"The men do notice you," Nancy commented in a voice that was
distinctly disapproving.

For a moment, the quiet sounds of silverware against china and
hushed voices murmuring the latest gossip from inside the Beltway
filled the air and seemed to become louder.

"I ordered champagne," Helene said lightly. "That always makes
people wonder what the celebration is. That's all they're noticing."

That seemed to please Nancy well enough. "Back to what we were saying. The celebration is for finding the perfect place to hold the fund-raiser. Now. Let's talk about your part in it, shall we?"

Helene was not in the mood for this. She had always hated this kind of conversation, all about a cause she didn't support and how she could lend a hand to help it. But she had no choice but to do her best, to offer the most she could, and to bring no shame or negativity down on the Zaharis name.

Sometimes that made her hate it even more.

When the waitress brought their drinks, Helene lifted hers in a toast with Nancy to the current president of the DAR—a toadlike woman who had once told several people that Helene was "once a shopgirl, so always a shopgirl"—and took what she intended to be her only sip.

After twenty minutes of Nancy's subsequent soliloquy on past DAR presidents, Helene gave in and finished the cocktail.

Why not? It gave her something to do other than nod stupidly at Nancy and pipe false laughter at her tedious jokes.

It was surprising how often Helene had these conversations, given how deeply uncomfortable they made her. Even more surprising was how oblivious everyone seemed to be to her boredom. Nevertheless, small talk was a huge part of her life, and as Jim continued on his path toward higher and higher political offices, it looked as if there was no end in sight.

So Helene accepted this lot in her life as peacefully as she could. People in Jim's circle ran on their own self-interest. It was very rare to meet one—no matter what age, sex, race, or sexual persuasion—who wouldn't run over their own grandmother in cleats to get to their goals.

Anyone who said Helene wasn't paying the price for the housewife deal she'd made was crazy.

Nancy continued talking.

Helene continued smiling and signaled the waitress for another champagne cocktail.

*

Later there would be hell to pay for turning off her cell phone.

Helene leaned back against the stiff faux-leather chair in the shoe department of Ormond's—her reward for her two-hour audience with Nancy Cabot—and turned the thought of her husband's anger over in her mind, like a piece of jewelry she was considering buying.

He hated it when he couldn't get in touch with her.

She, on the other hand, had grown to hate it when he could. And he did, more and more lately. No matter where she was or what she was doing, it seemed her phone would ring at the worst possible moment.

When she was dropping off canned foods at the Greek Orthodox church for the community food drive, she'd paused for a moment to admire the peaceful beauty that was the new stained-glass window, with a round icon depicting the Annunciation, and her phone had rung.

When she was balancing four paper bags of organic foods—all Jim would eat these days, though it would probably give way to the next newest trend soon—along with her purse and keys, while struggling up the long brick walk from her driveway to the front door, her phone had rung, but it was set on vibrate, so the unexpected vibration startled her so much, she dropped the bag with the eggs in it.

When she was taking homemade chicken noodle soup to the bedridden at the Holy Transformation Home, she'd been passing a just-microwaved bowl of hot soup to an elderly patient with diabetes when her phone had rung, startling her into spilling hot broth on both the patient and, less important though still aggravating, her Bally pumps.

Even today he'd called during her lunch with Nancy, turning one pointless lunch conversation into two, by telling her that he was having a late meeting and wouldn't be home until well after dinner, and that she should just go ahead and make do without him.

Nancy thought—and said repeatedly—that he was *a dear* for calling, but then again, Nancy didn't speak Jim's language. She didn't know "late meeting" was code for coming home smelling of someone else's perfume and dirty martinis.

The hypocrisy was worthy of psychological study.

Jim Zaharis (real first name Demetrius, but he'd decided it was too ethnic for American politics) was the charismatic junior senator from Maryland, but he was preparing for an aggressive sprint toward higher office. In a town like Washington, everything a public figure—and his wife—did was fair game, and he did *not* want Helene embarrassing him.

Yet, like many brilliant but stupid men before him, he believed his own indiscretions to be invisible, while at the same time he was very concerned about what Helene was doing while she was out in public.

She'd never, *ever* done anything that even *hinted* at scandal since she'd been married to him. No pool boys, no lesbian affairs, no insider trading . . . nothing.

Which was not to say she didn't have secrets. But at least she kept hers buried.

Meanwhile, she'd made a deal when she'd married him, though she'd been too naïve to see it at the time. It wasn't the housewife deal; it was worse. It was the Trophy Wife Deal, wherein she was required to look good; perform the occasional high-profile good deed; occasionally join the Ladies Who Lunch at the country club; take up a local charity as sponsor; and, most important of all, keep quiet while little pieces of her soul disintegrated.

Helene had grown alarmingly good at all those things.

"Helene!"

She was yanked out of her reverie by a bright, cheerful voice. She turned to see Suzy Howell, the county councilwoman, along with her teenage daughter.

"Suzy."

"You remember Lucy, don't you?" Suzy said, gesturing toward the sullen-looking teenager with limp black hair dyed into dullness by too many applications of those edgy hair colors they sold these days.

The girl looked completely out of place in the shoe department of Ormond's, and what's more, she looked like she felt it, too.

"Yes, I do." Helene had forgotten the girl's name and was glad Suzy had mentioned it. "How are you doing, Lucy?"

"I'm o—"

"She's doing marvelously well," Suzy interrupted, flashing her daughter a look that would have been more effective if she hadn't Botoxed the expression out of her face. "As a matter of fact, she's applied to Miami of Ohio. You went there, didn't you?"

Oh, no. This wasn't a conversation Helene wanted to have at all. Especially not now, when she was still tipsy from her lunch with Nancy Cabot.

"I did," Helene said slowly, hoping they couldn't smell the champagne on her breath. Then, because it looked like Suzy and Lucy might know a lot more about the place than she did, she added, "For some of my college education."

"Oh, you didn't complete your degree there?"

"No, I went for my freshman year only. Ages ago."

"Ah." Suzy looked disappointed. "Where *did* you graduate from?"

Helene knew she should have been taking notes on her fabricated history. "Marshall University," she said, because David Price had gone there and she used to visit him enough to know the campus pretty well.

David Price, who was the love of her life until she'd decided she could do better and left him.

She'd certainly gotten what she deserved.

"In West Virginia," Helene finished, hearing the melancholy in her own tone.

"West Virginia!" Suzy looked like Helene had told her she'd gone to school in a third-world country. "My goodness, how did a nice homecoming queen from Ohio end up there?"

Helene smiled, without a smidgen of sincerity. "That's a really good question."

"I don't want to go to West Virginia," Lucy snarked to her mother, without so much as a hint of apology to Helene for potentially insulting her.

That's how people around here were about West Virginia. Stuck in the crazy trap of thinking West Virginia was filled only with toothless rednecks who married their own cousins.

Suzy laughed at her daughter's objection, making it painfully clear that she shared Lucy's dismay at the idea. "Don't worry, darling, you're not going to." She gave Helene an overly bright smile. "Could you write a letter of recommendation for Lucy? For Miami of Ohio, I mean."

"I'd be glad to." What else could she say? Nothing. It was her job to say yes. "But," she thought quickly, "maybe Jim's recommendation would be more meaningful."

A light came into Suzy's eye. "Do you think he'd be willing to do that for us?" Clearly this was what she'd had in mind the entire time. Helene needn't have worried about it at all.

"Oh, I'm sure." Anything to get his name around. He was always signing his name to things he didn't mean.

Their marriage license, for example.

"I'll have his secretary give you a call," Helene promised.

"Thank you so much, Helene." Suzy nudged her daughter's ribs with her elbow. "Right? Isn't that nice of Mrs. Zaharis."

"Thanks," Lucy said dully.

"Any time." Helene gave her most polite smile.

She watched them go, thinking about how her life was full of this kind of artificial interaction these days. People wanted to use her as a connection for clout, but that was okay, because her husband took those opportunities to increase his own clout. And Helene had long, long ago made an agreement with the universe that she'd play the game in order to get the financial peace of mind.

So it worked out for everyone.

Well, everyone except Helene, as it turned out.

Ten years ago, she would never have believed it if someone had told her what her life would become. But it had changed in small, barely perceptible increments until one day she'd woken up to find she was living in some crazy cracked fairy tale.

It was bad, but the alternative—the life she'd lived before Jim—was still horribly clear in her mind.

Maybe it made her weak, but she couldn't think of a price she wouldn't pay to avoid going back. And if Jim knew the truth about that life, there wasn't a price *he* wouldn't pay to avoid it either.

And in turn, Helene could pay any price for anything she wanted. Which was what led her here, to Ormond's shoe department, where she ended up at least three times a week.

The pleasure she got here was fleeting—sometimes it didn't even outlast the drive home with her new boxes and bags—but the initial thrill of acquisition never failed her.

She'd lived too long without it to take it for granted now.

Now, as she sat back waiting for the dark-haired salesman— Louis?—to get the pile of shoes she'd asked for in a size 7½, she wondered if this life was worth it.

There was *definitely* something to be said for being able to buy whatever she wanted, particularly after the years of struggle she'd endured. Now it was easy. And it was a comfort.

She wasn't just buying *stuff*. Even in her current champagne-cocktail-woozy state she understood that.

She was buying herself some good memories.

In a life devoid of emotional warmth, she did what she could to have moments that could be remembered later as pleasant.

As something other than a waste of the time between birth and death.

So many times she'd been taken in by the allure of a certain perfume, a natural body lotion, an outfit that was killer on her, or—most of the time—a pair of shoes that raised her, both literally and figuratively, to exalted heights.

"Excuse me, Ms. Zaharis," a voice interrupted her thoughts.

Louis. Or Luis. Or, hell, maybe she had it totally wrong. Maybe it was Bob.

"Yes?" she asked, careful not to try to address him by any name, since the odds of being wrong were so large.

"I'm afraid your card was declined." He gingerly held her American Express card toward her as if he were holding a dead spider he'd found on his Caesar salad.

Declined? That wasn't possible. "There must be a mistake," she said. "Try it again."

"I ran it three times, ma'am." He smiled, apparently apologetically, and she noticed that one tooth toward the back of his mouth was a distinct dark gray. "The charge isn't going through."

"A six-hundred-dollar charge?" she asked in disbelief. The card didn't even have a limit!

He confirmed with a nod. "Perhaps the card was reported lost and you aren't using the replacement?"

"No." She reached into her purse and pulled out her wallet. It was stuffed with ones and fives—an old habit from the days when ones and fives made her feel rich—and credit cards. She pulled out a silver MasterCard and handed it over. "I'll figure it out later. Try this one. It shouldn't be a problem." Her voice rang with a shortness she couldn't remember adopting. As a matter of fact, her voice *often* rang with that impatient air, and she wasn't sure why, though the uncomfortable theory that it reflected more her own unhappiness, as opposed to a real dissatisfaction with *service,* did occur to her.

The dark-haired salesman—why didn't they wear name tags here?—eagerly strutted off with her platinum credit card, and Helene leaned back, confident that he would be back in a moment with a small slip for her to sign and then she could leave with her purchases.

Or rather her *prey,* as her therapist, Dr. Dana Kolobner, laughingly referred to it.

It *did* feel like prey. She'd acknowledge that. She sought it out to satisfy an appetite. Then, a few hours later, the satisfaction ebbed, and she needed more. Well . . . no. *Needed* was an overstatement. Helene was realistic enough to know this was all about *desire* not *need.*

Sometimes she thought she might eventually chuck it all, go off and join the Peace Corps. But maybe at thirty-eight she was too old. Maybe that was yet another opportunity that had slipped past her while she wasted years of her life with a man who didn't love her.

And whom she didn't love either. Not anymore.

The salesman came back, interrupting her thoughts. But something in his expression had changed. He'd dropped a certain veneer of cordiality. "I'm afraid this one didn't work either," he said, pinching the card between his index and thumb as he handed it back to her.

"This can't be right," she said, a very old but familiar feeling of dread snaking into her stomach. She dug out another card, one that was a rider on Jim's business account. It was for emergencies.

This was clearly an emergency.

Two minutes later the salesman was back again; this time his face communicated a distinct distaste. He handed her the card. . . . It was cut into four perfectly even pieces.

"They instructed me to cut it up," he said curtly.

"*Who* did?"

He shrugged narrow bony shoulders under an ill-fitting suit jacket. "The bank. They said the card was stolen."

"*Stolen!*"

He nodded and arched an overly plucked brow. "That's what they said."

"I think I'd know if my own card was stolen."

"I would think so as well, Mrs. Zaharis. Nevertheless, that is the message that was given to me, and that is the thing I must act upon."

She resented his condescending tone disproportionately, and tried to keep her anger in check. "You could have spoken with me before cutting the card, you know."

He shook his head. "I'm afraid not. They instructed me to dispose of the card on the spot, or else the store would be penalized."

Bullshit. She was absolutely sure he'd taken pleasure in cutting up the card, and especially in giving her the pieces. She'd known his type before.

She shot him a withering look and took her cell phone out of her purse. "Excuse me, please. I need to make a call."

"Of course."

She watched him walk away, fearing he would simply count to five and come back to hover over her again, flinging judgment at her. But as he got closer to the back, a girl poked her head out the door and said, "Javier's on the phone, Luis. He says you have a leaky pipe."

Luis. Helene made a mental note of the name, so she'd know exactly whom to reference in the scorching letter she planned to write to the store manager.

She took one of the credit cards that had been rejected out of her wallet and called the number on the back, impatiently pushing buttons through menu after menu until she finally got a human being on the line.

"This is Wendy Noelle, how may I help you?"

"I hope you can, Wendy," Helene said in the most gracious tone she could muster, under the circumstances. "For some reason my card was declined at the store today, and I can't figure out why."

"I'd be happy to help you with that, ma'am. May I put you on hold for a moment?"

"All right."

Helene waited, her heart pounding, while the hold music clashed in her head with the department store music.

"Mrs. Zaharis?" The bank representative was back after the first half of a Barry Manilow song had warred with the Muzak version of "Love Will Keep Us Together."

"Yes?"

"That card was reported stolen, ma'am." The girl was nice. She sounded sincerely apologetic. "It's been deactivated."

"But I didn't call in and report it stolen," Helene objected. "And I'm in the store now, but they won't let me use it."

"You can't use it if it's been reported stolen."

Helene shook her head, even though the woman on the phone couldn't see her. "This must be some sort of identity theft." It was the only explanation that made any kind of sense. "Who called it in and reported it stolen?"

"It was a Deme . . . Deme-et-tris—"

"Demetrius?" Helene asked in disbelief.

"Yes, Demeter's Zaharis," the woman fumbled. "He called to report the card was stolen."

"Why?" Helene asked before she could stop herself, even though she knew there wasn't an answer to that question. At least not one that would satisfy her.

"I'm afraid I don't know."

"Is a replacement card being sent overnight?" She was beginning to feel a little panicked. "Can you just authorize my purchase with the new card number?"

"Mr. Zaharis requested that we don't send another card out at this time."

Helene hesitated, dumbfounded. She wanted to object, to say there had been a mistake or that someone impersonating Jim had called and canceled the card, but deep down something told her there was no mistake. Jim had done this to her deliberately.

She thanked the woman, hung up the phone, and immediately dialed Jim's private line.

He answered on the fourth ring.

"Why did you call my credit cards in as stolen?"

"Who is this?"

She could picture his smug, laughing face as he taunted her. "Why," she repeated, her voice harder, "did you cancel all of my credit cards?"

She heard his chair squeak as he shifted his weight. "Let me ask you something," he said, his voice drenched with sarcasm. "Do you have anything you want to get off your chest? Maybe something you've been keeping from me?"

Her stomach tightened like a slip knot.

What had he found out?

"What are you getting at, Jim?" Oh, God, there were so many things it could have been.

"Oh, I think you know."

Too many possibilities came to mind. "No, Jim, I cannot think of anything I've done that was so bad it warranted you cutting me off and humiliating me in public. Did you think it would look good for you if your wife was trying to use bad credit cards?"

"Not as good as—oh, I don't know—a *family*."

Silence dropped between them like a Ping-Pong ball, bouncing just out of reach.

Jim was the first to take a swat at it.

"Does that ring any bells?" His chair squeaked again, and she could see him shifting around, agitated now. "I thought we were trying to get pregnant. Turns out we were just"—she could almost see his meant-to-look-casual-but-actually-seething-underneath shrug—"fucking."

She grimaced at the way he spat the word. "You didn't seem to be having such a bad time."

He wasn't so easily distracted from his point. "You lied to me, Helene."

"About what, exactly?"

"As if you don't know."

"You're insane," she said, the best defense being a good—or at least a strongly convincing—offense.

"I don't think so."

"Then tell me what you're talking about."

She was half-ready to dismiss his accusations as smoke and mirrors when he said, "I found out about the pills."

Guilt and anger coursed through her veins. "What were you doing looking through my bedside table?"

"Bedside table? I had to get a prescription filled at the G Street pharmacy today, and they asked if I was picking up your refill!"

Oh, shit. *Shit shit shit.* She'd tipped her hand. She still could have lied her way out of it, said it was an old prescription or a mistake on the pharmacist's part, but she'd offered too much information. She was caught, and there was no way out of it.

"Wait," she said, too late. "What pills?"

"Birth control pills. You've been getting them for months, so don't even try lying about it."

It was a quandary. Should she take the chance on denying it, or just come right out with the truth? "It was for medical reasons," she said, the lie coming almost as naturally as the truth. "I needed to even out my hormone levels in order to get pregnant."

The laugh of his response was ugly. "If that was the truth, you would have told me before."

"Because you're so warm and friendly and easy to talk to?" she asked, her voice hard.

"You're a liar."

"So you said. And so now you're punishing me."

"You bet I am."

She shuddered at his coldness. How the hell had she ended up married to a man like this?

"For how long?" she asked.

"How long do you think it will take you to get pregnant?"

"Are you *kidding* me? You're going to cut me off financially until

I'm *pregnant*?" She wasn't going to do it. She'd get a job. She wasn't going to ransom a child's future for her own shopping pleasure.

"I'll give you an allowance," Jim said. "For the necessities. Say, a hundred bucks a week."

"A hundred."

"I know, it's generous."

It was about sixty cents an hour for being married to him.

"You're despicable," she said, and flipped her phone shut.

She looked around the store, at the rich and unassuming patrons who milled around, oblivious of the plight she'd endured these past few years, looking comfortable and rich and carefree. Though at least some of them probably shared her uncomfortable situation.

Like that woman over there. Pretty. Too pretty to have been born rich. She'd been bought. She practically had a SKU symbol across her butt. Over the years, Helene had grown quite good at telling the real thing from the fakes. Like herself.

The fakes always had a little shadow of uncertainty across their pretty faces.

Like Helene. Somehow, despite the bank account she shared with Jim, she'd never fully reached that relaxed feeling of carefree spending that so many of the Ormond's patrons seemed to enjoy. There had always been some sort of threat hanging over her head.

The threat of Jim's disapproval.

Well, forget that. She wasn't going to live at his mercy, and prosper at his whim. And she definitely wasn't going to hang at his command.

As if in a dream, she bent down and put her Jimmy Choos into the Bruno Magli box and replaced the lid.

She stood up, feeling as if she were pushing against the force of Jim's disapproval as she made even that one small gesture. Yes, he'd knocked her down. Humiliated her, even, and then let a store clerk give her the news. But he wasn't going to win this round. He wasn't going to pull the leash in on her by cutting off her credit cards.

She took a step, thinking far more about the symbolism of walking out from under Jim's control than the fact that she was still, technically, wearing shoes she hadn't purchased.

But she'd be back, she told herself as she took another step. Ormond's wouldn't notice her leaving; she knew from her own retail experience in the suit department of Garfinkels—where she'd met Jim, incidentally—that the security sensors were at midbody level at the doors because that's where most shoplifters carried their goods.

Helene wasn't a shoplifter, though. She was a regular patron, who had probably contributed tens of thousands of dollars to the Ormond's coffers. Hell, she'd even left a perfectly good pair of Jimmy Choos back where she was trying the Maglis on.

She needed to do this. The Bruno Maglis she had on felt so damn good. And that wasn't true for everyone. Some people found them uncomfortable, but people with the *right* shaped feet loved them. So who wouldn't want to keep walking?

Well, maybe that was stretching it. She wasn't walking because the *shoes* felt good; she was walking because the *escape* felt good.

She'd pay later for the shoes, easily. As soon as she got home and either got her hands on some cash or talked some sense into crazy Jim so he'd release the credit on her cards again, she'd come back, explain that she'd accidentally left in the Maglis, and pay.

No problem.

It wasn't like she was *stealing* them, for heaven's sake. She almost chuckled at the thought. She hadn't stolen anything for thirty years, and even though she'd been good at it then, she wasn't about to pick up the habit again now.

Her heart pumped and she felt the flush in her cheeks. Jim was not going to win this time. It was exhilarating. She should get in her car and go get a bottle of champagne and drink it over at Haines Point, watching the planes take off from Reagan National Airport. Who was it that had taken her on a date to do that all those years ago? Woody? Yes, that was it. He was so cute. He drove a Porsche 914, back when that was cool. She wondered what had ever happened to him. . . .

She was nearly out, she could see the star-dropped twilight above an orange-and-pink horizon, and she could almost *feel* the balmy air on her skin when the security system began to wail.

It tripped her up for a second. It was loud. And were those flashing lights?

Guilt flushed over Helene and stiffened her gait, but she forced herself to keep moving. She kept walking, trying hard to ignore the sound. After all, that was a sound that was ignored—by patrons and employees alike—in most stores countless times per day.

She couldn't ignore the next alarm, though: the footsteps coming up behind her and the male voice at her shoulder saying, "Excuse me, ma'am. We've got a problem. Can you come back in the store with me, please?"

Chapter 3

I'm wearing my red leather stilettos. . . ." Sandra Vanderslice padded across the floor of her Adams Morgan apartment in bare feet, telephone to her ear, and stopped in the kitchen. She opened the refrigerator door very quietly.

"Oooh, baby," the man on the other end of the telephone line said, *"I like you in red. Have you got your little red thong on?"*

Carefully, Sandra took the orange juice out of the fridge and cooed, "Yes, baby, just like you like." She tipped her glass so he couldn't hear her pour. Two ounces. That was all she could have. She filled the glass the rest of the way with water.

"I'm ripping them off of you with my teeth."

Sandra moaned obligingly and screwed the top back on the orange juice bottle. "Oh—oh—oh yes!" Sip. "You're driving me wild!" She headed back to the TV in the living room. "Mmmmm. Yessss."

"Now I'm licking your wet pussy."

"Mmmm."

"Do you like it?"

"Oh, baby, you're so good." She'd said the words so often now, they were automatic. They no longer had meaning. It was just a mantra that she repeated in order to earn herself a dollar and forty-five cents a minute as an operator for A Touch of Class Phone Friends.

Class, indeed.

She moaned again, hoping to sound like she meant it, and sat down on the couch. "Ahhh . . . ahhhh . . ."

She picked up the clicker, hit MUTE, and scrolled through the TV channels until she landed on a repeat of last night's *Daily Show*.

"Perfect," she said, more to herself than to the caller, then proceeded to make more of the obligatory moans and groans her callers liked—and mirrored—so much, while she watched Jon Stewart interview the latest politician to be indicted for fraud, reading the closed-captioning.

"You taste so good," he muttered between what she'd come to think of as "spanker's gasps." *"I could . . . do . . . this all . . . fucking day."*

"Please do," she cooed, thinking of the Pliner boots she'd been eyeing online. A steal at $175. "Keep . . . going . . ." Camel or black? Maybe this guy would go long enough to get both. Nah, it would take almost two hours for him to cover just one pair. None of her callers had that kind of restraint. She'd just keep him going as long as possible and hope for another couple of long calls so she could log off. "Do it . . . do it to me." She panted a little bit, drawing the attention of her Persian cat, Merlin, who jumped onto her lap and spilled the glass of orange juice all over her.

"Shit!" She yelled it before she could think to stop herself.

Fortunately her caller, "Burt," liked that.

"Ooooh, yeah. Talk dirty to me," he grunted. *"Do you want me to eat your pussy some more? Huh? Do you like it like this? I'm sucking your clit."*

Once upon a time, this kind of talk had been seriously disconcerting to Sandra, who had grown up in a family so conservative that the word *damn* was the single worst curse, and it was saved for only the most severe situations.

But now, like her own telephone dialogue, it was just noise. Noise that acted as a means to an end. Rent, food, utilities, and her many, many catalog and online purchases.

It wasn't a bad living.

"Oh!" she cried, pulling her sticky wet shirt off. It was probably the first time she'd ever actually taken an item of clothing off during a call. "Oh! Oooooh!"

"You are so wet!"

"I am," she agreed, balling up the orange juice–soaked T-shirt and trying to dry herself with the small piece of it that was still dry. "I'm sooo wet. And I taste like fruit," she added, just to amuse herself.

"You do."

She sighed.

"Now I'm going to fuck you. I'm going to fuck you hard, bitch."

She rolled her eyes. Big tough guy. He was probably a total mouse in real life. In fact, she imagined he had a domineering wife or, better still, a female boss who thoroughly intimidated him.

So he paid for accolades.

And she provided them. For a price. "Oooh, Burt. You're so big. So hard."

"Say it again."

She did, adding a few elaborations, then set the phone down for a second so she could put something on. She grabbed the only thing handy—a tight size 22 blouse that she'd been meaning to throw away but kept hoping she'd fit into someday—put it on, and cradled the phone in the crook of her neck while she buttoned. Truth was, she wasn't even sure why she bothered with the shirt. She was alone. She was *always* alone. She could probably be naked for thirty-six hours straight and never run into a situation where she *needed* to get dressed.

Except maybe to avoid the prick of Merlin's claws.

The only prick she'd actually felt in . . . Oh, god, it didn't bear thinking about.

Burt reached his crescendo just as she pulled the final button over. It held for a moment, then popped off.

She could have cried.

Instead, though, she'd do what she usually did to make herself feel better in these situations.

She'd shop.

She booted up her computer, offering the occasional moan, groan, or exclamation as her caller's passion reached its death throes. When "Burt" finally finished, he was eager to hang up—he sounded like he was worried he'd get caught, probably by the boss Sandra had envisioned earlier—and she stopped the timer.

Twenty-seven minutes.

It wasn't great, but she'd had cracked-voice young guys who took much less time than that, so it would do.

She looked at the time on her computer screen. It was 12:45. Her appointment wasn't until four, so with any luck, she'd be able to fill the next three hours with calls and order the Pliners before FedEx went out tonight.

Thank goodness her job was so lucrative. Men loved "Penelope"— as she was known to them—and why wouldn't they? The picture she'd provided for her catalog bio was a killer. Penelope had Angelina Jolie's lips, Julia Roberts's nose, Catherine Zeta-Jones's face shape and eyes, mid-'80s Farrah Fawcett hair (tousled, not winged), and Cindy Crawford's 1991 body.

Sandra had put Penelope together with Photoshop herself, adding the small detail of replacing one of Catherine's earlobes with her own. Just so she had one small way to identify with Penelope.

It was fun to be tall, thin, and gorgeous—if only just in her imagination and that of countless lonely, horny men—when Sandra herself had been of average height and well-above-average weight all her life.

The fact that her family was very wealthy and lived in Potomac Falls Estates had never bought Sandra any favors when it came to social acceptance. In elementary school, her physique inspired such nicknames as Sandra Claus and, after an unfortunate experience on a field trip to a farm, Moo.

People also compared her—inevitably and unfavorably—with her older, very attractive sister, Tiffany. Tiffany the cheerleader, the homecoming queen, the average student who was remembered as a star by teachers and administrators alike because of her sparkling smile and outgoing personality.

Where Sandra's hair was the exact bland brown of a field mouse, Tiffany had dark golden blond hair, with subtle natural highlights of everything from strawberry blond to wheat. Sandra's nose was straight and unremarkable, where Tiffany's was the kind of thin, slightly tipped-up button women described to plastic surgeons all the time. Sandra's eyes were deep coffee brown, and Tiffany's? Grassy green. Again, the sort of thing most women could achieve only artificially.

Growing up with her sister had been like being trapped in a "before and after" diet ad, with the imbalance of affection toward Tiffany extending even as far as their parents were concerned. They would have told Sandra she was wrong about that, but she thought there wasn't a clearer eye than that of a teenager longing for attention and seeing it go to her more attractive sibling instead.

Tiffany was pregnant now, and Sandra was crossing her fingers that she'd start to show by the holidays so that, *for once,* Sandra wouldn't have to feel so conspicuously, and singularly, large and round at the family gatherings. Maybe it would even change her relationship with her parents, though she doubted it since the golden child was going to have the platinum baby.

Nevertheless, Sandra had taken this as the perfect opportunity to join Weight Watchers, albeit online. As Tiffany grew larger, Sandra would grow smaller.

That would be a nice change.

She thought of that now as she prepared a Weight Watchers recipe for Sweet Potato Gnocchi with Gorgonzola and Walnuts. It was a delicious dish. The problem was, the serving recommended seemed so small.

Sandra was pretty sure she wasn't the only Weight Watcher to feel that way. Even size 6 (when she wasn't pregnant) Tiffany ate four times as much, without ever putting on an ounce.

The difference was, Sandra was going to have to stick to the portion size, whereas Tiffany would never have to give it a thought.

A long time ago, Sandra had realized that life just wasn't always fair. And if she wanted to lose some weight, or do anything at all, she was going to have to play by life's stupid, cheating, biased, and badly refereed rules.

The phone gave a distinctive double ring.

Another customer.

Sandra grabbed a plastic fork—she kept them on hand for just such occasions, since they were so much quieter than stainless steel against the bowl—and hurried to where she'd left the phone on the counter.

She took a breath, quickly psyched herself into being Penelope, and pushed the TALK button. "This is Penelope," she squeaked. Penelope was like that sometimes. She was so delighted to get a call, she was practically Marilyn Monroe. "What's your name?"

"Hi, Penny," a familiar voice said. "It's Steve. Steve Fritz."

Oh, Steve. She'd told him a hundred times she didn't think he should be giving out his real name to people he didn't know over the phone.

Then again, maybe that *wasn't* his real name.

"Hi, Steve," she said warmly, dropping the sex voice with some re-lief. Steve was a Talker. He wanted sympathy, never sex. She loved it when he called, though sometimes she felt really bad that he was pay-ing two ninety-nine a minute to hand his metaphorical hat and coat to Donna Reed at the end of the day.

"It's been another one of those days," he said on a sigh.

"Oh, I'm sorry, honey," Sandra said, settling into a chair. "What happened?"

She wasn't Penelope on these calls, but she wasn't Sandra either. She was . . . It was hard to say. She was someone not quite motherly, but caring and maternal. Someone confident. Someone who had suc-cessfully navigated the obstacles of life and had come out on the other side, wiser and more serene.

Seriously not Sandra.

"You know how I told you about Dwight? The guy in the mail room who makes stupid comments every time he brings me the video game catalogs?"

"Yes, that jerk." She hated people like that. She'd gone to school with hundreds of them. "What happened?"

"Well." Steve's voice was tight. "I think he put my name on a news-letter for transsexuals."

"Oh, no." Asshole. Unimaginative asshole. Guys like Dwight picked on guys like Steve to make themselves feel better about their Chap-Stick dicks.

She'd probably talked to Dwight herself.

He was probably one of the ones that liked being "spanked" for being "naughty."

Steve wasn't finished. "He made a big production of bringing this newsletter in today. That means I'm going to be on all kinds of weird mailing lists, and Dwight is going to make an announcement every time something arrives."

Poor Steve. She wished she could tell him to take martial arts and kick the guy's miserable ass, but she'd read too many news stories about people ending up dead because of advice like that from people like her. Steve seemed like a nice guy, but it was impossible to get around the fact that there was probably a reason he was calling a sex phone operator instead of a friend. "You've got to tell your boss."

"If I tell my boss, I'll be calling attention to the fact that I'm on the mailing list. What if he doesn't believe Dwight's behind it? It's not like I can *prove* it."

"I know, but if you're really on these lists and dubious mail is coming in for you, your boss is going to hear about it whether you bring it up or not. Better for him to hear it from you, don't you think?"

There was silence. Sandra thought she was probably more aware than Steve of how much those seconds of silence were costing him. But it was against the rules for her to make private contact with her customers and, even though she did it sometimes anyway to save Steve some money, she was worried about getting caught and getting into trouble for it.

"He might not believe me."

"Maybe not, but he's more likely to if he hears it from *you*. Think about it: If you were trying to hide something like this, would you call it to his attention?"

Silence.

"Steve?"

"I guess you're right. . . ."

"So he'll see that."

"I don't know, Penny. He's not that smart."

She sighed. He was working in an office full of Dwights. Permanent junior high school.

It was one of the main reasons she did what she did for a living instead of joining the rest of the Beltway rats in the workplace.

"Steve, have you ever thought about getting another job?"

Another silence. "I've *thought* about it."

"Maybe you should think about it a little harder. There is absolutely no reason you should have to put up with this. You work for a network company, right?"

"We set up computer networks and databases, mostly for large retail and purchasing operations."

She wasn't really sure what that meant, but she knew it was cutting-edge technology stuff. "Then I'll bet your skills are in *demand*. Especially in this town." They'd already established that he lived in D.C. and she was in the area, too, but she didn't tell him exactly where. "Get out there and get yourself in front of the people who are hiring."

"I don't go out much."

"You should," she said emphatically, knowing she was a hypocrite. "It's important. Don't get so stuck in your ways that you can't get out of them. It's all about getting out."

For some. For others, like Sandra, it was all about being a homebody. If she didn't have this job, she'd just have some other job that didn't require much social interaction. That was just the way she was. It always astonished her when her parents told her she was a social butterfly of a child, because as soon as she'd reached grade school— some of her earliest memories—she'd wanted nothing more than to stay home and hide from the other children. She'd preferred reading to playing Red Rover on the playground.

Then again, she'd have preferred chewing on tinfoil to playing Red Rover, so maybe it wasn't that she had a problem being social so much as she had a problem being made fun of.

Sandra couldn't remember a time when she didn't feel self-conscious in the company of other people. Whether it was because of the external taunts of "blubber butt"—and all the other equally unimaginative but alliterative names—when she was at school, or because of her own internal dialogue—not so unkind as her classmates, but nevertheless harsh—when she was with her family, she didn't know.

Some people dealt with their childhood traumas by facing them head-on, bursting through them, and emerging on the other side so completely opposite of how they'd begun that people marveled at the transformation.

Others coped more quietly, functioning normally, if not remarkably, and trying not to think about the problems of the past.

Then there were the ones who got so stuck in the tar that they couldn't quite get it off their shoes. They might *appear* normal, under some circumstances, but there was always a personality glitch. In *extreme* extreme cases—Ted Bundy came to mind—things like serial murder and cannibalism.

But the rest of the extreme cases just had their own private demons to wrestle with; usually no one else got hurt. It may be a fear of dogs (*cynophobia*); fear of public speaking (*glossophobia*); or even a crippling fear of otters (*utraphobia*).

Sandra had no problem with otters.

No, Sandra's fear was of leaving the safety of home.

Agoraphobia.

As a matter of fact, thanks to the wonders of Internet shopping and grocery delivery, she hadn't left home in three months.

Oh, Sandra had issues. Not one of them was too big, too dark, too serious, but add her weight issues, self-consciousness, shyness, and the feeling that her parents preferred her sister all together, and you had one neurotic person who was in real danger of becoming a game show–watching hermit.

She didn't want that.

She knew she had to change.

She just didn't know exactly how to do it.

Chapter 4

Lorna walked through Montgomery Mall with a pair of shoes that—considering only two dollars of her monthly credit card payment went toward the actual principal versus the interest—represented twelve years' worth of payments.

It was ugly.

The mall was cool and festive, carrying the sounds of people talking and Muzak, and the smell of chocolate chip cookies, hamburgers, Boardwalk fries, and Chinese food. Usually the environment gave Lorna a lift, but walking back to the shoe department at Ormond's, she felt like she was carrying a boulder on her back.

She had to return the Delmans.

She had no choice.

"I need to return these," she said when she got to the counter in the shoe department.

It was Luis, the same salesman she'd bought them from—a tall, slight slash of a man with sharp features, small eyes, and dark hair slicked back in the style of a 1940s mobster.

Somehow, he hadn't struck her as quite so menacing when he presented her the Delmans at 30 percent off.

"You just bought them."

"I know that." She gave a *what can you do?* smile. "But I need to return them. They're just not going to work out for me."

"What's wrong with them?"

It was clear that Luis wasn't some teenage Wal-Mart employee who followed procedure without taking anything personally. No, Luis was going to *pursue* this; he was going to get to the bottom of things—probably in the most uncomfortable way possible, excavating all her financial insecurities—before letting Lorna leave with a credit receipt.

Even though his challenging attitude wasn't a surprise—she'd been shopping long enough to recognize someone clinging to his commission when she saw it—it still irked her. What irked her even more, though, was her own feeling of having to make up an explanation for this little weasel that would keep him from judging her.

"They didn't go with the outfit I had in mind for them."

He raised a dark eyebrow, and Lorna got a mental image of him plucking the middle of his unibrow every morning in a magnifying makeup mirror. "They're black leather."

"Yes," she forced herself to swallow further explanations, "they are." *Blue dress*, she thought but didn't say. *Wrong color black. The hardware is silver, and I'll be wearing gold.* A million lame lies came to mind, but she kept her mouth shut. She wasn't going to give him the satisfaction of an elaborate explanation.

With a look of undisguised disgust, Luis held out his hand, and she gave him her receipt and credit card.

Lorna stood and waited, wishing to God this transaction would just *end* so she could get out of the store and never come back. What was with Ormond's anyway? Why did they seem to have only this one salesman in the shoe department? Every single time she came in, she'd hoped for a different salesperson, but 90 percent of the time, it was Luis.

He processed the return, handed Lorna her receipt, and took the shoe box off the counter, flashing her a look that she interpreted as punitive. Maybe it was just the fact that she was bummed about having to give the shoes back that made her extra sensitive, but whatever it was, when she left the store, she felt like she was going to cry.

And she hated herself for feeling that way when there were people in the world with so many more serious problems.

But Lorna wasn't a fool, though her debt certainly appeared to be a testament to the contrary. Now that she knew where she stood, and what a colossal mistake she'd made, she was absolutely *determined* to make it right. She would cut up every credit card, work extra shifts— hell, she'd even eat beans and rice if that was what it took to save money and pay down her credit cards.

The only thing that concerned her, and she knew it was pitiful and shamefully self-indulgent to even *think* it, was how difficult it was going to be to stop buying shoes.

They made her happy.

She wasn't going to apologize for that.

Some people drank, some people used drugs, some people were sex addicts, some people even did truly *heinous* things to *other* people in order to make themselves feel better. Compared with all that, a new pair of Ferragamos here, some Uggs there . . . it just didn't seem that bad.

Now, before long, every pair she had would probably be worn out, and then where would she be?

Shoeless Lorna, too poor to resole her pumps.

When she got home and checked the answering machine, there was a call from a coworker, asking her to cover her shift at the restaurant, Jico, where they both worked that night. Grateful for the opportunity to put her debt-reduction plan into immediate action, she took the shift.

Nine hours later, she was on her last customer, Rick, a blowhard of a guy who'd been sitting at a table near the bar all night without getting anything more than one soda per hour and an order of onion rings. She'd waited on him before. Lots of times, in fact. He came at least once a week and somehow he always ended up in her section. Dumb luck. The guy was a lousy tipper.

Worse than that, he was a talker. Talk talk talk. He wanted to know all about the people at the bar and in the restaurant. She figured he was trying to find himself a date, but he didn't seem to have much luck. No wonder. The guy probably never paid for a date in his life.

And at the moment, Rick was the one thing that stood between Lorna and relaxation, so she was doubly irritated with him. When he finally asked for the check, she was relieved.

"Can I get you anything else?" she asked him, hoping against hope he'd say no.

He did. "Only the check."

She pulled it out of her pocket and set it down, saying, "I'll take that whenever you're ready."

"Hang on, sweetcakes, I'm ready now." He looked at the bill, then opened his wallet and peeled off a ten and a couple of ones. "Keep the change."

She hated getting stiffed, but she'd been raised to be courteous at all costs. "Thanks very much." She put the money in her pocket.

She'd chip away at her debt in tiny increments, if necessary.

Later that night, Lorna sat at the bar with her aching feet up, counting her tips.

"Lousy night?" Boomer, the bartender, asked, eyeing her. He was a big man, about six-five, with a craggy face, but the sort of watery blue eyes that always looked sympathetic. The rumor was that he'd been drafted by the Redskins a few decades back, but had been injured in training camp and so had been working in various bars ever since.

Lorna didn't know if that was true, because Boomer never talked about himself or his past, but, given his size, she could believe it.

"Let's see," she said, tapping the short stack of bills on the bar top. "The table full of Heathers who ogled the musicians all night and sucked down three hundred bucks' worth of Bellinis left five bucks, and that son of a bitch Earl Joffrey"—Earl Joffrey was a local newscaster with a reputation at Jico for being the worst tipper ever—"literally left the coins from his change. Seventy-six cents."

"Did you give him his change in ones?" Boomer asked, hauling a rack of mugs to the sink. "If you change him big bills instead of small ones, he gets pissed."

"I know that. I gave him *seventeen* ones."

Boomer drained a half-empty beer bottle and tossed it into the recycling bin with a clang. "And seventy-six cents."

She gave a dry laugh. "Yeah, and seventy-six cents. The cheap jerk. Don't watch Channel Six news."

"Never do."

"Me neither." Tod, one of Lorna's coworkers, stopped and set a check down on the bar top. "Last one of the night. Thirty-four percent tip. I saw Earl Joffrey coming, and I just prayed he wouldn't sit in my section." He gave Lorna an affectionate nudge. "Sorry, baby."

She rolled her eyes and put an arm around his rock star–thin waist. "You are not."

"No, I'm not." He gave her a squeeze. "Because *I* have got a date to-night."

"Now? It's so late!"

"Not for all of us, Mom." Tod gave a laugh.

She remembered feeling that way about dates. It seemed like a hundred years ago.

"I met the most amazing guy," Tod went on. "We're meeting at Stetson's at one-thirty. Then . . . who knows?"

"*I* know."

"You got me." Tod cracked up. Here was one guy who was totally comfortable with letting it all hang out. "Hey, live, love, laugh, and get laid, right?"

She mentally checked off which items she was *not* currently doing and got even more depressed, but she kissed Tod good-bye and told him to have extra fun for her. She had little doubt that he would do it.

"I don't know about that guy," Boomer said when Tod had left. "I hope he's being careful."

"Don't worry, I've had the Talk with him. He's a slut, but he's a cautious slut. I, on the other hand, am a tired nun."

"At least that'll keep you healthy." Boomer gave her an affectionate smile.

"There's that." She sighed and put her money into her purse. "I'm going home." She stood up. "Pass the word along that I'm looking to take over extra shifts, would you? If anyone wants me to cover for them, give them my number."

Boomer, who had been drying a wineglass, stopped and considered her. "Are you in some sort of trouble, kid? Something more than just being tired and single?"

Lorna smiled. "No, everything's fine. Really."

He looked unconvinced. "So what's with the need for extra work? If you need a loan, I could—"

"Oh, God, no." She laughed. "Boomer, you are so sweet, but no, thank you." Why he was so financially stable, she'd never understand. It probably had more to do with his NFL past than his bartending gig, that was for sure. "I'm working more to try and pay things *off*."

"Ah." He nodded sagely. "Credit cards?"

"And how."

He paused, then said, "I don't want to butt in where it's none of my business, honey, but there was a fella in here a couple of weeks ago who works as a credit counselor. Ever heard of that?"

A credit counselor. Sounded like something that would cost $150 an hour. And take credit cards. "What, exactly, does a credit counselor do?"

Boomer smiled. "Drinks a lot of Fuzzy Navels, for one thing. But what he said is his company helps people with debt to consolidate it and get lower interest rates."

She thought of the two credit cards she had at twenty-nine percent and sat back down. "Really? How?"

"He told me all about it." Boomer nodded wearily. "I mean *all* about it. They cut a deal with the companies. I guess the banks figure getting paid back at five percent is better than getting ignored at fifteen percent or something."

Fifteen percent. That would be like a gift at this point. But 5 percent? Lorna didn't have to get out a calculator to know that the lower the interest rate, the faster the problem went away.

"Any idea what the company is called?"

"He left his card. I've got it here somewhere." Boomer went to the cash register, opened it up, and pulled a business card out of one of the compartments. He handed it across the bar to Lorna.

PHIL CARSON, SENIOR CONSULTANT, METRO CREDIT COUNSELING SERVICES. Beneath that, it indicated it was A NONPROFIT COMPANY.

"Keep it," Boomer said, looking at her so earnestly, she couldn't refuse.

"Okay. Thanks." She put the card in her purse, along with her meager tip earnings for the night, knowing she'd probably forget about it before she got home. "Why'd he give you his card anyway?"

Boomer chuckled. "He wanted me to pass it along to Marcy. I think he's got the hots for her."

Of course. Who didn't? Marcy was a pillowcase-blond bombshell who routinely took home hundred-dollar tips and, occasionally, very wealthy older gentlemen whose needs apparently included size 38 DD silicone fun pillows and discretion. Marcy offered both, for a price.

And it wasn't a price Phil Carson, nonprofit credit counselor, was likely to pay.

"You should probably try to give it to her," Lorna said, reaching for the card again.

Boomer put up a hand to stop her. "I did. She took one look at the thing and said no way." He gave a crooked smile. "I think it was the *nonprofit* part that turned her off."

Lorna laughed. "Well, thanks. Maybe there's some kismet to this. Marcy's loss could be my gain." She thought about that for a moment. "Or my loss, depending how you think of it." She sighed. "I'm off. Remember to keep me in mind for extra shifts."

"Will do," Boomer said with a nod. Then he leveled his blue eyes on her, and she felt a wave of his concern come her way. "And you'll remember to let me know if you need help, right? It's a tough world out there, and I hate to see a nice kid like you struggling by yourself."

Lorna smiled, though she felt tears well in her eyes. Impulsively, she leaned over the bar and pulled Boomer into a hug. "Thanks,

Boomer. You're the best." When she pulled back, she saw his face had gone red straight down to his collar.

"Go on." He gestured with the wineglass he was wiping. "Get out of here."

Lorna got home at 2 A.M. As soon as she turned on the lights— relieved that the electricity was on—she went to her computer and turned it on, despite her exhaustion.

She had to *un*-order shoes from a few Internet sites.

Swallowing a lump in her throat, she switched her browser to Shoezoo.com, a site she had spent many happy hours browsing in the past. One click on MY ACCOUNT, and the words WELCOME BACK, LORNA showed up on her screen.

That usually made her smile, but tonight it just made her sad. And feeling sad about something she knew was so shallow made her feel even worse.

She clicked through to her most recent order—not an easy task, considering there were about twenty-five orders listed—and looked for the CANCEL ORDER button.

It was there. It was small, too. Like they knew their customers well enough to know they'd be reluctant to hit that button.

Lorna hit the hyperlink that opened her order. Pink Ferragamo slingbacks with a bow. She could already picture herself wearing them to some wonderful outdoor summer party, where the men cooked at the grill wearing KISS THE COOK aprons, and the women sipped wine spritzers and laughed at their macho counterparts while children raced around the perimeters of the party, shrieking with laughter as they ran through the sprinkler or wiped out on the Slip 'N Slide.

It wasn't glamorous; it was real life. Real good life.

Somewhere in her past Lorna must have been one of those happy kids, because the idea that this was what being a grown-up meant was so deeply ingrained that she couldn't shake it.

The shoes—suddenly more important than ever—were originally $380, but now they were just $75. For these timeless beautifully made works of wearable art! They defined a time, a place, in history. Without them, she felt the irrational certainty that she would actually *lose* something. Canceling the order was like giving up a great investment. Like telling a 1970s Bill Gates his ideas seemed too risky.

Maybe she needed to rethink this. Maybe it wasn't necessary to actually *cancel* these orders, considering what a great deal they were. Instead, maybe she should just vow to not keep looking.

Leaving the cursor flickering on her screen, she got up and paced the floor for a moment, considering the possibilities. There was no doubt about it: that seventy-five dollars would be money well spent. In fact, she could, theoretically, just keep the shoes in their box and sell them as vintage in mint condition someday. That could actually make a lot of sense.

She decided what she'd do was check her mail and see if there was anything pressing that would prevent her from this one tiny indulgence. The electric bill was paid. She was pretty sure the gas bill was, too. And, given the fact that West Bethesda Credit Union had let her charge go through with the power company earlier, presumably her credit cards—or at least that one—were current.

She went to the small pile of mail and started sifting through it.

One return address caught her eye: CAPITAL AUTO LOANS.

Her stomach dropped.

It *had* been a month or two since she'd made her car payment. Capital Auto was always so lax about it that it was one of the payments she'd let slide. At an interest rate of just under 6 percent, it didn't quite make sense to pay it off.

She tore the envelope open, bracing herself for two months' worth of payments at the worst. Two hundred and seventy-eight times two. Five hundred and fifty-six bucks. She'd have that . . . soon.

But when she took the letter out, words in bold font leapt out at her like something in a movie. SERIOUSLY DELINQUENT. THIRD NOTICE. REPOSSESS.

JULY 22.

Today was July 22.

They were going to repossess her car.

Lorna crumpled the paper and hurled it at the wall, shouting words that would have gotten her detention for a month in Catholic school.

How the hell had this happened? Heart pounding, she paced more rapidly now, trying to figure out where to put herself. Finally, she flopped down on the couch—the very one that would probably be repossessed next month, if this month was any indication—and put her head in her hands.

What was she going to *do*?

There was no way she could go to her stepmother again. Lucille had made it absolutely clear that the ten-thousand-dollar loan she'd given Lorna after her father's death was *it*. It was all Lorna would ever get in the way of an inheritance. And it was probably fair, given that at least some of the life insurance money had gone to pay off the mortgage on her father's house.

That ten thousand dollars had felt like a lifesaver seven years ago, and, though Lorna hated to use it on her own frivolous debt, she'd vowed then never to make another credit card purchase in her life.

How she'd managed to do it again, and again, and again, she couldn't say for sure. But there were some valid reasons interspersed in there—a medical bill here, food there—just enough to get her hooked again. Just enough to get her stuck in the "another few bucks won't make a difference" mentality.

It was financial death by dollars.

Lorna tapped her fingertips together, thinking. Thinking. She had to come up with something. Anything. Jewelry she could sell, extra jobs she could take on, convenience stores she could rob. . . .

She was going to *lose* her *car*!

How the hell was she going to get around?

The answer came to her so swiftly and clearly, it was frightening: she was going to need a damn good pair of walking shoes.

Silence followed that thought for a moment; then horrible self-realization fell over her.

This was fucked-up.

She had a problem.

Without giving herself the luxury of reconsidering, she signed on to one site after another, canceling orders and crying like a child who was watching her Christmas gifts being taken away.

She finished with the shoe sites and took out the card Boomer had given her earlier. The one she thought she'd never actually use.

Phil Carson, credit counselor.

Using the sensible caution she employed everywhere in her life but in shoe shopping, she looked his name up on the Internet, checking for signs of credibility as well as signs of fraud.

His company was listed as a member of the Better Business Bureau. That was good. Better still, his name didn't show up on any of the complaint sites, like epinions.com, scam.com, badbusiness.com, and so on. He was on the up and up, it appeared, and she was going to call him first thing in the morning.

Well, right after she called Capital Auto about her car loan. She paid with her credit card over the phone.

Then, in the dark of night, feeling as miserable as she'd ever felt without someone actually dying, Lorna got an idea.

She signed on to the local Gregslist.biz, the community bulletin board for everything from personals to babysitting and maid services to used mattress sales. It ran the gamut from sales of bizarre artifacts like shrunken heads to support groups for people with an addiction to Twinkies. Not Ho Hos. Not Ding Dongs. Forget Little Debbies. And mallow bar addicts were shit out of luck as well. Just Twinkies.

Lorna had no doubt that, somewhere on Gregslist, there was probably a special support group for people who ate only the orange part of candy corn.

Which made Gregslist the perfect place for Lorna to place the ad that would, if she was lucky, set at least one small part of her life on the right track again.

SHOE ADDICTS ANONYMOUS—Are you like me? Love shoes but can't keep buying them? If you wear a size 7½ medium and are interested in swapping your Manolos for Maglis, etc., Tuesday nights in the Bethesda area, e-mail Shoegirl2205@aol.com or call 301-555-5801. Maybe we can help each other.

Chapter 5

Helene showered for almost an hour that evening when she got home, trying to wash away the memory—and the smell—of her afternoon in a security office in the back of Ormond's. It had reeked of cheap coffee, hot Styrofoam, drywall paste, and something vaguely like urine.

She had sat, stock-still, as the pimpled and greasy young security guard had typed up a report, the words *shoplifting* and *arrest* leaping at her from his computer screen.

There were a lot of things she could have said. That she was flustered from the credit card debacle and had replaced the wrong shoes, that she was going to her car to get another card and hadn't thought to take off the shoes first; she could even have said that she was feeling flushed and needed a bit of fresh air, and that she'd purposely left her other pair of shoes there to indicate she'd be right back.

But Helene didn't want to give herself those excuses. Maybe later she would, but at that moment she simply sat still, neither accepting nor denying the charges. Later, she'd wonder why, but at the time she'd felt so beaten down that she hadn't been able to do anything more than wait.

It wasn't until the store manager came in and recognized her that she was able to move. Knowing who her husband was, and that this could be a public embarrassment to him and possibly to the store, the manager had let her go, muttering that he was sure this was just a misunderstanding of some sort.

They both knew—along with the security guard, the creepy salesman, a handful of other shoppers, and whoever was going to hear the story second- and thirdhand—that it wasn't really a misunderstanding at all.

Home was hardly a safe refuge. Jim wasn't there, and Teresa, the maid, was coolly courteous, as usual, when Helene came through the front door.

She'd gone upstairs to her bedroom. Jim called it her *boudoir*, but they both knew it was her space and he had his.

She'd taken off her clothes, put them away, gotten into a hot shower, shampooed, conditioned, shaved her legs and armpits, and rinsed thoroughly, allowing herself the brief luxury of hot water pounding down her back.

Afterwards, she put on her robe, combed and dried her hair, changed into a nightgown, brushed and flossed her teeth, put La Mer moisturizer on her face, and put everything away before finally allowing herself to sit on the edge of her bed.

And cry.

She allowed herself a good ten minutes to let it all out, to feel everything as deeply as she needed to before pulling the reins in on herself. When ten minutes passed, she straightened herself up, splashed her face with cold water, reapplied her moisturizer, and went back to her business as if nothing had ever happened.

Hopefully, the news wouldn't have gotten out. She brought her laptop computer to the bed, booted it up, and sat down in front of it. She typed in all the local news sites, Washingtonpost.com, Gazette.net, UptownCityPaper.net, and so on, entering her name in each search bar and waiting to see if there were any recent stories.

Fortunately, there were not. Not in any of the venues she could think of, even the obscure ones.

With considerable relief, she signed on to Gregslist.biz and pursued one of her other favorite online pastimes: looking up apartments in her favorite areas. She often fantasized about getting a little place all her own, where she could escape from Jim and her duties as "wife of." And maybe, somehow, someday it would happen.

Perhaps if she could do something innovative by herself, something that could gain her money without compromising Jim's station in society.

She typed in "Adams Morgan," one of her favorite D.C. neighborhoods; then "Tenleytown"; "Woodley Park"; and finally "Bethesda."

The usual apartment and town house offerings showed up in all the areas, and she'd seen a good percentage of them before, but this time when she typed in "Bethesda," something came up that she'd never seen before.

Shoe Addicts Anonymous.

The irony of it struck her immediately, and her first impulse was to go back and recheck the news sources to make sure they hadn't picked up the story of her shoplifting. But that was silly. This had nothing to do with that. It was just a coincidence.

Helene was a skeptic when it came to voodoo and fortune-telling and omens, but this time it was hard to deny: this had to be a sign.

And the fact that the ad had given her her first honest laugh in about as long as she could remember made her think she should at least write the information down before it disappeared forever into the dark recesses of Gregslist's archives.

It wasn't that she was going to join. Helene had always been a loner. But she *would* keep the information handy.

Just in case.

⁎

Maybe Helene was jaded, but she felt White House functions were always a bore. But they were nothing compared with the tedium of the post–White House Function parties she and Jim always had to make the rounds of.

They were on their way to Mimi Lindhofer's soirée in the heart of Georgetown when Helene's glass slipper flew off and left her flat on her ass on her karmic sidewalk.

"Got an interesting call today," Jim said, as if he were going to tell her his broker thought he should invest in pork bellies.

"Oh?" she asked absently, watching the quaint landscape of Georgetown pass by outside the window. She often wondered what it would be like to live in one of those cozy gingerbread town houses.

Then again, one couldn't live in one of those houses without a lot of money, and if there was one thing Helene had learned over the past decade, it was that people with money weren't always that great to live with.

"Were you going to tell me about your incident at the store?" Jim asked, still so casual, she had to wonder what he really knew.

Helene's heart pounded its panic in rapid Morse code. "Oh, good God, I'd forgotten about that," she lied. "Would you believe those people actually thought I was trying to *steal* a pair of shoes?"

He gave her a sidelong glance that made her blood run cold. "Was this before or after we spoke about your credit cards?"

"Oh, it was after," she said, matching his cold look with a frigid tone. "That's why I was going to the car to get some cash. I guess I was just so distracted by my husband's power play with me that I left the shoes on." Her face burned as hot as it had when that alarm had first gone off. She was grateful that it was dark in the car. "The stupid thing is that I left a *more expensive* pair of shoes behind, so *obviously* I was coming right back." She hated to call the store personnel stupid for catching her, but in this life, it was kill or be killed. "Moron," she muttered contemptuously.

"I thought there had to be a logical explanation," Jim said, sounding relieved. "I'll be sure my press secretary has the facts, just in case." He drummed his fingers on the steering wheel. "But I have to say, when I first heard about it, I was afraid your past . . . Well, you know . . ."

Son of a bitch. Yeah, she knew.

He was afraid everyone else would figure out what he already knew: that she wasn't good enough for him.

*

Helene noticed that a photographer—there were always at least a few around these events—who had been outside the Rossi party also showed up at the Lindhofers'. Which was odd, because these parties made news only if there was no other big news to be made. Usually one or two photos were stuffed into the "Style Watch" section of *The Washington Post,* and occasionally, if a party was good enough or if a movie star showed up to promote some cause or other, the photos would appear in *Vanity Fair.*

Likewise, if an intern turned up dead in the C&O canal or ended up with a politician's DNA on her dress, the archives of these party

shots were sometimes used, but generally they went the route of all
E-level celebrity photos and ended up in the trash.

So to see the same photographer at two events on the same night
was odd. Stranger still was the fact that he was fairly good-looking in
a bland, blond sort of way, something that couldn't be said with a
straight face about most of them.

Therefore when he approached Helene after a couple of hours of
boredom and a couple more glasses of chardonnay, she felt momentarily flattered.

"Mrs. Zaharis," he said, nodding.

She raised an eyebrow. "You are—?"

"Gerald Parks."

"Mr. Parks." She extended her hand, knowing she was approaching
drunk but allowing herself to enjoy just a moment of light flirtation.
"You're a photographer."

"Yes, I am." He held up his camera and pushed the button, sending
a quick flash her way.

She blinked, and his silhouette floated eerily in front of her for a
moment. Had he meant that to be obnoxious or flattering? Given the
miserable week she'd had, she opted to believe it was the latter. "Can't
you find something more interesting to photograph than me?"

"Actually, Mrs. Zaharis, I find you *very* interesting."

She plucked a glass of champagne from the tray of a passing waitress. "Then perhaps you don't get out enough."

Whatever Gerald Parks was going to say in response to that was interrupted by the appearance of Jim.

He hooked his arm around Helene, bringing to mind a vise.
"Sweetheart." He kissed her cheek, scratching her with the beginnings
of a beard. In public now, they were the picture of marital bliss.
"Who's your friend?"

She wanted to ask him if he was drawn over by the fact that she was talking to another man or the fact that the other man had a camera with which he could, potentially, record Jim's ascension to higher office, but instead she just gave what she thought of as her Political Wife Smile and said, "This is Gerald Parks. He's a photographer."

"So I gathered." Jim nodded at the camera and tightened his grip on Helene's waist. "Covering the power brokers or the wives?"

"Some of the power brokers *are* wives," Helene pointed out, wishing she had another glass of champagne since somehow the one she'd just taken was empty.

Jim chuckled. "You're right, you got me." He gave Gerald Parks an old boy nod of the head and added, "And nurses and stewardesses can be men."

"Stewards."

Jim's smile froze. "What?"

"If men are stewardesses," Helene said, "they're stewards." She heard the awkward sentence structure, but once it was out, she wasn't sure how to correct it.

It was time to go home and go to bed.

Jim gave a big laugh. "Touché, hon. You're hot tonight. Do me a favor, would you? Could you get me a Scotch?"

She was being dismissed. She'd gone one or two glasses of wine over the embarrassment line, and Jim wanted to get her away from anyone who could identify her with anything that wasn't perfectly middle-of-the-road acceptable.

Unfortunately, she knew he was right. She was two glasses past politely ignoring farts and about one away from karaoke singing. Since there was no way for her to sober up instantly, she agreed that she should remove herself from the situation.

"Of course," she said, removing his arm from her waist with a fraction more force than she needed to. She turned her smile to Gerald and met his eyes, feeling almost as if they'd just shared a tryst she didn't want her husband to know about. "Excuse me, Mr. Parks."

He nodded, and Helene noticed his finger twitched on the shutter of his camera, but he didn't take a picture.

She took that as a secret gesture between the two of them.

God, she was drunk.

She made her way to the bar and asked for a glass of wine, a chaser to the champagne she'd just downed. Jim didn't want a Scotch. Hell, he didn't even drink when he was at these functions. He just liked to *look* like he had a drink, so no one could accuse him of being a recovering alcoholic or, worse, not masculine enough. The John Wayne act had worked great for Ronald Reagan, and by God, it was going to work for Jim Zaharis as well.

She took a sip of her wine and looked around for someone bearable to talk to. Right off the bat she saw about ten people she'd like to avoid, so when Jim's young administrative assistant, Pam Corder, walked by, Helene snagged her.

"Pam!"

Pam stopped, turned to Helene, and seemed to go a shade pale. "Mrs. Zaharis."

Helene took Pam by the arm and said, "You've *got* to save me from these people. I mean, I know you work for my husband, but if you could get me out of another conversation with Carter Tarleton about fishing in Maine, I would be forever grateful."

Pam looked around uncertainly. "Um. Okay."

The girl was completely devoid of personality. Sure, she was cute, but she didn't seem to have much intelligence. Helene often wondered why Jim kept her on board instead of hiring someone more capable, more of a Betty Currie instead of Betty Boop.

"So." Helene took another sip of wine. Actually, talking to Pam might be *more* difficult than listening to an exaggerated catch-of-the-day story from Carter. "How's everything going?"

Pam took a barely perceptible step backwards. Barely perceptible, that was, unless you were a political wife hoping people didn't notice you were drunk. Helene's first thought was that Pam was recoiling from her alcohol-lit breath.

That was followed quickly by her second thought, though, which was that Pam had something caught between her teeth.

"You have something. . . ." Helene pointed at her teeth.

"Excuse me?" Pam looked at her blankly.

Helene narrowed her eyes and bent toward Pam, looking more closely and saying, "You have something caught between your front teeth."

It was during the infinitesimal fraction of a second in the middle of the word *teeth* that Helene realized exactly what it was stuck between Pam's front teeth.

It was a curly black hair.

And without a shred of hard evidence, Helene was 100 percent certain it belonged to Jim.

"I do?" Pam asked, still unaware that the person before her had figured out she had pubic hair caught in her teeth.

"It's . . ." Helene hesitated. There was no way to say it. And with the apparent certainty that it belonged to her husband, there was really no *reason* to say it. "It's nothing," she said. "Trick of the light."

"Oh. Okay." Pam gave a fake smile, clearly displaying the hair between her teeth.

Yup, there was no doubt about what it was. Even proper DAR women like Nancy Cabot would be able to tell. And there were plenty of them here tonight.

Helene was almost going to enjoy that.

"Do you know where I can find Ji— Senator Zaharis?" Pam was hanging herself, and Jim, with every word.

Whether it was the wine or the past ten years, Helene couldn't say for sure, but she answered, "Last I saw him, he was in the hallway by the foyer, talking to someone." She should have cared, but she didn't. At the moment, she didn't care about anything much.

She'd shoplifted.

And gotten caught.

And her husband's assistant, who called him by his first name—and who, come to think of it, had been missing, along with Jim, for some time after they arrived at this party—had a black pubic hair stuck between her front teeth.

It wasn't a good night for Helene.

"Mrs. Zaharis, we meet again." It was the photographer, Gerald.

Maybe Helene's buzz was wearing off in the wake of the administrative assistant revelation she'd just experienced, but suddenly Gerald looked a lot less handsome and a lot more feral.

"We do," she answered him, accustomed to answering at these events in as charming a manner as she could muster.

At the moment, that consisted of *we do*.

"I was sorry we were interrupted earlier."

She was entering a cynical mode. Something about this guy, his persistence, and the fact that he seemed to be everywhere she looked tonight, disconcerted her. "Why is that?"

"Because we weren't through talking."

"We weren't?"

He looked at her coolly. "No, I was going to tell you about one of the more interesting photo sessions I've had lately. In fact, it was just yesterday." He hesitated a moment longer than a kind person would have. "Did *you* do anything interesting yesterday?"

Apart from getting caught shoplifting? "Not that I can recall." Her alcohol haze was burning off.

"That's funny," Gerald said. "Because you figured prominently in the more interesting part of *my* day."

Helene looked at him. "Me?" She had a bad, bad feeling that she was going to get an answer she didn't like.

Gerald nodded. "I was at Ormond's department store yesterday. It's their semiannual sale, you know."

"Is it?"

They both knew she was bluffing.

He nodded, playing the game. "I took a few shots there."

"Photos, you mean." She arched an eyebrow. "Or were you drinking tequila in the men's room?"

He chuckled. "Good thing I wasn't, or I would have missed a damn good story."

"You don't look like the sort of guy who'd find *anything* of interest in Ormond's." She grazed an eye over his Super-Mart–quality suit. "Were you just passing through on the way to the parking lot?"

"As a matter of fact, I was. I'd gone to get a battery for my camera at one of those fancy jewelry stores. It always drove me crazy that I had to get a fussy little battery like that instead of a regular double A, but it turns out to have been one of the luckier things that's happened to me."

"Is that so?"

He nodded enthusiastically. "I was walking through Ormond's on my way to my car, and I was fidgeting with the camera to make sure the battery did the trick, when I stumbled upon an incredible scene. I didn't have any idea I was going to stumble across an actual story, but I did." He pulled an envelope from his pocket. "Take a look. It's good stuff."

He'd been planning to find and corner her tonight.

"I'm not very interested in your work, Mr. Parks." She didn't want to see what was in the envelope.

"Go on, take a look." He shook it at her, like a lion tamer shaking a steak in order to get his subject's attention. "I think you'll find it really interesting."

She glared at him wordlessly.

"Better that you see it from me, now, than on the news tomorrow."

Helene took the envelope reluctantly. At this point she was playing her role in the game she had no choice but to play.

Taking what felt like hours, she opened the envelope and pulled out the neat stack of five-by-seven black-and-white prints within.

The first was of her, from a distance, talking with Luis in the shoe department of Ormond's.

The second showed Luis returning with her credit card extended toward her.

The third showed Luis returning with her credit card extended toward her *again*.

The fourth was a really excellent close-up of the anguish on her face as she spoke to the credit card company on her cell phone.

The fifth . . . well, more of the same.

The sixth—that was the worst one. It showed her looking to the left in a way that clearly illustrated *seeing if the coast was clear*.

The seventh showed her putting one of the new shoes on her right foot, her old shoes clearly visible in the box at her feet.

The eighth was a great shot of the conflict in her face as she pushed the box containing her old shoes under the chair she was sitting on.

Nine, ten, and eleven showed her striding toward the exit with a gait that seemed confident and an expression that looked doubtful.

Twelve was opening the door.

Thirteen—this was a prize—was the security guard, with his super-serious Maryland trooper face on, hurrying after her.

And fourteen . . . was history. Along with fifteen through twenty-five. They were just moment-to-moment documentations of Helene's apprehension and arrest.

She looked the pictures over, then arranged them into a neat pile—as they'd been presented to her—and handed them back to Gerald Parks. "I'm not sure I understand why these would be of interest to anyone," she said, but her voice wavered just enough to assure the observant person that yes, she *was* sure.

She was painfully sure.

"Oh, because they are a sequence of photos showing you—frankly, I almost can't believe the luck—stealing a pair of shoes from a store and then getting caught and actually arrested for it." He explained it in a voice so friendly that he might have been a local forest ranger telling elementary school kids about the time he found a harmless black snake in his bathtub.

And took pictures of it.

It was America's Funniest Embarrassing Private Moments Caught on Film, and Gerald Parks had just won the grand prize.

"It was a misunderstanding," Helene said coolly.

"Meaning you weren't shoplifting?" He shook his head. "Not according to my source."

"And who is your source?" She wanted to stay calm, but it was obvious, just from looking at the pictures, that she was guilty as sin—and no one looking at them would believe the story she'd told Jim.

"Now, Mrs. Zaharis, if I told you that, I might endanger that person. And, more important, the story." He clicked his tongue against his teeth. "I think newspapers would pay a lot of money for this, I really do."

"Newspapers aren't interested in me."

"Don't be so modest." God, how could he sound so nice, so cordial, while delivering such a menacing threat? "You're married to what many people are saying is a future president of the United States. Your picture has been splashed around the 'Style' section of the *Post* and *Washingtonian*. You are, to purloin a criminal justice phrase, *a person of interest*."

When he finished, Helene looked at him in silence, astonished—and almost even impressed—by his incredible capacity for blasé evil. A person who didn't speak the language would have deduced from his tone that he was a respectful man expressing great appreciation for Helene's beauty and accomplishments.

"I see I've surprised you," Gerald said. "I apologize for that. Believe it or not, I gave this some thought in advance, and there's just no graceful way to sneak up on a subject like this. You have to just *bam!*—"

Helene flinched, startled.

"—get right to the point."

Again, his tone was so warm and casual that she couldn't figure out what he was getting at. Was he going to sell the pictures? Or was it possible that he was just warning her to stay on the straight and narrow because there were unsavory people out there who might not be so kind as he.

Helene had been around the block enough times to seriously doubt it was the latter, so she asked him straight up. "What do you plan to do with these pictures and your contentions of theft, Mr. Parks?"

His small dark eyes lit, like a teacher who was proud his student came up with a particularly astute question. "That's up to you."

"Up to me." If it were truly up to her, the man would dry right up and blow away.

He nodded. "I'm a working man, Mrs. Zaharis. I need to make a living, just like everyone else." He paused, and a telltale expression of disdain flickered across his eyes. "Well, like *most* people, anyway."

It was tempting to tell him that she damn well knew what it was to struggle to make a living, but she wasn't going to form any sort of camaraderie with him, even a vague one like that.

Besides, it was none of his business.

And he already knew too much about her.

So instead, Helene said, "Most people strive to make their livings honestly."

"Absolutely," he agreed. "That's exactly how I like to live. And you can rest assured that I have no intention whatsoever about lying to *anyone* about you." He nodded toward the pile of photos she still held. "Those pictures tell the truth, the whole truth, and nothing but the truth by themselves. No embellishment from me is necessary."

Helene shook her head. "What's the bottom line, Mr. Parks? I don't have the time, or the interest, to stand around and try to figure out your riddles."

He pointed a finger gun at her. "You're a sharp lady, Mrs. Zaharis. I like you. The bottom line is this: You pay me a lump sum of twenty-five thousand dollars right up front."

She gasped, then glanced around, hoping she hadn't drawn anyone's attention. "*Twenty-five thousand?*" she whispered harshly. "You must be joking."

"Oh, no. Not at all. See, I gave this a lot of thought. We don't want large withdrawals from the bank to call attention to you. You could easily explain a twenty-five-thousand-dollar withdrawal as a political or charitable donation, but more than that and your hubby might start asking for receipts and so on."

He had no idea. "My husband keeps a very close eye on his finances," she said.

"*His* finances? That's quaint. They're your finances, too. And you and I both know that, where you come from, ten thousand bucks and a stipend of, say, a couple thousand bucks a month is nothing."

A *couple thousand* bucks a month? And now, of all times, when Jim had pulled the reins in on her spending. "Where I come from," she said in an icy tone, "people wouldn't think of blackmailing as a legitimate way to get money."

"I don't like that term, *blackmail*."

"It's accurate."

"Yes, it is. But still I prefer to look at this as safeguarding you from your own truth." He chuckled. "In a way, I'm your own private Secret Service detail. Anyway, I'd like that twenty-five grand in the form of a cashier's check, no names or addresses. Get it and have it ready. I'll catch up with you later in the week."

"Where? When?"

"Don't worry about that. I'll find you."

Anger surged in Helene's breast. She'd worked too long and too hard for this life to let some sniveling little jerk like this take it all away from her, yet she didn't seem to have a choice. Here he was, proposing that she pay him twenty-five thousand dollars, probably again and again, according to his financial need.

Unless of course he wanted a *raise* for his hard work.

This could just go on and on, eroding her life in dollar-size fractions, until she finally crumbled.

She wasn't going to do it.

"I'm not giving you one flat dime. You have no idea what happened that day, or what you took pictures of." The flash. She remembered it suddenly. Outside, when the alarm was wailing, she thought it had lights, too. But it didn't have lights; that was just the pop of Gerald Parks's camera flash.

She should have figured that out a long time ago. She should have prepared for this moment, braced herself. Maybe even spoken with her lawyer in advance.

Except she couldn't speak with her lawyer without Jim finding out, and she did *not* want Jim to find out that, on top of everything else, now she was being threatened with blackmail.

Gerald Parks had her at a bigger disadvantage than he could have imagined.

It didn't matter. He knew enough. Even if she just wanted to keep the press from finding out, he had her.

And he knew it.

"You'll pay," he said, with utter confidence. "Have it ready. You'll be seeing me soon."

Chapter 6

It was Steve again.

Funny how he always seemed to call Sandra around three-thirty on her four o'clock days. She could almost count on it.

She kept an eye on the clock.

They were talking about his need for social activity again. And again it was raking in the big bucks for Sandra, while costing Steve a lot more than he should have had to pay for a friend.

"Didn't we talk about joining some sort of support group or something last time?" Sandra asked him, assuming her Professional Therapist Voice.

He wasn't the only caller who liked that voice. In fact, he probably needed it less than some of the others, but that was a different matter altogether.

"Yes," Steve said to her. "And I tried. It just didn't work out."

"What did you do?"

"For one thing, I looked on Gregslist to find a group or something I could possibly take part in."

"And? . . ."

"And the D.C. transsexual support group is full."

Sandra didn't know what to say.

"Kidding," Steve said, allowing for one of the first notes of levity she'd ever heard from him. "I called a cooking club and a gardening club, but apparently you have to bring something to the table, so to speak. You can't just join them to learn."

"That's too bad."

"Yeah, then I called this Parents without Partners number, but it's not enough to just *want* kids—you have to be a single parent."

Sandra waited for him to say he was kidding again, but this time he didn't and she found herself unexpectedly touched by the idea that this poor lonely man wanted kids.

"So *then* I came across this advertisement for people who like shoes. I figured, yeah, I like shoes." He snorted a laugh. "I like them a lot more than going barefoot."

Sandra was puzzled. "A meeting for people who like shoes?" He must have misunderstood.

"Forget it. It's really specific. You have to be a woman, for one thing, or at least—get this—a drag queen with narrow-to-regular feet. No wide sizes."

"*What?* Steve, seriously, what are you talking about? A group for people who like shoes but you can't have wide feet or be a drag queen?" And why did everything keep coming back to transsexuality with him? She wasn't going to ask, but she sure wondered.

"Okay, it's this." She heard him clicking on his computer. "Shoe Addicts Anonymous—"

Sandra straightened in her seat.

Was this for real? Because this was exactly the sort of get-out-of-the-apartment dream she often had. Having waited and waited for a nudge from God or Whoever, it would finally come true in a really specific form. And now that she was feeling more capable of getting out . . .

"—it meets in Bethesda every Tuesday night—"

See now, this was getting weirder and weirder. Sandra was free Tuesday nights.

Of course, she was free every night. Strike that from the "weird" column.

"And they trade shoes, I guess. It says something about trading Maglis—"

He pronounced it *mag*-lies instead of *mollies*, but she knew what he meant. There was a pair lying on the floor in front of the sofa right now.

"Oh! And you have to be a size seven and a half. *Women's* seven and a half. No eights. No fives. If you're a man with a size seven shoe, forget about it." He made a noise of disgust. "Talk about getting slapped in the face by an exclusionist group right when you're trying to get out and feel like you *belong*. Jerks."

Sandra, meanwhile, felt like she might be hearing about the first club in the history of the world that she could ever have been totally included in. So much so that it was suspicious.

Had he somehow found out where she lived, had come into her apartment, gone through her closet and ascertained her preferred shoe brand and her size?

"And you saw this on Gregslist," she said doubtfully, wondering if she should be getting her cell phone to call the police and have them trace Steve's call, or if she should turn on her computer and find this group before it disappeared into the world of fairy tales.

"Yeah," Steve said, so guilelessly that she couldn't believe her paranoia could be justified.

There was no way Steve could have found her. The company made really sure that calls were routed through several transfer hubs before ending up with the operators.

"So that wasn't the group for you," she said, still on guard but feeling quite a bit better than she had a couple of minutes earlier.

"Yeah. That's what you get for going on a free online bulletin board to find validation. Maybe what I need is a real psychologist."

Psychologist! Shit! She looked at the time.

Five minutes to four.

"You might consider that, Steve," she said, using a *wrapping it up* voice she rarely needed when she was being paid by the minute. "At least it would get you out and get you used to socializing with someone face-to-face. It might be a great first step for you."

"You really think so?"

She nodded, even though he couldn't see her. "Yes, I do."

"Well, what about medications? Psychologists can't prescribe, and maybe I need medicine—"

"A psychologist should be able to tell you whether you need to see a psychiatrist for psychotropic drugs."

"What?"

"Antidepressants."

"Oh." He paused again. It probably cost him a buck. "You really think so?"

"I really do. In fact—" She looked at the clock and saw she had two minutes until her four o'clock appointment. "—I think you should call someone right now. It's not that there's anything wrong with you, Steve," she hastened to add. "But I think there is help out there for someone sensitive like you who has a hard time getting out into this crazy world. Do it *now* before you lose your fire." *Fire* may have been overstating it a bit, but in Sandra's experience, men preferred overstatement.

"You may be right," he said, sounding hopeful for the first time she could remember. "I think I'll make some calls."

"Excellent!" Rarely did her calls end in such a crescendo for her. "And remember," she added, dispensing advice she knew she had to take herself, "small steps. Don't try to do it all at once."

"Penny," he paused, and she pictured him shaking his head and smiling, "you are the greatest."

"You, too, Steve," she said, wondering if either one of them was using a real name, or if this whole camaraderie was a mirage. "Now you let me know how things go, okay?"

"You got it." He sounded stronger than usual. "I'll be calling you back."

"Thanks, Steve." She pushed the END button on her phone and hesitated, wondering for the thousandth time if it was as wrong as it felt to let this poor guy call and pay so much per minute for a friend.

She knew it wasn't a *good* thing, but it was his choice. He chose to do it over and over again. Even though she'd warned him it was costing a lot.

How responsible did she need to be for that?

It wasn't a question she could answer, so she decided to pose it to Dr. Ratner, her four o'clock appointment. For which she was paying 130 bucks an hour.

Compared with what Steve was paying, it seemed like a bargain.

The conversation with Dr. Ratner went the same way it usually did.

"I'm concerned that you're not feeling confident enough to come to my office," Dr. Ratner said. "It's only six blocks away. You could walk here in ten or fifteen minutes and have the pleasure of knowing you beat one of your challenges."

Challenges. Right. It was a phobia. There was no spin on that. Sandra didn't like to leave her apartment. She knew it was called agoraphobia, she knew it was common, she knew it *could* be cured with some work . . . for some people. She knew a lot of stuff about it.

She knew she had to break through the fear by going out. It was practically Psychology 101, and it was time she did it.

"I've just been busy," she lied, wondering why she was paying so much per hour to lie to a therapist.

"Sandra, you need to make yourself a priority."

"I know. . . ."

"You've said that every week for almost a year," Dr. Ratner persisted. "I'm not sure you're really getting this. You can talk to me all you want, every week, every day, whatever you need. But you're not going to get *better* until you bust through that wall and get out of your safe environment."

"Every time you say that, it makes it sound like the world outside isn't safe."

"Maybe that's because you *feel* it isn't safe. Maybe that's just one more good reason for you to get out and face your demons." Dr. Ratner's voice was soothing, but what she said still felt undoable to Sandra. "Until you do, I don't think I, or anyone else, can truly help you."

"So what are you saying?" Good God, was her therapist *breaking up with her?*

"I'm simply saying you need to get out for an hour. Half an hour. Whatever you can make yourself do. Look, you drive to the grocery store and the library, and you've come into my office now and again. You know you can do it without running into any personal danger. All I'm saying is that you need to challenge yourself a *little* so that you can grow through this phobia." Dr. Ratner hesitated a moment, perhaps not realizing Sandra was sobbing silently on the other end of the line. "Does that make sense?"

Sandra nodded, then said in a small voice, "Yes."

"Excellent. So how about a trip to the movies?"

Sandra shook her head, unseen. "Too crowded. And movies are too long these days."

She knew what she had to try to do. And it wasn't some boring movie in a creepy dark theater. She needed to meet people she could feel safe with, people she had something in common with. The only way she could envision herself going out and leading any semblance of a normal life was to be with friends, to be talking about something interesting to her—as opposed to a party where all the skinny girls and hot guys were hooking up and she was working in the kitchen.

"Then what *are* you interested in?" Dr. Ratner asked. "What feels comfortable and appealing to you? It really doesn't matter what you pick—just pick something you think you can do."

"I don't know!"

"Okay." Dr. Ratner's voice was soft, but there was a firmness to the tone that Sandra had rarely heard. "That's fine, Sandra. But let's consider this an assignment for the next week. Find one thing—just *one* thing, and that's for the whole week—that you can go out and spend, say, more than an hour doing. Sixty-one minutes would be fine. It just needs to be more than one hour. And that will be progress. Are you up for it?"

One hour.

She could do that.

Couldn't she?

She wanted to. She wanted to get better. So she asked, "Are you talking about, like, a trip to the grocery store? Or the National Cathedral or the zoo or something?"

"No, Sandra. Those are all things that you picture yourself doing on your own—"

She was right.

"—what I'm suggesting is an hour of actual social contact. A town meeting, a homeowners' association meeting, whatever you can think of. It doesn't matter *what* it is; it only matters that you get out and do it." She paused for a moment and Sandra said nothing, so she continued, "I think it would truly do you a world of good."

"Okay," Sandra said, suddenly a petulant child. "*Fine*. I'll do it."

Dr. Ratner said, "Excellent. Sandra, I'm very serious about this. I think you would find that it isn't so hard as you fear it will be. It will change your life."

It will change your life.

If there was one thing Sandra needed, it was for her life to change. It almost didn't matter what the change was; she just needed a break from the routine she was stuck in before it devoured her.

After she'd hung up with Dr. Ratner, she turned on her computer and opened her browser to Gregslist.biz. From there, all she had to do was type in "Shoe Addicts, Bethesda," and the ad Steve Fritz had told her about popped right up.

> **SHOE ADDICTS ANONYMOUS**—*Are you like me? Love shoes but can't keep buying them? If you wear a size 7½ medium and are interested in swapping your Manolos for Maglis, etc., Tuesday nights in the Bethesda area, e-mail Shoegirl2205@aol.com or call 301-555-5801. Maybe we can help each other.*

She looked at the ad for a long time, trying to talk herself into making the call, but it seemed like such a big first step. Diving right into a meeting with people who would undoubtedly expect her to be sociable . . . As perfect as the group looked, Sandra needed to start herself off more slowly.

But she was interested. So she set up a couple of mini-challenges for herself.

The first was a trip to a fast-food restaurant. Since there was virtually nothing on the menu that was allowed by Weight Watchers, it was a quick trip. She went in, ordered a Diet Coke, sat down at a front window seat, and drank it, forcing herself to go slowly and use Dr. Ratner's trick of "floating" through her feelings of discomfort.

Twenty minutes passed like two hours, but when she left, Sandra felt like she'd accomplished something.

It was a small thing, and virtually everyone else in the world could do it daily without giving it a thought, but Sandra was learning to stop berating herself for her phobia, so as soon as she had those impatient thoughts with herself, she tried to stop them.

It didn't always work, though.

"The more you try and push your fear away, the more it's going to push back," Dr. Ratner said on the phone when Sandra called her later that day.

"But it's so stupid," Sandra said miserably. She wanted ice cream. Pizza. That ice box cake made from whipped cream and Nabisco famous wafer chocolate cookies.

She wanted *something* to give her pleasure, because drinking a diet aspartame soda in a greasy fast-food joint wasn't doing it.

"It is what it is," Dr. Ratner said. She came up with those maddening "philosophical" phrases sometimes, and they were no help at all.

"It *is*," Sandra said, "*ridiculous*. Everyone else in the world can walk down the street without getting palpitations. I *hate* this." Boy, she was really being a brat about this. But she couldn't help it. She *did* hate it.

She was just expressing her feelings. Normally, Dr. Ratner would have applauded that.

"Sandra, you went out for half an hour today and it didn't kill you. Doesn't that tell you something?"

It was on the tip of Sandra's tongue to give a flippant answer about how it told her she was a wimp for running home to get away from the big bad strangers, but she decided that would be counterproductive.

"It tells me I need to go on another field trip," she said.

"Good!" Dr. Ratner sounded truly delighted. She obviously thought this was progress.

And maybe it was.

"What's your next move?" she asked Sandra. "A museum? Maybe a sit-down meal at a real restaurant?"

"I made an appointment with a hypnotist," Sandra said, half-expecting Dr. Ratner to express shock and disapproval. "To help hypnotize my phobia away." There was a moment's silence and Sandra asked, "Do you think that's stupid?"

"Not at all," Dr. Ratner replied. "I'm just kicking myself for not suggesting it to you sooner."

"Really? So you think there's some validity to it?"

"What I know is that it works wonderfully for some people. If you're one of them, that's terrific."

"And if not? . . ."

"Then you're no worse off than you are now. In fact, I'd say you'll definitely come away from it better off because you'll learn some new self-relaxation tips that can help you in any anxious situation. Good work, Sandra. I'm proud of you."

Two days later, when Sandra was trying to talk herself into leaving her apartment five minutes before her appointment was due to start, she thought of Dr. Ratner's words.

She respected Dr. Ratner a lot. Too much, in fact, to call her Jane, even though she'd told her to countless times. To Sandra, "Dr. Ratner" felt a lot more comfortable when it came to revealing her most embarrassing inner thoughts. And she respected her so much that she didn't want to call and tell her that she'd chickened out of an appointment Dr. Ratner had felt so good about Sandra's having made.

So she took a deep breath and went out the door.

When she got to the small square brick building where the hypnotist had his office, she was ten minutes late. On her way up to the third floor in the little steel box of an elevator, she tried to think of excuses to give the officious secretary she was expecting to see. But when she got to the office, there was no secretary. In fact, there was only a cramped room filled with books and pamphlets and an attractive middle-aged man who looked exactly like you'd imagine a guy in a messy office filled with books to look.

"Sandra?" he asked, breaking into a warm smile.

"Yes, I'm sorry I'm late. There was so much traffic—"

"Don't worry about it." He waved a hand. "A lot of people change their minds at the last minute and don't show up at all. It's hard to face your fears head-on."

And getting harder by the minute. "Is there still time for . . . I'm sorry, I don't know how this works. Is there a set time?"

"It depends on you." He opened a door off the main room and gestured for her to go in. "I always block my appointments in hour-and-a-half slots so my client doesn't have a feeling of being rushed."

She went into the room and saw it was a smaller version of the one they'd just left. Bookshelves lined each wall and contained volume upon volume of psychology and hypnosis books, along with a good representation of other various health and well-being books and—Sandra noticed on its side at the top—a book on training your puppy.

"Have a seat." He indicated an overstuffed easy chair and sat down at a desk a couple of feet away.

Sandra sank into the easy chair and let out a breath she hadn't realized she was holding. "Wow. This is really comfortable."

"Isn't it?" He was unwrapping a cassette tape and looked up at her. "Twenty years old, and it's been patched more times than I can count, but I can't find another one that's nearly as cozy."

She nodded. "What's the tape for?"

"To record our session. Do you mind?"

Did she? She wasn't sure. "Why?"

"Often my clients like to take the tape home and listen to it in private, to practice the progressive relaxation techniques I teach them. It's completely up to you."

"So I take the tape?"

"Yes. It's for you. Value-added, you might say."

"Oh. Okay." She nodded. It made sense. And if she was serious about getting better—and she was—she needed to use every tool at her disposal. "Great."

He put the tape into a machine, pressed a button, and a red light went on. "Now, if you're ready to begin, lean back against the chair and close your eyes."

She did so.

"Listen to the sound of my voice. Let me be your guide as you enter a new world of carefree, worry-free, existence. . . ."

He had a good voice for this. Not too deep, but not too high. Mellow. Calm.

Familiar.

She tried to follow as he led her imagination down a flight of marble steps and into a great marble hall filled with doorways, but she was so distracted by trying to place his voice that she couldn't concentrate on the exercise.

"When you look at the doors, you'll notice each one has a word on it. Words like *love, hate, anger, fear* . . . whatever you see. It's entirely up to you."

She had it. He was one of her callers. Not frequent, like Steve, but she'd talked to him more than once. Whenever she asked him what he wanted, he'd say, "Surprise me. It's entirely up to you."

"Go through the door that says *relax* on it," he went on, completely unaware of the revelation Sandra was having. "See what's on the other side. See what makes you feel most at ease."

Whatever it was, she was damn sure it wasn't lying in a darkened room having a man who had, only a few weeks ago, told her to *spank me again, I've been a bad boy* lead her into the dark recesses of her psyche.

"What do you see, Sandra?"

"I—" She didn't know what to say. She wanted to leave. This was a waste of time. There was no way she was going to relax and take this seriously.

But on the other hand, she couldn't very well tell the poor guy she knew who he was and that he liked his balls sucked after having an orgasm.

So she did what she usually did with him.

She faked it until he was finished.

"I see a big green meadow. . . ."

Chapter 7

The first thing you'll need to do is cut up your credit cards and give them to me."

Lorna looked at Phil Carson—short, fifty-ish, bald—as if he'd just suggested she drop a kitten in a blender and push FRAPPÉ. "What, *now?*"

He laughed. He was kind, but he didn't seem to fully appreciate how hard this was for her. "No, no."

"Oh." Relief. "Good."

"First you have to read me the numbers and the bank names—" He took some scissors out of his drawer and passed them across the desk to her. "—*then* you'll cut them up and give them to me."

She looked at him, hoping for a sign that he was joking, but his small round face was still, his thin lips a straight line.

And he'd taken out a pen and poised it over a black leather-bound notepad on his desk.

"At that point, I'll call your creditors and negotiate a lower interest rate and payment plan," he went on, sweetening the deal marginally. "It will save you hundreds, maybe thousands, in the long run."

"But . . ." She knew what he was saying was true and that she shouldn't voice any objection to it at all. Still, she had to wonder, "What happens if I have an emergency? Will I be able to use the credit cards then?"

He glanced down, looked over the list of creditors and debts she'd printed out. "Emergencies? . . . I don't see anything much here that looks like an actual *emergency*."

Well, of course he wouldn't understand how a little retail therapy could cure her of otherwise deep emotional problems. Look at him! He was wearing a suit that was obviously poorly made—she could see the stitching. And his shoes! Good God, his shoes—they were probably from Payless or maybe the dollar store. They were a bright unnatural shade of tan. The kind of color her father always said "took hundreds of naugas to make." (For some reason, Naugahyde jokes were big in the Rafferty household.)

"I'm not *planning* an emergency," Lorna said, "but what if there was something like, I don't know—" What would he consider a reasonable emergency? "—I was stuck out of town. Or needed to pay medical bills. Or had car trouble," assuming she could hold on to her car for another month, "or whatever." She wondered if she should just keep *one* card, in secret. Just in case. But which would she choose? The Visa with the 9.8 percent interest rate but a $4,200 limit, or the American Express with the 16 percent interest rate but a $10,000 limit?

It was like *Sophie's Choice*.

Phil Carson looked at her across his desk. He was a small man, but he had his hydraulic chair pumped up high, so he looked like a little kid on a high chair, looking slightly down at her. "Lorna, I've seen this before. You're used to living a certain way, and you're insecure about changing that lifestyle."

He was right. He had her pegged. "That's definitely true. Isn't there another way to go about this?"

He shook his head. "Not at this point." He picked up one of the pieces of paper. "You're paying interest rates close to thirty percent. Your minimum payments take your debt-to-income ratio into the stratosphere. I'm no psychologist, and please don't take this the wrong way, but living this way has to be hard on you."

For some reason that last sentence, or maybe just the way he said it, made her suddenly feel like crumbling. Hot tears threatened to become a full-blown embarrassment. She swiped her hand across her eyes, looked down for a moment to compose herself, then said, "You're right. I can't keep doing this. I've got to do whatever it takes to get rid of this debt once and for all."

Phil smiled. "I'll be here to help. And I've got some ideas and suggestions for chipping away at the debt faster."

"You do?" That sounded hopeful. "Like what?"

"Ever sell anything on eBay?"

She'd never even *been* to eBay. She'd always just thought of online auctions as a place where grown-ups who should have better interests got online and bought Beanie Babies and *Who's the Boss?* lunchboxes and Hummel figures.

But maybe she was wrong.

The idea of selling stuff instead of taking on an additional job certainly appealed to her. "Like what? What do people sell, or buy, there?"

"*Anything*. Collectibles, cookware, knickknacks, clothes, even shoes—"

Shoes!

Oh, no, no. She couldn't. It was bad enough that she had people coming over tonight to perhaps *trade* shoes with. She wasn't going to sell them off to faceless strangers for money. Money that would just be thrown into a dark, deep, pool of debt.

She'd make sacrifices. Work longer hours. Babysit in her off time, if necessary. Mow lawns, like she did in junior high.

But she wasn't getting rid of the shoes.

No way.

"You know, I just don't think that's my thing," she said, cutting him off.

He stopped. "Okay. That's fine. It was just a suggestion."

"I appreciate it, don't get me wrong."

"You'll come up with something," he said. "Everyone has different levels of comfort with this. And I know it can be difficult to face at first."

"I'm facing it," Lorna said, perhaps a tad defensively. "Head-on. This is me facing it."

He looked at her. "That's good."

She felt like an ass. "It's just that . . ." The words dissolved. She was saying too much, without really *saying* anything at all. She did that when she got nervous. Better for her to just shut up now. "I've got a few ideas of my own about how to bring up my income," she lied.

She did, at least, have a good idea about how to get shoes now that she couldn't afford to actually purchase them, but something told her that Phil Carson wouldn't be very impressed by her plan or the fact that she'd taken care of that before thinking about the more serious matter of her income.

"Excellent. Now." He cleared his throat and held out his hand. "If you could pass all of your credit cards this way, we can get started. . . ."

*

"I'm going to place a small metal bar into the cartilage of your ear right here." Dr. Kelvin Lee pinched a spot on Sandra's earlobe.

"Will it hurt?" Sandra asked. A silly question, considering the fact that she was lying on the acupuncturist's table with about forty needles sticking in her at this very moment.

But Kelvin Lee had the tact *not* to point that out. "It might hurt for a moment when I insert it. But little more than a prick."

"So how long does it stay there?" she asked, wondering if the fifteen minutes for the needles had passed yet.

"A month."

"A *month*?"

"Auricular therapy is different from acupuncture," he explained patiently. "It continues to work as you leave the bar in."

The way it said that, *leave the bar in,* she pictured herself like one of those tribal women who put bigger and bigger tubes in their ears until eventually their lobes hung down lower than their sagging boobs. "I don't know about this—"

"I assure you, it will not be painful."

She swallowed. If it would help her get the hell out of her apartment now and then, she shouldn't care if it *was* painful. "Okay." She squinted her eyes shut. "Go ahead." She waited a moment while he felt around on her earlobe for the spot. She opened her eyes. "It's okay, you can do it."

"I just did." He smiled, displaying the kind of quiet confidence that made her wonder how she could have doubted him.

She lifted her hand to her ear and, sure enough, felt a little metal bar, much like the post of an earring, running through the back of her lobe. "That's it?"

He nodded. "That's it."

She was still for a moment, trying to see if she felt any different. But she didn't. "When will I notice a difference?"

"I cannot say for certain. It's different for everyone. More than likely you will notice what you're *not* feeling in terms of panic and stress, rather than feeling something new."

Three hours later, Sandra, despite a healthy dose of skepticism, started to think maybe he was right.

It was hard to pinpoint exactly what the difference was. It wasn't like she was suddenly ready to get on a crowded Metro car, but the idea of going out and, say, picking up groceries wasn't quite so daunting as it would have been even yesterday.

The next morning, the improvement was still there. In a way, Sandra felt like she could take on the world, but she knew there was a bit of false confidence to that. If she went out and hopped on a bus, she'd probably be clawing her way out of it at the first stop.

So the bus was out. But the corner grocery store seemed doable. She went out for salad fixings and Skinny Cow ice cream bars. And while it wasn't exactly a party, she found she wasn't panicking so much as she usually did.

She went back to her apartment in some amazement, wondering if that little stick in her ear could *really* have the power to help her get over her agoraphobia.

There was one pretty good way to find out.

Tomorrow was Tuesday. The day Shoe Addicts Anonymous met. She could just go once, she told herself. If it worked, great. If it didn't, she could at least say she'd done it and move on in her therapy with Dr. Ratner.

She'd do it.

Just once.

Just once.

She repeated that chant to herself as she went to the phone and picked it up to make the call.

∗

The people were due to arrive in fifteen minutes, and Lorna was hav-ing serious second thoughts. What if they weren't who they said they were? What if they weren't women even? What if one was a deranged man who wanted to strangle her with her own underpants, take her belongings, and leave her to rot in the apartment until the smell drew the attention of the neighbors (something that could take a while, considering how foul the garbage outside sometimes got when the trash collectors were on one of their many strikes).

It wasn't impossible. What about that guy who'd called? That was so weird. He kept insisting that he "needed to get out" and that he could *buy* women's size 7½ shoes and participate in the swapping. Like they were baseball cards, or Hello Kitty puffy stickers, or something, and they'd all meet on the playground to swap. Really, it had been hard to get him to take no for an answer. Maybe he was just some hound dog who figured he could meet women that way, but on the other hand, maybe he was a psycho who had called back, done a convincing imitation of a woman's voice, and gotten her address so he could come cause trouble tonight.

She'd been cautious and put her cell phone number in the ad so she couldn't be traced—so much for Phil Carson's suggestion that her cell phone might not be an expense she needed!—but when Helene, Flo-rence, and Sandra had called, Lorna had readily given them her ad-dress after a short chat.

Maybe one of them . . . like Florence. Was anyone *really* named Florence, or had Lorna fallen for a really stupid ruse, perpetrated by some deranged *Brady Bunch* fan?

With a knot of anxiety in her stomach, Lorna went to the door and made sure the bolt was on. She could look through the peephole and make sure whoever came looked . . . normal.

Then she waited.

The first knock came at three minutes to seven. Lorna hurried to the door and looked out. It was a very tall, thin woman with frosted black hair that reminded Lorna of Cruella de Vil. She was holding three large shopping bags, and she was frowning.

Lorna opened the door. "Hi," she said, suddenly aware that she hadn't concocted any sort of opening line. "Welcome to Shoe Addicts Anonymous. I'm Lorna."

"Florence Meyers," the woman said, bustling through the doorway and knocking Lorna with a bag as she passed. "First thing, we've got to change the name."

"Change the name?" Lorna repeated.

"Absolutely. It sounds like a drug or alcohol rehabilitation program. We don't want that."

Actually, that's exactly what it felt like to Lorna. "We don't?"

"Mm-mm. How does everyone else feel about it?"

"I don't know yet."

"You haven't talked to them?"

"Not about that, no."

Florence looked exasperated for a moment, then shrugged. "Where should I put these?" She lifted the bags.

"What are they?"

Florence looked like Lorna had just asked her what came after three. "Shoes, of course."

That was a lot of shoes. "All of them?"

Florence began opening the bags, lifting out shoes, and laying them across the floor. Some of them were scuffed, a fact undoubtedly made worse by throwing them into a bag together, but most of them were . . . Well, they were ugly. And unrecognizable, style-wise.

"See these?" Florence lifted a pair of what looked like the kind of patent leather sandals Lorna would have *adored* as a child. They were the color Lorna thought of these days as *biological pink*. "Jimmy Choos. Limited edition."

"Jimmy Choos?" Lorna repeated skeptically.

Florence nodded. Smug. "He almost never does flats."

"Well, he does . . ." No sense arguing. Lorna reached for one of the shoes and examined it. The label *looked* like the real thing, but it was glued on a little unevenly. "Where did you get them?"

"New York." Florence took the shoe back. "On the corner of forty-eighth Street and Fifth Avenue."

"I'm sorry, I don't really know New York that well. What store is that?"

"It wasn't a store," Florence said, like Lorna had just said something incredibly stupid. "It was a guy who had a bunch of high-end shoes and purses for sale. I've sold a lot of them online. Made a fortune. But these." She glanced admiringly at the shoes. "They're special. Someone might have to give me *two* pairs for these."

"So you're saying you bought them from a street vendor."

Florence shrugged. "I know they're probably stolen, but that doesn't make them any less valuable."

It was on the tip of Lorna's tongue to point out that the fact that they were knockoffs *did* make them less valuable, but she stayed quiet. She'd been raised too polite for her own good.

Fortunately there was a knock at the door, and Lorna had to get up to answer it. Her fear of a dangerous man had gone, replaced by the fear of spending the evening with a bunch of crazies in her apartment, trying to trade orange man-made uppers for butter-soft leather Etienne Aigners.

Lorna didn't even look first; she went ahead and opened the door to find a statuesque redhead in a fitted ivory linen dress and *exquisite* brocade Emilio Pucci mules. She had a Fendi baguette purse in one hand and a small Nordstrom shopping bag in the other.

It was obvious it had a shoe box in it.

Lorna could spot that kind of thing a mile away.

The woman smiled a bright white movie-star smile and said, "Am I in the right place? Are you Lorna?"

Lorna had been too dazzled by the woman—and the *shoes!*—to speak first. "Yes," she said at last. "I'm sorry, you are—?"

"Helene Zaharis." She held out a bottle of wine, revealing a slender, evenly tanned arm. "It's nice to meet you. I wasn't sure what this was going to be like, but I figured wine was always appropriate."

"That was really nice of you." Lorna shook her hand warmly and stood back to usher her in. "I *love* your Emilio Puccis. I don't think I've seen that pattern before."

"I haven't seen it here either. I got them in London." Helene smiled and looked at Florence. "Hi."

"Florence Meyers," Florence said briskly. "Don't you think we should change the name?"

"I'm . . . sorry?" Helene looked puzzled.

"Shoe Addicts Anonymous." Florence shook her head. "It just sounds bad."

Lorna resisted the urge to roll her eyes at her own guest. "I don't mind changing it. It was just sort of, I don't know. A joke."

"It's cute," Helene reassured her. "I like it. And I *am* a shoe addict. I'd be embarrassed to tell you the lengths I'd go to." She hesitated, then smiled.

She looked familiar for some reason, but Lorna couldn't quite place her.

"Me, I can take them or leave them," Florence said, her voice still as crisp as ever. "But my customers like them."

Lorna glanced at the clock on the wall. This had the makings of a really long evening. Wasn't someone else coming? Sandra?

"What can I get you all to drink?" Lorna asked. "There's beer, wine, soft drinks. Helene, we could crack open that bottle you just brought."

"How about a Dubonnet?" Florence asked. "Do you have any of that?"

Dubonnet. Jeez, Lorna hadn't thought about that in years. Like, since the seventies, when they played those "Dubonnet for Two" commercials all the time.

"I'm sorry," she said. "I don't have that. But—" What *was* Dubonnet anyway? Wine? Brandy? "—maybe something else?"

"White zin and club soda," Florence said, continuing to set one cheap, ugly pair of shoes out after another. "Like a spritzer? That would be all right, I guess."

Lorna caught Helene's eye as she went into the kitchen and asked, "Anything?"

Helene gave a sympathetic smile. "Not right now, thanks."

In the kitchen, Lorna glanced out the window and noticed, directly below outside, there was a man leaning against a car—a small nondescript economy car—and looking up in the direction of Lorna's apartment.

Her nerves tightened. Was he the guy who had called her about Shoe Addicts? Was he so pissed that she'd rebuffed him that he'd come to stalk her or something?

No, that was crazy. It was a largish apartment complex, and plenty of people came and went every day. She was letting her imagination carry her away. Still, she tried to make out his description, just in case she'd need it later: bland, blond, medium build. Could've been anyone.

She turned her attention back to searching the fridge for some club soda to make Florence's drink. She mixed the club soda with chardonnay, since she didn't have white zinfandel and she doubted Florence would notice the difference.

There was a knock at the door, and Helene called, "Do you want me to get that?"

"Would you?" Lorna asked gratefully. She could already tell Helene was fabulous. She was the kind of person who walked into a place and just felt right at home, taking command of whatever she could in order to make life easier for her hostess.

Now this was the kind of guest Lorna liked.

Florence, on the other hand . . .

Lorna took a generous gulp of the wine herself before putting it back in the fridge. In the other room, she could hear Helene talking to another woman.

Good. It was definitely a woman. There was no way a man could imitate one that well. She glanced out the window and noticed that, although the car was still there, the man who had been leaning on it didn't appear to be around. So he was probably just visiting someone.

It was nothing for Lorna to worry about at all.

At least not this time. There was plenty of time to worry later, and she had all the reason in the world to do it.

Chapter 8

Lorna took the spritzer to Florence and saw a short, heavy woman with long light brown hair hanging midway down her back. She wore granny specs under thick, dark eyebrows.

Lorna tried to hide her surprise, but the woman looked so unlike her voice that it took her aback. "Hi," she said, overcompensating with a wide smile. "I'm Lorna. You must be Sandra."

Sandra touched her ear with a hand that seemed to tremble slightly. "Yes. Sandra Vanderslice. I hope I'm not late. Or early?" She looked at the flea market–style shoe display Florence had just finished arranging. "I didn't bring that many shoes."

"I only brought one pair myself," Helene said quickly. "Well, two counting the ones I'm wearing."

Lorna's heart quickened. Was Helene willing to trade those amazing Puccis?

"Would you like a drink, Sandra?" Lorna asked. She decided she'd have some wine herself. She needed it. "Beer, wine, soda?"

"Um." There was definitely a tremor in her voice. The girl was nervous as a cat for some reason. "Soda would be good. Thanks."

"Coke okay?"

Sandra nodded and took a breath.

"Helene?" Lorna said. "Are you sure I can't get you something? Some wine?"

"You know, on second thought," Helene said, with a downward glance that went by so fast, Lorna almost missed it. "White wine would be great."

"Oh, I'll have one, too," Sandra chirped, then added, "instead of the Coke. If that's okay." She reached up and touched her earlobe again, then, catching Lorna's glance, went pink and pushed her glasses up the bridge of her nose.

"You got it." Lorna poured the drinks and brought them in.

Helene had taken the box out of her bag, and Lorna saw that it was a pair of pink high heels.

"Oh, my God," Lorna gasped.

Helene looked startled. "What's wrong?"

"Are those Pradas?" Lorna pointed at the shoes.

"Oh. Yes. They're a couple of years out of date, though. I wasn't sure what kind of thing to bring."

Lorna was in heaven. "I *love* them! I wanted those so badly when they came out, but I twisted my ankle"—one of many embarrassing shoe stories she could tell later if things got too quiet—"and my crappy insurance didn't cover it, so I couldn't get them." She looked closer. The shoes appeared to be in perfect condition. Like they'd never been worn.

"I have them in black," Sandra said. "And some Kate Spades that look sort of similar, but the heel doesn't suit me."

Oh, this was good.

Lorna had had a very hard time picking out three pairs of shoes to bring out for trading—she knew, as hostess, that she'd be sort of obliged to trade at least one pair since the whole thing was her idea—but now she was thinking she might have to run back and get more.

"So." Florence slapped her hands against her thighs. "How do we do this? Like an auction?" She picked up the purple fake Choos. "These are very special, as I was telling Lana here. I was thinking I'd need two pairs in exchange, but since everyone only brought one or two pairs, I'll settle for one. This time." She held them up. "Anyone?"

There was a polite silence.

Lorna got uncomfortable. "Can I see them?" she asked, although she didn't have any genuine interest in looking them over.

Once in her hand, the lack of quality was even more evident, if possible. Clear glue had dried around the edges of the soles, and the stitching on the patent leather was uneven. Lorna didn't know how to comment on that, though, without sounding too insulting to her guest. Fortunately, there was a *10* stamped on the sole—another giveaway—and it gave her the out she needed.

"These are size ten," she said. Then, suddenly uncertain, she asked, "Didn't I say seven and a half in my ad?" Oh, God. Had she messed up and wasted everyone's time?

"Yes," Helene said quickly. "You did. That's what I brought."

"Me, too," Sandra said, finishing her wine. She seemed to be a little more comfortable now.

Of course, wine had a way of doing that.

"Oh, come on," Florence said, "with nutrition as good as it is today, ten is the new seven and a half." She looked down at her own Jurassic feet, for which she undoubtedly had to order shoes specially.

Lorna got up and went to the kitchen to grab the bottle, saying,

"I'm sorry if it wasn't clear, Florence. If we're all the *old* size seven and a half, we can't swap for a different size."

"I've got a whole bunch of sizes here," Florence said, a little snappishly. She began to rummage, roughly, through the shoes. "Here's . . . let's see . . . ten. You've made it clear that won't do. Five. Ah—seven." She set that pair aside. "Those might work. You never know if the sizes run large."

"I've never heard of Bagello," Sandra said, peering down at the label in the shoes.

"It's a Super-Mart store brand," Helene said, without judgment.

Florence turned a sharp eye on her. "Is there something wrong with Super-Mart?"

"Of course not." Helene looked like she was suppressing a smile. "But I don't think a size seven Super-Mart shoe will fit anyone here." She waited a beat before adding, "They actually tend to run small."

Lorna poured more wine into Helene's glass and wondered how a woman so elegant and obviously cultured knew anything about Super-Mart fashions.

"Well," Florence said triumphantly, pulling out a pair of gray flannel flats. "Ralph Lauren should suit you, then." She handed them to Helene and gave a smug smile. "Those babies cost a whole lot."

Helene turned the shoes over in her hand and nodded. "They're Ralph Lauren, all right. Vintage, even. I'd say 1993 or '94."

Florence looked very pleased with herself.

Lorna looked at the shoes while she poured more wine into Sandra's glass.

"So. Who wants to make a deal?" Florence asked.

Sandra, who had already picked up her glass and taken a sip, said, "I'm too short to wear flats."

Lorna looked at the shoes in dismay. They were very scuffed. Still, she was afraid it might be her hostess-y duty to make an offer.

She was about to do so when Helene said, "All right." It was clear she was just being polite. Her amusement still shone plainly on her face, and she didn't even look at the Ralph Laurens again. "I'll trade you these Puccis for them."

Lorna felt an actual pain on her chest. "Oh, no, not the Puccis! Wait—I've got . . ." She thought frantically. "Some Angiolinis you might like better."

Florence glanced from one woman to the other.

Helene just looked at Lorna. "Oh, no. Not the Angiolinis. Those are way more expensive than these." She winked.

She knew.

Sandra, on the other hand, had an undisguised look of confusion.

Lorna kept running with Helene's game ball. "You may be right. . . ." She was *sure* Florence would leap at the chance to score shoes that were *too expensive* to give up.

So it was a shock when Florence shook her head. "Sorry, ladies. These suckers are worth *two* pairs. Two *designer* pairs," she added, as if everyone else had brought shoes they picked up at the grocery store.

Helene gave a rueful sigh. "You're too rich for my blood," she said. She was really a master at working people. "I don't think I can help you out."

"Me neither," Sandra interjected quickly.

"I've only got a few pairs myself," Lorna said, hoping her nose didn't grow or twitch with the lie. "I thought mostly we'd sit around and, you know, talk about shoes." She hoped she had Sandra and Helene pegged right, because she really didn't want to turn them off.

"Okay," Sandra said. Her face was slightly flushed, probably from the wine, and she had loosened up considerably. "Did you know that ancient man invented the first sandals by strapping a flat piece of wood or animal hide to his feet with the intestines of his prey?"

There was silence for a moment, while everyone looked at Sandra with surprise.

"I read a lot," she said with a shrug, her face turning red like the top of a cartoon thermometer.

Lorna smiled. "Tell us more."

"Well, shoes came after that, for people in colder climates. They just took the sandals and added tops made from animal skins. It's pretty much what we wear today, if you think about it."

"So, sociologically," Lorna improvised, badly, "we're not as evolved as we think we are."

"Exactly!" Sandra said. "We share a great deal with our prehistoric ancestors."

"Fascinating. So—"

"Uh, wait." Florence held up a hand. "Excuse me. I've got to get going." She started throwing her shoes back into her bags without regard to organization. I didn't realize this was going to be like a book club or something. This isn't my bag."

Lorna's impulse was to feign disappointment and object, but she squelched that. "I'm sorry it didn't work out," she said to Florence, walking to the door to prevent the woman from stopping and trying to cut a deal for Helene's Emilio Puccis.

"Yeah, well . . . if you want some of my shoes, you'll have to go to eBay. Look for 'Flors Fashions.' I'll cut you a deal on shipping, since I know you guys live local." She bustled out of the apartment. "Remember, that's Flors Fashions."

Lorna closed the door behind Florence and took a breath before turning to the other two women to see what their reaction was.

There was a moment of tense silence, during which Lorna imagined everyone was sizing the others up.

Finally, Sandra, on her fourth glass of wine, said, "Those poor shoes."

"Don't defend the shoes," Lorna said immediately, parroting one of the funniest quotes from Tim Gunn on *Project Runway*. Immediately she remembered she didn't know these women and they'd probably think she was crazy, so she tried to explain what suddenly seemed like an increasingly lame joke. "That's from this show—"

"*Project Runway!*" Sandra said. "Oh my God, I *love* that show. And when Tim Gunn said that about Wendy—"

"Pure gold," Helene interjected. "And she totally deserved it, those shoes *were* dowdy . . ."

Everyone laughed, and the relief seemed to fill the room like warm water.

It was at that moment, over something as inconsequential as a television show, that Lorna decided this really might work. This was a bonding moment. The mood in the room had lightened completely, and everyone was laughing and chattering now about designers and would-be designers from the show, and about the moment they'd realized they loved shoes, and finally about Florence.

"You panicked when I offered her the brocade Puccis, didn't you?" Helene said to Lorna. "I saw it in your eyes. I'm really sorry about that." She took off the shoes and handed them to Lorna. "Here. Take them. You deserve them after what you went through to bring us all here."

Once again Lorna found herself saying the *right* thing instead of what she meant. "No, really. Thanks, but I can't just *take* them. That's not the point of the meeting."

"But I don't mind." Helene looked at Sandra. "Do you?"

Sandra shook her head. "Not at all. I'm ready to give you mine, too.

You must have been really surprised when Florence came in here and started unloading."

Lorna laughed. "I *was* a little nervous that I hadn't communicated very well in the ad."

"Honey, there will *always* be people who don't get it," Helene said, like one who knew from painful experience. "I thought you handled it really well. Are you, by any chance, in sales?"

Lorna shook her head. "I'm a waitress. At Jico, over on Wisconsin Avenue."

Helene smiled. "That's where your people skills come from."

"What do you do?" Lorna asked, then shifted her gaze to Sandra. "Both of you, I mean."

Helene was silent for a moment, so Sandra volunteered, "I work telecommunications."

"Telecommunications?"

Sandra nodded but looked uncomfortable. "It's not very interesting, but it pays the rent." She gave a small laugh. "And the shoe bills."

Lorna nodded. It seemed they were all in the same boat, basically. "How about you?" she asked Helene.

Still the hesitation. "I used to be a salesperson at Garfinkels. Before they went under."

"Really? Garfinkels?" Lorna had always thought of that as a store for old people, her parents' friends and so on. And that was back before it closed, which was, what, ten years ago now?

Helene nodded. "I worked in men's suits. The department, not the clothing." She smiled and shrugged. "I met my husband there, so I guess it worked out as it was supposed to."

"That's Demetrius Zaharis, right?" Sandra asked.

Helene looked startled. "Yes. How did you know?"

Sandra shrugged. "I read a lot. A lot."

"I *thought* you looked familiar," Lorna said. "Your picture is in the 'Style' section sometimes." It was probably in other sections, too, but Lorna only read the "Style" section.

Helene looked down for a moment, but then said, in a voice more casual than the expression on her face, "Those pictures are always so awful that I hope no one recognizes them as me." She laughed lightly, but there was something chilly about it.

Lorna doubted it was possible to take a bad picture of Helene, but she could tell Helene was uncomfortable with the subject, so she changed it entirely. "Let me just get those Angiolinis, then. And a mirror. And let the trading begin!"

The trading took only a few minutes, but the conversation went on for another hour, and all the women grew more comfortable as the time—and the wine—wore on.

When things began to wind down, Lorna said, "So tell me, do you all have other shoes you want to swap? I mean, do you want to come back? I don't really know how to go about organizing this."

"I have a million pairs," Helene volunteered. "And, to be honest, it's nice to have a social occasion that doesn't involve stuffy political causes and publicity."

"Great." Lorna was thrilled. Always one to be afraid no one would come to her parties, setting this group up had been a leap of faith that appeared to be working out. She turned to Sandra. "How about you?"

Sandra's cheeks flushed slightly. "I don't get out much," she said, then shrugged. "But I *do* have a lot of shoes." She took a quick breath in and nodded. "So . . . sure. I'm in."

"Fantastic. I still have the ad on Gregslist, so I guess I'll just let it run a little longer, in case there are more of us out there."

Helene smiled. "Oh, there are plenty. The question is, how many are willing to come out of their overstuffed closets and be counted."

From there, the conversation grew easier, and at the end of the evening, the women had agreed to meet the next week, and to bring more shoes than they had this time.

When Sandra and Helene eventually left, Lorna was feeling optimistic about Shoe Addicts Anonymous. Things had gone so well. She carried the wineglasses into the kitchen with a new bounce in her step—probably thanks to her new brocade Puccis—and stopped to look out the window as Sandra and Helene parted ways under the lamp in the parking lot.

Lorna was about to turn away when she noticed the taillights on the car the man had been leaning against earlier flare to life.

Interesting coincidence.

A black BMW drew smoothly out of its parking space. Helene's, Lorna assumed. But after a moment, the car she'd been watching backed up and left the parking lot.

Lorna watched for a moment, expecting to see Sandra's car pass, but it didn't. She was just beginning to wonder if the man had driven Sandra over and waited in the car the entire time when there was a knock at the door.

Lorna hurried toward it, secured the chain, then opened it just enough to see that it was Sandra.

"I left my purse," she said.

"Oh! Wait." Lorna shut the door, undid the latch, then opened it again. "I didn't even notice. Come on in."

Sandra did so. "I'm really sorry to come back to the door so late."

"Don't worry about it. Actually, I have a question. Did you notice a guy in a little blue compact car when you were in the parking lot?"

Sandra considered. "I don't think so. Why?"

"Well, it's nothing, really." Lorna hesitated. Anything she said would sound paranoid at best, and would make Sandra nervous at worst, and to what end? The guy was gone. She'd watched him drive away. "I thought I saw an old boyfriend of mine out there, but it must have just been my imagination." She gave a laugh. "He wasn't really the stalking type."

Sandra eyed her shrewdly. "Are you sure?"

"Oh, yeah. It was nothing."

"Stalking is nothing to take chances with," Sandra went on very seriously. "If you think there's any chance this guy is dangerous, I think we should call the police."

Lorna was touched. She hadn't really had any close girlfriends since high school, and while this didn't exactly qualify as "close" or maybe even real "friendship" yet, she liked Sandra and Helene, and she was glad they were coming back next week.

"Honestly, it's nothing," Lorna assured her. Then, to make things seem even more benign, she added, "Just wishful thinking, I guess."

"Oh." Sandra nodded, her eyes understanding. "Well . . . sorry. But if you broke up, maybe it's best if it wasn't him."

"Probably so." Lorna gave a rueful smile.

Sandra retrieved her purse and said, "So I guess I'll see you next week."

"Can't wait."

Sandra hesitated by the door, then turned back. "I want to thank you for doing this." She gave a small smile. "I wasn't really sure I was going to come out here more than once. Like I said, I don't get out much. This . . . well, it was really nice."

Lorna felt warm. "I'm really glad."

Sandra left and Lorna went back to the sofa, thinking about what Sandra had said. More than that, she thought about how Sandra had looked. Like she really meant what she said.

Lorna had gone into this as a way to solve her own problems, to make herself feel better. She'd never anticipated her silly little shoe swap might mean much to someone else.

Chapter 9

B art—*Bart!* Don't lick that!" Jocelyn Bowen held one of her charges—twelve-year-old Colin Oliver—with one hand and reached for ten-year-old Bart Oliver with the other. His mother was having a cocktail party, so naturally Colin and Bart had decided to sneak out of bed to come down and make their presence known.

Colin did it by blowing spitballs at guests through a long narrow sterling silver straw.

Bart did it by licking the cheese puffs one by one and putting them back on the tray.

"Excuse me for just a moment," their mother, Deena Oliver, doyenne of the Chevy Chase nouveau riche neotraditional housewives, came rushing over to her children and Joss with a pained expression trying to poke through her Botoxed face. "What are they doing down here?" she asked Joss through gritted teeth.

"I put them to bed, but they were determined to come down and see who was here."

"So you *let* them?"

Joss wanted to point out that she was just their nanny and that, technically, since it was eight thirty at night, she was off-duty, but she wasn't a person who enjoyed confrontation. "I tried to stop them, but the minute I went to my room they shot out of theirs like bullets." She loosened her grip on Colin, whose wriggling was getting more intense. "Why don't you tell your mom why you wanted to come down?"

"I wanted to say good night."

"We already said good night, Colin," Deena said, her expression frozen but her irritation clear in her eyes. "After dinner. I told you I was having company and I had a lot of work to do."

One of the caterers walked by at that moment, stopping to offer Deena a glass of wine from a tray. She took one, and the waitress turned her gaze to Joss.

Before Joss could decline, Deena snapped, "She's *working,* she's not a *guest.*"

The red-faced worker moved on quickly.

"*Please* get these kids *out of here,*" Deena hissed at Joss. "Then come back down. I need you to run over to Talbots and get more wine. We're running low."

"We want to say *good night,*" Bart whined.

Deena stopped just short of rolling her eyes and patted Colin, then Bart, gingerly on the head, saying, "Good night, boys. Don't forget you and Jocelyn are going to the library tomorrow."

It was news to Joss, just like the wine run. "I'm sorry, Mrs. Oliver, but tomorrow is my day off."

"Oh, is it?" Deena looked surprised, as if she hadn't even realized Joss was supposed to have any days off. And, actually, given the way she treated her, it seemed she *wasn't* aware of it, since she was constantly asking Joss to go above and beyond the call of her contractual duty without regard to time or day.

"Yes, it is," Joss said, biting her tongue to keep from following up with some overstated apology.

Deena eyed her skeptically. "Do you have plans?"

Ah. Joss had gotten caught in this trap before. Staying in her room on a day off, or otherwise revealing she didn't have solid plans for the day, had gotten her roped into extra hours (with no extra pay) on more than one occasion. It was hard, but she was trying not to fall into that trap, even though it meant she sometimes had to just go sit and read at the library or wander around the mall aimlessly.

It wasn't that she didn't like taking care of the children. They weren't exactly angels, God knew, but caring for them was still easier than killing eight hours in a mall.

Just recently she'd begun looking into groups that met on her time off. The little southern Virginia town of Felling, where she came from, had a Kiwanis club, but that was it. Here in D.C. there were groups for everything—volleyball, softball, bikers, writers, puppeteers, you name it. Unfortunately, Joss wasn't super athletic, and the grief groups were just too depressing. Still, she had to find *some* way to get out of the house when she had the chance or else she'd spend the rest of her life catering to Deena Oliver's whims.

It was the principle of the thing. Joss wasn't being paid for overtime and being a general cook and bottle washer, so she shouldn't be doing it.

She also shouldn't be doing laundry, scrubbing floors, picking up dry cleaning, grocery shopping, painting kitchens, or weeding the garden, but somehow, despite her resolutions to say no, she always ended up wimping out and saying okay.

"I do have plans," Joss forced herself to say. And she was going to get plans for all these days, somehow, so she'd have a place to go. Maybe the karaoke club, though the one time she'd gone, there had been a really creepy guy who spent the whole night singing songs to her by some old group called Air Supply. "I've got this . . . meeting. Sorry."

Before Deena could object or, worse, ask for details, Joss began herding the children off. "Let's go upstairs, boys. Time for bed!" She knew those words were music to Deena's ears, and, sure enough, Deena turned and went back to her party.

As soon as she and the kids were out of sight, Joss relaxed a little. "You shouldn't have gone down there," she said to the two red-haired, pajama-clad boys who slumped up the steps in front of her. "She told you she was having a party and didn't want to be interrupted."

"So what? She's always doing something." That was Colin, the older of the two, who was beginning to get his mother's number already.

"Someone in the kitchen was smoking pot," Bart said, folding his arms in front of him.

Joss stopped, midstep. *"What?"*

Bart nodded, his expression faux-grim. "Mrs. Pryor was smoking pot. She always smokes pot. She is so dumb."

Joss thought a moment, then remembered who Mrs. Pryor was. One of the older, richer neighbors. A woman with blue hair and facial skin so tight, you could bounce a quarter off it. "No, no, Bart, honey, she was smoking a cigarette."

"What's the difference?"

"It's . . ." How the heck did he know about smoking pot but not about smoking cigarettes? Clearly the kid had his facts mixed up. Joss needed to give him just enough information to be correct, without overeducating him. "It's tobacco. People smoke it, but it's not illegal like pot is."

"What's *illegal* mean?"

"It's—," Joss began.

"It means the police will put you in jail, idiot," Colin said, perfectly mimicking the spirit, if not the wording, of his mother's impatience.

"If something is illegal," she said, shooting Colin a silencing look before turning her gaze back to Bart, "that means it's against the law. And yes, when people do things that are against the law, the police can arrest them and put them in jail."

"Is killing someone illegal?"

"Yes. Big-time."

"What about stealing?"

"Yes, stealing is illegal, too."

"Then that's why my Uncle Billy is in jail."

"Shut up, stupid," Colin interjected. "It is not."

"Uh-huh. I heard Mom telling Dad he was stealing Coke." Bart screwed up his face. "Why would anyone steal a Coke?"

Ooh, *that* was a little fact the Olivers probably didn't want bantered around. "Let's go up to bed, guys," Joss said before they could repeat any of this loud enough to embarrass Deena and Kurt. Both of them prided themselves on their stations in D.C. society—stations secured and assured by Kurt's booming German import car dealerships, Oliver's Motorcars—and Joss shuddered to think what they might do to shut their children up if they heard them talking about Uncle Billy's jail stint.

Joss took the boys up and told them they couldn't play computer games anymore, then supervised tooth-brushing and face-washing, told them again that they couldn't play computer games, put them into their beds, tucked them in, then stood outside their door and said a prayer that they would stay in bed so she could have a little break for the night.

She knew she should be firm with Deena about her work schedule. It didn't matter, or at least it shouldn't have, that she was at the house anyway; she was supposed to have her evenings off after 8 P.M. and all day and night off on Tuesdays and Sundays, but if she was in the house, she was inevitably at Deena's service.

Joss sat outside the boys' room for ten minutes, watching the hall clock tick away into her supposed free time. When she was finally convinced that the boys were going to stay put, she went to her small room and took out the *City Paper* to read up on what other twenty-somethings were doing with their lives.

It was a pretty sure bet that most of them weren't being held prisoner in Chevy Chase homes.

Around ten thirty, Joss's stomach began to rumble, and she realized she hadn't had anything to eat since the peanut butter and jelly sandwich she'd had with the boys at lunchtime. The party was still going strong downstairs, so she figured she could slip into the kitchen the back way and grab a few of the hot appetizers without Deena spotting her and asking her to—who knows—mow the lawn or something.

"What a *bitch*," one of the caterers, a middle-aged brunette woman who looked like she'd seen it all, was saying to another when Joss entered. "She's one of those freaks that likes to yell at *the help* in front of her guests so she looks cool."

"We should have made the spinach feta puffs so she'd have spinach stuck in her teeth," the other woman, younger and blonder but with the same basic look, agreed. "And what about that forehead? Did you notice? She's had so much collagen pumped in, it's sticking out like she's Cro-Magnon!"

The other laughed. "So instead of looking ten years younger, she looks two million years younger!"

They laughed.

"Thing is," the younger of the two said. "She seemed so nice over the phone when she hired us."

"Don't they all?"

"Yeah, I guess. We've got to build a reputation somehow. Even if it means putting up with this shit sometimes."

The brunette nudged the blonde and shushed her when she saw Joss coming in.

"I'm sorry to interrupt," Joss said. "I was just hoping to grab a bite to eat."

"Oh, sure, honey." The brunette went to the oven and began putting an assortment of beautiful little puffs and dips on a plate. "I noticed you weren't eating earlier when you were down with the kids."

Joss smiled. "Unless it's peanut butter, pizza, or spaghetti, I don't really get the chance to eat it."

"Lady of the house keeps you under wraps, huh?" the blonde asked.

"Carrie!" It was the brunette, looking alarmed at her coworker's indiscretion. "Sorry about that—Carrie sometimes speaks"—she shot Carrie another warning look—"without thinking. I'm Stella, by the way."

"Oh, so you own the company," Joss said, thinking of the Occasionally Yours minivan out front that had the words STELLA ENGLISH and a phone number underneath it.

"We both do," Carrie said, shooting Stella an affectionate look. "It's sort of a family business."

They didn't *look* like family, but Joss didn't ask questions. The food was delicious, and that was all she cared about right now. She chowed down on cheeses she'd never seen before, thinly sliced meats that tasted like bacon, puffed pastry things that looked sweet but tasted savory. Back in Felling, they didn't ever serve this kind of food. If a clip-art picture of it wasn't available for purchase to put on a restaurant wall, Joss had never eaten it.

The door from what Deena called the great room swung open, and one of her guests edged in, a diminutive woman with glossy dark hair and a tight green dress painted over her trim figure.

"Hello, ladies," she drawled in a sharp Southern accent, her gaze lingering for just a moment longer on Joss than on the other two. "You did a marvelous job, just marvelous, on the food. Fan*tab*ulous. I just love those little cheese pies, what do you call them?"

"Quiche Lorraine?" Stella suggested.

"Is *that* what they were? I've only had that in big slices. Well, they were fantabulous, let me tell you." She looked at Joss again, holding her gaze. "And you were really something, too."

Joss felt uncomfortable.

"I mean with the boys," the woman went on. "That Bart can *really* be a handful, and I know it. He's in my Katie's class, and my goodness, Ms. Hudson sometimes has to put him in time-out for the entire morning."

Joss didn't doubt it. Bart was on his way to being a real hellion. Joss was able to get him under control sometimes, but Deena invariably undid all her work by ignoring everything he did wrong when she was around. If Joss tried to discipline him at a time like that, Deena would object, favoring quiet over tantrums at all costs.

"Where are my manners?" the woman went on. "I'm Lois Bradley."

Joss had heard Kurt Oliver talking about Porter Bradley's pool and patio business several times, so Joss figured Lois must be his wife. "Joss Bowen," she said. "It's nice to meet you."

Lois put a hand on the small of Joss's back and guided her farther away from Carrie and Stella, to a darker corner of the kitchen.

"Is there something I can do for you?" Joss asked uncomfortably. She didn't know what Lois Bradley was up to, but in Felling people didn't touch people they didn't know.

Everything was different up north.

"As a matter of fact, there is," Lois said in a hushed voice. "And I think there's something *I* can do for *you*."

Instinctively, Joss glanced around, looking for an exit, or maybe emergency intervention from Carrie and Stella. But Carrie and Stella were banging around with dishes, not paying attention to Joss and Lois.

"I don't understand," Joss said, looking down at Lois, who had gotten disturbingly close.

"If you come work for me, I will give you a twenty percent raise," Lois whispered, glancing around herself, just as Joss had a moment before. "And I can *guarantee* you that my Katie is a whole lot easier than Bart and Colin Oliver." She practically spat the boys' names out.

Joss was taken aback. "Gosh, Mrs. Bradley, that's flattering, but with everything I'm doing here, it just wouldn't be possible for me to fit another job in."

"You wouldn't be working *here* anymore—"

The words were like the angels singing.

"—you'd just work for us. You could have whatever two days off you wanted every week, though I'd prefer you took the weekends off—"

The *weekends off*! Joss might actually be able to have a social life!

"—plus, of course you'd have your own car, and your suite at the house—"

Suite!

"—has a private entrance and full bath." She stopped talking and looked at Joss expectantly. It was like the quiet between *One!* and *Happy New Year!*

"Thank you so much for the offer, Mrs. Bradley." This was painful.

"But I can't leave the Olivers. My contract is for a year, and that's not up until next June."

Lois looked at her as if she'd just said she preferred squirrel over filet mignon. "Are you saying you prefer to work for the Olivers?"

Lord no, Joss wanted to say, but she knew she couldn't be quite that honest about her employers. "Well, I have a contract," Joss said evasively. "I'm committed through June."

"And there's no way I can persuade you to leave it?"

"I'm sorry, I can't." Not for the first time, Joss wished to heaven she'd never signed that document, but it was thorough and included a no-compete clause, meaning she couldn't work for anyone within fifty miles of Chevy Chase for the next year.

Lois's expression was a mixture of disappointment and irritation, but there was also a small shine of admiration in her eyes. "I wish I'd gotten a hold of you first," she said, a bit wistfully. "Please at least *think* about it, would you?"

It was foreign to Joss, this apparent longing for her. Even Joey McAllister hadn't looked at her with this kind of desire, and she'd gone out with him for *two years*. She'd never even *heard* the term *blue balls,* or learned of the condition's supposed ill health effects, until Joey had pleaded with her for sex in the backseat of his 1985 Chevy Impala, and even he hadn't looked at her with such intense interest.

That was just sad.

"I'm really sorry, Mrs. Bradley."

Lois Bradley reached into the little purse she had slung over her shoulder and handed her a card. "That's my home phone number and e-mail address," she said. "If you reconsider, or even if you just want to talk about the possibilities, *please* contact me. I'll be very discreet."

"I really don't think I should—" Joss tried to hand the card back, but Lois closed her fingers over it.

"Shhh. Keep it. Just in case."

Rather than argue, Joss decided it was best just to keep the card and dispose of it later so as not to embarrass anyone. "I appreciate your interest, Mrs. Bradley," she said, sounding like an operator who was trying to sell a magazine subscription or something. "Thank you."

Lois left, as stealthily as she'd come in, gesturing as she went for Joss to put the card into her pocket.

After she'd gone, and Joss was still staring after the door, Carrie came over to her. "Was she trying to nanny-nap you?"

Joss turned to her. "What?"

"That woman. She wanted to steal you and have you come work for her, right?"

"How did you know?"

"Oh, honey," Stella said, coming over to join them with three glasses of Mrs. Oliver's champagne in her hands. "We see it *all* the time. More business connections are made at these little rich-folk get-togethers than you could imagine."

"So what did you say?" Carrie asked.

"I told her I had a contract with the Olivers." Joss sighed, taking the glass that Stella had offered. She'd never tried champagne, but she'd always wanted to. "It's too bad, because she seemed so nice."

"They *all* seem nice when they want you," Carrie said, and Stella nodded her agreement. "All that changes once they have you. The nannies are always prettier on the other side of the fence."

In the distance, though as loud as if it were in the next room, Joss heard a shriek of laughter.

Colin!

She knew—she just *knew*—Deena had heard it, too, and she was probably on her way upstairs to reprimand Joss right now for letting the boys be so loud.

"I've gotta run," Joss said, setting the glass down untouched. There was no time to regret lost alcohol opportunities now, though. "Thanks, ladies, you've been real nice."

"Good luck, honey," Stella called as Joss hurried from the room.

✳

"What are you two *doing*?" Joss demanded when she found the boys in front of the computer in her room.

Two faces, illuminated by the dull greenish-white glow of the computer screen, turned to her in surprise.

"Nothing," Colin said, instantly belligerent.

"Yeah, nothing," Bart added, not helping his brother's case one iota.

"Okay, guys, move over." Joss didn't wait for a response, but pushed between them to get to the computer screen before they exited out of whatever godforsaken Web site they'd wandered onto.

"What the heck is Gregslist?" she asked, more to herself than the boys, as they clearly weren't going to give a straight answer.

"I was, uh, just looking for used dirt bikes for sale," Colin sputtered. "My mom thinks you're stupid, you know."

"You must, too," Joss responded, looking closer at the list on the computer screen. "Unless the dirt bike you wanted was a blonde with blue eyes and—" She looked closer. "—a passion for stargazing."

Colin looked at her slack-jawed. "Huh?"

She turned her gaze to Bart. "Was it you or Colin that wrote back to this *dirt bike* saying," she read, "'*I like your tits. Meet me at Babes Friday at seven*'?" Joss turned her attention back to Colin. "That sounds like a *very* interesting dirt bike."

"Don't tell our mom," Bart said impulsively. He was always the first to break in these situations.

Colin flashed his brother a silencing look, then said to Joss, "Yeah, she'd be really mad at you for letting us on your computer, so you better not tell."

"You know darn well I didn't *let* you on this computer," Joss said. "You were supposed to be in bed. And unless I miss my guess, your mom is probably on her way up here to find out why you're being so loud right now." She stopped and listened for what she honestly thought would be footsteps on the stairs, but heard nothing. Still she said, "I think I hear her now."

Colin looked like he'd seen a ghost. "I'm outta here!" Leaving his brother behind, he dashed back to his bedroom.

Bart stayed still, apparently frozen with fear. "You're not gonna tell her, are you?"

Joss's anger relaxed a little. Poor Bart was more a victim of his brother's bad behavior than anyone. Bart was *always* the one who got caught during the getaway.

"Not this time," Joss said, more gently. "But you have to go to bed."

"Will you read to me?" He glanced reflexively toward the door, clearly hoping his brother wasn't there to taunt him for his request.

"Sure." Joss smiled. These kids needed so much—if she could help them even a *little* bit, it was worth trying. Ever since she'd found a black snake tied to her bedframe with kitchen string, she'd been pretty sure it was too late for Colin, but she thought Bart still had a chance. "Let's go."

She took him to his bedroom, where he picked a picture book called *A Day with Wilbur Robinson* from his shelf. It was a children's book, probably a little young for him, but Joss figured the significance of his choice shouldn't be overridden.

So she read.

Bart fell asleep before she finished the book the second time, and

Joss pulled his sheet up over his shoulders, the way he liked, and put the book away before turning off the lights and leaving his room with a real feeling of freedom for the first time that day.

She went back to the computer and checked her e-mail. There was one from her mom, chatting about her dad's new project: a 1965 Mustang he was fixing up so they could drive across the country.

There was also one from Robbie Blair, the guy she'd dated since senior year of high school. Joss had broken up with him last Christmas, but he still wanted to get back together with her. She read his note with a combination of dread and melancholy.

joss, your mom told me you werent having such a great time there and I'm sorry to hear it maybe you should come home soon. me and my brother are starting our own plumbing company so I can support a wife ha ha. ceriusly come on back babe you know i still love you. robbie

Joss sighed. Robbie was a nice guy, so her feeling of overwhelming horror at the very idea of going back to Felling and becoming Mrs. Blair felt really mean. But Robbie didn't want anything more than to be a plumber in Felling, with a nice little wife and a couple of kids, and to watch TV with a beer in hand every night and all day on the weekends. There wasn't anything wrong with that plan, but it wasn't what Joss wanted.

What Joss wanted was to travel the world, to see things that she'd seen only in the out-of-date books in the Felling public school system. She wanted to have her own business, and to make a difference in the world she would explore.

Being Mrs. Robbie Blair was so much like death in her mind that it made her stomach hurt for him even to suggest it like it was possible. She shut down the e-mail program and was about to turn off the computer when she noticed the Gregslist window was still up from the boys' little adventure. It seemed to be a virtual classified Web site full of local D.C. events.

This could turn out to be lucky.

She went to the search bar and typed in "Sunday meetings support groups" and pulled up a long list of hits.

This was *great!*

But when she browsed through the list, she saw that most of them were either religious groups or substance abuse groups. Joss was neither religious nor a substance user—heck, she hadn't even been able to try her first sip of champagne tonight!—and she was pretty sure that joining in with either group would be catastrophic.

There was, however, a ski club that met in Dupont Circle at 3 P.M. on Sundays. With the Metro ride down and back alone, Joss could kill a couple of hours. And it wasn't like the group would be skiing anytime soon. After all, it was summer and still hot as blazes.

She clicked the link and gave her e-mail address for more information.

Then she typed the same information in for Tuesday nights. It was the usual assortment of sports groups—volleyball, badminton, softball, and bowling. There was also a grief group at the Episcopal church right down the road, but Joss had already tried one of those, and it was a lot more depressing than dealing with Deena Oliver.

So she continued to click until she saw the weirdest, most quirky ad she'd run into yet.

Shoe Addicts Anonymous.

She read the ad with interest. The fact that her feet were six and a half might be a problem, but the likelihood that this was a bunch of women who would sit around talking about something other than depressing stuff was great.

Therefore, Joss would make sure the shoe size wasn't a problem. There were vintage shops all over the place where she could find good shoes in the right size for not too much money. All it would take was a little research, and a little legwork.

Fortunately, taking time for both would be time spent away from the Oliver house so, with that criterion alone, it was perfect.

Chapter 10

"Ms. Rafferty, this is Holden Bennington from Montgomery Federal Savings and Loan. Again. There is a confidential matter that I need to discuss with you as soon as possible. If you could call me at 202-555-2056 as soon as possible, I'd appreciate it."

"I don't think so," Lorna said lightly to the answering machine before pushing DELETE. Holden Bennington was *always* calling her when her balance was getting low and he thought she might have checks or charges coming in that would bounce. Granted, it *seemed* like a nice thing for the bank's assistant manager to take the time to do, but Lorna was convinced that he was simply angling for a raise by taking on the Big Debt Girl as his pet project.

She'd met him a couple of times at the bank, and he struck her as a real prig. He was probably in his late twenties but had an air of seriousness about him that made him seem older. Although . . . his face was actually sort of handsome, and it looked like he might have a decent build under those stiff Brooks Brothers suits, but who could possibly tell for sure?

Lorna could totally picture him forty years from now, still looking and sounding very much the same, wagging his finger at every customer who had the misfortune to dip a tiny bit lower than they should in their account.

Like it really cost the bank so much as a dime when a person bounced a check.

The phone rang.

Lorna, who had always had a weakness for a ringing phone, answered it immediately, and to her regret.

"Ms. Rafferty, I'm glad I caught you."

It was, of course, Holden Bennington of Montgomery Federal Savings and Loan.

Caught, indeed. "I'm sorry?" Lorna asked, still unsure whether she was going to play this like it was a wrong number, or like she was a friend answering the phone while she, Lorna, was out—or if she'd bite the bullet and take the call for herself.

"This is Holden Bennington from Montgomery Federal Savings and Loan in Bethesda."

In one of the stupider impulses she'd had since seventh grade, she decided to play it as a friend. "Oh, sorry, you must mean Lorna." In her attempt to do a false voice, she ended up with an accent that sounded between Britain and New Jersey.

There was a long silence.

"You're not really going to try to fool me with a bad accent, are you?" Holden asked.

Lorna's face burned, but she persisted. "Sorry?" The less said, the better. She pulled her shirt up over the mouthpiece the way people did on TV when they wanted to disguise their voices.

But then she didn't say anything else, so she stood there like an idiot with her shirt yanked up and over the phone, waiting for Holden Bennington to make the next chess move.

"Ms. Rafferty, come on. I've heard your outgoing answering machine message enough to know every inflection of your voice." Brief silence. "You're not fooling me."

"She's not here," Lorna said to her shirt. "Can I take a message for her?"

Another long pause.

"Yes, if you could tell *Miss Rafferty* that the manager of her bank called—"

Lorna resisted the urge to point out he was the *assistant* manager.

"—and tell her to call me back as soon as possible, I might *perhaps* be able to save her quite a lot of money in returned check fees."

"Really."

"Yes. So you can tell your, uh, *friend* Ms. Rafferty that if she doesn't come in and get this straightened out, I'm going to return the checks *and* assess her the thirty-five-dollar charge that everyone else has to pay under the same circumstances."

Lorna knew she should cut her considerable losses and hang up then, but she couldn't stop herself from saying, "Isn't that confidential business? You probably shouldn't be leaving it in a message with someone other than the account holder."

"Under any other circumstances I wouldn't," he assured her, then hung up without so much as a good-bye.

Jerk.

She closed her eyes hard, thinking. He was on to her. Of course. He'd have to be a moron to not be on to her. How stupid was she, putting on a fake accent like a big old pair of size 12 Uggs, and hoping he wouldn't notice? Jeez, she *deserved* the bounced check fees.

Except she really, really couldn't afford them.

"I'll give her the message," Lorna said sarcastically to herself, sounding to her own ear like Dick Van Dyke in *Mary Poppins*. Good thing he was no longer on the line.

She hung up the phone, thought for a fraction of a second, then did what she knew she needed to do.

She hurried to the bank.

About seven minutes later, she stopped outside the doors of Montgomery Federal, catching her breath for a moment before ambling in as if casually coming by to see what Holden Bennington had wanted.

She expected to see him immediately upon entering, so when she didn't, she was taken aback. She was even more surprised when someone tapped her on the back of the shoulder.

"Ms. Rafferty?"

She whirled to face him. "Mr. Bennington."

"That was fast."

Her cheeks warmed. "What was?"

He held her gaze for one knowing second before saying, "Can you come back to my office so we can talk?"

She followed him through the paper-and-ink-scented lobby. No place had bubbled up so much anxiety in her since she'd walked the halls of Cabin John Junior High fifteen years ago. Not wanting to let on that anxiety, though, she said airily, "When I picked up my messages a few minutes ago, I heard that you'd called, so I thought I'd stop by since I was in the neighborhood."

"You live in the neighborhood, don't you?"

She shrugged. "It's about a te—a fifteen-minute walk. Or so."

"I'll bet you could run it faster." He looked like he was suppressing a smile.

Now, if she hadn't just spoken to him, she would probably ask what the hell he was getting at. Then again, if she hadn't just spoken with him and didn't *know* exactly what the hell he was getting at, she might not think anything of what he was saying at all. She might have just thought it was small talk.

She decided to take that tack.

"I'm not much for running," she said, gesturing vaguely at hips that were a little too curvaceous to belong to someone who exercised regularly. Of course, the slight breathlessness she was still feeling from running four blocks to the bank was also ample evidence of that.

"I don't know, you look like you could get someplace fast if you wanted to," Holden said, still looking like he was suppressing amusement.

That irked Lorna. "I don't have a lot of time, Mr. Bennington, so if you could tell me why you called—"

"Let's go to my office," he said again. "This is a private matter."

She followed him to an office so narrow that when he opened the door, it extended halfway into the room. Lorna struggled to get around it and sit in the chrome-and-mahogany-fabric chair before the desk, while Holden, much more lithe than she, maneuvered himself into his chair in what seemed like one smooth move.

"So what is this all about?" Lorna asked.

"Let me pull up your account." He began typing on his keyboard, staring intently at the computer monitor.

Lorna waited in silence, like a teenager waiting for the principal to pull up records of a bad report card.

"Here we go. Check number eight seven one two came in yesterday in the amount of three hundred seventy-six dollars and ninety-five cents."

"Well, okay, but I also deposited a check for four hundred and fifty something."

"That's not from our bank."

Lorna looked at him in surprise. "So what?"

"So it will take two days to clear."

"Other banks' money isn't good enough for you?"

"Because we can't verify the funds on site, we have to wait from clearance from the other bank." He leaned back and looked Lorna over like a painting he'd decided not to buy. "Surely this concept isn't new to you."

"I know you hold out-of-town checks," Lorna said evenly. "But that bank is half a block away. You couldn't park your car closer to this place than that bank. In fact, you probably *pass* it regularly on the way to the parking lot."

"That's not the point," Holden said.

Actually, make that *Holden Bennington III said,* because Lorna's eyes had fallen on the name plate on his desk and decided, in an instant, that he could never possibly understand what it was not to have enough money.

"But *you know* the bank is right there. You *know* you could verify the funds, or whatever, instantly. In fact, I think I've heard that these days funds *are* verified instantly because everything's done electronically." She was working herself up. "In fact, this whole notion of hanging on to a check for days comes from, like, the pony express days."

"But those are the rules," Holden said, looking for a fraction of an instant as if he might actually agree with something of what Lorna had said. "You agreed to them in writing when you opened your account."

"Which was, by the way, fifteen years ago."

Holden bowed his head in agreement. "You are a longtime customer. That's why we try to take special care of you."

"Huh," Lorna said, looking into blue eyes that weren't altogether displeasing. If she were a few years younger, that was.

And if he were a few ratchets less anal about *her* money.

"But we cannot continue to cover for you when you don't do your part," he went on.

"When I don't do my part," she repeated, disbelieving. The guy was, what, seven, eight, maybe nine years younger than she was, but he was accusing her of *not doing her part*, like he was a science teacher reprimanding her for letting Kevin Singer do all the dissecting of their frog in seventh grade.

"Exactly." Holden smiled insincerely, showing two nice rows of even white teeth, and some creases—*almost* dimples but not quite so pert—that Lorna hadn't noticed before.

All at once, Lorna knew there was no fighting this. The guy was too good at parental-style disapproval. There was no way in the world she could charm him into bending the bank rules.

"Okay, okay, I get what you're saying," Lorna acknowledged. "I do. But just this once, can you clear the check? I mean, come on." She gave what she hoped sounded like a very laissez-faire laugh. "The check in question is from Jico. They've got a reputation in this town. You don't seriously think it's going to bounce."

"No way to know." He was lying. He had to be.

Lorna sighed. "Then can you just give it a day. Just a *day*? I'm sure it will have cleared by then."

Holden gave a noncommittal nod, then said, "But the problem is, there are these other three checks." Again with the clicking on his keyboard. In a room as tiny as this one, that clicking was disturbingly loud.

Lorna shrank a little inside. Three more checks? For what? She racked her brain. Usually she used a credit card—she knew because she felt so damn guilty afterwards each time—so where could she possibly have written three more checks in the past week?

Macy's. That was one. *But* that had been to pay off the remaining forty bucks on her Macy's charge, so that was certainly . . . well, if not *noble* exactly, it was at least *worthwhile*.

And . . . where? Oh, yeah, the grocery store. Literally two dollars and ten cents. Literally. She'd gotten a quart of milk and some gum.

But she couldn't remember another check.

". . . this one for two dollars and ten cents will end up costing you thirty-seven ten," Holden was saying. Then he turned those blue eyes on her and said, "Can't you see that's ridiculous?"

"Can't *I* see that's ridiculous?" Was he *joking*? "Yes, *I* can. Of course *I* can. A child of three could see that's ridiculous. The question is, why do you do that to us?"

"Those are just the terms—"

"Stop blaming everything on some stupid terms I agreed to a thousand years ago." She heard herself, felt appropriately embarrassed, and pulled some of the hysteria out of her tone. "You know darn well those papers contain a million words a page in negative ten point Ariel sans readability font."

He gave another quick bow of the head, a gesture she was quickly coming to recognize as his acknowledgment that the bank was totally out to screw its customers. "I can't change the rules."

"And I can't change the facts," she said, waving an arm in the direction of his computer. "You can see my situation. I don't want to pay a bunch of overdraft fees, and I don't want you to send my checks back, so what can I do? Did you call me here just to shame me?"

Holden Bennington III looked genuinely surprised, then hurt, by this accusation. "I'm trying to *help* you."

"I appreciate that," she said, and meant it even though it sounded completely sarcastic, even to her own ear. "No, really. I do."

"Can you just promise me that you'll make sure you have the funds in your account *before* writing checks from now on?" he asked. All at once he looked like a tenth-grader playing a weary dad in a high school play.

But it touched her anyway. He cared. He actually *was* trying to help her. And she'd just been a snarky bitch to him.

"I will," she vowed. "I promise." It was on the tip of her tongue to tell him about Phil Carson, but that would have been going too far. She didn't need to trot her problems out like dolls at show and tell, especially since she hadn't had enough time to prove she could stick to the program. No, it was better just to let it go at this and be grateful he was going to waive the bounced check fees this time.

"Good," he said, and did another couple of clicks on the keyboard. "I was able to override two of those nonsufficient funds fees," he added triumphantly.

His triumph, at least with Lorna, was premature. "Two of them? Does that mean two are still being charged to me?"

"I'm afraid so."

"*Seventy* bucks?"

He nodded. "I can't reverse them all."

She wanted to whine *Why not?* but it didn't matter if it was because he literally couldn't or he wouldn't-couldn't; he obviously wasn't going to change his mind.

And he obviously felt she didn't deserve a totally free ride on this.

She had to be gracious. Anything less would have been childish. "Thank you very much for your assistance," she said, standing up and holding her hand out to him.

He looked at it for a moment, then shook it awkwardly. "You're welcome, Ms. Rafferty. I'm glad I could help at least some."

If you want to help, you could transfer a million or two to my account and stop charging me seven bucks a month for the privilege of having a no-interest account here, she thought. What she *said* was, "Well, working double and triple shifts like I am, it's hard to keep up with these things. Every once in a while I even come across a paycheck I forgot to deposit." It was a stupid lie. He could probably look and see that the one thing that she did like clockwork was deposit her check from Jico every other Friday.

"I see."

She was sure he did. "But I'll try to do a lot better with that now."

She struggled through a narrow pathway carved out by his desk, her chair, and the now-open door. "Thanks again, Mr. Bennington," she said, lowering her voice halfway through his name because they were in the main bank vestibule and she didn't want anyone there to figure out she had banking problems as opposed to, say, so much money she had to open a new account in order to be fully FDIC-insured.

He nodded stiffly. "Ms. Rafferty. I hope to see you again soon. Or, actually, I guess I hope *not* to see you again soon." The joke had the dual disadvantages of being both awkward and obvious.

Lorna could have strangled him for it. But, let's face it, she wasn't in a position to strangle *anyone* for pointing out her debt issues.

The sooner she took responsibility for them, the sooner she could leave them behind.

The world according to Phil Carson.

✳

Lots of laundry detergent commercials talked about removing blood, chocolate, and wine stains, but they never mentioned vomit.

Joss pulled her vomit-soaked shirt carefully over her head and balled it up so all the wet was on the inside. Then she threw on a T-shirt, grabbed a trash can, and hurried back to Bart's room, where he was lying in bed with a stomach flu.

"How are you doing, buddy?" she asked gently, setting the T-shirt inside the trash can for the moment and sitting on the side of the bed. "Any better?"

"No," he whimpered miserably. "But can I have some Coke?"

He seemed so small now. So innocent and vulnerable. It reminded Joss what she had gotten into this business for—she loved kids. She wasn't so crazy about hellions, and she certainly had her doubts about whether or not it was too late for Colin, but Bart managed to touch her heartstrings.

"Sure," Joss said, recalling the thick Coke syrup her mom used to pour over ice and give to her when she was nauseated. "I'm going to pop down and start a load of laundry and then I'll bring it right up."

"And some Count Chocula," Bart added.

It wasn't the flavorless shredded cardboard cereal Deena usually tried to get Joss to feed the kids, but Deena wasn't here, and Joss was ready to do anything to make this poor kid feel better. "Okay, but just a little."

She took the T-shirt out of the trash can and took it down to the laundry room, ready to do one small load.

So she was surprised to find two large laundry hampers in front of the washer with a piece of paper on top of them that had Joss's name in big, black Magic Marker.

Dreading what she knew was coming, Joss picked up the paper.

Joss: Separate the whites and colors and do all loads in <u>cold water only</u>.

No *please,* Joss noted. Not that it would have made her feel very much better about the demand. For a moment, she considered the possibility of turning around and leaving the room as if she'd never been there and never seen the note, but for all she knew, Deena Oliver had cameras set up and was tracking her moves.

She was better off just doing what she was asked when she was on duty, and getting the heck out of the house whenever she wasn't.

With a heavy sigh, she took both hampers and dumped the contents on the floor, making piles for colored clothing and whites. Or things that *should* be white, she amended mentally, coming across a pair of Mr. Oliver's briefs that bore unfortunate evidence that Bart wasn't the only one in the house with stomach issues.

Nanny was one job description. *Maid* was something else entirely. Joss had *not* signed on to be a maid. So why was she here, in a basement in Maryland, cleaning someone else's biological stains up for what amounted to something like two fifty an hour?

Times like this, Robbie Blair's offer seemed more and more attractive.

Then again, times like this even a convent seemed more and more attractive.

Later that night, when Joss was relishing a moment of quiet between the end of Bart's flu and the return of Colin from martial arts class, Deena Oliver called her into what she called "the parlor" but which, in Joss's house, would have been called "the fancy living room with furniture you can't use."

"Joss," Deena said without preamble. "Is there something you want to tell me?"

Oh, there were a lot of things Joss wanted to tell her, but she seriously doubted Deena was referring to the same things. "I'm not sure what you mean," Joss said.

"No?" Deena arched an eyebrow and waited, in silence.

A guilt she had no business feeling crept over Joss. It was the same feeling she got when she walked through those security sensors at the library—hoping she didn't get "caught" even though she'd done nothing to be "caught" at. "I don't think so," she said, her voice twisting into a question.

"What if I said to you the word *underwear?*"

If Deena's expression, on that leathery tanned face under a brittle cloud of bleached hair, hadn't been so menacing, Joss would have laughed. "I'm sorry, Mrs. Oliver," she said, her stomach clenching. "I still don't know what you mean." Unless Deena somehow had the psychic power to have picked up on Joss's distaste earlier when she'd encountered Mr. Oliver's underwear, but who *wouldn't* have felt distaste at that?

Deena eyed her coldly for a moment, then leaned forward and produced a wad of tiger-striped fabric from behind her back. She hurled it at Joss, and even though it had the velocity of a Kleenex, Joss jumped.

"That," Deena said. "Is what I'm talking about. Care to explain it?"

Explain it? Joss didn't even want to pick it up and find out what, exactly, it *was.* "What is it?" she asked.

Deena stood up and began the kind of dramatic pacing Bette Davis would have used in one of those movies where she was a horrible bitch. All Deena lacked was the cigarette trailing smoke punctuation. "You know damn well it's a man's thong."

Joss was at a loss. "I didn't even know men *wore* thongs!"

For a fraction of a moment, Deena looked surprised. Then perplexed. Then anger returned and settled on her face. "I found that under my bed, Joss. Under *my* bed."

"I—I can't explain—," Joss stammered. "I'm not even sure what you're asking me."

"I'm not asking you anything. I'm *telling* you that this stops now. And if I get so much as a *suspicion* that you are bringing men into my home again and taking them into *my* bed, I will not only fire you on the spot, but I will sue you for every penny I've paid you, do you understand?"

Joss was horrified. She felt the blood drain into her toes, leaving a cold path behind in her chest and stomach. "Mrs. Oliver, I *swear* I have never seen this—this thing before and that I haven't had *anyone* over."

There it was again, that expression that said Deena was less comfortable with Joss's denial than she would have been with a confession. "Have I made myself clear?" she demanded.

"Yes, but—"

"*Have* I made myself *clear*?" It was as if she'd gathered all her energy into her voice and was erupting with the fury of a Disney villain.

Joss was no fool. It was better just to concur and get out than to argue. "Yes, ma'am."

Deena gave a satisfied nod. "That's all."

Joss left, wishing Deena hadn't mentioned the part about suing her for back pay, because that firing wasn't sounding too bad right now.

*

"Are those Max Azrias?" Thank God for these Tuesday-night meetings. It was the only way Lorna was able to get any material satisfaction at all these days.

Sure, there was satisfaction in beating her debt down, but could you slip a shrinking debt onto your feet and totally change your mood? Nope.

Lorna needed shoes for that.

Helene nodded and handed the Max Azrias to Lorna. "You know, they're gorgeous, but they just never fit me quite right. Try them on."

Lorna slipped into the shoe, and it was like the proverbial glove.

"Oh, my God. What are these, *massage* shoes?" She took a few steps. "They feel amazing." It occurred to her that might be rude since Helene had just said they weren't comfortable to her. "On me," she clarified. "It could be my weirdly shaped feet."

"More likely it's mine." Helene smiled. "Now pass me those Miu Mius." She took the box. "By the way, where's Sandra?"

"She called about an hour ago and said she couldn't make it tonight," Lorna said. "It was kind of odd. At first she said she had an appointment, but at the end of the conversation she said she was sick. So I'm not sure which it is. Hopefully it's not something I did to keep her away."

"I'm sure it's not." Helene reached across the coffee table and refilled her wineglass. "She's probably just overbooked."

Lorna nodded, though she wasn't so sure.

"Is anyone else coming?" Helene asked.

Given that it was twenty past, Lorna doubted it, but there was the one person who had called. "There's a Paula something," she said, trying to remember the last name. It had been unusual. Like a holiday. Not Paula Christmas. "Valentine," she remembered after a moment. "Paula Valentine."

"It's funny, at first I thought there would be a lot more of us coming to these meetings, but I think a lot of women keep their shoe addiction in the closet." She laughed. "So to speak."

"Then there are the women whose addiction spills out of the closet and into the surrounding rooms. Literally."

There was a pounding at the door, so hard that it rattled the pictures hanging on that wall.

Helene and Lorna looked at each other.

"Expecting a Valentine?" Helene said, barely cracking a smile.

Lorna laughed, and hesitantly walked to the door to peer through the tiny peephole.

The stupid thing had always been insufficient, and never had it felt like it mattered as much as it did now. All she could see was a tall buxom figure in the hallway, silhouetted by the dinky overhead light.

"I guess it's her," Lorna whispered.

"Are you going to let her in?" Helene responded in a stage whisper, then cracked up laughing.

Lorna joined her. "I'm getting paranoid," she said, then took a steadying breath and opened the door.

The person before her was tall, at least six foot three. The wig couldn't have been more obvious if it had been made out of cotton candy. The makeup was likewise pronounced, as was the man's Adam's apple. His dress, on the other hand, was superb—it looked like vintage Chanel, though in that size it couldn't have been. But the earrings and Chanel pearls were the real thing, and they served to illustrate the word *irony* better than anything Lorna had ever seen.

She wondered, for one panicked moment, what to do. She didn't have an anti-transvestite policy at all, but this guy's feet were clearly twice the size of hers. Whatever he'd brought in that large silk Chanel bag, it wasn't size $7^1/_2$.

"Hi," Lorna said, in a voice much stronger than the uncertainty she felt. "Paula Valentine?"

The guy—come on, there was no question!—opened his eyes wide, looked at her in stunned silence for a moment, then glanced behind her, where Helene sat on the sofa. It was as if he were assessing the group and it didn't measure up.

The silence grew uncomfortable.

"Paula?" Lorna repeated. His weren't the eyes of a deer in the head-lights. They were the eyes of the guy behind the wheel suddenly see-ing the deer in the headlights. "Paula Valentine?"

The man's eyes grew even wider, and he nodded rapidly.

It took only one or two extra seconds for this to feel insanely bizarre, and Lorna glanced uncertainly back at Helene, who had pulled her cell phone out like a gun. It was open, and she had her thumb poised over the call buttons.

Which was a good thing, since Lorna was afraid she might have to signal Helene to call 911.

Before she reached that point, though, Paula Valentine turned tail and ran, his shoes clapping thunderously down the hall to the stairwell.

Lorna watched in stunned silence until she heard the stairwell door slam shut.

She turned back to Helene. "I don't think she likes our style," she said.

They both dissolved into laughter.

✳

Helene and Lorna spent a long evening talking and laughing, and burning through two bottles of wine and an entire twelve-cup pot of coffee. It wasn't until almost 1 A.M. that Helene finally left.

Judging from her own state of inebriation, Lorna guessed that she herself had probably consumed the lion's share of the wine, since for at least the past hour Helene had been drinking water.

So when Lorna went to the kitchen and noticed a car sliding out of the parking lot after Helene's BMW, at first she didn't think anything of it.

Then, when it occurred to her that it might be the same car that was in the parking lot last week, she thought she had to be imagining things.

But the thought nagged her for hours, even keeping her from sleeping. Finally, just after 2 A.M., when her conscience told her it was better to make an ass of herself warning Helene of a threat that didn't exist than to ignore what might be a *real* risk, she called Helene to tell her she thought she might be being followed.

Chapter 11

Helene woke with a start to the theme song from *Bewitched*.

It was her cell phone, the ring she had designated for social calls. Fun stuff. Political calls came in with the ominous opening to Beethoven's Fifth Symphony.

She opened the phone quickly to stop the noise, then looked at Jim, sleeping heavily next to her. His snores could have rattled the windowpanes. Thank goodness he normally slept in his own room. Tonight had just been a conjugal visit, the price she paid for her material comfort regardless of whether she and Jim were actually getting along.

When he'd confirmed, while undressing her, that she'd stopped taking the pill, she said of course she had. It was a lie. But she had, at least, remembered to remove them from the drawer and hide them in the lid of a shoe box in her closet instead. She was surprised Jim hadn't gotten to them first, actually. Two entire days had passed between her arrest and her remembering what had instigated the whole thing in the first place.

She crept away from him now, feeling a mixture of emotional detachment from him and a lingering tingle from his sexual skills. It was at least one reward for fulfilling her duty.

"Hello?"

"Helene?" It was a woman. With just the one word, it was hard to figure out who it was, though the voice sounded familiar.

Of course, familiar wasn't always good.

"Who is this?" Helene spoke in an urgent whisper, padding silently across the room in bare feet so as not to wake Jim.

God only knew what he would conclude about her getting middle-of-the-night calls.

Actually, *she* didn't know what to make of this either. "Who's calling?" she asked before the caller had the chance to respond to her the first time.

"It's Lorna Rafferty," the woman said quickly, and the mystery of whose voice it was fell into place. "I'm really sorry to be calling so late," she went on.

Helene's shoulders sank with relief. But what had she been afraid of? Who had she feared the call was from? Mom and Dad? Ormond's? Maybe . . .

Gerald Parks?

Bingo!

She had tried not to obsess over him, but even the thought of his name sent a shiver of nausea through her.

"Lorna," she said, relieved but unsettled by the thought of Gerald Parks. "Is everything okay?"

"I hope so. That is, I think so. God, you'll probably think I'm the biggest idiot for calling." She sounded flustered, stumbling over her words. "I probably should have waited until morning. Or until next week—"

"What's going on, Lorna?"

"Okay." Lorna took a breath that hissed across the telephone line. "I'm just going to spit it out, even though I think it probably doesn't mean anything."

Helene was getting anxious now. "Lorna, what *is* it?"

"I think maybe . . . I think maybe someone's following you. Do you have security or something?"

"No. Why?"

"Well, I thought maybe with your husband in the public eye, and being a politician and all, that maybe they gave you Secret Service—"

"I mean, why do you think someone's following me?" Helene knew she sounded sharp, and she didn't want to, but she'd had the same uncomfortable feeling, and it was nothing short of shocking to hear it from this person she'd only just met.

"Last week when you were here, there was this guy leaning against a beat-up old car in the parking lot, looking up in the direction of my apartment. That was why I was so nervous about who was coming."

Helene remembered that. Lorna had looked out the window about twenty times. Helene had just figured she was waiting for a boyfriend or something after the meeting.

"Anyway," Lorna went on. "I was sort of looking out there, keeping an eye on whether he was there or not—I don't know why—and I noticed that when you drove away, he drove out, too. At first I thought it was Sandra—"

"And it wasn't?"

"No, she forgot something and came back up to my apartment right after you left."

Dread settled in the pit of Helene's stomach. "Is that it?" She had a bad feeling it wasn't.

And she was right. "Well, it happened tonight, too," Lorna said. "Same car and everything. Of course, it could totally be a coincidence. In fact, maybe someone else in the building has some sort of Tuesday-night thing going on, and I'm just overreacting. Or maybe it wasn't even the same car."

Helene doubted it. "What did the guy look like?"

"Blond. Blah. Nondescript, really. Medium weight, medium height, medium build.

Gerald Parks. "Did he have a camera, as far as you could tell?"

"No." On this point, Lorna was firm. "He just stood there at the trunk of his car with his arms crossed in front of him. You don't have to worry about pictures, I don't think." She hesitated, then added, "Not that you were doing anything incriminating."

Not this time. "Thanks for letting me know," she said, thinking this *had* to be a coincidence. Gerald Parks was not shy; if he was following her, he'd probably just as soon confront her. After all, he still wanted money.

Her own paranoia was probably just contagious, and Lorna had picked up on it. Helene would keep an eye out, certainly, but she didn't want her new friendship to be shadowed by any discomfort. "Sometimes local photographers have absolutely no other stories, so they'll follow me looking for something." And sometimes they found it. "It's irritating, but nothing to worry about."

Lorna let out a breath across the line. "That's a relief. Look, I'm really sorry for bothering you. You must think I'm such a ninny."

Helene laughed. "Of course not! I think you're a friend who was concerned, and I really appreciate it."

After they hung up, Helene lay in bed for a long time looking at the glow of the driveway lights on her ceiling. She was in her own room, her sanctuary. The only place she even came close to feeling like herself.

But having Jim there changed the feeling entirely.

Another bad sign about their marriage.

She got out of bed and padded quietly across the cold wood floor to the front window. She wanted to unlock it and let in the summer night air, maybe smell the jasmine that she knew was blooming outside because she herself had planted it.

But she couldn't open the window or the alarm would go off.

Instead she leaned on the narrow sill and looked outside at the deep purple sky, the scattering of stars overhead, and the faint glow of the city reaching upward.

At times like this she longed for the big sky of her childhood, so filled with stars at night that it looked like sugar spilled on a dark tablecloth. She could almost smell the deep green scent of West Virginia, and she was half-tempted to get in her car and drive north for an hour and see it.

Of course she couldn't. Helene had no real business there, and if she went—and if the wrong people found out about it—it would raise questions she didn't want to answer.

So she went back to her bed, opened the bedside table to take out the bottle of sleeping pills her doctor had prescribed her during Jim's last political race, and took two of them.

That way, for a few hours at least, she could block out the present, the future, *and* the past.

✳

The woman on the box had long, gleaming, dark blond hair, with subtle highlights that added dimension and made her blue eyes look bright like colored glass. The color was called Deep Palomino.

What Sandra had ended up with was dark grayish green, with frayed and fuzzy ends.

Her blue eyes *did* look bright, however. They always did after a good cry. And so far Sandra had cried her way through *Jeopardy!*, *Survivor*, and *Law & Order*. She was headed for the evening news, and if the entire jar of mayonnaise—well, Miracle Whip—she had applied and sealed on with a plastic grocery bag didn't work, she would probably make it all the way through *The Tonight Show*.

Calling the number included with the instructions had been of no use.

"Unfortunately, you're going to have to wait a month before you can do anything," the woman had said after Sandra had waited on hold, listening to one instrumental Henry Mancini song after another, for about half an hour. No doubt there had been hundreds of other green-haired callers before her, because she had followed the directions *exactly*.

"A *month?* Why would I have to wait a *month?*"

"Because you opened the cuticle by using the product and, from the condition you described your hair as being in, if you put another product on, the developer might burn right through the hair."

Sandra pictured herself with half her hair short and shaggy and the rest breaking off slowly.

She could definitely see why they'd recommend against that.

"What if I put on some of that gray coverage color, like maybe in dark brown or something. Wouldn't that cover it?"

"No, because your hair was highlighted, some of it will grab the color more than the rest, and you could end up with a calico pattern."

Sandra mentally weighed that image against the long green she had now and wasn't immediately sure which was worse.

"What if I go to a salon?" she asked, though the whole point of buying the box and doing it at home was that she hadn't had to go to a salon. "Could they fix it?"

"They might say they can, honey, but their products are just as capable of burning your hair off as something you might buy yourself. I wouldn't chance it. If you wait a month for the cuticle to lie flat again and the condition of your hair to improve, then you can go to a salon for color correction."

"That's it? That's all you can suggest?"

"I'm sorry, ma'am."

"I bought your product in good faith. How can you get away with turning people's hair green and telling them they have to live with it?"

"The directions do say not to use it on highlighted hair."

"Where? Where does it say that?" Sandra had read instructions one through four word for word.

"Check the small print at the bottom."

Sandra was exasperated. "No one reads that!"

"Unfortunately, lawyers do," the woman said, sounding sympathetic for a moment.

This was devastating. She was finally starting to get out again, and this happened. "Well, thanks anyway. I guess."

"Certainly, ma'am. And as a gesture of goodwill, we'd be glad to send you a coupon for a new box if you could give me your address."

Were they kidding? A coupon for a new box? Sandra supposed she'd need it in the unlikely event that she was able to get her hair to return to a normal color and found herself with the urge to go Grinch again.

She'd hung up in disgust and trolled the Internet for home remedies. One of the most popular was to apply a strong dandruff shampoo and let it sit for an hour to lift the color. But that would require not only going out to the store, but doing it with hair that looked like something that had been plucked out of sewage and placed atop her head.

Mayonnaise seemed like the better option tonight. Something about the vinegar lifting the color and the egg conditioning her hair. Hopefully Miracle Whip Light had the same magical hair-mending properties. She'd used the last carefully measured tablespoon of her mayonnaise on a turkey breast sandwich for lunch.

It was so stupid, really. She could have afforded to go to a salon; it was just her damn phobia getting in her way again. After a really good week—kicked off by her meeting with the Shoe Addicts—she'd suddenly, out of the blue, had a panic attack this afternoon as she was getting ready to go to Lorna's.

It was weird because up until then she had thought the auricular therapy was going so well. The panic had felt like a major setback. Instead of going out to Lorna's, she'd stayed in her apartment twisting her hands, trying to catch her breath, and wishing to God she were someone else.

That's where the hair coloring had come in. She'd bought it a few months back when she was in a similar mood, but the mood had passed—a fortunate thing, she realized now—and she'd never used the color. But tonight, as she watched *Wheel of Fortune* and admired Vanna White's hair, she remembered the two boxes of Deep Palomino in her linen closet (she'd bought them previously in a bad mood) and decided to change her look, and therefore her life, for the better.

It never occurred to her to examine the bottles inside to make sure they both said "Palomino" and not "Dark Ash Blond," and even if it had, she wouldn't have realized that dark ash blond would grab her previously highlighted hair and turn it the color of rotten asparagus.

It was perfectly fitting for her to top it with salad dressing.

The question was, what was she going to do next? Giving green hair to a person who didn't want to leave the house on a *good* day seemed unusually cruel. But Sandra was one who was always looking for signs, and she had to wonder if this was one.

Maybe she needed to do the very thing she didn't want to—maybe she needed to go out and just . . . submerge herself in the embarrassment.

In psychology they called it *flooding*.

She thought about it for a moment. It was Thursday night, a little after eleven. The streets would be crowded—they always were in the Adams Morgan area—but not quite so crowded as they'd be tomorrow night. Not that that mattered, because if she told herself she'd wait and do it *tomorrow*, then *tomorrow* would always be a day away.

She was going to do it.

It was impossible to say just what possessed her, or where she got the nerve to go out—hatless—and be seen, but twenty minutes later, she was glad she had.

"Sandra?"

For a moment, it seemed like this was going to be the realization of a nightmare.

She turned to see a great-looking guy with a slight build, perfect wavy brown hair, chocolate brown eyes, and skin so smooth, it screamed *exfoliation!*

"Sandra Vanderslice?" Her name was formed by beautiful, movie-star-quality lips.

The voice, however, was a little bit high. A little short of masculine. Not that that meant anything. He was just a high talker.

What was strange was the fact that he knew her name.

How?

"I'm sorry. . . ." She reflexively raised a hand to her head, remembered the green, and felt a contrasting red fill her cheeks.

This had been a bad idea.

"It's me," the guy said, raising his eyebrows and looking at her expectantly.

No idea. She was drawing a complete blank, and she could feel it written all over her face. "I—"

He rolled his eyes. "Mike Lemmington?" Pause. "From high school?"

Her jaw dropped. Mike Lemmington! How was that possible? Mike Lemmington was the one person in high school who she could stand next to and feel, if not *slender* exactly, at least comparatively less fat.

"Mike!" Her own self-consciousness disappeared in the face of his incredible transformation. "Are you serious? Oh, my God, what—?" She shook her head. "I've got to ask, what did you do?"

He smiled, revealing perfectly even white teeth. "I just lost a little weight."

"Mike." If anyone could avoid the bullshit about weight, it should have been these two. "You lost a lot of weight. *How?*"

He shrugged. "Weight Watchers."

"Really?" She thought of her own Weight Watchers membership and wondered if a little more attention to it could result in as amazing a change as his.

"Every Thursday afternoon." He smiled. "But look at *you!* Look at *your hair!*"

How she'd forgotten for a few moments, she couldn't imagine, but the embarrassment was back. "Oh, it's—"

"It's *green!*" He reached over and fluffed it.

"Yes, that's because—"

"That is so bold," he went on, looking at her with what seemed like admiration. "Honey, I thought you'd never come out of your shell."

She frowned. Had she had a shell for that long?

Who was she kidding? She'd been born in a shell. She was practically Botticelli's *Venus* only without the curvaceous body or angelic Renaissance face.

"Good for you for expressing yourself that way. And it makes your eyes look so blue!"

"Really?" She needed this. She really needed this.

"Totally."

Sandra decided to go ahead and be the girl who had dyed her hair green out of confidence instead of the kind of insecurity that's drawn to boxes of blond hair coloring on a bad day. "Thanks, Mike. So," she continued on in the role of the kind of woman who would purposely dye her hair green to make some sort of bold and confident statement. "What are you doing in this part of town? Visiting? Or do you live here?"

"I've got a place right over in Dupont Circle," he said, smiling that glorious smile again. Had he had work done on that, too, or did it change that much with the diminished body weight? "But I come over here to Stetson's a lot. My pal tends bar there."

"Oh. I've heard great things about that place." She'd never been there. It had a reputation as a gay bar, though she wasn't entirely sure that was true. Either way, it was supposed to be nice.

Mike pursed his lips and looked her over. "I'm on my way there right now—why don't you come with me?"

Her heart leapt. Was this gorgeous guy actually asking her to go out for drinks with him? Maybe this green hair was the luckiest thing to happen to her this year.

Then again, it *was* green. And it was on her head. And no matter how much she might *want* to be at ease with that, she really wasn't. "Gosh, Mike, I don't want to intrude on your evening."

"Are you kidding? I'd love it. Besides, there are some interesting people there. You might meet someone. Unless—" He looked like he'd just stepped in something. "—you're already involved with someone? . . . I can't believe I didn't already ask."

"It's okay," she assured him. "And I'm not. So—sure, yeah, it looks like we're a go."

"Great! You are going to *love* Stetson's. And I can't wait for you to meet my friend Debbie. I think you guys will really hit it off."

Friend Debbie. Okay. If she was his girlfriend, he wouldn't be asking Sandra out. "I can't wait to hear everything you've been up to for the past—" She calculated. "—thirteen years. Jeez, has it really been that long?"

"Seems like a lifetime to me," Mike said breezily, putting his arm around Sandra's back. "I'll tell you what, my mother would have loved it if we'd hooked up a long time ago. She hates my lifestyle now, of course."

Sandra wished she were a little Twiggy-ish waif, so he could put his arm all the way around her and draw her close, the way the hero always did at the end of a romantic movie, but she wasn't going to quibble with that kind of detail right now. "Swinging bachelor?" she asked, hoping his response would help her gauge his current romantic situation.

"Right." He gave a laugh, then stopped and looked at Sandra again. "It is just so good to see you. I've thought about you so much over the years."

"You have?" She wished she could say the same, but the truth was, she'd tried pretty hard to block high school out of her mind entirely. "That's so nice of you to say."

"It's the truth." They began walking again. "From now on, we're going to be seeing a lot of each other, I just know it."

Sandra beamed. This was, officially, a *great* night. She'd remember this the next time things seemed to be going badly. You just never knew what was right around the corner.

Come to think of it, maybe you never really knew what was in your past. She'd definitely never seen this gorgeous hunk of man in Mike Lemmington.

She hadn't even seen the potential.

Maybe it was like that with life, too. Sometimes you just didn't see the potential in an ugly day.

Three hours ago, she'd been despondent, sure she was such a neurotic fat mess that she'd never really be thin or happy. Hell, she'd been afraid she might never leave the apartment again, becoming instead one of those weird stories that shows up in the *Post* every now and then about someone who was found two weeks after death when the neighbors finally realized the smell *wasn't* the awful Hunan restaurant down the street.

Now here she was, arm in arm with a man so gorgeous that heads were turning—both men's and women's—as they walked down the street together. She was on a date, though admittedly it was to what might well be a gay bar, with a great-looking guy. A guy who knew her from her past and accepted her anyway.

Things were definitely looking up.

*

"I need another panic bar," Sandra said to Dr. Lee. "In my left ear this time."

"Miss Vanderslice, it does not work that way. There is only one spot for that anxiety, and we are utilizing it. I assure you one is sufficient."

"I think I *am* noticing a difference," she agreed eagerly. "That's why I want another one. Because I'm not quite *there* yet, you know? But maybe another one would tip me over the edge." *Make me normal again,* she thought, but she couldn't voice something quite so pathetic.

Dr. Lee looked her over doubtfully, and she remembered her green hair. Did she need to explain? Nah. He probably saw weirder things than that on a daily basis.

"Miss Vanderslice, we can do another acupuncture therapy, since you're here, but your auricular therapy is perfectly set."

She nodded. "Okay, I understand. I was just so excited about the way this was working that I wanted more."

He nodded, and smiled kindly. "It will continue to get better."

He proceeded to perform another acupuncture treatment on her, and she left feeling like a million bucks. She couldn't wait to tell Dr. Ratner. It had been a long, long time since she'd had anything good to report in the way of progress.

Finally she did.

Chapter 12

Fortunately, when Joss found the torn top of a condom wrapper on the floor, under the lip of the kitchen cabinetry, she was alone.

Now, what *she* was doing under there made sense—Deena Oliver had, as usual, left her dishes in the sink with detailed and painstaking instructions on how to wash each piece by hand so when she'd dropped a small sterling silver mustard spoon, she *had* to retrieve it—but what any kind of contraceptive evidence was there for, it was hard to imagine.

The idea that it had anything to do with the Merry Maids who came twice a week was absurd, so Joss dismissed that thought as soon as it occurred to her. And the boys had revealed that Kurt Oliver had had a vasectomy. Which left her with only one conclusion, since she knew it wasn't herself: Deena Oliver was having an affair.

And when she'd gotten careless and left the evidence of it under her bed—or her safari vehicle, if the thong had been indicative of a theme—her first defense had been a pretty decent offense: blame the nanny. Right to her face.

Just in case push came to shove.

Heaven knew if Kurt Oliver had found them, but if he had, the elusive yet vaguely intimidating man of the house thought Joss was screwing around with some guy when the family wasn't home.

He might have thought they were Joss's, too.

The potential was humiliating.

But, like so many other humiliating aspects of this job, it didn't allow for an easy way out of her contract. Getting fired would have getting sued tagged on, Deena had made that clear, so Joss could only guess that displeasing Deena by breaking the contract in any way would end in the same result.

She was stuck.

And everything Deena Oliver did made her even more aware of that uncomfortable fact.

"I don't want you talking to my friends. It's a bother for them to have to take the time to be polite and chat with the help," she'd chastised one day after one of the mothers at Colin's overly elaborate birthday party had asked Joss where the bathroom was.

"Would you go pick up Kurt's dry cleaning? I can't find the ticket, but don't worry, they always know which stuff is his." It had turned out they *didn't* always know which stuff was his, or even who he was, so, after six calls back to Deena, they had finally found the brown Armani suit . . . only it wasn't a brown Armani suit but a gray Prada jacket.

"Merry Maids had to cancel today because of the weather or some other nonsense. When you're finished cooking dinner, would you please go clean the bathrooms? With this flu that's been going around, they're a mess."

And then there was Joss's most reviled interruption:

"Are you almost finished in there?" Deena had asked from outside the bathroom door one day when Joss was changing a tampon. "The boys are waiting for you."

It was a living hell.

So Joss returned, over and over, to the quest to find Something Else To Do on her time off, and of the offerings she had found for Tuesdays, Shoe Addicts Anonymous had seemed like her best bet.

Which meant she had to get out there and get her first real look at designer footwear.

∗

Joss wandered slowly through Something Old, a used and vintage clothing shop in Georgetown. The bus ride down had taken almost an hour, so she was going to take her time. After all, she had the whole day to kill until seven thirty, when she was going to Bethesda to the Shoe Addicts Anonymous meeting. She figured as long as she made it out of there by ten, she'd be able to catch a bus back to Connecticut Avenue in Chevy Chase, and walk the rest of the way to the Olivers' house.

Surely by then Deena would be asleep and unlikely to request any additional work. Unless, of course, she walked in her sleep. Which, given the volume of her requests, didn't seem out of the question.

"Can I help you find something?"

Joss turned to see a slight girl with long straight hair and the kind of billowy, flowing shirt and skirt that Joss used to call "gypsy clothes" when she was playing dress-up or getting ready to go out on Halloween.

"Thanks," Joss said. "I was just browsing, but I was hoping to find some shoes. Like, designer shoes? Size seven and a half?"

"Designer?" The girl looked as blank as Joss felt. "I don't know what *kind* of shoes we have, but they're all over here."

Joss followed the girl, catching a faint whiff of pot trailing behind her.

She stopped in front of a wall of shelves with shoes arranged on them like books. "This is what we have."

"Thanks," Joss said, spotting a price tag that read seventy-five dollars on what looked like a pair of her grandmother's old cast-offs.

"Sure," the girl answered faintly, and drifted back where they came from.

As soon as she was gone, Joss began digging through the shoes for something cheaper—she had to find the right price first, *then* she could look at the make—but there wasn't one pair under fifty dollars. She recognized the names on some of them from her Internet research: Chanel, Gucci, Lindor. Finally she settled on a pair of slightly scuffed Salvatore Ferragamos—a name that had come up repeatedly in her research—and handed over the fifty dollars plus tax.

It was an expensive initiation into this club, but she didn't have time to look around more. She'd figured it would be easy to find cheap designer shoes. Her mistake had been in going to a vintage shop in the most expensive part of D.C. Next time she'd go farther out, maybe to West Virginia, and find a true thrift store.

She was getting on the bus when her cell phone rang.

"Where the hell are you?" Deena snapped at her, so loudly the woman next to Joss turned and looked at her.

"I'm on a bus in Georgetown," Joss said quietly, trying to counterbalance Deena's volume.

It didn't work. *"What?"*

"I'm in Georgetown," Joss said, a little louder.

"Georgetown! What about your *job*?"

The people around Joss weren't looking at her, but she felt like they could all hear Deena, which was embarrassing in the extreme. "The boys are in school," she said.

"Does that mean you get the day off?"

Joss was confused. What did Deena want her to do? Sit in on their classrooms? And, if so, both? At the same time? "No, I'm going to get Bart in an hour and a half, then—"

"Get back here *immediately!*"

Joss's face burned hot. The bus pulled to a stop outside one of the fussy little shops on Wisconsin Avenue, and Joss made her way off, too humiliated to continue this conversation in front of everyone. "I don't understand," Joss said, wincing inwardly because she knew she'd get a lashing for it. "The boys aren't there, so—"

"So their laundry is! It's piled halfway to the ceiling in Colin's room."

A lie. Joss had done the boys' laundry yesterday and, as of last night, each of them had had only one day's outfit in the hamper in the bathroom. "He must have taken clothes out of his drawers and put it on the floor instead of putting it away." And he'd probably done it on purpose.

There was a seering silence; then Deena said, "You're skating on thin ice, you know that?"

Why? Joss wanted to scream, but she knew there was no point. Logic didn't work with Deena Oliver. "I'm sorry, Mrs. Oliver. I'll be right there."

"You've got fifteen minutes."

That wasn't possible, even given the cab Joss was already hailing. But she said, "I'll be there."

The driver pulled over to the curb, and Joss was opening the door when her phone rang again. She was tempted not to answer it, but it could have been anyone.

It could have been an emergency.

But it wasn't. "Stop at the Safeway," Deena barked before Joss even said a word. "Pick up milk and those Lean Cuisine dinners I like. That way your little excursion won't be too big a waste of time."

As she settled into the torn cloth seat in the back of the cab and looked at the meter, it occurred to Joss that this hour she'd spent out of the Oliver house would, when all was said, done, and paid for, have cost her about seventy-five bucks.

It was a pretty big investment in a group she wasn't actually interested in. She could only hope it would be worth it.

✱

Shoeho927.

It had a certain ring to it. Lorna entered a brand-new password into ebay to go with her new user name, waited for a confirmation e-mail, clicked the hyperlink and got the message, WHAT WOULD YOU LIKE TO FIND?

Could it be this easy?

She typed in the words *Marc Jacobs.*

Bingo, 450 hits in women's shoes! She scanned the page for size 7.5 and immediately saw *Bone Leather Boots NYC Marc Jacobs.* She clicked the link and read the description:

Brand-new in box. Sexy leather boots feature a rounded toe, side lace-up detail, side zipper closure, and chunky stacked heel. Leather lining and insoles. Size 7.5 M. Heel 3.75", shaft height 18"

Oh, my.

The starting bid had been $8.99, and for a moment Lorna felt like she couldn't breathe—$8.99 for *genuine* Marc Jacobs boots? They had to be fakes, or— Oh, there it was. Bidding had escalated the price considerably. It was now at $99.35. But that was still a savings of, what, five hundred bucks or so.

Worth it. So worth it. Good lord, if she needed to, she could sell them back, maybe even at a profit. She could certainly sell something else she had, if she absolutely needed to.

This was bargain shopping. The shoe-shopper's equivalent of Sav-A-Lot Foods. She eagerly typed in $101.99 as her top bid and beamed as the screen changed and said, YOU ARE NOW THE HIGH BIDDER.

If things didn't change, in one day, two hours, and forty-six minutes, the boots would be hers. At an *amazing* price. It was practically stealing, but it was legal.

Phil Carson would be proud of her.

Well, okay, Phil Carson wouldn't exactly be *proud* of her. He'd probably think this was another extravagance, but he just didn't understand. It was cheaper than therapy.

She'd maintain that to her dying day.

EBay was awesome. If she'd discovered it years ago, she probably wouldn't have gotten into that financial mess at all.

For the rest of the afternoon, Lorna kept finding herself drawn back to the computer, clicking the REFRESH button over and over to see if she was still the high bidder. Every time she did, there she was: *High bidder, Shoeho927 (0)*. And the time clock kept ticking down.

She couldn't wait to tell the other shoe addicts tonight.

But just after five o'clock—with twenty-three hours and eighteen minutes left in the auction—the message on her refreshed page switched to, YOU HAVE BEEN OUTBID.

For one ugly moment, Lorna sat there, feeling like Snow White's stepmother being told, "You're okay, Your Highness, but frankly someone better has come along."

Who had outbid her?

Lorna scanned the page—she was quickly becoming an eBay expert—and saw that the new high bidder was *Shoegarpie (0)*. The zero in parentheses, Lorna had learned, was for new users who didn't yet have feedback from other users.

So she'd been outbid by a newbie! Never mind that she was a newbie herself, the sight of *Shoegarpie (0)* really ticked her off. Especially since the bid that trumped her was $104.49.

A piddly two dollars and fifty cents higher than her own bid.

Without thinking too much about it, she raised her bid. $104.56. A nice, weird number. If her anonymous opponent had bid $104.50—as most people would—she'd beat her by six cents. Ha! Take that *Shoegarpie!* And take your *(0)*, too!

But instead of the blue YOU ARE NOW THE HIGH BIDDER message she'd been hoping for, Lorna got a dirt brown YOU HAVE BEEN OUTBID.

Shoegarpie!

A competitiveness she didn't know she possessed took over Lorna, and she put in her maximum bid at $153.37, still feeling like odd numbers would work for her.

And they did. She immediately got the YOU ARE THE HIGH BIDDER message and, with a satisfied nod, left the computer—on—to get ready for her guests.

As before, Helene was the first to arrive, dressed impeccably in an olive green linen suit that made her look positively vibrant. Her shoes were leather strappy sandals, in a green so deep, it was almost black.

"Prada," Helene said, in answer to Lorna's unasked question.

"Amazing."

"New." Helene smiled. "You may see them on the table in a few weeks."

Lorna laughed. "I certainly hope so."

Carrying on the green theme, Sandra arrived next, with startling green hair. Not that it was neon or anything—it was enough that it was green. And absolutely fried.

"I know," she said, before Helene or Lorna could comment. Not that they would. "I had a little mishap with some home hair coloring."

"My girl Denise could fix that right up," Helene volunteered immediately. "She's at Bogies, right on the northern end of Georgetown. I can give you her number. . . ."

"Thanks," Sandra said. "But this," she gestured at her head, "is apparently how I have to look for a month if I don't want to be bald. And, believe me, I've weighed the options. Green for a month versus growing out for two years . . . unless you can point out something I'm not seeing, I'm going with green."

"I guess there is a danger of your hair breaking if you process it too much," Helene said, nodding. "But when you're ready, make sure you give Denise a buzz. She works miracles."

And looking at her gorgeous auburn hair, with a cut so perfect that no matter which way she turned it fell in flattering layers, who wouldn't take the chance to go to the same stylist?

If Lorna hadn't just committed more than a hundred and fifty bucks to a pair of boots—she was beginning to have a little buyer's remorse on that one, and was hoping *Shoegarpie* had outbid her while she wasn't online—she would have made an appointment herself.

After a quarter of an hour or so, there was a knock at the door. Everyone looked to Lorna.

"I forgot to mention we have someone new coming tonight," she said. "Jocelyn."

"I hope she stays longer than last week's addition," Helene said, then explained to Sandra about the man/woman who had taken one look in the open door and had fled wordlessly. "We attract some weirdos," she concluded. "I mean, apparently *we're* weirdos, but that attracts even scarier weirdos."

Fortunately, that didn't appear to be the case this week, Lorna thought as she opened the door to a young woman with the fresh-scrubbed shiny-brunette good looks of the All-American Girl Next Door.

"Hi," the girl said, her looks made all the more charming by a slightly crooked smile. "I'm Joss Bowen." She held up a Pier 1 shopping bag. "I'm here for the shoe addiction thing? . . ." She followed Lorna's gaze to the bag and quickly added, "Don't worry, they're not made of wicker. This was the only bag I could find."

They both laughed, and Lorna, remembering her manners just a little late, stepped back and ushered her in, making introductions and explaining Sandra's hair issue so that Sandra didn't have to tell the story again.

Despite the fact that she was about ten years younger than the others, Joss fit right in, and they passed the evening gabbing away about their lives, loves, and jobs. Joss worked as a nanny for the Oliver family. Lorna had bought a car at Oliver Ford once—before they'd gone highfalutin and started selling only German "motorcars"—and had been so disgusted with the high-pressure salesman and total lack of support when she had mechanical problems that the very name *Oliver* made her shudder. She wasn't surprised to learn that the Olivers themselves were as obnoxious as their sales staff.

"Why don't you quit?" Lorna asked, though it had to be admitted that was pretty much her solution to any and all work woes. That was why she was working at Jico instead of, say, an office where she could use the English degree she'd gotten from the University of Maryland. "I bet there are hundreds of people in this area looking for a good nanny."

"I've got a contract," Joss said, the weight of her signature on that contract clear in her eyes.

"Break it!" Okay, so maybe Lorna wasn't the best one to be dispensing work advice. It was better, only a little, than her giving financial advice, but it was still inappropriate.

Fortunately, clearer heads prevailed, in the form of Sandra and Helene.

"How much longer do you have on your contract?" Sandra asked.

"Nine months. Four days." Joss smiled. "And about three and a half hours."

"Have you shown the contract to a lawyer?" Helene asked. "Perhaps see if there's a loophole that could get you out? I'm guessing cleaning and grocery shopping, and working after hours aren't in your job description, so that might be your ticket right there."

Joss looked hopeful for a moment, then shook her head. "I can't break a contract. If I did, who'd want to hire me? The Olivers would trash me, they'd make sure no one would even give me an interview."

"Then you must *at least* make sure you get out at every opportunity so she can't snag you into doing her bidding for her," Lorna insisted.

"I agree," Sandra said.

"Maybe we can go shopping—" Lorna stopped herself midsentence. Shopping was not in her immediate future. But what social thing could she propose that didn't cost money? Bridge? Power walking?

Get real.

"—or something," she finished, in a voice somewhat weaker than the one she'd begun with.

By the end of the evening, Lorna had scored a pair of gold Hollywould Marilyn sandals and some Jil Sander open-toe black heels, and was definitely feeling guilt about having bid so much on the boots on eBay. She turned on her computer, hoping to see *Shoegarpie* had swooped in and gotten herself a *(1)* for already having purchased and paid for the boots.

It didn't happen. As soon as her reluctant fingers signed her in, she saw the boots listed under ITEMS I'VE WON. $153.03. Plus shipping, which she hadn't even thought of. That added another fifteen bucks to the grand total.

Shit.

Shit shit shit.

She clicked on the picture again. They *were* nice. Really nice. And they'd go with just about anything. As soon as winter came around, she'd be damn glad to have them.

Feeling bolstered, she reviewed the auction information to find an address to send the payment. She was all ready to write a personal check when she noticed the seller would take only a cashier's check or money order.

The next morning she went to the bank to get the money order. Thankfully, Holden Bennington the Pretentious Third was nowhere in sight, and when she got up to the teller's window, she thought she was home free.

But when the teller clicked into her account, he got a strange, sort of *uh-oh* look on his face, and said he needed to get his manager.

Lorna could barely sputter an objection before he was gone. For one wild moment, she considered running, and when the teller returned with Holden, she wished she had.

"Ms. Rafferty."

"Mr. Bennington."

"How about coming back to my office?"

The temptation to refuse was overwhelming, but what could she do? She *had* to pay for the boots. "Such personal service," she commented, and followed him back to what was rapidly becoming a familiar walk through the bank.

"A hundred and sixty-eight dollars and three cents," he said, gesturing for her to sit in what they would both no doubt be coming to think of as *her* seat.

"That's right."

"Your bank balance is currently two hundred twenty dollars and forty-nine cents—"

She splayed her arms in a broad shrug. "Sounds like a go to me."

"Except you've gotten approval for—" He clicked into the computer, and Lorna resisted the urge to suggest he simply put her account on his *favorite places* list. "—two hundred and four dollars and sixteen cents." He looked at her. "One of which was a dollar preapproval at the gas station for what was probably more than a dollar's worth of gas. So I'm guessing that takes us back into the red."

Lorna swallowed. She did *not* like living this way. And she could get snarky with Holden, but what would be the point? She needed the guy in charge of her bank account to be on her side, not against her.

"Look," she said. "I'm working on this. And I won't lie, it's been a struggle. I'm sure you can see that." She gestured toward his computer monitor. "But I really need to get this cashier's check today."

"I can't just give you money you don't have."

"Well, you *could*." She smiled. "Isn't that what banks do?"

To her surprise, he smiled back.

And to her even greater surprise, she thought he looked sort of cute when he smiled.

He worked more on the computer, looking like he was really wrestling with the problem, but then said to her, "I'm sorry, but there's nothing I can do."

She wondered what the penalty was for being an eBay deadbeat. She'd probably be banned. No sooner had she found this wonderful bit of heaven, where she could buy designer shoes at discount store prices than she'd have to give it up forever.

Then she remembered the tip money in her purse. "Oh! Wait!" She dug through her bag while Holden waited silently on the other side of the desk. Then she found what she was looking for: an untidy wad of money she hadn't even counted yet. "I need to make a deposit."

She counted it out—$204, sixty-four dollars of which were ones—and handed it over to Holden.

"I can get that cashier's check now, can't I?" she asked.

He looked pained. "Yes. Though I'm inclined to advise against it."

"Yeah, well, duly noted. But you can cut the check, right?"

He sighed, looked her dead in the eye—she hadn't noticed the unusual greenish blue of his eyes before—then nodded. "I know this is going to come back to haunt me," he said. "But legally, I can't refuse."

She gave a quick smile. "Buck up, Bennington. It will be fine. Honestly."

Chapter
13

"I can't help myself. . . . I love you and nobody else. . . ." Sandra wasn't usually one to bounce out of bed in the morning, but today she was in an excellent mood, singing the song she suddenly couldn't get out of her head. Mike had called while she was at Lorna's last night and left a message asking if she wanted to go to Cosmos tonight for karaoke night.

She would never, ever get up in front of people and *breathe,* much less sing, but she was glad to go and have some martinis with Mike. Hell, she'd be glad to go and do just about *anything* with Mike.

How had she managed to go all these years without giving him a thought? And, more to the point, how lucky was she that he'd turned up in her life just when she needed it most.

" . . . *no matter how I try, my love I cannot hide . . .*" She booted her computer and danced around the room to get the phone and call Mike back. She got his voice mail and left a message. Then she called

Helene's stylist. The soonest appointment she could get was in a month. She toyed with the idea of asking for someone else, but the green hair had sort of brought her luck. If she'd just been blending into the woodwork as usual, maybe Mike would never have noticed her that night.

Besides, he liked it.

So . . . okay. She'd keep it a little longer. Why not? It wasn't like she looked in the mirror a lot and had to face it.

She sat down at the computer and started clicking around. She had her routine. E-mail, Zappos, Poundy.com, Washingtonpost.com, eBay, and usually at least two or three Google searches on whatever might have caught her curiosity the night before.

Lately she'd been Googling Mike Lemmington a lot. He'd gotten some academic achievements in college that were still listed on the site, and a brief bio, along with a tiny picture, was posted on his advertising company's Web site. She'd looked at that picture a lot. If she hadn't been so afraid that he'd end up seeing it sitting out somewhere, she would have printed it out.

She completed her routine, then did the thing she always saved for last on Wednesdays—she went to the bathroom, peed, stripped off every shred of clothing, including any hair accessories, and got on the scale. She had to do it once a week, and she chose Wednesday because it gave her a reasonable amount of time to recover from the possibility of a fattening weekend. (Lonely Friday and Saturday nights often resulted in the consumption of empty calories.)

She took a breath and stepped onto the scale. She hated seeing the number. Especially since lately it hadn't gone down much, if at all. Two weeks ago, she'd actually been up half a pound, and last week she hadn't been able to stand the idea of getting on at all.

This week was different, though. She was happy. Excited. *Optimistic.*

Jeez, when was the last time she could have said that? So she stood on the scale and waited for the numbers to settle.

She was down four pounds.

Four! She got off the scale, let it reset, and got on again. Same result. Down four pounds.

She couldn't believe it. She knew she hadn't been thinking about food so much, but this? This was a surprise.

She put her clothes back on and eyed the scale again, almost confident enough to get on it fully clothed.

But that was going too far. She slid the scale back under the sink and promised herself to keep up the good work and not get on again until next week.

With everything in order, and ready for tonight, Sandra went to work. She called the central number and logged in, then waited for the first call while watching a morning talk show, where two women were duking it out over a tall thin guy with a tuft of pale peach fuzz on his chin.

It didn't take long for the first call to come in.

"Penelope," he said, his voice thick and slurred. "Pen . . . el . . . o . . . *peeeee.* You got me hot, babe."

"Hey, baby," she cooed. "Who are you?"

"Jis' call me Long Dong Silver. . . ." He laughed at his own joke for a good long time. At least a buck fifty's worth. "Ge' it? Long dong . . ." He laughed again.

Excellent. With any luck, this would be a case of whiskey dick that would take a good long time to satisfy. She could use the money to buy Mike some shoes. He was woefully undereducated and undersupplied in that department.

She giggled for him. "You're funny!"

"Aw, man, I gottamillion of 'em."

He proceeded to give her a litany of crude puns, one after the other, as the dollars on his phone bill racked up into the tens, the twenties . . . Finally he stopped and said, "You spose' be talkin' to *me*. Get me hot, babe. I wanna feel ya. Talk to me, Pen-el-o-*pee* . . ."

Sandra leaned back on the sofa, put her feet up on the coffee table, and said, "I'm wearing black patent leather hip boots. . . ."

It was a good day. A *very* good day. She didn't know what it was about this particular Wednesday that had so many men going hot and heavy, but when three o'clock rolled around, she'd logged a good solid six hours. More than enough to go to Ormond's and get that pair of pale suede Hogans she thought would be just perfect for Mike. Not so casual that they looked cheap, yet not formal at all, the Hogans were the perfect, elegant choice.

When she got to the shoe department, it was, of course, Luis who was working there. She'd never quite forgiven him for the icy, condescending way he'd treated her when she'd first encountered him. As if he'd looked at her and instantly decided she must be looking for the thrift store down the street instead.

Their exchange, and her resulting purchase, had apparently made her more memorable to him, because when he saw her he raised his eyebrows and addressed her by name, "Ms. Vanderslice. It's been such a long time since we've seen you! But it's always a pleasure," he hastened to add.

Not always, she remembered.

"I'm looking for a pair of Hogans for my boyfriend," she said. Though she'd only used the term *boyfriend* because it was shorter than saying *this guy I'm seeing and hoping to develop a relationship with*, but she liked the sound of it nevertheless.

Boyfriend. She'd never really had a boyfriend, so some part of her was still stuck in a fifth-grade mentality, trying on "grown-up words" to see how they felt.

"Hogans," he said, and a light went into his eye. "Good choice. I, myself, am partial to them. Tell me, what size does your boyfriend wear?" Something about the way he asked it made her think he was skeptical of the relationship, but that could have been her imagination.

"He wears a nine." Under the guise of using the bathroom, she'd checked out his closet when they'd gone by his place on the way to Stetson's one night.

Luis snapped his fingers and pointed at her. "You know, we just got some Zenders in as well. I think you might like them even more than the Hogans. Take a seat, and I'll go get you some to choose from."

"Thanks." She sat down and was startled when he asked, "Would you like a cup of coffee?"

She shook her head. "No, thanks."

"Tea? Anything?"

Truth be told, she really resented his overly solicitous approach to her now, but she wasn't going to confront him about it. Instead she just tried to act like she was above it all. "Nothing, thanks."

He hurried off and was back within a couple of minutes with five boxes. He set the boxes down and removed the tops, telling Sandra, "The Zenders are about a hundred dollars more than the Hogans, but who can put a price on style, am I right?"

Sandra smiled politely.

He set the shoes up expertly, showing them off to their greatest advantage. "The color of these Bruno Maglis, I'm sure you'll agree, is just magnificent." He set down a pair in a deep, rich burgundy.

She had to admit, they were nice. But too formal. "My friend—my boyfriend, that is, does a lot of walking in his job, and I think those are just too formal. I like the Hogans because they're such comfortable walking shoes."

"Absolutely." Luis moved the boxes around so the Hogans were closest to Sandra. He was also careful to make sure it was the more expensive pair that was in front. "What does he do? Your boyfriend, I mean."

"He's in real estate."

Luis nodded without real interest. "These are perfect for any discerning man." He nudged the pricier pair toward her.

She deliberately picked up the less expensive pair. Actually, she liked them better anyway.

"Luis!" An older woman Sandra had never seen before came out from the back room. "Javier's on the phone. Again."

"Tell him I'll call him back," Luis snapped. Then, perhaps realizing his tone, he explained, "We have a policy not to leave customers unattended."

Sandra thought that was odd. "I think I can fend for myself if you need to take a phone call."

"No, no." He gave an exasperated sigh. "It's a new policy." Then he added, in confidential tones, "It's because of what happened with the senator's wife."

"I'm sorry, it's because of what?" She couldn't even imagine what could have happened with a senator's wife that prevented Luis from taking a phone call. Had she had some sort of weird accident while no one was here to take care of her? Perhaps she'd been attacked by a pair of alligator pumps?

"I'm not supposed to talk about it," Luis said, in the voice of one who had already talked about *it*, whatever it was, repeatedly. And who had no intention to stop talking about it. "But I can trust *you*, I'm sure."

Sandra's life was already so uncomfortably full of men's secrets, that the words *I can trust you, I'm sure* made her instantly aware that he was about to say something she probably didn't want to hear. "I wouldn't want you to get in trouble," she began. "Honestly, you don't—"

"She was caught *shoplifting!*" He pressed his lips together and nodded, watching Sandra for a reaction.

"Who was?" Sandra was confused. Had she missed something? Surely Luis wasn't saying that some senator's wife—

"The senator's wife," Luis said in a stage whisper. His glee was evident. "Helene Zaharis."

⋆

The party was excruciating.

Of course, most of these political fund-raisers were, but this one was at the home of the controversial Mornini family—rumored to be involved in organized crime, though Helene doubted it—which should have spiced things up considerably.

Maybe she was just too tired to appreciate it tonight. Surely she and Jim would be leaving soon. It was already . . . Helene looked for a clock and found one on the mantel. Eight fifteen? That was *all*?

Good Lord, she was sure it was past eleven.

She tried to shake off some of her exhaustion and headed for the open bar to order her fourth Red Bull of the evening. The caffeine would undoubtedly kick in full steam in a few hours, right about the time she was lying down to sleep.

"Another one," she said to the bartender, smiling and shaking her head. "Maybe make it a double."

He gave a charming smile and took out a small can and poured the contents into a short crystal glass.

"Goodness, you look as bored as I feel!"

Helene turned to see Chiara Mornini, the gorgeous, petite, *young* Italian wife of patriarch—and septuagenarian—Anthony. They'd never met, but Chiara's picture regularly showed up in the *Washington Post* "Style" section, and the *Washingtonian* magazine.

"Chiara Mornini," Chiara said, holding out a manicured hand.

"Helene Zaharis," Helene said, and thought she noticed something flicker across Chiara's expression. She could only hope it wasn't that she disliked Jim's politics. "I apologize if I look bored, I'm really just tired." Usually her game face was better than this.

"Oh, honey, this is *boring*," Chiara said with a laugh. "We just do what we have to do, for the men." She gave a trill of laughter.

"It pays the bills," Helene joked, then took a step and stumbled slightly. A mistake. That was far too indiscreet. She needed to get some coffee before she embarrassed herself and, heaven forbid, Jim.

But Chiara didn't look like she cared one whit. In fact, Helene's stumble only served to call Chiara's attention to her feet. "My goodness, are those Stuart Weitzman?"

Helene looked at her in some surprise. "Yes. Good call."

"Oh, I *love* him! I nearly talked Anthony into buying me his diamond-encrusted Cinderella Slippers, but he felt two million was too much for a pair of shoes." She sighed. "He'd drop it on a necklace but not shoes. I couldn't convince him it was the same thing, even though Alison Krauss wore them at the *Oscars,* for heaven's sake."

Even Helene would have a hard time rationalizing that, but she was in awe of Chiara's attitude. "I can't see my husband going for that either."

"They just don't understand, do they?"

Oh, there was so much Jim didn't understand. "No," Helene said simply.

"So . . . you're a shoe person?" Chiara asked.

Helene laughed. "You might say I'm an addict."

Chiara smiled. "I knew it! I could tell we had something in common as soon as we met. Quite a few things, I'll bet. As a matter of fact," Chiara paused a moment, then whispered, "come upstairs with me for a moment. I have something I want to show you."

Helene glanced uncertainly in Jim's direction.

"Oh, yes, of course he'll be mad. Anthony as well. Forget them." Chiara took Helene by the arm in instant camraderie. "If they want us to stick around, next time they better invite some pretty young boys for us to look at."

Helene liked this woman.

They went upstairs, through a gilded hallway more ornate than anything Helene had seen outside of a church, and Chiara led her through a red room with a massive round bed with red satin sheets, to what appeared to be a large empty room lined with doors.

"What is this?" Helene asked, thinking how great that bed had looked and how much she'd like to just take a small nap.

"This? This is my closet." Chiara sashayed over to one of the doors and pulled it open.

Lights flashed to life in the little room, revealing floor-to-ceiling trays with pull-out boxes.

Shoe boxes.

Each one of them had a label with some sort of cataloging number. Chiara went straight to C-P-4 and took out the most beautiful stiletto T-strap sandals Helene had ever seen.

"Look at them, darling. You won't believe it."

"They're lovely," Helene understated, turning the shoe in her hand to examine it like a work of art.

The arch was a graceful waterfall perched on a heel so exquisitely shaped, it could have been made of crystal. The leather was as soft and supple as Egyptian cotton sheets.

Helene looked for a label, or even a size stamp, but there was none.

"Where did you get these?" she asked.

Chiara smiled and raised an eyebrow. "My nephew, Phillipe Carfagni."

"Nephew?" Chiara couldn't have been older than twenty-six or twenty-seven. How old could her nephew be?

Chiara shrugged. "He's my age, but my father was married before, you see. My sister, from his first marriage, is already middle-aged."

Which explained a lot about Chiara's choice of husband. Chiara's father was probably Anthony's age.

"Anyway, my nephew makes these shoes, wonderful shoes. Go—try them on."

"What size are they?"

"Oh, of course. Your feet would be too big for them." Chiara clicked her tongue against her teeth. "It's a shame, because they feel like little tiny hands are caressing your feet."

Helene laughed at the image. "Where does he sell them?"

Chiara shook her head. "He does not. Not yet. I've only just learned of his talent, and Anthony—" Chiara interrupted herself to let fly a brief, staccato string of Italian. "Anthony will not support the young man's efforts. The investment would be great, of course—" She gestured at the shoes. "—you can see that. But Anthony . . . I think he is jealous. Phillipe is very young, and very handsome."

Suddenly Helene wanted nothing more than to have a pair Phillipe's shoes in her own size. She didn't even care that much if they were comfortable; they were beautiful enough to make up for a whole host of aches and pains.

It had always been that way for her, ever since she was a child. If someone told her she couldn't have something, she was driven to prove them wrong. To have it, whatever it was.

That was how she'd gotten where she was today—by proving to her father, a man who told her she'd "never amount to anything," that she could have any material thing she wanted.

It didn't make a difference that her father was dead, that he'd been gone long before she'd left home.

She still had something to prove to him.

And now she had something to prove to Jim as well.

She approached him about the idea of investing in Phillipe's designs as they were driving home from the party.

His answering bark of laughter had been her first indication that he wasn't going to be impressed with her suggestion. "Leave it to you to come up with a way to make money off of shoes." He glanced at her from the driver's seat, the streetlights flickering across his face so quickly, she couldn't read his expression. "I admire that, really."

"You should. I'm sure you'd rather I make money *from* shoes, than spend it *on* them."

"Or steal them," he added.

That stung. He'd never let her forget it. They both knew that. "I don't think that's fair," she said to him.

"It's just the truth, babe." He reached over and put his hand on her thigh. "You know I'm nothing if not honest."

She thought of the pubic hair between Pam's teeth a couple of weeks ago, and decided she didn't want to pursue this conversation with Jim. She might be able to persuade him to back the plan, but suddenly she was thinking that maybe she didn't *want* him to reap the rewards of this plan.

She was going to do it herself.

※

"This place smells funny!" Colin Oliver said, loudly enough to turn the heads of several patrons of the Goodwill thrift store.

"Colin!" Joss whispered harshly. "That's not nice."

He put his hands on his hips and managed, somehow, to look down at Joss while looking up at her. "My mom says it's better to be honest than nice."

And there was Deena Oliver in a nutshell. Opting for masturbatory "honesty" rather than basic consideration for others, then patting herself on the back for it.

Once again, Joss really wished she'd gotten to know the Olivers before signing a contract to live with them for a year.

"It's important to be nice, too," Joss said, taking a stab at diplomacy instead of telling the child his mom was wrong. "And it's especially important to be polite."

Colin shrugged. "It stinks in here."

"Yeah." Bart agreed, pinching his nostrils shut.

"Then we'll be quick." Joss took each boy by the hand and dragged them through the store to the far wall, where she could see shelves of shoes and shoe boxes.

The boys protested all the way, putting up such a fuss that people probably thought she was kidnapping them. She was sorely tempted to make a deal with them, to promise some great treat if they'd behave themselves, but she just couldn't bear the idea of rewarding them in any way for this behavior.

She just couldn't contribute to putting that kind of person out in the world. Deena would be doing plenty of damage on her own; Joss had to stick to her standards.

She got to the shoes, and yes, it *did* smell somewhat unpleasant. Worse, the shoes were just jumbled onto the shelves without regard to size or the expected gender of the wearer.

This was going to be ugly.

Fortunately there was a toy section about twenty feet away from the shoes, so she dragged the protesting boys over there and let them each pick out a germ-filled deathtrap of a toy to look at while she tore through the shoes.

Colin took a short-wave radio with a broken antenna, and Bart took a Tweety Bird Pez dispenser with a couple of old pieces of orange Pez still stuck inside.

Fine. As long as it kept them occupied for a few minutes, Joss was all for it.

She took a list out of her pocket. Before coming, she'd printed out the names of some of the better shoe designers. To her surprise, finding designer shoes wasn't hard. But finding them in a 7½ and in decent condition was more of a challenge. Most of the soles were worn, sometimes almost all the way through. Heels were broken, leather scuffed, buckles bent.

After twenty-five minutes of power searching, Joss was able to find one perfect Gucci pump. The size was right, but there was only one of the shoes.

"Excuse me," she said to a passing employee, a tired-looking woman with hair that was mahogany on the ends, and black at the roots. "Do you know where the other one of these is?"

"That's where the shoes are," she said, limply gesturing to the wall of shoes.

"I know, but there was only one of these, and I wondered if you knew where I might find the other one." Joss frowned. "You wouldn't put out just one shoe, would you?"

"No, we don't do that. Unless it's like, a medical shoe or something."

Joss wondered what that meant but didn't have time today to ask. "So the other one should be there somewhere?"

"It *should*." She shrugged and pushed her purple hair back. "Unless someone stole it."

Joss considered asking if a one-legged woman with expensive tastes had been in recently, but the employee's eyes widened as she looked at something behind Joss.

"Is that your kid?" she asked. "I think something's wrong."

"What?" Joss turned to see Bart, bug-eyed and deathly pale, clawing at his neck. "Oh, my God!" She ran to him. "Bart! What's wrong?"

He didn't answer. He didn't make a sound. He just continued to panic and turn a frightening shade of blue.

That's when Joss saw the Pez dispenser, less Tweety's head, lying on the floor.

"Are you choking?" she gasped, and, without waiting for an answer, flipped him around and performed the Heimlich maneuver on him.

Nothing happened.

It didn't work.

"Colin!" she shouted, pulling the other boy's attention away from bending the antenna out of shape. "Get my cell phone out of my purse. Call 911."

"Why?"

"Godalmighty, Colin, just *do it*!" She clasped her hands tighter and thrust them against Bart's solar plexus again.

Still nothing.

Joss felt cold terror wash over her. Colin appeared to be moving in slow motion, and the employee who had pointed out that Bart was having trouble was still just standing there, watching.

"Call a fucking ambulance!" Joss yelled at her, thrusting hard with panic and anger.

This time Bart gave a low, almost inhuman cough, the plastic Tweety Bird head flew out of his mouth and banged against a cement pillar about twelve feet away.

Bart coughed and gasped for air.

"Are you okay now?" Joss knelt before him. "Can you breathe? Is anything still stuck in your throat?" She knew the coughing was a good sound. As long as he was coughing, he was getting air.

Finally the coughing subsided somewhat, and the color gradually returned to Bart's cheeks.

"Can you breathe?" Joss asked him again.

He nodded, gasping and working his mouth like a fish.

"Okay." She pulled him into her arms. "It's okay. Stay calm." Holding him against her rapidly beating heart probably wasn't doing much to calm him down.

"I was scared," he said, in a voice so small and vulnerable that her heart felt like it was breaking.

"It's okay now. I need to make sure there's nothing still stuck in your throat, okay?" she said to him. "So stay right here. Take big, deep breaths. I'm going to just go get the toy, okay?"

He nodded and she went to pick up the bottom of the Pez dispenser and looked for the top, stopping every two and a half seconds or so to look back at Bart and make sure he was still standing, breathing, and pink.

She knew the direction the plastic piece had gone and that it had bounced against the pillar, so she searched around that area until finally she saw it lying on the floor behind a threadbare wingback chair that reeked of cigar smoke.

Joss got down on all fours and reached under the chair for the Tweety Bird head, but she felt something else first, something hard and furry with dust. She pulled it out.

The other Gucci pump.

There was no time to examine it now, though, so she reached under again, trying to ignore the tumbleweeds of dust and finally felt the little hard plastic head.

It was coated in dust, but she was able to fit it perfectly onto the other part. Good. There were no slivers of plastic working their way toward Bart's lungs or intestines.

She slumped against the pillar for a minute, relieved but spent by the experience.

"Excuse me, ma'am."

Joss looked to see the employee standing in front of her. "Yes?" She hoped the woman wasn't going to make a big deal about Joss being a hero or anything. In Felling, the news would cover this kind of thing, and the last thing in the world Joss wanted was to be the center of attention.

She needn't have worried.

The woman gestured at the plastic Tweety Bird she still had clutched in her hand. "You're going to have to pay for that, you know."

Chapter 14

T he thing is," Lorna said to Phil Carson, who was sitting at the bar during her shift at Jico, "I'm meeting my bills, but I don't feel like I've got *anything* left over to have fun with."

"Maybe you should come over to the bureau and speak with me during business hours—"

"Oh, come on, Phil." She had no patience for this nonsense. "You can see what I do." She gestured around. "I'm pulling double and sometimes triple shifts here. And you're sitting right here. What have you got to lose by talking to me for a minute."

"It's not that—"

"What are you drinking?" She eyed his glass. She had a gift for this. "RitaTini with a Cointreau floater?"

He looked at his half-empty glass. "How did you know?"

Actually, it was what all the guys with midlevel management jobs were drinking. "I pay attention, Phil," she said. "I'm good at my job.

And I'm working as hard as I can. So can you just give me a little advice without making me go all the way to your office?"

"I guess I can."

"Great." She looked to the bartender. "Boomer!" She pointed down at Phil. "Another one here. On me."

"You don't have to do that." Phil looked like he was blushing. "Actually, you *shouldn't* do that. You can't afford it."

"I get it at cost and then you tip me on it." She winked. "I'll make a profit, trust me."

"So do that a few hundred more times, and your problems will be solved." Phil gave a loopy smile.

"Funny." Lorna sat on the barstool next to his. "I need to know if you can negotiate a lower interest rate with any of my credit card companies."

"They're already low!"

"Discover only went to nine-point-nine," she said. "Their introductory rate is a lot lower than that!"

"Yes, but it's introductory. They lure people in, and then—you know the rest."

Lorna was disheartened. Yes, she knew the rest. She knew it way, way too well. "But I can't even buy shoes!"

Phil chuckled. "Now, come on, you're exaggerating. You have enough to cover the basics. And you should feel so good about the progress you're making."

"I feel good about the progress," she said. "Just not so good about the lack of money."

"Does this job have benefits?" Phil asked. "Health insurance, that sort of thing?"

"No, I have to get that myself."

"What's your hourly wage?"

She told him, and he gasped. "But that's because I make tips. Sometimes with tips it amounts to fifteen, twenty bucks an hour."

"Every hour, every night?"

"No," she admitted. "It's definitely variable."

"Miss Rafferty—"

"Lorna."

"—you might want to consider getting a more . . . reliable job. One with benefits, and a 401(k), and a salary that you can plan on. You have a college education, don't you?"

She gave a shrug. "A bachelor's in English." Reading had seemed like a *great* major until she went out in the world and tried to find a job doing it.

Phil's second drink arrived, and he drained his first one more quickly. "You could have a much better job."

Boomer stopped and gave Phil a cautionary look, but Lorna waved him off, mouthing the words *It's okay.*

"But I can barely afford to eat!" she said. "There's got to be something you can do."

"You're still spending, aren't you?" he asked, eyeing her with a lucidity he hadn't displayed before.

She felt her cheeks grow warm. "What do you mean?"

He gave a knowing nod. "We went over your budget very specifically. Even with the variable income, the low-end average should have given you enough to make the payments on your debt as well as your rent, utilities, and food." He shook his head. "You're still spending. I've seen this before."

She tried to swallow the guilt that was balling up in her throat. "I have not been to the mall in *weeks.*"

"So what is it, online shopping? With your check card?" He knew he'd nailed her. "As far as I know, it's the only one we didn't destroy."

So, what, was she one of his only clients? How could he remember the details of her meeting with him with such clarity? "No, I just had a couple of unexpected expenses. My car," she added, for credibility. And it was true, she *had* given them a considerable back payment. "And also utilities." So it hadn't been in the past week—it wasn't as if she could admit she'd been on eBay. A guy like Phil Carson would never admit that there was virtue in bargain shopping if it took the place of therapy.

"Well." He took a sip of the drink she'd bought for him. "You obviously need more income. The budget we set up should work, but if it doesn't, you've got some leaks in your spending, and the only way I can think of to stop them is for you to be bringing more money in." He shrugged. "I worry. I wish I could make this easier for you, but it's really the only way."

"Thanks, Phil." It sounded sincere when she said it, but she didn't really feel it.

Sure, he was right. She was spending outside her budget. And if he said he was unable to negotiate a lower rate, she had to believe him because what reason would he have to lie to her?

She spent the rest of her evening going through the motions of work, smiling and describing the night's specials, all the while trying to think how or *where* she could fit *another* job into her schedule.

She took a fifteen-minute break in the middle of the evening to put her feet up and look at the classified section of the *City Paper*.

Nothing.

Unless she could drive a bus or a truck, teach English as a second language, or create more hours from thin air and take on a secretarial job that paid less than she averaged as a waitress, she was out of luck.

She flipped idly through the rest of the paper, feeling despondent and more sore and tired than she could remember ever feeling. She was getting old, she decided miserably.

And, worse, her gorgeous new Jimmy Choos were killing her. Soon she was going to have to wear big white orthopedic nurse's shoes to work just to save her back.

Around 11 P.M., Lorna was surprised to see Sandra coming through the door with a very attractive man. Sandra had mentioned she was going out with an old friend from high school, but this guy had leapt right off the pages of *GQ*.

Sandra looked every bit as surprised to see Lorna, and after an awkward reunion, she stepped back and introduced her friend. "This is Mike Lemmington, my friend from high school. I told you about him."

"Yes!" Wow, had Sandra hit the jackpot. This guy was *hot*. Maybe even a little too hot. A little too . . . manicured. But, whatever. She'd ask Tod to check him out and use his gaydar later.

"It is so nice to meet you," Mike said, taking Lorna's hand in a soft greeting. "God, I just *love* your shoes!"

"Oh!" She looked down at her new Choos and smiled. "Hey, you're a customer. Maybe the fact that you've commented on them makes them tax deductible."

"Why not?" He laughed, and Sandra laughed. Maybe just a little too loud. She seemed nervous.

"So we're meeting some of Mike's friends here," Sandra said. "Then we're going to Stetson's. I'd love it if you could join us. Do you get off work soon?"

"Not for another couple of hours." It was the constant lament. Lorna loved socializing during work, but at the same time, sometimes when her friends popped by and were moving on to another bar, she felt like the kid who was stuck with a 7 P.M. bedtime in the summer while all his friends were outside riding bikes in the still-light twilight.

"Too bad," Mike said. "We're going to meet my friend Debbie. I've been *trying* to get this girl out to meet her for *ages*." He pulled Sandra in with one arm, and she laughed. "Tonight you're doing it."

"We're doing it," Sandra agreed, and gave Lorna a small *I don't know, but I like it* look.

"Mike!"

All of them turned to see a tall stunning woman in a Diane Von Furstenburg wrap dress and strappy high heels Lorna couldn't identify, walking toward them in the bar.

"Margo." Cute Mike went over and embraced her.

Lorna noticed Sandra stiffen at the gesture. She didn't blame her. The woman was a knockout.

"Everyone—" Mike led his friend to Lorna and Sandra. "—this is Margo St. Gerard."

"It's nice to meet you," Lorna said, putting out a hand.

Sandra just said, "Hi, there." And she watched as Mike gazed perhaps a hair too affectionately at the statuesque blonde.

And, really, she must have been at least six feet tall. No more than 125 pounds, though, so she was as trim and flat-chested as a supermodel. What she lacked in womanly curves, though, she made up for in facial bone structure.

She was so striking, it was, frankly, disconcerting.

Lorna was concerned that Sandra must be hating this.

"I'm so glad to meet you," Margo said, in a smooth, modulated voice. She sounded like a broadcaster.

An awkward moment passed.

"So . . . Sandra has told me so much about you," Lorna said to Mike, hoping to return his attention to the woman he'd come in with. "It's great to finally meet you."

"You're one of the shoe addicts, right?"

She laughed. "Oh, yeah."

"She's the one who started it all," Sandra said.

Mike laughed. "What a fabulous idea! If I had a size seven and a half in ladies', I'd be joining you myself."

"We've had men inquire before," she said, trying not to be dismissive while, at the same time, hoping to god this guy wasn't interested in joining them. "But they didn't have the right insole." She glanced at his undeniably wide feet.

"Oh, the midoperation transvestite?" he asked.

Sandra obviously told him a lot.

"Better off without that sort," he finished in a whisper. "If they're not proud of who they are, it's just going to result in a lot of tension. You don't need to deal with someone else's shit."

"I couldn't agree more."

They all stood around talking for a few more minutes. Mike was really cute, and Sandra was obviously really enamored of him, so Lorna pushed aside the small irritation she felt when he went off on recent political events she didn't happen to agree with him about.

"I don't know, Mike," she said, trying to sound light. "If we all felt the same way about everything, this would be a pretty boring world. Division makes democracy."

"Shouldn't we go?" Sandra asked uncomfortably.

Lorna looked at the clock over the bar. *She* definitely had to go. She had to get up and work again in eight hours.

"So, Lorna," Mike said, thankfully not holding a grudge that she disagreed with him. "We're going to Stetson's, do you want to join us? I'd love to continue our debate there."

Like she had the energy to *debate*.

"Oh, yes!" Sandra exclaimed. "Please!"

Lorna really wanted to help her out, but she was exhausted. She had, after all, been on her feet in the restaurant since 11 A.M. She needed a break. There were theories out there that God had created the earth in seven hours, not seven days, so if that was correct, and he rested on the seventh hour and wanted us all to do the same, Lorna was currently about five and a half hours past church-endorsed relaxation. "I'm really sorry," she said, mostly to Sandra. "I'd love to, but I'm almost too tired to drive home. There's no way I can get into town, stay upright for another couple of hours, then drive home."

"You *could* stay at my place," Sandra said. "But I understand you're tired."

"Next time," Lorna promised.

She was about to overapologize when Tod rushed by. She tried to stop him—she thought he'd like to meet Sandra and Mike at least, but it was as if he took one look at them and huffed past, nose in the air.

Lorna made a mental note to tease him about being a bratty little child later, but she didn't think much more about it until after Sandra, Margo, and Mike had left and Tod approached Lorna in the parking lot.

"Do you *know* that jerk?" he asked.

Lorna looked around, half-thinking he might be talking to someone else nearby, and half-thinking he might be talking *about* someone else nearby. "Who?"

"Mike Lemmington. Mr. *Live, love, laugh, and get laid.*" Tod gave a disgusted snort. "I didn't know he meant with different people every night."

"Oh." Then Lorna remembered how excited Tod had been about a date the other night. "*Oh.* He's the— Oh, Tod, I'm sorry. That must have been awkward to see him."

Tod gave a tight-lipped nod. "Especially with *her.*"

"Sandra?"

"Oh, is that her name? I've seen her at Stetson's. She makes me sick."

Sandra *had* mentioned Stetson's, though Lorna could hardly imagine her inspiring this kind of disgust in someone as nice as Tod. Though jealousy did strange things to people.

It had to be because she was so tired, because with all this mental juggling, it occurred to Lorna only afterwards that what Tod was saying was that the guy Sandra was dating was gay. Or at least bi. "Are you sure he's the guy?" she asked him.

He gave her a withering look. "Gee, I don't know, Lorna. Let me go through the mental catalog of guys I had sex with that night." He put a finger to his chin and mocked *The Thinker.* "Yup. Yup, that's him. The son of a bitch." He bit his lip and shook his head before adding, "Isn't he beautiful?"

"He's hot. No doubt about it."

"The hot ones are always like that. *Always.* I hate it."

"I do, too."

Tod looked at her then with concern. "Look at you. You're being so nice to me about my failed love life, and I haven't even asked what happened to that guy you were dating."

"George? George Manning?" She shook her head. "That was over like a month and a half ago." Lord, she had such a stockpile of failed and unmemorable relationships. The thought of it struck her suddenly and made her profoundly sad.

It must have shown on her face because Tod looked concerned.

"God, I'm such a selfish prick." Tod was back on his self-flagellation kick, thereby proving his point. "I didn't even know."

"It doesn't matter. Really, there were no high hopes there." The truth was, she hadn't had high hopes, or even medium-high hopes, for a long, long time. She'd gone out with George Manning for like two months and just now it had taken her a moment to remember his last name. "But back to Mike."

Tod scoffed.

"Are you absolutely sure he's gay?"

"Honey, I've known plenty of men who claimed they were straight as they zipped up after a good time. Mike isn't one of them. He's as homo as they get." He sighed. "And he's really damn good at it, too."

"Then what's he doing with Sandra?" Lorna asked. "And more importantly, should I tell her?"

"She knows," Tod said with a judicious nod. "Believe me, she knows."

⁕

"What did you think of Mike?" Sandra asked eagerly at the next meeting. She was *dying* to know what Lorna, who seemed to have such excellent taste all around, thought of her boyfriend.

"He was really nice," Lorna said quickly. She sounded really definite about it.

"And isn't he cute?"

"Very cute. Yes." Lorna glanced at Joss and Helene. "Really."

Normally Sandra might have found Lorna's clipped affirmatives odd, but not tonight. She was in too good a mood. "I've got to say, I wish the girls in high school could see me now!"

"Don't we all," Helene murmured.

Joss looked uncertain.

"Jeez, not me," Lorna said. "The girls I went to high school with are all doctors or lawyers or Forbes 400 executives, or they're married to doctors or lawyers or Forbes 400 executives." She shook her head and revealed a secret she'd barely acknowledged to herself. "Sometimes I wonder if I was always subpar with them or if that happened somewhere after the time we all graduated."

"Subpar?" Helene repeated, surprised. "You? How could you say such a thing?"

Lorna smiled a sad smile. "Well, maybe that wasn't the best choice of words, but there was a time when I used to drive past those little ranch houses down River Road in Potomac, thinking I was going to do *way* better than that. Now they're selling those places for one, two million, and I can barely make my rent." Her face turned warm, but now that she'd put it out there, she didn't know how to take it back.

She didn't have to, though, because Sandra chirped up quickly, "God, I know what you mean. Everyone I went to high school with, even those mean bitchy girls I hoped would pay later, ended up married to great-looking guys and living in houses that were worthy of *Architectural Digest*." She shook her head. "Honestly, it wasn't that I was planning on being one of them, ever, but I was pretty sure that at least a few of them would be like *me*. You know, single and . . ." She frowned. "Struggling. Not financially so much, but just . . ." She shrugged. ". . . personally."

"But you seem to have it all together," Joss said, apparently amazed that Sandra didn't.

Lorna looked at her in surprise. She had all the respect in the world for Sandra, but she was still surprised by Joss's total shock that Sandra wanted more.

"Oh, my God, that is the best thing you could say to me," Sandra said. "Because it's totally not true. Well, it *wasn't* true, but now it's better. See, I went to see an acupuncturist a few weeks ago, and he put this metal bar thing in my ear." She touched the ear that Lorna had noticed her fiddling with before. Not that it was that shocking; she only had two ears.

"Ouch!" Joss said. "They put, like, a *needle* in there?"

"Yeah, you can feel it. It's like the post from an earring, only smaller, and it's in a different place." She let go and shrugged. "Look, I'm as skeptical as the next person but before he put it in, I was nervous about leaving the house and now I'm a *lot* better."

"You were agorophobic?" Helene asked.

"Big-time." Sandra nodded. "And I tried everything—Prozac, therapy, Xanax, hypnotherapy. Honestly, I really doubted anything could help, much less acupuncture, but I really think it has. It's not like I was expecting it, too, you know? If anything, I went into it more cynical than most."

"What's agorophobic?" Joss asked. "Sorry, I don't mean to sound dumb, but—"

"It's okay," Sandra said quickly. "I was nervous about leaving my apartment. I'd get nervous in a crowd. Even on the street or in the grocery store."

Joss nodded, but it was clear from her expression that she'd never heard of such a thing.

"And this guy put a needle in your ear and you're all better now?" Lorna asked skeptically. "Really?"

Sandra shrugged. "I'm here, aren't I? Six months ago I couldn't have done this." Her face went pink again. "I hope that doesn't make you guys think I'm some huge loser or anything."

"Oh, no!" everyone objected at once, and Lorna went on to say, "I just always thought I was the only person I knew with human foibles. It's great to hear I'm not."

"Okay, what are yours?" Sandra challenged, looking to Helene and Joss for support. Though Helene looked away and Joss looked so innocent, it was impossible to believe she could ever have anything to fess up to.

"All right." Lorna straightened her back. "I had one good boyfriend when I was sixteen, but I screwed it up and I haven't been able to find anyone to replace him since then."

Helene sucked in a long breath. "Really?"

Lorna nodded. "Chris Erickson. I know it's easy to glorify first love, but even when I think about it objectively now, I think he really was The One. Or at least someone I could have spent my life with."

Sandra looked teary. "What happened to him?"

Lorna swallowed an old, inappropriate lump in her throat. "Oh, I screwed it up in a stupid, fickle, teenage way and we broke up and now he's married and has a new baby and all is wonderful in his world." She gave a short laugh. "I'm sure he's better off without me."

"I bet he still thinks about you," Joss said, looking at her with big, sincere blue eyes. "Honest. My high school boyfriend, Robbie, still wants me to marry him."

"And—?" Sandra asked, raising her eyebrows so her glasses slipped down her nose and made her look every inch the schoolmarm she sounded like. "You're not thinking about going back, are you?"

"No," Joss admitted. "It would feel like a compromise."

Helene, who had been watching this exchange in thoughtful silence said, "Do you think it's possible to meet your soul mate in high school and then be too stupid to know it and blow your life forever?"

All eyes turned to her.

Lorna wanted to ask *Did you do that?* but the answer seemed so obvious that the question would have been insulting. "I think things ultimately work out the way they're supposed to," she said, meaning it. "Even if it's not always the most comfortable, cushy way."

"I agree," Sandra said quickly, and unlike Lorna, she didn't have a trace of uncertainty in her eyes. "If someone's right, they'll come back to you eventually." She nodded, so certain that what she was saying was true that one could almost feel her certainty as another entity in the room.

And even though Lorna privately wondered if Chris had been The One That Got Away, it was so patently wrong with Sandra and Mike that she had to believe Fate would take care of things in the end.

Chapter 15

Helene was definitely being followed.

She'd gone out for the afternoon, making a few runs to some of her charity organizations, and she'd noticed the fairly nondescript blue car following her between the second and third stops.

If Lorna hadn't told her she thought Helene was being followed, Helene might never have noticed. Not that the guy was that slick. He was always within about three car lengths of her. But it still made her very uneasy.

She couldn't tell for sure what he looked like. It *might* have been Gerald Parks. Then again, it could have been Pat Sajak. She just couldn't get a close look at him.

It didn't matter; she could see his car, and she'd been seeing entirely too much of it lately.

With one eye on the road and one hand on the steering wheel, she took out her cell phone and called 411 for the police nonemergency number. She didn't want to call 911 because, here in traffic and in the safety of her locked car, it just didn't feel like an emergency.

"Operator 4601, this line is being recorded."

Helene glanced in the rearview mirror. The car was still there. "Hi," she said awkwardly. "I'm calling because . . . well, it's not necessarily an *emergency*, but . . . anyway, I'm on 270 heading north, and there's a car following me."

"Has the driver confronted you in any way?"

"No. But he's definitely been following me for some time now."

"Can you see the driver, ma'am? Is it someone you know?"

"I think so. But I'm not sure. I can't really get a good look."

Helene was beginning to feel really foolish, although it didn't diminish her feelings of anxiety any.

The operator's response made it clear that was exactly what she was thinking, too. "Ma'am, I'm sorry, but we can't really send a car out to pull someone over for being on the same road with you. If someone physically threatens or harms you, dial 911."

Nice, generic answer. Helene couldn't blame her, though, so she thanked her and hung up, hoping the police nonemergency operators wouldn't trace her number and note her as a crazy who shouldn't be taken seriously if she called again.

She pulled off on an exit, with the blue car three cars back, and wound her way back to Route 355, which spanned from beyond northern Maryland all the way down to Georgetown, in Washington, D.C.

She thought at one point she'd lost him, but soon thereafter she noticed the blue car had reappeared and was now directly behind her. She looked at the driver, making mental notes for a police report, while simultaneously trying to keep an eye on the winding road in front of her. It was obviously Gerald Parks. He wore Jackie O. big round dark glasses, and his fingers clutched the steering wheel like long thin hot dogs.

She drove rapidly along the curving contours of Falls Road, half-hoping to get stopped by the police so she could point Gerald out and have them apprehend him. But she knew he'd probably just keep driving and she'd sound like a nut as well as a reckless driver.

When she got to Potomac Village, she ran through a yellow light to cross over River Road, where she'd normally turn.

In the rearview mirror, she could see that the blue car was stopped at the light. She turned into the shopping center parking lot and weaved through behind the shops to pick up River Road and head home. After a mile or two of driving without being followed, she began to relax a little, though her heart thumped to beat the band against her rib cage.

As she crossed over the D.C. line, she took a deep breath, feeling like she was at last home free, when he appeared again. He turned right off Little River Turnpike—a whole different route!—and ended up behind her *again*.

As bad as this guy was at staying undetected, he was a master at following his prey, and for the first time Helene felt real anger mingling with her fear. Part of her wanted to pull over and confront him, but she knew that would be extremely foolish.

As she turned onto Van Ness Street, where her house was, she wondered if she should pass her driveway so he wouldn't know where she lived, but in the end it didn't matter, because he turned off right before her block and disappeared into traffic.

She put her car in park and sat, locked in, for about fifteen minutes, trying to calm her breathing.

Then she did the thing her desperation drove her to. She called Jim.

"I think someone's following me," she said to him when he picked up the phone.

"What?"

She told him what Lorna had said about her being followed a couple of times from the parking lot, and about the fact that he'd been behind her today for forty-five minutes. She left out the part about calling the police, though. No sense in giving Jim an out by quoting the police. "I want private security," she finished.

"That's nuts," Jim said immediately.

Hurt niggled at the pit of her stomach. "You think it's nuts for me to want to be safe from wackos in a city that's seen more weird abductions and political assasinations than any other?"

"It's nuts that you're worried about this. You said the guy didn't follow you home, right?"

"Right."

"So this is a crowded city. You can't blame someone for being on the same road with you."

"Even if they're on the same *ten* roads, right behind me, for twenty-five miles?"

"It's a coincidence. You're being really egotistical, thinking this is all about you."

That was incredibly insulting. "If someone is following *me* it *has* to be about me, doesn't it?"

"No one's following you, Helene. Don't make a fool of yourself."

"Make a fool of myself?" she echoed stupidly. "How?"

"Well, for one thing, don't even think about calling the police."

Good thing she hadn't told him about that. "Why not?"

"Because the story will get around, and you'll waste a bunch of city resources while they dig around into nothing. Reporters would have a field day blaming me for that."

"But what about my safety?" she asked, hating how small and childlike and *weak* she sounded. But she felt really weird. She was obviously being followed; the police couldn't do anything about it even if they did believe her, which they didn't; and she couldn't hire her own security, because Jim had completely cut off her financial access and *he* didn't believe her. Or he didn't care.

She was at his mercy, yet he was her only hope.

"If I have to open myself up to public criticism every time you have a bad dream, I'm politically fucked," Jim said. "Don't do that to me."

"This isn't about *you*!" How had the man she married become so cold? "I'm *scared*, Jim. I really am."

He made a noise that was the verbal equivalent of rolling his eyes, then said, "I've got to go. Lock the doors and put in a movie. We'll talk about this later tonight."

"Later might be too late," she said, recent headlines running through her mind like a scrolling marquee.

But Jim wasn't listening. He was talking to someone else in the room, probably Pam. She'd probably come in with the whipped cream and G-string, ready for action.

"I gotta go," Jim said to Helene. "I'll be late tonight. Don't wait up."

Jerk. *We'll talk about your concern for your safety tonight—oh, but I won't be there, so go on to sleep*. It was so typical of him that it shouldn't have hurt her feelings, but Helene hung up the phone feeling like she was going to cry.

Even more than that, though, she was overwhelmingly tired. Maybe it was the postadrenaline reaction to the chase, or maybe it was the fact that she was deeply unhappy with her life and couldn't see a way out.

Or maybe something was seriously wrong with her.

Whatever it was, she had to go in and lie down for a little while. She didn't wake up again until the next morning.

And when she did, she was alone.

*

It was easier having just Bart, without Colin there to influence him to do bad things.

The good news was that Colin had begun a two-week stint at day camp, allowing Joss times like now, to take just Bart to the park alone. The bad news, though, was that Deena interpreted this as being something less than what she was paying Joss for, and she felt all the more free to ask Joss to do little extra things.

As the grocery list in Joss's pocket proved. Five items, five different stores.

At least she got to use the car when she was on official duty. The one time Deena had asked her to "pick up a few things" on her way home from the ski club meeting one Sunday—a bust, by the way, don't even ask—she'd ended up wrestling with two large, heavy paper bags on the Metro.

Still, on a glorious sunny summer day like this, it was almost possible to forget the bad stuff. Unlike most of the other nannies and moms, she ran with Bart on the playground and went up and down the sliding boards with him about twenty-five times.

"This is fun!" Bart squealed as he reached the bottom again. "What should I do next?"

"Whatever you want." She looked around. "The swings?"

Bart looked excited; then doubt crossed his eyes. "Colin says swings are for sissy girls."

Oh, that Colin. She could throttle him. He was a bad influence on Bart. She was more and more convinced of it. "Do you see any sissy girls on the swings?" she aked. The only kid on them was a boy who looked to be a couple of years older than Bart.

"No," Bart admitted.

"Maybe Colin just says that kind of thing to make himself look cool for *not* going on the swings," she suggested. "Not that he has to or anything. But, heck, maybe he's even *afraid* of the swings." It was probably unfair, calling Colin out like that when he wasn't there to defend himself, but she was sick and tired of how Colin's dos and dont's colored everything Bart did.

Because, frankly, Colin was a jerk.

"I *do* like the swings," Bart said, eyeing them.

"Me, too—let's go." She took him by the hand and led him to the swings, helping him onto one and then getting behind and pushing him as he laughed and laughed and yelled, "Look how high I'm going, Joss!" over and over again.

So maybe she'd defamed Colin's meager character. At least she'd made sure Bart had a good time.

"You keep going," she told Bart after a while, laughing and catching her breath. "I've got to take a little break."

"Keep watching me!" Bart called. "My feet are touching the sky!"

"Cool!" Joss waved, and he swung off into the wild blue yonder again.

"Jocelyn?"

Startled, Joss turned to see a tall woman with blue-black hair and startling light blue eyes. "Y-yes?"

"You're Jocelyn who works for the Olivers, right?" She gestured at Bart, who was swinging past, calling that he was going up again.

Joss smiled and waved at him and turned back to the woman. "Yes. Who are you?"

"Felicia Parsons. That's my son, Zach, over there." She pointed to a dark-haired kid, about seven, who appeared to be bullying a smaller boy while a heavyset young woman tried to separate the two. "I need a nanny, and I want to know how much you charge."

"I'm sorry, Mrs. Parsons. I've already got a job." A job she hated, admittedly. A job she'd do almost anything to shrug off.

But she couldn't.

Felicia Parsons looked at Joss as if she were a moron. "I know that. I just asked if you worked for the Olivers. What I want to know is how much will it cost me to trump their offer."

Joss couldn't believe that this was the second time someone was approaching her for a job even knowing that she was contracted to work for the Olivers. A contract was a contract, and these women should understand that. It wasn't like Joss could just jump ship at a better offer, even if she wanted to.

"I'm really sorry," she said, keeping her eye on Bart, who was climbing on the rope knots now. The woman's son was, at the same time, being physically held back by the girl who'd been trying to keep him away from the other boy a moment earlier. "I can't break my contract." She gestured toward the child. "It looks like your son might need you."

The woman glanced in his direction, then waved the scene off. "Oh, she'll take care of it."

Because a nanny is a nanny, even if she isn't your nanny? Joss wanted to ask. But she didn't.

"Please keep me in mind if you change your mind," Mrs. Parsons said. "Do you have something I can write on?"

"No, sorry."

The woman sighed dramatically and dug through her own purse to come up with a pen and a torn piece of an envelope, the back of which bore the return address of an attorney. "This is my cell phone number. *Only* call this number. Do *not* look up my home phone number and call me there under *any* circumstances."

No danger of that. Joss didn't reach for the paper. "Mrs. Parsons,

I really don't want you to think there's any chance of hearing from me, because I honestly am occupied with the Oliver family through next June."

"You say that now." Mrs. Parson's physically grabbed her hand and pressed the paper into it. "But you may change your mind." She went off in the direction of her son, bellowing something either to him or to the girl who was trying to help with him.

Joss shuddered at the thought of working for a person like that.

She returned to Bart, but at this point he was playing with a little red-haired girl named Kate, and he didn't seem to want anything to do with Joss on this date, so she told him she'd be sitting on the bench waiting for him. She went and joined the other nannies, keeping a keen eye on the youthful boy–girl drama between Bart and Kate.

"Did Felicia Parsons ask you to work for her?" a young African-American girl asked.

Joss frowned. "How did you know?"

"She's asked most of us now." She looked at the girl who'd been separating Mrs. Parsons's son from the other boy. "Poor Melissa. I'm Mavis Hicks, by the way." She held out her hand. "I don't think we've met yet."

"Joss Bowen." Joss shook her hand. "What do you mean poor Melissa? Is she the Parsonses' nanny?"

Mavis nodded. "And she's really good, as far as I can tell. Don't you think, Susan?" She tapped the shoulder of a stout woman in her mid- to upper thirties.

"What?"

"That Melissa's good with that Parsons kid."

"Yes." Susan noticed Joss then. "Oh. Did you get propositioned by Fickle Felicia?"

Joss nodded. "Yes. Just now. I feel just awful about it." She looked at

Melissa, who was clearly trying mightily to deal logically with the dark-haired hellion that was her charge.

"Don't worry, she knows," Mavis reassured Joss. "It's not the first time this has happened to Melissa. She'll probably take the next offer someone makes *her*."

"It happens that often?"

Both Susan and Mavis looked at her like she was from outer space.

"Are you joking?" Susan asked.

"Well . . . no." There was no sense in pretending she was familiar with this game, because it was *all* new to her. New and disconcerting. These women might be really helpful with that. "But it's happened to me twice now. Once at a party the Olivers were hosting."

Susan shrugged. "It goes on all the time. When word gets around about a good nanny, everyone wants her."

Joss was surprised. "I had no idea Mrs. Oliver was saying anything nice about me at all."

"She's not," Susan said simply. "It doesn't come from the employers. The word gets around via the Mom Network. They observe whose nanny is doing what; then they decide their nanny isn't good enough, and they sneak around behind her back to try and hire someone new."

"But doesn't everyone have a contract?" Joss asked. "Doesn't that bind the employer as well as the employee?" She'd gone over hers with her dad, and they were pretty sure she was guaranteed gainful employment plus room and board for a period of one year.

Susan and Mavis both laughed.

Then Susan caught Joss's eye and said, "Oh my God, are you serious?"

This was nuts. "Yes, I'm serious."

"Oh, honey. You don't know?"

Joss was beginning to feel like she was in some bizarre parallel universe, where everyone knew what was going on except her. "Don't know what?"

Susan and Mavis exchanged looks; then Susan nodded at Mavis.

"Mrs. Oliver asked me at a party last week if I wanted to work for her," Mavis said. "I thought for sure you knew."

Joss tried to think where the Olivers had gone last week, and right away three parties came to mind. Three parties for which Joss had covered their parenting duties free of charge.

And they thought they were going to do *better* than her? What other nanny on the planet would work during so much of her time off? What other nanny would pick up food, wine, dry cleaning, other people's children, and anything else Deena could think of?

What other nanny would take that kind of treatment and still stick with her obligation to the Olivers instead of cutting her losses and running for the hills?

"Are you *sure*?" she asked Mavis. "Maybe you misunderstood."

Mavis and Susan exchanged looks again, in a motion that was already clearly code for *You take this one* or *Go on, tell her*.

"Joss," Susan said, reaching over and putting her hands on Joss's. "She's sure. And so am I. Three weeks ago, Deena Oliver offered me salary and a half to take over within a week."

Chapter 16

"Oh my God, are you sick?"

Sandra was alarmed at the way her sister was looking at her. "What do you mean? I'm not sick. Why?" She raised a hand to her face. Did she look that awful? Had she lost her color?

Or was it just the green hair?

"You're so *skinny*!"

"I am not!"

"Well, not *skinny* for a regular person," Tiffany said, as obnoxiously honest as ever. "But skinny for *you*. How much weight have you lost?"

"I don't know." Yes, she did. It was 24.8 pounds. But for some reason, it embarrassed her to talk about the details with Tiffany. Maybe it was because life was always so effortless for Tiffany that Sandra didn't want to have to admit how much she herself struggled. "I've just been trying to eat sensibly."

"Not me." Tiffany patted her slightly protruding belly. It was barely noticeable. "I've been such a pig." She ushered Sandra into the huge gleaming white kitchen that overlooked hole number five on the Coronado golf club's newest course.

Tiffany had been a pig during her first pregnancy, too, seven years ago, but at the end of it she'd gotten both a perfect daughter—Kate—and her figure back. It was maddening.

"Do you want some coffee?" Tiffany asked, then made a face. "It's decaf."

"Sure." Sandra settled into a cushioned barstool. "So how's it going?"

"Just fine." Tiffany put a mug in front of Sandra, then went to the fridge and got out a creamer and put it down on the counter as well. "I had my eighteen-week sonogram the other day, and they say the baby's perfectly healthy. Kate's over the moon with excitement. Charlie, too." She hesitated a little longer than Tiffany might have expected. "Me, too, of course."

"That's wonderful." Sandra poured some cream into her coffee and stirred, watching the swirl fade. She looked at Tiffany. "Do you know if it's a boy or a girl?"

"The technician could tell, but Charlie wants to be surprised, so I have no idea. I think it's a boy, though."

"Wow, a boy! That would be so weird, wouldn't it? We grew up in such a girly house."

"I know. I—"

Sandra set her spoon aside, then looked at her sister. To her surprise, Tiffany was crying. "What's wrong? Tif, what's the matter?"

Tiffany put her hands up over her face and shook her head. "It's nothing."

"Is the baby really okay?" Sandra put an arm around her sister, wishing their mother were there to handle this. Sandra had no experience at all dealing with an insecure Tiffany. "Is there something you're not telling me?"

"The baby is fine." Tiffany sniffed and carefully wiped the tears from under her eyes without messing up her makeup. "It's just . . . This is so selfish, I can't even say it."

"What *is* it?" Sandra was alarmed. Was Tiffany about to reveal an affair or something? That was it, Charlie had probably had an affair. Sandra had never fully trusted him. He was cold. And a little mean. "Look, maybe we should call Mom and ask her to come over."

"No," Tiffany snapped. "The last thing I need is her here telling me how wonderful everything is, and how perfect my life is, and on and on and *on*."

Come to think of it, Sandra wasn't really fond of those conversations either. She grasped Tiffany's narrow shoulders and looked into her eyes. "What's the matter? Tell me."

Tiffany closed her eyes for a moment, her mouth quivering some with unspoken horror, then admitted, "I don't . . . ." She swallowed. "I don't know what to do with the penis."

This wasn't a phrase Sandra had ever heard before, so her first reaction was no reaction. "You don't know what to do with the penis? What do you mean?"

"The *baby*. I don't know what to do with a baby boy. It's not like we had brothers or male cousins or anything like that. When I found out I was pregnant, I was all ready for pink nursery walls and frilly bedsheets, and baby dolls, and Disney princesses. . . ." She dissolved into tears.

"Oh, Tif." Sandra patted her back, unsure what else to say or do. "It'll be okay. Really." She didn't want to add that she thought Tiffany was a victim of her hormones right now, but she did think that was at least part of the problem.

"I'm sorry," Tiffany said through shuddering breaths. "I love the baby—I really do. Part of me is disappointed that it's not a little girl, but mostly I'm just afraid I can't be a good enough mother to him because I don't know how to teach him to be a boy."

"I'm pretty sure that will come naturally."

"Not necessarily. What about hygiene? When will he start to shave? What about wet dreams? I don't know how to explain that stuff to him. I can't even imagine having that conversation."

Sandra laughed softly. "Well, for one thing, you can't imagine having the conversation partly because you haven't even met the little guy yet. All these things will come to you in time. And don't forget Charlie's going to be around to take over those tough guy talks."

"What if he's not?" Tiffany wailed.

Sandra answered cautiously. "Do you have some reason to think he won't be?"

"No." Tiffany took a tissue from the box on the counter and blew. "You must think I'm crazy."

"No, not at all. I think it's got to be really hard to be pregnant. You've hardly felt *any* of this stuff before."

Tiffany nodded. "But that doesn't mean it's not real."

"No, it doesn't. It means it might not need to be so scary, though."

"God." Tiffany closed her eyes tight and shook her head. "I just wish I could have a martini."

"I'll bring one to you in the hospital in four months. What do you want, Appletini?"

"Cranberry." Tiffany managed a smile. "But my cravings may be different by then."

They laughed, and after a moment, Tiffany said, "You know what scares me the most?"

"What?"

"What happens when he wants to know about his family history?"

Sandra laughed. "Are you kidding? Dad will get out that family tree he spent three years building at the Library of Congress, and—"

"I mean his, you know, his *blood* family."

Sandra frowned. "I'm not following. Whose blood family?"

"The children's!"

"Right. Okay, so, as I was saying, Dad can—"

"Sandra, I'm not going to lie to him!"

"To who?"

"Kate and the *baby!*"

"What are you *talking* about?" Then something occurred to Sandra. "Wait, is Charlie adopted or something?"

"Not *Charlie*," Tiffany said impatiently, looking at Sandra with sharp eyes. Then her expression lifted slightly. "Oh my God, are you kidding me?"

This was too weird. "About *what?*"

"Don't you know?"

"So help me, Tiffany, I don't care if you are pregnant, if you don't tell me what the hell you're talking about, I'm going to shake it out of you."

"Sandra." Her eyes, which moments before had been glistening with self-pity now held pity for Sandra. "Charlie's not adopted. *I* am."

Dear ~~Occupant~~ Ms. Rafferty:

We have enjoyed running the Bethesda Commons Apartments and getting to know all of you over the past fifteen years. However, times change, and we have decided to convert all of our units to condominiums. You, as the occupant, have the first right of refusal, and you also have the unique opportunity to buy in at a discounted price.

All units will be priced at $346/square foot. This means that those of you in 1-bedroom dwellings will pay an average of $340,000, and the *two-bedroom units will be approximately $416,500. We feel this is very competitive and fair pricing, and with interest rates at their lowest in some time, the pleasures of ownership can be yours for only a modest increase over what you are paying currently.*

The last of your leases is up on October 1, and as a courtesy to all of you, we will allow you to rent on a month-to-month basis until then if your lease is up sooner. We feel this will give you ample time to make your decision and either get financing for your purchase, or find a new place to live.

Again, we have enjoyed meeting all of you and wish you the best of luck whatever your choice.

Sincerely,
Artie and Fred Chaikin,
Your Management Team

Obviously Lorna was going to have to stop opening her mail. It was always—*always*—bad news.

Three hundred and forty thousand bucks. Like her debt wasn't high enough. She went online and looked for a mortgage calculator. With no money down—and that was the *only* way she could even *consider* getting a mortgage of any sort right now—the monthly payment would be over $2,200 a month. That was a thousand dollars more than she was paying now!

They called that "modest"?

To say nothing of the condo fees, whatever they might be. Lorna had heard figures into the hundreds for some local places.

So now what? She was in debt up to her neck, her credit was a mess, and she was about to lose her home. She had to do *something*; it wasn't as if she had a choice to just sit on this information and hope for a change.

No, no, that was bullshit. She didn't have to *hope* for a change, she had to *make* a change. She needed a better-paying job, or maybe an additional job.

But first she needed a new place to live.

She took out the newspaper, which she'd already put into the recycling bin unread, and sat down on the sofa to look for other rentals in the area.

Turned out prices had really gone up in the five years since she'd moved into the Commons. To live in a place in this neighborhood, she was going to have to pony up at least three hundred more than she was paying right now. And that was for some of the crummier apartments.

Unless she could get a better job, she was going to have to move farther out in Montgomery County. Maybe even to Frederick County. But the thought of driving fifteen, twenty, even twenty-five miles to work from some generic suburban enclave was just too depressing.

She flipped through the help wanted section and circled a few things that sounded terminally dull but promising in terms of pay and benefits.

She went to her computer and printed out several copies of her résumé to send to the P.O. boxes in the ads.

Then she signed on to eBay to reward herself with a little something *fun* after the depressing task of looking for a job. Maybe she'd find a pair of Pradas for $4.99 because the seller had typed in *Predas* accidentally. She was discovering these tricks as she went along. Unfortunately, *Shoegarpie* was learning them, too, so they still ended up competing over most of the same shoes. But Lorna hadn't made the mistake of overbidding by so much again.

She'd also discovered Paypal.com, so she could pay for her auctions directly, without having to go in to the bank and put her dignity on the chopping block to beg for a cashier's check.

She clicked her way through the size 7.5 designer shoes and was thrilled to find a pair of perfect vintage Lemer spectators for just $15.50. The heels were magnificently high, and the arch curved so gracefully that, were it not for the uppers, these could have been sexy strappy sandals.

So far *Shoegarpie* didn't appear to have seen them, and with less than six hours left until the end of the auction, Lorna's hopes swelled.

That's when she had a revelation.

If she looked at this objectively—and it was time she did just that—she truly *was* a shoe addict. She had *no* control over herself or her impulse to buy more shoes. Credit, cash, it didn't matter, she could rationalize her purchases no matter what, and it was *ruining her life*.

Starting Shoe Addicts Anonymous had been a good first start. It wasn't like she was addicted to substances, so the shoes themselves weren't harming her. It was the spending . . . the overspending. Which made eBay . . . good. Right?

She wasn't *sure* about that, but she was sure of one thing: it was time to do what she should have done a long time ago.

She went to the freezer and took out the Neapolitan ice cream she'd bought for a fussy dinner party she'd had six months ago. She set the box in the sink, lifted the lid, and ran hot water over the crystalized ice and ice cream until it melted enough to reveal the secret within:

Her Nordstrom credit card.

Perhaps because it was a department store credit card, it hadn't shown up on Phil Carson's list when he'd made her turn over her cards. So she'd kept it, just in case, a sort of emotional retail crutch she could use in case she really needed to.

She'd already used it twice since then, for online purchases, because she'd long ago memorized the number.

Hiding it in the ice cream had only made it messier for her to dig it out and take it to the store.

Well, all of that had to end now. She had to get rid of this final string that tied her, financially, to her addiction.

She went to the phone and slowly dialed the number on the back. Someone in the credit department answered right away, fortunately, so Lorna forced herself to speak before she could talk herself out of it.

"I need to cancel an account," she said.

From now on, it was cash or nothing.

It wasn't a *perfect* plan, but it was a start.

When the Shoe Addicts arrived two hours later, the star of the evening was Joss, who had brought a pair of fabulous Gucci pumps. Lorna swapped her dark blue John Fluevogs for them, but it was worth it. The Guccis must have been from the sixties or so, but they were in fantastic condition. One of them was a little scuffed, though it looked like it had been cleaned up. No matter. Lorna had a special saddle soap that would get that scuff right out.

Sandra told everyone about her sister's pregnancy, and the fact that she had just learned for the first time that her sister was adopted.

"Why would they tell her and not me?" she mused aloud.

"Maybe they didn't want you to be smug about it," Lorna suggested, and when Helene shot her a look, she shrugged and said, "I'm not saying she *would*, I'm just saying that might be what they were worried about."

"You might be right," Sandra conceded. "But the weird thing is, I grew up feeling exactly the opposite. I could never understand why they seemed to go out of their way to make Tiffany feel good when she already had so many obvious assets. I mean, really, she's gorgeous. Tall, blond. I think I got into shoes partly so I could bridge the height gap between us. That and the fact that your shoe size doesn't change even if you gain weight."

"I don't know about that," Helene said. "I've put on a couple of pounds recently, and my shoes have been feeling really tight."

"Are you about to get your period?" Lorna asked. "I swell like a water balloon beforehand."

Helene nodded. "I think it is some sort of hormonal thing. Water retention. When I got to the sugar pill days on my pill this month, I didn't even get my period."

"That happened to me for three months in a row once," Sandra said. Then, in answer to everyone's attention, she added, "I was on it to try and regulate my period. Eventually it worked, but those first three months nothing. I would have really enjoyed it if I wasn't afraid it was going to start any minute." She laughed. "I wore pads every day for those three months. It was like wearing diapers again."

"I hate to tell you this, girls, but in my case it might be perimenopause." Helene nodded grimly. "It can happen anytime from thirty-five on. So maybe I've been on borrowed time for the last three years."

"No way, you're far too young," Joss objected. "I don't believe it."

Helene shrugged. "I've got all the symptoms. Tired all the time, vaguely ill, weight gain, food cravings and aversions—What? Why are you all looking at me that way?"

"Because it sounds like pregnancy, too," Sandra said gently. "Believe me, I've been going through this with my sister for five months."

Helene shook her head. "Believe me, if I weren't on the pill, that would be the first thing I'd be worried about."

"Then it's the pill!" Lorna said. "I've never been sicker than when I was on the pill. I hated it! Still, maybe you should see a doctor."

Helene waved the idea away. "Oh, let's forget about me. I'm just whining. What's going on with the rest of you? Joss? You've been awfully quiet."

Joss's face went slightly pink, just highlighting her dewy youth. "Actually, there is something I'd like to get your opinion on. You know how I told you I kept getting job offers from other families?" Everyone nodded. "The other day I found out that Mrs. Oliver has been propositioning other nannies herself."

Lorna gasped. "You mean she's been offering other people *your* job behind your back?"

Joss nodded. "Isn't that weird?"

"It's grounds for breaking your contract," Lorna huffed.

"I agree," Sandra said. "That's like finding out your boyfriend is seeing someone else. It had to hurt."

Joss turned to her, with gratitude in her eyes. "It did. Even though I'm not very fond of Mr. and Mrs. Oliver, I think I've done a good job for them. The boys respond well to me. I've done everything I was supposed to and then some." She sighed. "It's a slap in the face."

"But you've had other offers," Helene reminded her. "Were they from people like Mrs. Oliver, who already have nannies?"

"I think so," Joss said ruefully. "Actually Lois Bradley might not."

"So keep her in mind," Helene said earnestly. "Just in case. You wouldn't want to work for someone who was cheating on a nanny she already had."

"No," Joss agreed. "But what about someone who'd try and steal someone else's nanny?"

"It's kill or be killed in this world," Lorna said.

"Amen." That was Sandra, nodding her still-greenish-blond head in agreement.

"That may be a little cynical," Helene said, then shrugged. "True, but cynical. Listen, Joss, please see a lawyer. At least let someone look over your contract to see if you have any legal way out of it."

"Well . . ." Joss looked uncertain.

"Would you rather wait until she springs it on you that she's hired someone else and is firing you for some made-up reason?" Lorna had no patience for people like Deena Oliver. She saw them all the time at the restaurant, and she'd never seen a spark of humanity light their eyes. "See a lawyer. Then decide what you're going to do with it later."

"You've got nothing to lose," Sandra added.

Finally Joss said she'd think about it, maybe call one of those TV lawyers who say the first consultation is free.

But Lorna had a feeling she wasn't going to do it.

"I hate to say it, but I've got to go," Sandra said, close to 11 P.M. "I'm supposed to meet someone."

Lorna raised an eyebrow. "Big date?"

Sandra blushed, but didn't cower from the question. "Yes," she said, pride ringing in her voice. "Yes, it is."

"Ooh! Who is it?" Joss wanted to know.

"A guy I went to high school with. Funny enough, I never really gave him a second look, at least romantically, and now . . ." She sighed. "He's really hot. We've been seeing a lot of each other."

Everyone gave a squeal of appreciation for this positive turn in Sandra's life.

Sandra blushed again. "Jeez, he's got me giddy. I'm so embarrassed."

"Don't be," Helene said, laying a hand on Sandra's forearm. "We're so happy for you. And I'm thinking you're pretty happy yourself. You look it."

"And you've lost a ton of weight," Joss added.

"Twenty-five pounds," Sandra replied, then pumped a fist in the air. It was incredibly uncharacteristic of her, and Lorna smiled at her unabashed joy. "It's been *hard work*."

"Congratulations!" Lorna said earnestly, and the other two concurred, adding their congratulations and comments on how obvious and spectacular the change was.

The evening ended on that very positive note. Everyone was so happy to see Sandra, previously so shy and insecure, coming out of her shell, that they set aside all their other worries to celebrate with her.

When everyone had gone, Lorna cleaned the dishes and wineglasses and then went back to her computer and logged in to eBay.

Shoegarpie had been there!

The bidding on the Lemers was up to $37.50.

Now, Lorna had sworn to herself that she wasn't bidding over twenty bucks, and she knew that even that was probably too much for her budget to handle.

But she was getting a new job; everything that had happened this week had made that clear. So obviously she'd have a more reliable income soon. And she could keep Jico's night shift, so, really, she'd have double the income. Soon. Because businesses didn't advertise job vacancies unless they were ready to fill them.

Where would she ever find specs like this again? They were *vintage*. This was the *last chance* she'd *ever have* to own something like this.

She could already picture herself showing them to the Shoe Addicts.

Time was running out. The auction had only five minutes and forty-six, forty-five, forty-four—

She typed in $61.88 and waited with bated breath.

YOU HAVE ALREADY BEEN OUTBID, the screen said.

"Crap!" She typed in $65.71.

YOU HAVE ALREADY BEEN OUTBID.

She looked at the screen. *Shoegarpie* again. Of course. With four minutes and under ten seconds to go, *Shoegarpie* might actually win this thing unless Lorna got on the stick.

234 * Beth Harbison

$99.32.

YOU ARE THE HIGH BIDDER.

"Ha! Take *that*, Shoegarpie!"

She refreshed the page. She was still the high bidder. Good. She continued to refresh as the minutes ticked down. Three minutes and ten seconds . . . two minutes and fifty seconds . . . two minutes and thirty-five seconds . . . two minutes and ten seconds . . .

Boom! There it was!

YOU HAVE BEEN OUTBID.

Logic left Lorna like a great swoosh of wind. She was going to beat *Shoegarpie* at this no matter what it took.

It was just maddening that this woman—or man—was sitting on the other side of a computer screen somewhere, typing in bids that were costing Lorna money. And for what? There was no way she was going to let *Shoegarpie* win.

She typed in a maximum bid of $140.03.

YOU ARE NOW THE HIGH BIDDER.

The price leapt to $110.50—obviously *Shoegarpie*'s max—but held steady.

Heart pounding, Lorna hit the REFRESH button over and over, glad to see she was still the highest bidder It was under a minute now. She was coming in toward the finish line. The spectators were hers. They were within reach. In just a few seconds, it would be official.

Ten, nine, eight—Lorna refreshed the page—five, four—she was still the high bidder!—three, two, one—she hit REFRESH again, confident in her victory.

And there it was.

$152.53. Winner: *Shoegarpie*.

Lorna couldn't believe it. She felt sick. *Shoegarpie* had jumped in at literally the *last second* and trumped Lorna's highest bid. By a mere

$12.50! Only $12.50 stood between her and that amazing pair of vintage Lemers! It was such a small amount.

Shoegarpie had stolen Lorna's shoes.

After the initial outrage had faded, and Lorna regained her perspective, she realized that the shoes she had lost had not, in fact, cost just $12.50. She'd been willing to shell out a hundred and a half, plus shipping, despite the fact that she was about to lose her home.

That was not rational.

She had to force herself to get her act together. That began by calling and making . . . She stopped and thought. Three, she came up with, *three* job interviews. She was going to make calls and fax résumés—in *bare feet*, no less—until she had lined up three interviews.

Chapter 17

You don't want to work on Capitol Hill," Helene told Lorna. She was the first to arrive for the meeting, and Lorna had told her she was interviewing with Senator Howard Arpege the next morning. "They blame everything on their administrative assistants. When they're not screwing them, I mean."

"Ew." Lorna made a face. "I don't think *that's* going to happen."

Helene pictured Howard Arpege and felt her stomach seize. "No, but it's almost as bad if he's trying to get you to. Maybe worse."

"Come on, there's no way that old man is interested in sex."

Helene raised an eyebrow. "You'd be surprised what I've heard."

"Oh, God, don't tell me."

There was a knock, and the door opened slightly. "Can I come in?" Joss asked, peeking around the corner.

"Of course." Lorna stood up. "I've got to pee. Just keep the door open so Sandra can come on in when she gets here."

She disappeared into the back, and Joss sat down next to Helene on the sofa.

"What've you got this week?"

Joss took a shoe box out of her bag and produced a pair of lime green Noel Parker sandals.

"Hey, I used to have a pair of those. Let's see 'em." Helene took the shoes and examined them. Yes, she'd had a pair like this. She'd had a pair *exactly* like this. Right down to the faint black mark on the left shoe, where she'd dropped a Sharpie permanent black marker and couldn't get it off the shoe.

That's why she'd given them to Goodwill.

"They're fantastic," she said warmly, handing them back to a disconcerted-looking Joss. "I miss mine. I wore them so much, they got totally worn out."

Joss looked relieved. "But they're good shoes, right?" she asked, eagerness in her eyes.

"Oh, yes. They're great."

Lorna returned to the room and was taken aback when she saw Sandra, who had just arrived. She'd finally gotten clothes that fit since she'd lost all that weight. Tonight it was a pair of jeans and a fitted black top. On her feet, she wore a gorgeous pair of extreme heel spectators.

"I can't believe it!" Helene gasped. "Are those Lemers?"

Sandra grinned. "Yes, aren't they fab?"

"Wonderful. They only made that style for two years, you know." Helene gave a low whistle. "Lemer spectators. Where on earth did you get them?"

"*What?*" Lorna came running into the room. "Lemer spectators? Let me see those."

Sandra pointed a toe out to show off the shoes.

"Holy shit," Lorna breathed.

"I know!" Sandra beamed. "You'll never guess where I got them."

"EBay," Lorna said.

Sandra looked shocked. "How on earth did you know?"

"Oh, my God, I can't believe it. You're *Shoegarpie?*" Lorna asked, her voice rising to near-hysterical pitch.

For a moment, Sandra frowned; then understanding crossed her face. "*Shoeho927.*"

"Yes!" Lorna shrieked. "Do you know how much money you've cost me?"

"*Me?* You jacked these babies into the hundreds!"

Lorna laughed and held out her hand. "Well, let me congratulate you face-to-face. If I'd known how great they were, I probably would have bid higher."

Sandra laughed, too. "Thank God you didn't. I could barely afford them as it is. So you scored the Marc Jacobs boots, huh?"

Lorna nodded. "I'll show them to you."

"*What* are you two *talking* about?" Joss asked, looking bewildered. "Are we supposed to have nicknames?"

This sent Sandra and Lorna into gales of laughter, and when they finally calmed down they told Helene and Joss that they'd been bidding against each other on eBay.

Sandra tried to hand the specs over to Lorna, but Lorna wouldn't let her, and instead they decided to share custody of the specs and the Marc Jacobs boots.

That set the tone for one of the most relaxed evenings they'd had together. It was funny—Helene had come into this looking for an escape; she'd never dreamed she'd end up with true friends.

"Tell us about this guy you've gotten all slimmed down for," Joss said to Sandra, digging into the Doritos and watching Sandra expectantly.

"First, keep those things away from me." Sandra smiled and shooed the bowl of Doritos away.

"They're baked," Lorna offered.

"Really?" Sandra reached toward them, but stopped and drew her hand back. "I can't start. Three pieces of a sensible snack are fine. Thirty are another thing altogether. I'd go for the thirty."

"Me, too," Helene said, though the truth was she'd always had a wobbly stomach that felt ill if she ate too much of anything. Some people were jealous of her seemingly effortless ability to stay slim, but it was hard work feeling sick half the time.

And nerves just made it worse.

Tonight she was a nervous wreck.

"Go on, Sandra," Helene said, forcing herself to sound and act normal. "You're not distracting us with Dorito talk. Tell us about the guy."

"Okay." Sandra blushed prettily, though the contrast with her green hair made it a little less attractive. "I've actually known him since high school. We were both the fat kids. No one ever gave either one of us a second thought, I'm guessing. But they'd be stunned to see Mike today."

"That's his name? Mike?" Joss asked.

Sandra nodded. "Mike Lemmington." She blushed again. The girl obviously had it bad if just the *thought* of the guy, or saying his name, made her blush like that. "He is unbelievably good-looking. I mean, seriously, like a male model."

"I can vouch for that," Lorna said, smiling at the obviously proud Sandra. But something about the smile looked like . . . pity? "I saw him at Jico. Very good-looking. And he's nice, too."

"That's the best part. He's sweet and sensitive, and we just talk and laugh for hours." She gave the "okay" sign. "*Totally* in touch with his sensitive side."

"Are you sure he's not, maybe, a little *too* in touch with his feminine side?" Lorna suggested carefully. It was clear to Helene she'd picked up on a vibe that Sandra had missed.

"What do you mean?" Sandra asked, looking sincerely puzzled.

"Oh, nothing, really." Lorna was struggling. "I just dated this guy once who seemed perfect. You know, sensitive, great-looking, the whole nine yards. But it turned out he was gay."

"Oh my God!" Sandra looked shocked. "How *awful* for you."

"It was. It really was. And the thing is, I missed all the signs. Really obvious signs."

"I don't want to sound like too much of a rube, but if he was gay, why was he dating you?" Joss asked.

Lorna shrugged. "I guess he wanted a beard."

Joss's mouth dropped open. "A—?"

"A cover-up," Helene explained. "A woman to date so people thought he dated women."

"Ooooooh." Joss nodded. "I get it. Yikes, that must have been up-setting."

"It was," Lorna said pointedly. "I just wish I'd figured it out sooner." She met Helene's eyes.

Helene made sure no one was looking and mouthed the words *Is Mike gay?*

Lorna grimaced and nodded.

Helene's heart sank. Poor Sandra. Here she was, head over heels for the guy, probably thinking she'd finally met Mr. Right, and she was headed for heartbreak.

"I can't even imagine what that must have felt like, Lorna," Sandra said. "Truthfully, if I hadn't known Mike for so long, I'd worry about the same thing."

"Did he date a lot of girls in high school?" Helene asked.

"No, but only because he was fat. Or, as he would put it, *weight challenged.* Girls in our high school didn't pay any attention to guys who weren't either hot or rich, since most of the guys there were, so he was lost in the shuffle."

"At least you found him now," Joss said. "Does he have any available friends?"

Sandra shook her head. "As far as I can tell, most of his friends are women. *That* drives me nuts."

"Ew, it would drive me nuts, too," Joss agreed. "I prefer a guy who's a loner. You know, the dark, brooding type."

"That's asking for trouble," Helene said, thinking of her own dark, brooding husband. But her marriage was a dark corner of her psyche that she didn't want to examine too closely right now. "Trust me, there's a lot to be said for the bland accountant who drives a sensible car and remembers your birthday."

"Amen," Lorna agreed.

"That's who my sister married," Sandra said. "Well, he's a banker. And his car isn't sensible so much as it's German. But he's bland."

"That's what counts. And it's a good thing, too, because your sister's pregnant, right?"

Sandra nodded. "Oh! And remember how I found out she was adopted?"

"Yes."

"Well, it turns out she'd often play the 'you don't love me as much as Sandra because I'm adopted' card on our parents."

"She *told* you that?" Lorna asked.

Sandra reached for the Doritos and nodded. "She admitted it." She crunched into a chip and nodded. "She was totally honest."

"Did that piss you off?" Lorna asked.

"No way. It made me feel *great*. All these years I thought they loved *her* more than me and it turns out they were just trying to *reassure* her."

She laughed. "And she wasn't even depressed; she was just playing them in order to get out of being grounded or to get a raise in her allowance or whatever. Everyone wins."

"And you spent years having no idea?" Joss shook her head. "It's like a bad movie. How do things like that happen to real people."

"Oh, you'd be surprised what weird things real people go through," Helene said.

"Isn't *that* the truth?" Lorna stood up. "Who wants more wine? Sandra, I got seltzer water, so we can cut yours in half the way you like. I'm going to do that myself with the wine Joss brought."

"I wouldn't mind trying that," Helene said.

"Not me," Joss said. "It took me a long time to get to twenty-one. I want mine straight."

"You got it, young one." Lorna laughed and went to the kitchen to get the wine.

"So tell me something," Sandra said to Helene. "Is it my imagination or are *you* getting even skinnier lately? I hope you're not on a diet."

"No, no," Helene said, trying to sound light, though she really felt as if she might get sick. She took a deep belly breath, like her yoga teacher had taught her. "It's just . . ." She shrugged. "Nerves."

Everyone seemed to move in closer, including Lorna, who was carrying a tray of wineglasses. "That's it," she said, setting the tray down and handing a glass to Helene. "What's going on?"

"Nothing."

Lorna looked at the others, then said, "You look unwell, honey. Last week you looked tired, but this week you look tired *and* rattled. Is there something going on?"

"You can trust us if you want to talk about it," Joss said, moving in to put a hand on Helene's shoulder.

Something about the gesture was so sweet, so soothing, that Helene found her eyes tearing up.

"Oh, no, it's okay." Sandra moved closer and put her arm around her, too, and before she knew it, Helene was in the middle of a big group hug, sobbing her eyes out.

As bad as she felt, though, it felt good to let it go. Finally. She let fly with everything—all the pain she'd felt for years, her whole life.

"I'm sorry," she said, drawing back at last. "I'm really a mess."

Six concerned eyes looked back at her.

"How can we help?" Lorna asked.

Helene hesitated. This was a chance to tell someone about the guy following her and not to have them laugh at her or dismiss it out of hand. After all, Lorna was the one who'd noticed him first.

But if she told them, she might worry them, and she didn't want to do that.

"You're slipping away," Sandra said, giving her a squeeze. "I've seen this before. You were about to tell us, and now you're changing your mind."

Helene couldn't help but laugh. "You should be a psychic. People could call you on a 900 number, and you'd make a fortune."

Sandra's cheeks went pink, and Helene was immediately sorry for having made light of her concern.

But before she could say anything, Lorna said, "Why are you afraid to talk about it?"

"I'm not *afraid*," Helene began, then looked at the women. Her friends.

They were her *friends*.

"I *am* afraid," she admitted. "Lorna, do you remember a few weeks ago when you called me because you thought someone was following me?"

"Of course."

"You were right."

"I was?" Her eyes widened. "I *knew* it! That son of a bitch has been out there every single time you've come over, and I kept telling myself it was a coincidence, or that Thugs R Us was also meeting here on Tuesday nights." She shook her head. "Who is he? Let's go out and get him." She honestly looked like she was ready to spring into action.

"Wait a minute, what are you two talking about?" Sandra asked; then her mouth dropped open. "The guy you asked me about that first night when I came back for my purse?"

Lorna nodded.

Sandra gave a low whistle.

"Well, who *is* he?" Joss wanted to know. "Why would someone be following you anyway?"

"Helene has a pretty powerful husband," Sandra began patiently. "He might be running for president someday."

Helene felt another wave of illness well up in her.

"I know who he is," Joss said without sounding defensive. "Do you think someone's following Helene to try and catch her doing something bad?" She turned her baby blue eyes to Helene. "Is that what you think?"

"I don't know. All I know is that he knows where I live. When I leave my house, he shows up within a couple of blocks, and when I go home, he turns off a block or two before my turn usually. He's always behind me, so there's no way for me to whip around and see where *he's* going."

"Not without some pretty fancy driving anyway," Joss agreed, furrowing her brow. "I know a guy back home in Felling who's *excellent* at that kind of thing. When they came to the town next to ours to film *Runaway Truck,* he actually did stunt driving for them."

Helene couldn't help but smile at the idea of the people in Joss's small town being excited about a film called *Runaway Truck*. It was like that where Helene came from as well. Oh, sure, there were pockets of intellectuals, pockets of artistes, pockets of just about every kind of person, but those pockets were sometimes mighty small. If *Runaway Truck* had premiered in her town, you could have broken into just about any house in town without getting caught.

"I don't suppose you've done any stunt driving?" Sandra asked her.

"Hardly." Joss laughed. "But I'm a heck of a lookout."

"That can come in handy." Sandra lifted her wineglass to her lips but was stopped by a sudden exclamation from Lorna.

"Wait! Nobody drink."

Sandra set her glass down as if she'd just seen a cockroach floating in the top.

Joss went ahead and took a sip before putting hers down.

And Helene hadn't been able to take so much as a sip without feeling ill at the very idea.

"*What?*" Sandra asked. "You scared me half to death."

"Sorry. But I have an idea. I have a *great* idea." She got up and hurried to the kitchen, flipping off the light as she went in.

"Have you lost your mind?" Sandra asked. "What are you doing in there?"

But Helene was starting to get an idea of where Lorna was headed. "Is he out there?"

Lorna emerged from the kitchen, looking like the cat who had the canary cornered. "Why, as a matter of fact, he is."

"What do you want to do, go out and confront him?" Sandra asked.

"No," Lorna said.

"He'd get away," Helene added quickly.

Lorna nodded. "Exactly."

"So what's the idea?" Joss asked eagerly. "Call the police?"

"I already did that," Helene said. "They can't do anything until he maims or kills me."

"But we can't let that happen!" Joss cried.

"We won't," Lorna assured her. "We're just going to get him at his own game."

"Ahhh." Sandra nodded. "I think I see where this is going."

"*Where?*" Joss's face was knitted with confusion. "I feel so stupid for not getting this!"

"Okay, here's the plan," Lorna said, sitting down in front of them and talking quietly, even though there was no way the guy could hear them from outside. "First we conference call between all of our cell phones."

Helene was starting to like this. "Okay . . ."

"Then Helene drives out first. He follows, right?"

"Definitely," Helene said dryly.

"Perfect." Lorna looked at Joss. "Do you have a car?"

She shook her head. "No, I take the bus."

"Good, then you can go with Helene and keep lookout, just like you said."

"But will he follow her if she has someone else in the car?" Sandra asked.

"Good point." Lorna looked at Helene. "What do you think?"

"I have no idea. I haven't had anyone else in the car with me. But maybe we shouldn't take the chance."

"I'm a little nervous behind the wheel," Sandra volunteered. "Maybe Joss could drive my car. If you're comfortable with that, I mean, Joss."

"Sure."

"Great." Lorna's eyes were bright with excitement. "So you two go second, watching for any moves he might make that Helene can't see from in front, and I'll drive behind so I can follow him if he deviates off course."

"This is crazy," Sandra said. "But I like it."

"Me, too," Lorna said. Then she looked at Helene. "Do you think he'd follow you down River Road, around Esworthy? It's off the beaten track."

"He's followed me up 270 to Frederick, he's wound down 355 to Germantown behind me, he's managed to keep chase through every damn light on Wisconsin Avenue." She nodded. "I'm pretty confident he'll follow me through the Potomac. Child's play."

"It sounds like it," Lorna agreed. She stood up again and got a piece of paper and a pen, and began drawing a rudimentary map. "Is everyone familiar with that area down by the locks?"

"I used to take horseback riding there," Sandra said.

"I used to have romantic dates with Jim there," Helene said. "Back when I used to have romantic dates with Jim, that is."

"Well, you know the part of Siddons Road that does this?" She drew the unusual double *D* pattern of Siddons road, and everyone nodded. "What I'm thinking is, Helene, you park here." She drew an *X*. "Sandra and Joss will block him in on the east, and I'll come through the west. He won't have any way to get out without smashing his car or driving into the Potomac River."

"What if smashing a car is his choice?" Joss asked.

"Hm." Lorna tapped her chin. "Good point."

Helene had liked the idea until Joss pointed out that obvious and serious problem. She didn't want anyone to get hurt, especially not because of her.

"So either Joss or I will keep one of our phones free so we can call 911 if we need to."

Lorna snapped her fingers. "Perfect."

"I'm in," Joss chirped.

Helene had been ready to let them all off the hook, and here they were bounding like enthusiastic puppies into God-knew-what.

"As the old lady of this bunch, I really think I should talk you guys out of this," Helene said, feeling a rush of tears threatening again. "Though I can't tell you how much it means to me that you care enough to go to such lengths for me."

"Are you kidding?" Sandra was looking flushed. "This is more excitement than I've had in *years*. Let's go!"

Everyone got up and collected their things, chattering nervously about how this was going to solve the problem once and for all.

Helene waited behind and caught Lorna on the way out.

"Thank you so much," she said to her, fighting tears. She didn't know why she was so emotional lately, but if there was ever a good reason to feel like crying, this was it.

Lorna looked surprised. "For what?"

"For everything. For thinking of this idea and rallying the troops." Here came the waterworks again. "For starting this group to begin with. Really. Thank you."

Lorna gave her a hug and held on just long enough to show it was sincere. "Any time."

"I'm a mess."

"No, you're not. But you've got reason to be. Come on," she gestured, like the general leading the troops, "let's go get this bastard. He'll be sorry he ever messed with you."

"I'm sure he will. By the way," Helene said, and Lorna stopped and turned to her. "This is just a hunch, but you watched *Scooby-Doo* a lot as a child, didn't you?"

Lorna smiled and nodded. "Every Saturday morning."

Chapter 18

S andra was glad Joss was driving, because even sitting in the passenger seat, she felt like her heart was going to beat its way right out of her chest.

She'd made a lot of progress over the past couple of months in terms of getting out and meeting people, but she wasn't quite to the "driving a high speed chase" level yet.

Though, truth be told, she was psyched to be part of this. She'd never been part of anything that felt thrilling or important before. Even when she was taking her phone calls—maybe *especially* when she was taking her phone calls—she felt like she was wasting her time and her callers' time, and that she really should be doing something more worthwhile, if only she didn't need the money.

"This is the most fun I've had in a long time," Joss said.

"I bet. It's got to be a real drag being stuck in that big house playing Cinderella all the time."

Joss shrugged. "I hate to complain. . . ." She hesitated. "Yeah, it's been pretty awful. But I really feel like I can *help* the boys." She reconsidered a moment. "Well, the younger one, anyway. I honestly think I'm getting through to him."

"How many women have said the same thing to justify staying in a difficult situation?" Sandra asked. "Granted, it's usually a *man* they're talking about, but the point's the same. You can't sacrifice yourself at the altar of Deena Oliver's bad parenting, because no matter how you slice it, you're still just an employee."

"But—"

"You can't *fix* what's wrong with their family."

"I know." Joss sighed. "Sometimes I wonder if it's doing them more harm than good seeing how their mother pushes me around. Does the good of my caring for them outweigh the bad of them seeing someone who cares about them treated like a doormat?"

Sandra tried to puzzle that out, but she didn't know the answer. "Look, just consider the fact that maybe this isn't the right job for you."

"Maybe not, but there's the contract."

"I know we've talked about that before, and it's really honorable that you want to stick to the letter of your contract, but look, if your *boss* is willing to break the contract, why shouldn't you be?"

Joss was silent for a moment, and Sandra got the feeling that, for the first time, she was actually considering it. "You may be right," she said at last.

"I *am*. And consider the fact that you're being asked, maybe even bullied, to do all those things that aren't part of your job description. That's not in the contract."

"No. Those things are definitely not in the contract."

"I've got an idea. I know a lawyer who I'm pretty sure would do a phone consultation with you." This was going to be one of the strangest barters Sandra had ever heard of, but she *did* have a regular caller—one of the talkers—who was a lawyer. She was pretty sure it wouldn't be hard to set up an anonymous call so Joss could get some advice. "Would you be interested?"

Joss glanced at her. "You're one of the nicest friends I've ever had," she said with a completely guileless smile. "I can't believe you'd do that for me."

Sandra was surprised by how much this touched her. She'd never had any close friends, and until recently she hadn't really realized how much she was missing.

It was amazing how much her life had turned around in these past few months. Mike. Weight Watchers. That mind-altering conversation with Tiffany.

Sandra had never been so happy.

"I'm glad to do it," she said. Then, embarrassed by her own emotion, she looked at the road ahead and said, "We're going to be turning left in about a quarter of a mile."

The blue car was still in front of them, though someone had whipped their Land Rover out between the blue car and Sandra's, and when they went around a bend in the road, Sandra noticed Helene's black BMW about four car lengths in front of him.

Sandra's phone rang and she flipped it open.

It was Lorna. "Hey, it's me. Helene, are you still on?"

"I'm here," Helene's voice said.

"Cool! I did it right!" Lorna's voice reflected the excitement Sandra was seeing in Joss. "All right, so we're all here. Is the stalker there, too?"

"I see him," Sandra said. "He's a little bit behind Helene."

"This is crazy," Helene said. "Does anyone have anything we can use as a weapon if we need to? Umbrella? Anything?"

"I've got Mace," Sandra said.

"Wow, really?" Joss said, next to her.

Sandra pointed to the fat Mace pen on the key chain in the ignition.

"I've got a chain dog collar in my glove compartment," Lorna said. "If you whip it around, it's actually a great weapon."

"Lorna, is there something you want to tell us?" Sandra joked. "Why would you keep a dog collar in your glove box?"

"What?" Joss asked.

Sandra laughed and whispered, "It's for protection."

"For just this kind of occasion," Lorna said. "You never know when a friend might prevail upon you to chase down a stalker."

Everyone laughed.

"Okay, I'm turning off," Helene said. "This is your last chance to bail."

"No way," Lorna said.

"We're with you," Sandra said, and, to her utter amazement, the last traces of her fear dissolved. "All the way."

The street before them was dark, and the night sky was filled with stars, the way only a remote place can be.

They had to act fast.

As planned, Helene drew to a halt, turning her car sideways, Joss whipped in next to her—so close, Sandra was amazed they didn't hit Helene's bumper. Lorna pulled in, equally close, blocking the hapless stalker in without room to turn around, and no way to escape unless he wanted to back right into the river and swim for it.

They all left their headlights on, so Sandra could tell the guy looked like he was contemplating the water.

What followed went so quickly, there was hardly any time to think. They leapt out of their cars and surrounded the guy.

Joss tossed the keys to Sandra and said, "I don't know how to work that thing."

Sandra removed the cap from the Mace and stood ready.

"I *knew* it was you." Helene's voice shook with anger. "Why have you been following me?"

The guy got out of his car, keeping his hands up in plain view. Either he'd been through this before, or he'd seen too many police shows on TV. Like the rest of them.

"Whoa, you guys are good." He stood about five feet ten inches tall. He had a blandly handsome face, like a soap opera actor, with blond hair that was almost the color of his skin.

He didn't *look* like much of a threat.

"Who *are* you?" Lorna demanded.

"His name is Gerald Parks," Helene said. "He's a photographer who's been trying to blackmail me."

"I'm not a photographer. I'm a private detective."

"Since when?" Helene asked, looking genuinely shocked.

"I have been the whole time. I said I was a photographer as a cover story."

"I don't think detectives are supposed to blackmail people," Sandra said.

"The blackmail wasn't for real. That was the story I was hired to tell."

"Okay." Lorna stepped forward and held her hand out. The thick silver chain glinted in the headlights. "Who hired you, then?"

Sandra had to suppress a laugh at how positively menacing Lorna and her chain looked.

He frowned at the chain. "Are you crazy?"

Joss opened her phone and held it up in front of her.

Lorna whipped the chain around like some kind of matador.

"Shit, you *are* crazy," Gerald Parks said. "Either that or you're on the rag."

Lorna whipped the chain close to him. "Nothing's more dangerous than a crazy woman who's just been accused of being on the rag by a dumpy little caveman." The chain came so close to him, at such a rapid speed, that he must have felt the breeze from it.

"Stop it!" he shrieked.

"Who hired you to follow Helene?" Lorna demanded, and tapped him with the chain.

"I'm not telling you that. You can hit me with your goddam chain all you want. It's confidential." The guy's eyes darted around and landed on Joss. "What the hell are *you* doing? If you're calling the police, *you're* going to be the ones to get in trouble. And a lot of it."

"I'm not calling the police," Joss said, in a calm voice. "It's way worse than that. I'm taking a video of you cowering away from a few helpless women. I gotta tell you, Gerald, it's not a flattering view. In fact, you look pretty funny. I think if I put it on the Internet, it's going to make the rounds." Then she pulled out her trump card. "Remember the *Star Wars* Kid? He was all over the Internet. *Everyone* forwarded that embarassing video along."

"Okay, okay, okay," Gerald said, putting his hands up again. "Nothing's worth this." He turned to Helene. "I'll tell you the truth."

Sandra recalled Luis's story about Helene shoplifting. If he really was a detective, did he have something to do with that? Should Sandra somehow try to stop him before he said it out loud and everyone else found out? She froze with the desire to help and the complete uncertainty as to how to do it.

"Go on," Helene said evenly.

Sandra cringed, anticipating his answer.

"I don't know why he told me to blackmail you. I guess it was to scare you. Keep you complacent. Who knows? I don't ask why. I just do what I'm paid to do."

"Who paid you to do it?" Helene asked. She looked like she was going to be sick. "Who hired you?"

"Your husband."

"My husband," she repeated dully, her suspicions finally out there, admitted.

"Yeah, Demetrius Zaharis."

Sandra hurried over to Helene and put an arm through hers to help prop her up.

"Right," Lorna said. "Why would we believe her husband hired you to blackmail her?"

"Because it's true," Gerald snapped. "Look, I've got his private number on my cell phone." He reached in his front pocket.

"Slow," Sandra said, half-enjoying the *Cagney & Lacey*–ness of it all. "Put it on the ground and kick it over to her." It was a good safety precaution.

Joss giggled, but turned it into a cough.

Sandra tried not to do the same thing as Gerald did what she'd asked and kicked the phone over.

Helene picked it up and looked. "That's it, all right."

"Call him, Parks," Lorna said. "Let Helene hear him talk to you."

"Yes, call him," Helene said stiffly.

Sandra took the phone from Helene and tossed it back to Gerald.

"What do you want me to say to him?" he asked Lorna.

"What do you normally say to him at the end of the night?"

"I report where she's gone and what she's done."

"Then do that. Only leave this part out." She looked at Joss. "Are you still filming?"

Joss nodded. "I already uploaded the first part, and now I'm filming again."

Lorna looked at Gerald. "Isn't technology great?"

He rolled his eyes and dialed the phone and put it on speaker.

"Do you mind if we all hear?" Sandra whispered to Helene.

She shook her head.

"Zaharis."

"It's Parks here."

"What have you got for me?"

"Nothing much to report. Are you at home?"

"No, I'm at . . . a friend's. What do you care?"

Sandra felt Helene stiffen.

"Well, she's at home now. First she went to the Rafferty chick's place, and hung out with them."

"Anything unusual happen?"

Even in the headlights, Sandra could see Gerald blush. "Nope. Looked like it was just the same as always."

There was a woman's voice in the background, but it was impossible to tell what she said.

Gerald glanced at Helene. "That's all."

"Got it. Ciao." Jim Zaharis clicked his phone off.

Sandra was disgusted. What a creep Zaharis was! Here he had a great wife like Helene and he was off messing around with another woman. *And* had the gall to have a detective tailing Helene while he did it.

Pig.

And that smarmy *ciao*—that had really tipped him into creep territory.

"I don't want to go home," Helene said quietly.

"Come to my place," Sandra volunteered immediately. "How about you all come over, and we'll talk Helene through this."

Gerald, whom she'd forgotten for a moment, said, "Sure."

"Not *you*," Lorna snapped. "Are you nuts?"

Helene looked at Gerald. "What have you told him about me?"

He met her eyes. "Just what you do, where you go, who you see, and how long you do it. That's what he asked me to do."

"Did you—?" She hesitated and cleared her throat. "Did you tell him anything else?"

"You mean like the fact that your name's not really Helene and you were never even *in* Ohio, much less born there?" He shook his head, keeping his eyes level on hers. "I haven't told him that part. Yet."

Chapter 19

How about some tea?" Sandra offered. She focused her attention on Helene. "You look like you could use a nice, soothing cup."

"Thanks." Helene nodded. "I'd appreciate it." She looked at Joss and Lorna, who were sitting around her on Sandra's big soft sofa.

"Take some deep breaths," Lorna suggested. "You've had a hell of a night."

"I'm fine," Helene insisted.

Sandra came back in with a cup of tea and handed it to Helene before sitting on the floor in front of her. "Listen, you can stay here as long as you want to, okay?"

Helene smiled. "Thanks, but I'm going back tonight. I'm going to have to face the music sooner or later."

"Isn't Jim the one who needs to face the music?" Joss asked. "He's the one who hired a detective to follow you."

Helene shrugged. "I'd have more of a leg to stand on if the detective hadn't been able to find out such juicy stuff about me." She raised an eyebrow. "Now don't pretend you're not wondering what he was talking about."

"You don't have to tell us anything you don't want to," Lorna said, though she was wildly curious about what Gerald had meant when he said Helene wasn't . . . well, Helene.

"You really don't," Sandra agreed, and Joss nodded.

"You guys are liars." Helene gave a small laugh. "But, to tell you the truth, I think it would do me some good to get this off my chest. I've been hiding it for a long time." She took a sip of tea, and everyone waited, practically holding their breath, for her to continue talking. "Gerald's right. The name I was given when I was born was Helen. Helen Sutton."

"That's practically the same!" Joss argued.

"That's not the whole story. I grew up in Charles Town, West Virginia, by the racetrack. It wasn't . . . glamorous. There were a lot of times when I literally had to walk to school barefoot."

"Ohhh." Joss looked like she was going to cry.

Lorna felt like she might, too.

But Helene held up a hand. "No, no. No pity. I'm just telling the truth. And as you all know, I lead a privileged life now, so there is no room for you to feel sorry for me. Anyway, suffice it to say, it was a pretty ugly life. For my family, that is, not necessarily for everyone in our town. But my father was an alcoholic, and he was brutal to my mother and me. When Mama died, the doctor said it was a stroke, but I swear I think it was from being pushed too hard one too many times by my father." Helene took another sip of tea, and Lorna noticed she held the cup with shaking hands.

"Did he ever get in trouble for it?" Sandra asked.

"Oh, hell no," Helene said, uncharacteristically blunt. "That's not how it worked there. And I can't prove it was his fault, regardless. Though it was definitely his fault she had such a miserable quality of life while they were married." She shrugged. "Then again, she chose her own hell. We all do."

Lorna thought of her past relationships, some of which she'd stayed in way too long, just because she was too lazy or maybe too afraid to be alone. "We sure do," she agreed.

Sandra was nodding, too, with a faraway look in her eyes.

And Joss was just watching them all.

"So that's *it*? That's all this guy's got on you?" Lorna asked. "Because, I've got to say, I was hoping for something a lot more scandalous."

Helene laughed. "Well, I didn't *kill* anyone. But the thing is, I made up a whole history that wasn't mine. I invented a fictional past growing up in the Midwest, gave myself fictional dead parents who were clean-living and supportive. I was a fictional cheerleader and first runner-up in the Homecoming court my senior year."

"First runner-up?" Sandra questioned. "Why not go all the way and be queen?"

Helene smiled. "I had to keep it realistic. Add fictional disappointments to my fictional perfect life."

"I think that sounds like fun!" Joss said. "We should all do that, just make up who we want to be. People would probably be a lot happier if they did that."

"So when Jim came along, you were working in Garfinkels, right?" Lorna asked.

Helene nodded. "And going to school."

"So it really ended up being a Cinderella story," Lorna said. "I mean, in a way. You got your palace, if not your prince."

"Oh, he seemed like a prince at first," Helene said, smiling at some fond memory. "He's not all bad, even now. He's a good man, for the most part. He's just not a great husband."

Lorna wanted to yell *But he had a detective following you!* but she didn't because if Helene had made the choice to stay with the kind of creep who would do that, it wasn't Lorna's place to correct her.

Lorna had stayed with plenty of creeps herself, and for a lot less money and prestige than Helene got out of the deal.

"I still think you could have come up with something more dramatic and shocking," Lorna teased. "I wouldn't buy a tabloid with that headline."

"How about the fact that I got caught shoplifting at Ormond's in July?" Helene asked, eyebrows raised.

Joss gasped.

Lorna's mouth dropped open.

Sandra . . . Weirdly enough, Sandra didn't really look surprised. "All right, forget the tea. This calls for margaritas. Everyone in?"

Everyone was in.

"Are you *serious*?" Joss asked Helene when Sandra had gotten up and moved to the kitchenette, where she banged around making the much-needed libations.

Helene nodded. "It was an incredible lapse in judgment. A moment of anger, because Jim had cut off my credit cards and I just decided the hell with him, he's not keeping *me* barefoot, and I walked out of the store with a pair of Bruno Maglis on. I left a pair of Jimmy Choos, but apparently Ormond's isn't in the business of bartering." She tried to be casual, though her face was red. "Who knew?"

"And you were *caught*?" Lorna asked, disbelieving.

Helene winced. "Oh, yeah. As I said, it was stupid from start to finish. And there"—she splayed her arms—"you know all my worst secrets. And you know why I'm in huge trouble if—*when*—Jim finds out. He'll be publicly humiliated when everyone learns that his wife's résumé, which is printed in countless charity catalogs and political bios, is complete horseshit."

"Do you ever think about leaving?" Sandra asked carefully, entering the room holding three glasses. She handed one to Helene. "Not that I'm saying you *should*." She handed drinks to Lorna and Joss as well.

"Oh, of course I should," Helene said, waving a hand and picking up the margarita. She took a long sip before continuing. "God, if I were listening to this story, I'd be asking why the hell this dumb woman hadn't left ages ago instead of suffering the stress of living a lie for so long." She gave a dry laugh. "And the answer to that is just that I'm weak. Or I was. I've been giving the idea a lot more thought lately. Divorce isn't so bad, politically, as it used to be. If Jim and I divorced now, he could still run for higher office in the next few terms."

Sandra came back into the room with her drink, sat down, and had a sip.

"Sure. You'd just be his Jane Wyman," Lorna said. "No one ever thinks about her as Ronald Reagan's first wife. She's just Angela from *Falcon Crest*."

"That's right," Sandra said, setting her glass down. A third of the drink was already gone. "I was trying to remember what show she was on."

"I know my *Falcon Crest*," Lorna said, thinking maybe she should offer to go into the kitchen and make a pitcher of the drinks, since it looked like they were going to need them.

Sandra must have been thinking the same thing because she said, "We're going to need more margaritas." She started to get up, but Lorna stopped her.

"You relax, I'll make them. Is everything out?"

Sandra looked grateful. "Yes, it's all on the counter."

"I'll be right back." Indeed, Sandra had an excellent bottle of tequila reposado, Rose's lime juice, triple sec, and Grand Marnier. The girl knew how to party.

She threw the ingredients together, along with some ice from the machine on the door of Sandra's stainless steel fridge, and took it back into the room just as Sandra was starting to tell her story.

"Since we're opening up, I have a secret identity, too," she said, and took another pull of her drink. "Actually several of them."

"Okay, out on the table," Lorna said, refilling Sandra's glass to keep her talking. "Who are they?"

"I am," Sandra cleared her throat and sat up straight, ticking the names off on her fingers, "Dr. Penelope, sex therapist; Britney, the naughty schoolgirl; Olga, the Swedish dominatrix—"

This was weird.

"—Aunt Henrietta, the mean old aunt who always spanked; and the ever-popular Lulu, the French maid." She smiled. "Among others. I am a phone-sex operator."

This was way—*way*—more shocking than Helene's story. Sandra? A phone-sex operator? She seemed so shy! So conservative! So—so— *un*sexual.

Lorna downed half her drink.

"What does that mean?" Joss asked. "Like those ads in the back of *City Paper* where people call and pay tons of money per minute?"

"Exactly. I make a dollar forty-five a minute."

"Wow!" Immediately Lorna wondered if she could bring herself to talk dirty on the phone with strangers.

The money was certainly right.

"So those are the *communications* you talked about when we asked what you did for a living, eh?" Helene wagged a finger at Sandra. "Shame on you. For not telling us sooner, I mean. I *love* that. It's so risqué!"

"It can be." Sandra seemed completely unaffected by it. "Some of the callers want really kinky stuff, but you'd be surprised how many just want someone to talk to. Even at two ninety-nine a minute." At Joss's puzzled look, she said, "The company I work for gets a little more than half, and I get the rest."

"Yes, I get that," Joss said. The world was getting pleasantly wobbly for Lorna, but Joss still looked completely sober. "I was just trying to figure out what the revenues for the company itself are, having a team of women doing this for them twenty-four hours a day, seven days a week. Now *that's* the business to be in."

Lorna couldn't believe sweet little Joss wasn't shocked at the job, but instead was thinking it was a good business. "You little businesswoman," Lorna said, smiling. "Next thing we know, you'll be a madam."

"There's money in it," Joss said seriously. "Oh, my God, old Mrs. Cathell, back in Felling, made a fortune doing it. And she gave to the community, put money in the basket at church, and no one ever said a word about it being inappropriate." Then, in response to everyone's silent gaping, she added, "But I'm just interested in the business plan, not the business." She looked embarrassed and added, "I took business and Web design in community college."

Sandra agreed. "My checks come from a bank in the Cayman Islands. I wouldn't mind sitting on a beach somewhere, letting the money roll in like that."

"So what made you get into that line of work?" Lorna asked, fascinated.

"Agoraphobia." Sandra gave a short laugh. "Actually, that's true, but it's only half the truth. I've always been a bit . . . self-conscious. I don't like going out much in public."

"Why?" Joss asked.

Sandra looked at her as if she was trying to figure out if Joss was kidding or not. "I've been the Fat Girl all of my life. In school, the other kids made fun of me. And out in the real world, grown people—people you'd like to think knew better—did the same thing. People can be so cruel."

Helene put a hand on Sandra's and twined her fingers with hers. "You didn't deserve that."

Sandra smiled. "I'm starting to realize that. Ever since I met you all, actually. I've gotten out more these past few weeks than in the past five years. I met Mike"—she blushed—"everything's gotten so much better." Her eyes grew bright. "Oh, jeez, now I'm going to cry."

"Don't do that—you'll get us all going," Lorna said. Her heart felt like it would break.

Sandra sniffed. "Okay, enough. This isn't supposed to be a sob story. It's a *good* thing. Shoes were always my friends. My mother had to specially order my elementary school uniforms, and I couldn't buy trendy clothes at the mall like all the other girls, but shoes *always* fit. Off the shelf, from a catalog, it didn't matter. No matter how heavy I got, no matter what size jeans I wore or what section of the department store I had to go to to find them, in shoes I was size seven and a half, and that was that." She snapped her fingers. "If I was ordering shoes from a catalog, asking for a seven and a half didn't say a thing about me. I could have been Jennifer Aniston for all they knew. Which, come to think of it, is sort of what it's like being a phone-sex operator."

"That's probably not a coincidence, then," Helene commented. "Do you enjoy your work?"

"Sometimes I do." Sandra laughed. "I have never *ever* confessed *that* to anyone. Not even myself."

"But that's *good*," Joss insisted. "It's important to like your work. I sure wish I did."

"I wish you did, too, sweetie," Lorna said. "I can't wait until you talk to Sandra's lawyer friend." A thought suddenly occurred to her. "Wait a minute, this lawyer . . . he's not one of your . . ." She raised her eyebrows in question.

"So who's next?" Sandra asked, winking at Lorna. "Lorna, got any skeletons in *your* closet?"

Okay, subject changed.

"Along with all the shoes, you mean?" Lorna nodded. "As a matter of fact, I do. Truthfully, I came pretty close to sticking a pair of Fendis under my shirt and sneaking out of Ormond's myself last month. They were so gorgeous—" She recalled the black leather, the perfect little buckles. "—I would have bought them, but I'm broke." A moment of silence. "Dead broke. I have more than thirty thousand dollars in credit card debt, so I saw a counselor who cut up all of my cards and put me on a budget."

"Are you okay now?" Helene looked at her closely. "Because if you need money, I'd be glad to help out. Really."

Lorna felt warm inside. "That means a lot, Helene, but actually— I've got to knock wood when I say this—I think I'm starting to get it under control. I rebudgeted the other night and put a few pairs of my babies online for sale—"

"The Gustos," Sandra breathed.

"Yup." Lorna remembered how psyched she'd been when *Shoegarpie (1)* had bid on the shoes, and how amazed she'd felt when some new person, *shoeshoesheboogie (0),* had swept in and outbid her, taking the Gustos up to an incredible $210.24. "Sorry you missed out on those. But honestly, I only paid one seventy-five for them at an outlet in Delaware. No tax even."

"I see a road trip in our future," Sandra said, then, thinking better of it, she added, "The distant future, that is. Once you feel comfortable buying retail again."

Lorna nodded. "I need to get a new job. That should change everything. Or at least make it so I can buy an *occasional* pair in a box."

"In the meantime, though, you started this group," Helene said, nodding. There was admiration in her eyes, rather than the judgment Lorna might have expected from someone—someone like Lucille—upon being told that incredible sum of debt. "That was good thinking."

"Yeah, it would be, if I weren't also bidding against Sandra for shoes on eBay and giving up meals to save for more shoes anyway." Lorna laughed and shook her head. "I'm truly an addict."

"Me, too," Helene said, resigned.

"Me three," Sandra added.

"Um . . . I'm not." That was Joss. She was looking at them with wide eyes and pink cheeks. "If it's time for admitting secrets, I've got one of my own."

Lorna's heart skipped a beat. Surely she wasn't going to say she didn't like shoes!

"Well, for one thing—" She took off the Miu Mius she'd gotten from Sandra last week and took a wad of tissue out of the toe. "—I'm a size six."

"But—" Lorna wasn't sure what to say. "That can't be comfortable!"

"Actually, it's not as bad as some of the SuperMart shoes I've worn. I can see why you guys like these. I just never had the opportunity to wear good shoes before. I joined the group because I needed to get out of the Olivers' house on Tuesday nights and a shoe meeting sounded better than a sexual dysfunction group." She cast a sly glance at Sandra. "No offense."

Sandra laughed out loud. "You made the right choice."

"I did." Joss's expression grew earnest again. "I really did. But you three are so wonderful, I just don't know what I'd do if I hadn't met you!"

"Well, we're not letting you go now, size six or not," Lorna said. "But where on earth did you get all those fabulous pairs you brought with you?"

"Thrift stores, vintage stores, Goodwill." She looked at Helene. "When you said you'd had a pair like those green shoes, I was absolutely terrified you might have given them to Goodwill and I'd bought them and brought them back."

Helene laughed. "Oh, no!"

Joss nodded. "I was!"

"Well, we had no idea those weren't your own treasures," Helene said, still looking surprised at Joss's admission. "What did you do with the shoes you traded from us?"

"I've got them all in my closet at the Olivers house. I'm like a magpie with all these pretty things I've collected. But now that I've come clean I'll give them back to you, obviously."

"I'd say you don't have to, and you don't, but what else can you do with them?" Lorna said. "Though I wouldn't mind having those Miu Mius of Sandra's." She nodded at the pair Joss had just taken off, then looked at Sandra.

"Take them," she said. "They're yours."

"Maybe you can loan me a pair of socks to wear home, Sandra." Joss handed the shoes over to Lorna, and everyone laughed.

"I've got one more secret to tell," Helene said when the group quieted down.

"Oooh! Do we go around again?" Lorna asked.

"I hope not," Sandra said. "You guys do *not* want to know what I did with Vice Principal Breen's championship golf ball in seventh grade. What is it, Helene? Give us the scoop."

Helene looked from one to the other of them, with a strange expression of mingled happiness and what looked like fear. "I think . . . ," she began, then took a long breath and tried again. "I think I'm pregnant."

Chapter
20

In Felling, a woman going to the drugstore for a pregnancy test was something that got noticed. Inevitably the cashier would know her, and word would spread through town about who it was, where she'd gone. It probably wasn't quite so attention-grabbing here, Joss thought, unless *four* women went to the drugstore for a pregnancy test.

But that's what they did, flanking Helene like her own super Secret Service protection. Anyone watching wouldn't have been able to tell exactly who the test was for, and that's the way they wanted it.

They went back to Sandra's apartment with two double-packs of EPTs, and fifteen minutes later, four positive sticks sat on the side of Sandra's sink.

"So that's definitely positive?" Joss verified.

"Look at the picture." Lorna passed one of the instruction sheets over to Joss. "One line negative, two lines positive."

"There are eight lines here," Helene said dully, staring at the tests. "It's true."

"How did this happen?" Sandra asked. "I thought you were on the pill."

"Jim threw them out when he found them." Helene continued to stare at the pregnancy tests. "I got more, I couldn't have missed more than three days, and I doubled up but . . . I guess that wasn't good enough. Obviously that wasn't good enough."

"I've read that even if you miss one day, you're way more vulnerable and should double up protection," Sandra said.

"God." Helene covered her face with her hands. "I didn't even *want* to make love with him. *Especially* after what he did." She took a shuddering breath. "It was just easier to comply and let him get it over with than to argue." She shook her head. "Spoken like a really foolish woman, huh?"

Lorna came over and gave Helene a squeeze. "Look, we *all* do things we don't want to sometimes just because it's the path of least resistance. Life is hard enough—no one wants to add arguments on top of everything else. You can't blame yourself for it."

"Of course I can," Helene said with a little laugh. "I have to. It's my fault."

"Forget all that," Lorna said. "It doesn't even matter anymore. The question now is what do you want to do?"

Helene swallowed. "I don't know."

"I'm about to be out a job," Joss said. "I can help you out. Honest. I've got loads of experience with babies."

Helene looked at her gratefully. "I'd like that." Then she looked around at the rest of them. "Should we get out of the bathroom?"

That broke the ice, and they went back to Sandra's cushy sofa and settled in, moving in close to Helene.

"This does complicate your plans for your marriage, doesn't it?" Lorna said.

"That was my first reaction," Helene said. "And the truth is, I'm not sure what to do about that. Either way the marriage is over, but is it better to stay in the same house for the sake of the child?"

"I think it's better to do whatever is going to make you feel the most peaceful and happy," Sandra said. "If a child grows up in a strained environment, that has a lot more impact on him than growing up in a happy environment—or two—where he visits his dad on alternate weekends and has two sets of everything." She sighed. "My parents had a very tense marriage. Separate rooms, which they never explained, stony silences, Dad had a lot of late nights out *at work*. Now I wonder."

"Gosh, that and the feeling that Tiffany was their darling must have made it really rough on you," Joss commented.

Sandra shrugged. "A lot of people had it a lot worse. If I'd been stronger, I wouldn't be such a neurotic mess now."

"But you're not!" Joss hated to see Sandra say that kind of thing, especially now, when she seemed to be getting so much confidence, maybe for the first time in her life.

"No, you're just slogging through the stuff life has dished out," Lorna agreed. "We've all got some of that."

Helene looked at Lorna for a moment, frowning. Then she looked from Sandra to Joss. "I've got an idea," she said, and it was clear that some positive force—hope, optimism, whatever—was coming into her. "I might have a really good idea."

"About slogging through life?" Sandra asked.

"Actually, in a way, yes. Lorna, you need a new job, right?"

"Amen."

"Joss, you're about to need a new job."

This sounded really promising. "Definitely."

"Sandra? I know you're okay with your work, but would you be interested in a little entrepreneurial venture on the side?"

Sandra looked curious. "With you all? You bet. What have you got in mind?"

"I was at a party a few weeks ago at the Mornini house—"

"Ooh, partying with the mob?" Lorna asked.

"Those stories are *not* true," Helene said. "Probably. Anyhow, Chiara took me upstairs and showed me the most exquisite shoes I have *ever* seen, bar none." She described the shoes in great detail, and Sandra and Lorna squealed at the description. Joss was just lost. Shoes were shoes. She loved these women, but she'd never completely understand why they were so nuts about shoes.

"Where do we get them?" Lorna asked eagerly.

"That's the thing," Helene said. "The guy needs financial backing. And an American distributor. Chiara wanted her husband to get involved, because she was sure it would be a hugely profitable business, but he didn't want to be associated with that particular kind of business. Not manly enough, I suspect."

"And you think we can do it?" Lorna asked. "Really? That sounds like something that would cost a hell of a lot of money."

"So we get a loan," Joss said, remembering her Incorporation 102 class. "We incorporate, get a loan, set up the business as a separate entity, and we're safe. Of course, that's a little easier said than done, but that's how we'd do it."

And suddenly a strange excitement came over Joss. She'd come to D.C. hoping to get a taste of life in the big city. Nannying was just the first step in her plan. It wasn't the end; it was only the beginning. She was going to orient herself in the town and find new opportunities to build a bigger life than she'd have if she stayed in Felling and married one of the boys she went to high school with.

This was just exactly one of those opportunities.

She did, however, have to fight a feeling of failure at not having been able to stay on and at least try to help fix some of the things that were so clearly wrong in Bart's and Colin's lives. They received no gentle adult guidance from their parents, no warmth, no affection. And without someone steady there to run interference and shield them from the freak show that was their parents, they were bound to pick up some bad influences.

Bart had shown such sweetness now and then, such vulnerability. . . . Joss shuddered to think of him losing that and becoming exacting and demanding like his mother. Or emotionally detached from his family, like his father.

Or—terrible possibility—both.

But Joss had done everything she could. There was no question that if she continued on there, things would get worse. No doubt. So this new business was—what was the word?—*serendipity*. It couldn't have come at a better time, or with better people.

Helene was talking now, more excitedly than ever, about the business opportunity she'd proposed. "I have plenty of contacts within local stores. I've had to tap them repeatedly for donations and so forth. I'm almost certain the big five stores around here would want to carry Phillipe's shoes. I'm certainly willing to pitch them."

"What about home parties?" Sandra suggested.

"What, like Tupperware?" Lorna asked.

"Well . . . yeah. Or any number of things. But direct sales with the right clientele. That could go even faster than retail."

"Better still if it's in *conjunction* with retail," Joss said. She was beginning to like this idea.

Helene yawned.

Sandra picked up on that immediately. "Okay, girls, it's been a long and eventful night. God knows. Let's reconvene tomorrow, okay?"

"Yes," Lorna said.

"Absolutely," Joss agreed. "As long as it's after eight P.M." She looked to the others. "Can you guys meet that late?"

"I can," Helene said.

"If you can make it closer to ten, I can, too," Lorna said, and looked relieved when everyone nodded.

"Done," Sandra said. "In the meantime, can anyone find out what would be involved in getting a bank loan for start-up money?"

"I could probably squeeze it in in the morning," Helene began.

"No," Lorna interrupted. "You need your rest. I don't go to work until noon tomorrow. I'll go to the bank first. I have a contact there anyway. Sort of."

And with that, Joss's future began to change.

All their futures did.

✳

Helene couldn't sleep.

It was a lot to take in. Not only her husband's betrayal, which was legion and worthy of weeks of contemplation if it weren't for more important circumstances, but the more important circumstances.

She was pregnant.

It wasn't what she'd wanted. When she'd done the first test and seen the double lines, indicating a positive result, she'd toyed with guilt. But as she'd continued to dip the sticks and read the subsequent three pregnancy tests in Sandra's bathroom, she'd come to the conclusion that it didn't matter what she wanted. She was pregnant and, unless she decided to terminate the pregnancy, she was going to remain pregnant until she gave birth.

So far, she hadn't decided what to do.

As a result, she'd spent the longest night of her life struggling with the turmoil of trying to answer a question she had, until recently, been positive would never be asked.

In the murky swirl of thoughts that kept her from falling asleep, she kept returning to her own childhood. The life she'd left behind. The life, in fact, that she'd sworn off.

It hadn't been all bad. The trees, the creeks, the fact that she could smell the color green every spring when the grasses started to come up again. The dramatic winter nights so filled with stars you couldn't be sure which one was the Eastern Star that led the wise men to baby Jesus.

Those were the thoughts that pulled her out of bed at 5 A.M., like strings on a marionette, and led her to her car for the drive north. She didn't look to see if Jim was home before she left. She didn't care. She just got into the fussy little Batmobile he'd insisted she drive, and she'd beaten the rush hour traffic onto River Road, the Beltway, 270 north, 70 west, and finally, the road she never thought she'd travel again, 340 west into West Virginia.

The main roads had changed. There were gas stations and food stops and souvenir shops where once there had been green trees, dark shadows, and dirt roads. Signs all around pointed to Harper's Ferry and various hotels and motels and fast food restaurants from which to appreciate what had once been a majestic view of the hills, the trees, and the river below.

Helene felt an unexpected surge of pain, as if it had been her personal responsibility to keep this landscape pristine and, by leaving, she had let Mother Nature down.

Or maybe it was just the personal feeling of loss, at having spent so much time away that she didn't even know this development was taking over the land, that brought her so close to tears.

In any event, she drove on through the misty morning toward the house she'd grown up in. Her mother was long gone, and she'd heard from a neighbor when she was working at Garfinkels that her father had died in a car accident with a tree. It hadn't surprised Helene. And it hadn't grieved her either.

The most melancholy thing for her was thinking about David Price. Funny, cute David, who threw snowballs at her when they were ten, passed her notes in school when they were twelve, kissed her badly when they were fourteen, and coerced her out of her virginity when they were sixteen.

Actually he'd done that pretty well.

The last time she'd seen him he was nineteen, and she was leaving for less green pastures in the city. For all the things that she didn't remember from long ago, and all the memories she had that were foggy with time, she could see the heartache in his sweet brown eyes when she'd told him things were over.

Now, as she drove through the semi-familiar landscape, wondering if he still lived around here, she had to ask herself if she'd been right to leave and completely lose touch with the one good thing from her past.

Her old house was still there, remnants of the log facing still apparent in front. But several additions had been built onto the place, and there was a minivan parked in the gravel driveway. It looked insanely out of place, like a space shuttle superimposed on a Civil War picture.

Good. The place had brought nothing but bad to her as a child. She was glad it was different now.

She got back into her car, marveling at how little she felt when she looked at the place where she'd spent almost the first two decades of her life.

There was another place that would bring the emotion, though. And she had to see it, even though she knew damn well it was like touching a bruise to see if it still hurt.

David's house.

She drove through the little town center, which now had a coffee shop and video rental in the block that used to house a low-roofed warehouse with broken windows. Left on Church Street, right on Pine, and straight down the long, winding road to the lone house at the end.

Only it wasn't the lone house anymore. An entire development had cropped up, with tiny trees and big signs announcing SINGLE FAMILY HOMES FROM THE LOW $300s!

Helene drove in openmouthed amazement, straight to the end where she was astonished to see David's house still stood.

Of course, it had always been a pretty nice house, reputed to have belonged once to George Washington's brother. David's parents had been much better off than Helene's, and there had been talk even back then of designating the place as a historical landmark, for tax purposes.

Helene stopped the car across the road and looked at the house for a few minutes. It looked exactly the same. Then again, it would, since the old oaks were already over a hundred years old twenty years ago, so it wasn't like they'd gotten appreciably bigger.

She got out of the car and walked slowly toward the house, trying to see in the windows, but the sun bounced off the glass in bright rays that blocked her view and brought tears to her eyes.

What would she say when she got to the door, she wondered as she trudged slowly toward the front porch. Would she ask for David or ask if they knew what happened to David? Was she prepared for the answer to either question?

No, she decided, as a wave of nausea nearly overtook her. No, she wasn't up for this. It had been a bad idea and an even worse execution. She had no business here in West Virginia and, after twenty-some years' absence, she *knew*, damn well, she wasn't wanted here anymore.

She turned back to her car when she heard the front door open and that old familiar screen door creek forward.

"Can I help you?"

She turned to see a curvy woman with dusty blond hair and a red-haired baby situated on her hip. The woman looked to be in her early thirties, and her expression, though tired, was pleasant.

Helene took a quick breath, unsure what she was going to say until it came out. "No. Thanks. Actually . . . I . . . I used to know someone who lived here."

The woman narrowed her eyes.

"Twenty years ago, I mean," Helene clarified, so as not to get the woman's husband into any sort of trouble. She waved the years ago. "An old boyfriend," she was babbling, "ancient history. I'm sorry to have bothered you."

"Wait a minute. Are you . . . Helen?" The woman stepped forward, and that screen door clattered shut with the exact same clang that punctuated so many of Helene's memories.

Helene froze, hearing the woman clatter across the wood porch toward her.

"I *knew* you looked familiar," the woman said. "Don't go—you're in the right place."

Helene turned back to her. "I'm not sure I am," she said with a smile, more to herself than to the woman.

"David's going to be back any minute," the woman said, hurrying toward her, bouncing the baby on her hip as she ran. "He forgot his lunch today. Go figure. He takes it with him every single day; but today?—he forgot. And he *never* forgets. Oh, my goodness, he's going to be so surprised. You *are* Helen, aren't you?"

Helene nodded, momentarily unable to find her voice.

"Oh, my goodness, wait until David sees you. I'm Laura, by the way. David's wife. And this is Yolande." She touched the baby's nose.

"Oh. Well. It's—"

"I've heard so much about you! You left quite an impression on my husband." She said it without any hint of jealousy or discomfort. "Of course, we've seen you on TV now and again. Who hasn't? You're very pretty, you know. But then I'm sure you know that. You probably hear it all the time. Do you think you'll be First Lady of the United States someday?" She pronounced it *You-knighted States*.

"N-no, I—I'm not sure." Helene tried to smile. "You know, I'm really pressed for time this morning, so if you could just tell David I stopped by to say hello—"

"There he is now," Laura said. "Look at that, he made it just on time. He's like that, you know. Always lucky. Everything happens just in the nick of time for him."

Helene watched the scuffed-up Toyota Highlander pull into the old drive. "I guess so."

"That's how David is, always . . ."

Helene stopped hearing. Every sense she had was focused completely on the man who was getting out of the old car. He was, of course, thirty-nine now. A grown man with a sweet, chatty wife, and at least one little redheaded baby. A man with a job, and a home, and a family, and a distant memory of a high school girlfriend who'd shot out of town like a bullet and never looked back.

But as he walked toward her, frowning with concentration, she saw and recognized not the man, but the faded pastel ghost of the boy who had given her her first kiss. The brown eyes that scrutinized her now were as familiar as her own, even all these years later.

It seemed to take forever for him to get to her. Time enough for tears to burn behind her eyes and spill down her cheeks, dissolving her into silent sobs for all she'd lost.

She struggled to pull herself together and stood tall, facing him, though still crying. Her voice wouldn't come to her. She could only look at him, and marvel at how clearly she saw the boy in the man before her.

"Hell, it took you long enough to get back here." He pulled her into a big bear hug that absorbed twenty years of tears in one long heartfelt embrace.

When Helene was finally able to collect herself enough to speak, she drew back and said, with a smile, "Why didn't you pay the ransom?"

He got it immediately. Just like she knew he would. Even when they were kids, they had the same dark sense of humor.

"I knew they'd give you back eventually," he said. "You were too ornery to keep around forever."

She sniffled and nodded.

He put an arm out, and Laura fit herself into the crook of it. "You met Laura? And my daughter, Yolande?"

"Yes." The syllable left Helen's lips without her control. "They're both beautiful."

Helene and David locked eyes.

"Come on in," he said. "To hell with work, we've got some catching up to do."

✳

When she pulled her car out of the driveway three hours later, Helene felt like a new person. A void she hadn't even fully realized was aching within her was finally, *finally* filled. David was okay. And he remained there in the same old house, guardian of the past.

"You've done real well for yourself," he'd said to her, over coffee made with Folger's instant crystals. *"Looks like you were right to get out when you did."*

But when he talked about his own life with his wife and kids, she could tell he was really and truly happy.

To Helene, this was the real fairy tale.

She drove home feeling like she had a whole new lease on life. Finally she could let go of the past. It wasn't exactly resolved, it would never be *resolved*, but it was, at least, more settled.

When she'd driven north that morning, she'd been unsure what she was going to do about her pregnancy. But driving back, she knew she was going to welcome it, and the baby, no matter what changes it brought.

As she drove, she marveled over the newfound peace she felt at her decision, wondering if it was in part the result of that visit or if there was something to the pregnancy hormones everyone talked about.

There was certainly something to the fact that pregnancy made a person absentminded, because it wasn't until she was crossing back into Montgomery County, Maryland, that she realized Gerald's blue car was behind her again. Or still. He had to have been following her the entire time, and she just hadn't noticed, because there was no way he could have just happened upon her here in the north end of the county.

Furious, she pulled off onto an exit from 270 and headed toward Lakeforest Mall, making sure to go slow enough that he could follow her. This time she didn't want to lose him; she wanted to catch him.

She drew to a halt in a parking space by the food court entrance, and Gerald pulled up next to her, making no effort whatsoever to hide the fact that he was there.

"What the hell are you doing?" Helene demanded, her heart rate instantly escalating.

He put his hands up in front of him. "Don't get mad."

"I thought you got the message."

"I did! I'm not following you."

She looked at him in disbelief.

"Okay, okay, I *did* follow you," he said. "I admit that, but it's because I have something for you."

It suddenly occurred to Helene that she should be using a lot more caution in a situation like this, especially since she had the baby to be concerned about now. She glanced around, and was glad to see a couple of twenty-something guys putting antifreeze into a car in the next row.

"What do you mean you have something for me?" Helene asked, backing up and feeling for the car door handle behind her, just in case. "Why would you have something for me?"

He gave a half shrug. "I, uh, I felt bad about following you. See, I sort of felt like I got to know you since I was watching you every day and, you know, I think you deserve better than that scum you're married to."

She didn't know what to say. He was trying to compliment her, she supposed, but it was coming across as sort of creepy, too. "I appreciate that you felt bad for following me," she said. "But you're following me now, too. It's got to stop."

"Absolutely." He nodded. "Right away. Pronto."

"Good. Then we have an agreement." She pulled the car door handle and opened the door.

"Wait a minute." Gerald put a hand up, then turned and opened his car door to get something off the front seat.

Helene positioned herself behind her open car door, though if he pulled out a gun, it wasn't going to do her a hell of a lot of good to stand behind the door.

"Here." He produced a manila envelope.

She looked at it skeptically. "What is it?"

He approached her, holding it out. "Just something that might come in handy for you." He shook it at her. "Go on, take it. It's not gonna bite you."

Slowly, she reached out and took it. "Thanks. I guess."

He gave a quick nod and dragged his hand along under his nose. "Just, uh, just save it for a rainy day."

She frowned and started to open it.

Gerald, meanwhile, got into his car, started it up, and drove away, his little blue car spitting a small black stream of smoke behind it.

The envelope contained papers. Photos, she saw when she looked closer. She pulled them out.

"Oh, God."

They were full-color eight-by-ten photos of Jim and Chiara Mornini, naked in Chiara's big round red satin bed. There were hands, legs, tongues, and fairly graphic shots of other body parts.

There was no doubt what was going on.

Helene felt sick. She put a hand to her chest and sat down in the driver's seat, closing and locking the doors before looking at the pictures again.

She wasn't sure which was more upsetting to her, seeing Jim, whom she knew to be a philanderer, or seeing Chiara, who she'd *thought* was her friend.

For a long time, Helene just stared at the pictures. Anyone passing by and glancing in at her would have thought she was some sort of sicko looking at porn in a public parking lot.

If only she had the money, the access to her credit cards, she would have gone right into the mall and spent these worries away. But she didn't. Thanks to Jim.

Thanks to Jim.

The realization dawned on her like sunrise on time-lapse film. Gerald had just done Helene a *huge* favor. So had Chiara, come to think of it, though the bitch certainly hadn't intended to.

Neither Jim nor Chiara would want the press—or, more important, Anthony Mornini—to see these pictures.

If she acted fast, Helene could write her own divorce settlement.

※

Joss went home and fell dead asleep in bed. It had been a totally exhausting night.

The next morning, her alarm went off and, half sleepwalking, she got Bart fed and dressed and took him over to his friend Gus's house. Fortunately Gus had a very cool older nanny named Julia, who took one look at Joss and said, "Honey, go home. You look like you can use the rest."

"No, I'm fine," Joss objected, but she stifled a yawn halfway through the sentence, which detracted from her point.

Julia laughed. "I was twenty-something once. Go home. And someday you can spell someone else the way I'm spelling you now." She gestured for Joss to go. "Don't worry, they'll never know. I'll give you a ring when it's time to come get Bart."

Joss didn't need much more convincing than that. In fact, she was genuinely afraid that if she stayed and watched in nanny-ish silence, she'd fall asleep in her chair. "Thanks," she said gratefully. "Really. I owe you one."

"Forget it," Julia said, waving her hand. "I was young once, too. I remember having a life."

If she only knew. Still, Joss was more interested in going back to the house and getting some much-needed sleep than explaining the less-interesting truth of where she'd been the night before. So she thanked Julia and drove back to the Olivers' house.

Alone. She was finally going to be alone. This would be the first time in, what, three months? Joss was giddy with anticipation as she pulled her car into the driveway.

She noticed the dark green Saab parked outside on the street, but since it was parked closer to the neighbor's property than to the Olivers', it didn't register as anything of any importance.

Not until she got inside and heard a strange man's voice—well, no, that wasn't accurate, it was more of a strange man's *grunts* (but they were distinctly too high to be Kurt Oliver's)—coming from the Olivers' bedroom, two doors down from Joss's.

She froze for a moment, wondering what to do.

Here it was, the proof that what Deena was accusing her—trying to *convict* her—of was the thing she, herself, was guilty of. Theoretically, Joss could take her handy-dandy camera phone to the door and get pictures of Deeena in the act. It would make her life a lot easier.

But . . . eew.

She couldn't do it. No matter how horrible Deena had been to her—and Deena had definitely been horrible—Joss couldn't go to the door and take pictures of her having sex with some guy.

Then again, she couldn't very well stay here, acting like she didn't notice anything was amiss. Obviously Deena wasn't expecting anyone to be here, since she'd left her bedroom door halfway open.

Joss scurried, as quiet as a mouse, into her room and called Sandra. "Help."

"What's wrong?" Sandra asked, not questioning who was on the line.

It was nice that they'd become good enough friends that they didn't have to announce who they were on the phone.

"I left Bart at a play date," Joss whispered, getting as far from the door and bordering walls as she could get. "And I came home and there is some sort of raunchy sex going on in the Olivers' bedroom."

"Ick," was Sandra's first reaction. Then, "But I guess they're entitled since it *is* their house and they thought you'd be taking the child out."

"It's not him," Joss whispered urgently. "I heard a man who is *not* Mr. Oliver. I think she's having an affair. And, as much as I'd like to humiliate her by catching her, I'd much much *much* rather get out of here and pretend I have no idea what's going on."

"Now, wait a minute," Sandra said. "The way she's been treating you . . . you do know this could be to your benefit."

"I know, but—" Joss shuddered. "—no way. So what do I do?"

"In that case," Sandra's voice was strong and definitive, "you keep the phone on your ear and if someone comes in, start chatting like you've been listening to me, and not them, all along. I'll wait on the line so the phone doesn't ring in your ear unexpectedly."

"Okay." Joss took a steadying breath. "Okay. I'm opening the door. . . ." She opened the door to her room. "And I'm stepping quietly into the hallway."

"*Oooh!*" came from the Olivers' bedroom, just before the door burst open and a thin arrow of a man, with white-blond hair and a white-white goatee, flew into the hall, buck naked and sporting an almost comically large hard-on. "Come and get me, big boy," he said, clearly unaware of Joss's presence, "if you dare."

"If I dare!" The voice, shockingly, was not that of Deena Oliver.

It was Kurt Oliver.

Joss knew it because he leapt into the hall after the blond, equally naked, equally hard, but not nearly so big.

All Joss could think, as she backed frantically back into her room, was that she'd seen too much.

Way too much.

"Joss?" Sandra was calling over the phone. "Are you okay?"

"I'm fine," Joss rasped, trying to catch her breath, although at this point it was surprise, in addition to panic, that had gotten a hold of her. "But it's *Mr.* Oliver."

"Oh, Mr. Oliver is with Mrs. Oliver?" Sandra questioned.

"No," Joss whispered. This was too weird. Things like this never happened in Felling. Or, if they did, people kept it well hidden. "It's Mr. Oliver and some other guy."

"Oh!" That got Sandra's attention. "Then, for God's sake, get some pictures with your phone."

"*Pictures!* God, you want to *see* this?"

"No, they're for *you.* Keep them, just in case you need them later, as evidence, or blackmail, or something."

"But—"

"—but, nothing. This might be your best defense against Deena Oliver if she accuses you of anything else. Seriously, Joss, I know you don't want to, but get out there and take some picures. You don't *have* to use them, but if you need to, at least you'll have them."

"I *can't.* I don't even want to *look!*"

"You don't have to look, just hold up the phone. Trust me," Sandra urged, "you've *got* to do this. For your own protection."

"Okay, okay, but then how the heck am I going to get out of here without them noticing me?"

Sandra laughed. "Honey, from what you tell me, they're not that interested in what's going on around them."

It was true. After Joss hung up the phone, she peered around the corner from the door, and the two men obviously had no interest in anything but each other. So she drew back quickly, closed her eyes against the image that was now burned into her gray matter, and held her camera phone out to take two pictures.

The noises didn't stop, so she gathered she had managed to go undetected. However, given the fact that they were in the hallway, she doubted she could manage to leave without being noticed.

She had to wait until they were finished. Or until they moved. Fortunately, the hall led to two different stairways in two different parts of the house. Unfortunately, the men were currently in between both.

So she leaned back against the wall, hiding, waiting, and—so ironic—hoping *she* wouldn't get caught.

It felt like hours, but in reality it was more like ten minutes before they went downstairs to the kitchen.

Joss crept stealthily down the stars like a child on Christmas Eve trying to catch a glimpse of Santa Claus, only in her case, she was trying to *avoid* the odd bearded man in the house.

She opened the front door and looked into the surprised eyes of Deena Oliver.

They must have mirrored the surprise in her own eyes. Or at least some of it. Given what Deena was about to walk in on, though, she had more shock coming.

"What are *you* doing here?" Deena demanded. "You were supposed to take Bart to a play date."

Joss wondered frantically if she should talk loud, to warn the men someone was coming, or if she was better off pretending she knew nothing.

She decided this was *not* something she wanted to get in the middle of.

"I took Bart over, but Gus's nanny had things under control, so I came back here to take—" She couldn't admit she'd come to take a nap; Deena would have her head. "—*get* something."

Deena raked a hostile gaze over her. "You left my child in the care of some stranger?"

Well, why not? That's what Deena herself did, ten minutes after meeting Joss. "She's the nanny, she's absolutely capable of taking care of Gus and Bart."

Deena put a hand on her hip. "What was it that was so important you had to come back here for it, hmm?"

Joss thought fast. "My phone. I thought I should have it in case of an emergency."

"Well, this is absolutely inexcusable." Deena shook her head, looking as disgusted as if Joss had just puked on her shoes.

"I'll go back right away," Joss said, starting toward the car.

"Wait a minute," Deena barked.

Joss turned back. "What is it?"

Deena narrowed her eyes to lizardlike slits. "You're acting awfully jittery."

Ironically, it was the first time Deena had ever been perceptive about Joss's feelings.

"I'm not jittery," Joss lied. "It's just that you're obviously not comfortable with Bart being over at Gus's without me, so I'm just—"

"Wait right here," Deena snapped. "I'm going to call Maryanne and make sure Bart is being looked after until you get there." She rolled her eyes. "I cannot *believe* I have to bother with this, with everything else I have to do."

"Look, I'll just go back there, it's only a fifteen-minute drive—"

"You'll *wait here* because *that's what I told you to do,*" Deena snapped viciously before turning and going in.

Good lord, Joss did *not* want to be part of this. She did *not* want to stand here and wait for the fireworks to go off. How long was she supposed to wait? Because this was obviously going to take some time—

Deena was back within minutes, looking pale and shaken.

For a moment, Joss felt sorry for her, but only for a moment.

That's all it took before she started in on Joss. "Your boyfriend is in there," she said. "Now I know why you came back, for a little midday tryst."

Joss was stunned. "Mrs. Oliver, you know that's not true, don't you?"

"I know what I saw," she said, her voice wavering.

Joss knew what she saw, too.

"One more infraction like this," Deena went on, seeming to come back to life with every angry word, "and you will be fired so fast, your head will spin. And I'll take you to court, don't think I won't."

It occurred to Joss that Sandra had probably been right about taking those pictures to protect herself. But she couldn't imagine taking them out in court. Eventually word would get out, and the boys would be the ones to pay the highest price.

She couldn't do that to them.

Chapter 21

"Ms. Rafferty." Holden Bennington looked surprised to see Lorna. "I didn't think you were having any account problems."

"I'm not here about account problems," she said, then added in a stage whisper, "And you might want to be a little more discreet when addressing your customers in the lobby."

Holden looked around. "There's no one here but employees," he pointed out.

She could have argued with him about whether all of them knew about her account issues, but she decided against it. "I'm here to talk to you about a loan."

He laughed out loud. Sincerely. Then, noticing she wasn't laughing, looked at her, sobered, and said, "You can't be serious."

She held her head high. "I'm completely serious." Then, before he could dismiss her out of hand, she added, "I was hoping to get your advice. Please."

He considered her for a moment, then took a breath and said, "Sure. Okay. But I'm going to need some coffee for this, I think. Want some?"

"Sure. Black is great, thanks."

He nodded. "Go ahead to my office. I'll meet you there in a minute."

She went into his office and sat down on the uncomfortable chair. There was a picture of a kid in a baseball uniform framed on the desk, and Lorna wondered if it could possibly be his own. That would put a whole new, unexpected twist on her perception of him, though it would explain why he was so damn didactic.

"Sorry it took so long." Holden entered and set a Styrofoam cup of coffee on the desk in front of Lorna, sloshing the obviously creamed coffee up over the edge and onto the desk. He cursed and started to reach for a tissue from the box on his desk, but Lorna stopped him.

"Don't worry, I've got it."

"The machine was off, so I had to start a new pot."

She nodded, and took a sip of the thick liquid.

"You asked for black, didn't you?" Holden thumped his forehead with the heel of his hand. "Man, I'm sorry. Let me go get you another one."

"No, no, this is good. This is fine." She took another sip. "Though I've got to say I think we've found something *I* know more about than *you* do."

He shrugged. "I'm lost in the kitchen."

"Maybe you can teach me how to get a start-up loan for a business, and I can teach you to make a decent cup of coffee."

"Deal." He took a sip of his own coffee and made a face.

"Is that your son?" Lorna asked, pointing to the picture. Suddenly she hoped it wasn't.

She was in luck. He shook his head. "It's my nephew. I don't have kids. Or a wife."

Why did that make her glad?

"Me neither," she said unnecessarily.

He laughed. "Finally, we have something in common." As soon as he said it, though, he looked like he regretted getting personal, even in that small capacity. "Now, what is this business you wanted to talk about? Something you're actually planning or is this theoretical?"

"I'm actually planning it."

He lifted his brows. "Oh."

"You sound surprised."

"I am."

She couldn't believe he was so blunt. He didn't even try to disguise his amazement. "Don't sugarcoat things for me."

He leaned back and folded his arms in front of him. "You're not the kind of woman who likes things sugarcoated."

He was right. "Except chocolate," she agreed. "So let's cut to the chase. Say I want to start a business with several other people and we need a loan to get things started. What do I do?"

"What kind of business is it?"

"Importing. Sort of. Importing and distributing."

"Why don't you tell me exactly what you have in mind?"

"Okay, I have a friend who has a very powerful friend, someone whose name you'd recognize but I can't mention, and her nephew is an Italian shoe designer. A really good one. And, believe me, I know shoes."

Holden nodded seriously. "That I believe."

Of course. He'd seen all the charges at Ormond's, Nordstrom, Zappos, DSW, and the like. "All right, so this guy makes beautiful shoes, and we want to import them. Be the sole distributor. No pun intended."

Then something amazing happened. Holden Bennington III actually laughed. And he actually looked good doing it. "All right, so do you have a business plan?"

"Apart from what I just told you?"

"Something formal. A written description of the proposed business, projected costs, possible profit, and so on."

"Yes. Joss, one of my—" She hesitated. "—business partners is working on that."

"Good. Have you thought about venture capitalists?"

Her time in college hadn't been a complete waste. "Getting people to invest, you mean?"

"Yeah. Now, a lot of people think that means going to big, established companies to get investors and that's where they go wrong. Big, established companies don't *need* to invest in upstarts. You need to talk to successful new companies, maybe three to five years old."

"And bypass a bank loan altogether?"

"Not altogether. But investors essentially give you equity. That makes you more attractive to banks."

She was liking Holden right now.

He went on, enthusiastically telling her all the creative ways she might go about getting financing, and finding investors. He suggested a collateral loan might be the way to get the balance of the start-up costs if Lorna or any of her partners had something of value to put up, like real estate. Turned out business was his real love, but he needed the work, so when the bank had come knocking, he couldn't refuse.

After nearly an hour had passed, Holden looked at his watch and said, "Shoot. I've got a meeting to go to." He looked up at Lorna, and seeming surprised at his own question, asked, "Would you like to go to dinner? We could discuss this some more."

She was certainly surprised at her own answer. "I'd love to."

She walked home with more of a bounce in her step than she'd ever had leaving the bank.

Holden Bennington.

She was going to dinner with Holden Bennington. It was hard to believe. Then again, most of what had happened in her life lately was hard to believe. Not the least surprising was Sandra's revelation that she was a phone-sex operator. Lorna would never, ever have pegged her as one.

It just went to show how little you could tell about people, even if you thought you were an expert at reading them after years in the bar business.

*

Later, Lorna could barely remember the dinner they had at Clyde's.

What happened after dinner blew it all out of her mind.

They went back to Lorna's place, and she offered Holden a beer.

"Sure," he said. "But you stay put, I can get it. You don't have to serve me."

"I don't mind," she said, thinking of all the embarrassing things he might spot in her fridge—cartons of half-eaten Chinese food, peanut butter pie in a takeaway container from Jico, almost every kind of cheese in existence, and cans of Slim-Fast that were so old, they had the company's previous logo on them.

Turned out it didn't matter, because they both stood at the same time and took a step toward the kitchen, knocked into each other in the small space, and then—how it happened, Lorna couldn't quite figure out—ended up in each other's arms, locked in a kiss so hot, it could have melted wax lips.

Holden was artful, knowing exactly what moves to make to rachet her passion up to high in the shortest amount of time.

Two weeks ago, she would never have believed she would even *think* about having sex with him. Now she couldn't wait one more second to rip his clothes off.

Which was crazy.

She wasn't supposed to be so impulsive anymore.

She pulled back and said, breathlessly, "What are we doing? Maybe we should consider this a little before we go any further."

He gave a short laugh, and she couldn't help but notice the way his gorgeous blue eyes crinkled in the corner when he smiled. "I've wanted to do this since I met you," he said, then kissed her again.

"But—" She drew back. *Consequences,* she reminded herself. She was supposed to think before acting.

"Shut up," he said with a smile, then crushed his mouth onto hers again, twirling her insides into whipped cream.

"Wait a minute." She drew back again. This wasn't right. She should ask what it meant, how they could possibly have a future. If things worked out, would he be one of those guys who put her on an allowance—? "The hell with it," she said, realizing now was *not* a good time for her to start thinking about consequences before acting.

There would be time for that later.

✶

Apart from the fact that Sandra's lawyer contact kept referring to Sandra as "Penelope," the call Joss had with him went really well. He assured her that if she was being coerced into doing things that were not part of her job description, she did not have to stay on the job.

It would be considerate of her to give them notice, he said, or to stay on until they found someone new, but she wasn't obliged to do any of it.

Still, Joss wasn't all that confident when she went in search of Deena Oliver to give her the news.

Deena was doing her nails and watching an afternoon talk show on the TV.

"Mrs. Oliver." Joss wished she could be more assertive, but she'd never had to quit a job because she didn't like it before, only because she was leaving for school, and she wasn't looking forward to it. "May I speak with you for a moment?"

Deena Oliver made a point of looking at the TV, then back at Joss. "I'm in the middle of a show."

"Yes, but the boys aren't here right now, and I really need to talk with you privately."

With a huge sigh, Deena pointed a remote at the TV and froze the picture, then turned back to Joss with a hideous hardness in her eyes. How one human being could feel justified talking to another human being that way, Joss couldn't understand.

"What is it?" Deena asked on a heavy sigh.

Joss noticed she didn't ask her to sit. Par for the course. Good. That made it easier to leave the room when she was finished. "I need to talk to you about my work here."

"What about it?" She filed her nails with a brisk grinding sound. "Apologies aren't going to change anything, you know."

Apologies? "I—I'm not satisfied with the work." No, that sounded wrong. *Satisfied* was the wrong word. "I mean—"

Grind grind grind. "What do you mean you're not satisfied? Are you supposed to be *satisfied?*" Deena shook her head, answering her own question. "You're a nanny, not some kind of superstar."

Joss took a short breath. "Okay, what I mean is, I'm not—I don't—I love the boys, but I don't think I can help them anymore. Maybe I never could." This wasn't easy, and Mrs. Oliver's pointed refusal to look at her just made it worse. "So I'm giving you my notice."

Deena stopped working on her nails. She looked up at Joss, while somehow still managing to look down at her. "Notice? You have a one-year contract."

"Well, yes, we had a contract." She'd practiced this over and over in her room, but it was so much harder in real life. "But the terms were that if one party feels the other isn't living up to the contract terms, they could give a reasonable notice and, well, I don't feel like I'm doing the job I was hired to do."

Deena snorted. "We agree on that."

"I mean," Joss said, getting a little angry, "that I think you're asking me to do far more than the job description entailed." There was an awkward, shivering silence, so Joss went on, despite her better judgment, "And that's why I'm giving you notice. So you can find someone more suitable for your needs."

"Fine." Deena arched an eyebrow. "I consider nine more months' reasonable notice, since that's what I've been planning on."

"That's too long," Joss said. "I was thinking two weeks or so."

"Two weeks doesn't help me one whit," Deena spat. "I hired *you*, and by God, you're going to stay on and do the job you signed on the dotted line for."

Joss shook her head. "I can't stay. I'm sorry."

After a long scrutiny, Deena said, "You're serious, aren't you? Jesus H. Christ, after all we've done for you!"

"All you've—?"

Deena was instantly hysterical, tears and all. "We've given you a home, we entrusted you with our boys' very lives, and this is the way you repay us!"

Joss really wanted to object, to point out all the extra things she'd done without complaint, all the extra hours she'd put in, but there was no point. Deena Oliver was the sort who would argue to the death, no matter how patently wrong she might be.

So instead of rebutting her, and pointing out her husband's romp with the skinny Santa Claus look-alike and the fact that Deena had actually blamed *Joss* for it, Joss swallowed her pride and said, "I think if you would calm down and consider it, you'd understand some of the reasons I can't stay." It was pointed, and she hoped Deena would get the hint, but she couldn't help softening it by adding, "I'm sorry."

"Sorry," Deena echoed.

"Yes," Joss said sincerely. "And if I could still see the boys and keep up with them a little, that would be so great—"

"You want to see the boys." Deena laughed. "You don't want to care for them, but you want to pop up occasionally in their lives and pretend you had an impact." She gave a cold, humorless laugh. "I don't think so."

"Oh, please don't say that, Mrs. Oliver. This isn't about you or me or Mr. Oliver. Honestly, the boys need to know that they're cared about and that none of this is their fault."

"None of *what?*" Deena asked incredulously. "You're quitting, despite your contract, and you're making like it's a big issue that all of us share?"

Joss had to bite her tongue to stop herself from saying the ugly things that Deena deserved to hear, about her life, her husband, and the thin veneer of perfection she seemed to believe was her life. "I want the boys to know I care about them," she said instead. "I think it's important that they know that."

"Don't make this about you," Deena said with what sounded like true hatred in her voice.

"I'm *not!*" Joss objected. "Jeez, don't you think it would be easier for me to just cut my ties and run? If I didn't genuinely care about your sons, and want the best for them, there's no way I would ask you to let me keep seeing them now and then."

"Meaning you think you're the best?" Deena asked, as haughty as the Queen of Sheba.

"Meaning, I think anyone who has cared for them should stay in their lives, at least on the outskirts, so they don't think people leave because of *them*." Joss was hot with anger. "It's not about me, but it's also *not about you*. Or at least it shouldn't be."

"Just go." Deena waved her away. "I'm going to call my husband and tell him we need to replace you right away. Thanks a lot, Jocelyn, thanks a lot."

Joss swallowed. She wasn't used to this kind of scene. "Listen, I really think we need to put the boys first, so if I pick them up—"

"I said *go*!" Deena screeched. "And I mean go *now* or I will call the police, I swear I will." She leveled a steely gaze on her. "Collect your things and get out of the house. I don't want to see you again."

"But—today?"

"Now!"

Crap. Where would she go? What was she going to do?

What difference did it make? Anywhere but here would be better.

"You have *one hour*," Deena went on. "Whatever's left then goes to charity. Or, better still, the trash."

Only Deena Oliver would think the trash was a preferable place for the clothes than charity. It was tempting to tell her just how *enormously* she fell short of her husband's needs.

But as angry as she was, Joss couldn't form the words.

Instead, a lump formed in her throat. This was so ugly, because this woman was the mother of two boys Joss had cared for. One that she had really grown attached to. "Can I at least say *good-bye* to the boys? I don't want them to think I totally abandoned them."

"Again, it's all about you, isn't it?" Deena snapped.

"No, I want them to know I care about them. For *their* sake." Joss looked at the ugly sneer on Deena's face and thought if Deena's society friends could see her now, they wouldn't think very highly of her. "It's *important* that they know the people in their lives care about them, even though I'll be leaving." She hated to plead for any more time in the house, but she felt strongly about it. "Please, Mrs. Oliver."

Deena stood up, her toes wedged in hot pink foam toe separators, and hobbled over to Joss. She was shorter than Joss, but her presence was enormous. "Listen, missy. I told you to get out of the house. If you don't do so within the hour, I'm calling the police. Is that clear enough for you?"

"Perfectly." Joss nodded, and swallowed the lump in her throat. There was no way she was going to let Mrs. Oliver see one more shred of emotion from her.

She turned and walked from the room as calmly and coolly as she could. As soon as she was out of Mrs. Oliver's sight, she rushed upstairs to call Sandra and see if she could pick her up and give her a place to stay for a night or two.

It took only a short while for her to collect all her things. Hoping that Deena wouldn't get curious and come looking for her, she went to the computer room and signed on.

Working quickly, and glancing nervously over her shoulder every few words, she typed a note for the boys.

Dear Colin and Bart:

By the time you get this note, I'll be gone, and I don't know what your mother will have told you about why. That's why I'm writing this note—I want you to know that just because things didn't work out as far as my working here goes, I am not leaving because of you. You are great kids, and it's hard for me to leave you because I care a lot about you.

Colin, I know you didn't always like having me here, but I hope you'll read this note to Bart and let him know how special he is to me and how much I loved spending time with him, too.

If you guys ever need anything, whether you're in trouble or you just want to talk, please write down my cell phone number. It's 240-555-3432. You can also e-mail me at this address: NewShuz@gregslist.biz.

Take care, you guys. I'll always remember you!

Love, Joss

She pushed the SEND button and hurried down the stairs, hoping to escape without any further attention from Deena.

She should have known better.

"Stop!" Deena yelled. She was standing a few feet from the front door, still barefoot, but she'd removed the foam pedicure pad.

"I'm finished packing." Joss lifted her bag. "I'll be out of your hair now." She started toward the door, but Deena stepped in her way.

A tremor of fear crossed Joss's chest. Scenes from bad horror movies flashed through her mind in rapid succession.

"Is it a raise you want?" Deena asked.

Considering the fact that Joss had been half-afraid that Deena was going to pull out a knife and hack her to death, it took a moment for the question to sink in. "A *raise*? What do you mean?"

"I *mean* is it more money you're after? Is that what this game is about?"

"I'm sorry, but I don't understand. What game?"

"This quitting game. You're not *really* going, are you?"

That was it, Deena had popped her clutch. Joss looked at the bag in her hand. "Yeah, I really am."

"I'll raise your salary by ten percent."

"*What?*"

"Okay, twenty. Plus," Deena eyes flashed a little wildly while she thought, "I'll throw in holiday bonuses. Big ones."

"Well, that's really . . . generous . . . of you." And really weird. Really, really weird. "But I just don't think this is going to work out."

Deena shifted her weight from one side to the other, looking for all the world like a sullen teenager. "What, do you want me to beg or something?"

This was surreal. "No."

"Fine. *Please* don't go. There. Satisfied?"

"Mrs. Oliver, I don't want you to beg. This just isn't working out."

Deena's face went pale. It looked as if she was realizing for the first time that everything Joss had been saying was true and that she really was leaving.

Only someone like Deena would look at quitting as a viable way to request a raise.

"I can't do this alone," Deena said, so quietly she was practically whispering. "I can't deal with the kids."

Guilt shrouded Joss, and for one wild moment she thought about staying so she could protect the boys from this crackpot. But she couldn't. There was no protecting them from Deena. Or Kurt, for that matter. "They're good boys," Joss said. "Especially Bart. Colin needs a little more discipline." That was an understatement. "But they both have so much potential."

"I can't do it!" Deena's voice was approaching hysteria. "Don't leave! You're the only person who's ever stayed longer than three weeks! I thought we had an understanding."

"I'm sorry," Joss said. This was really getting uncomfortable. "It's not working out."

"I'll raise your salary by fifty percent!"

306 ★ *Beth Harbison*

"No, thanks." She had to get out of here. This was just too weird. "I've got to go, Mrs. Oliver—"

"I don't know what to do with the boys! Wait!"

There was no way she was waiting. She turned and hurried out of the house, with Deena's voice still echoing behind her. "No! Joss, don't go!"

✳

"I've got a date tonight," Sandra said, taking one of Joss's suitcases out of the back of her car. "But I can cancel it if you want me to stay in with you."

"Oh, no, don't be silly!" Joss was so grateful to Sandra she had almost cried three times on the drive to Adams Morgan. "I'll be fine. I'm going to call the agency and see if they have anyone else they can send me to interview with. A lot of people want you to start right away, you know."

They hauled the bags up the steps of Sandra's building and a guy who was coming out the front door rushed over to Sandra and took the suitcase out of her hand.

"Let me help you with that, Sandy." He was nice-looking. Late twenties probably. A little short, brown hair parted conservatively on the side, and big blue eyes that kept his face from being ordinary. But he looked at Sandra as if she were a goddess.

"Thanks, Carl, but I've got it." She gestured at Joss. "By the way, Carl, this is my friend Joss. She's going to be staying with me for a while."

"Oh. Nice to meet you." He put out a hand. It was warm and soft. "Carl Abramson. I live upstairs from Sandy."

"Very nice to meet you." Joss looked to Sandra for some indication that she was interested in him, too, but she looked positively oblivious. "I hope to see you around."

He nodded. "You gals sure you don't need some help?"

Sandra shook her head. "We've got it. But thanks anyway."

"Uh, listen. Sandy." He moved closer to Sandra and spoke in a lower voice, looking so self-conscious, he was practically circling his toe on the ground in front of him. "I was wondering if you might be free to go to the movies some time this weekend."

She looked surprised. "Carl, that is so nice of you. And I'd love to"—he looked hopeful for a moment—"but my boyfriend might get jealous. I'm really sorry."

"Oh, that's okay. Can't blame a guy for trying. I should have known you had a boyfriend."

Sandra flushed as she smiled and said, "Thanks, Carl."

He gave her one last lingering look, then went on down the sidewalk.

"Wow," Joss whispered. "He's got it bad for you."

"You think?" Sandra looked after him. "It's funny, I had a crush on him when he first moved in a few months ago, but I was never brave enough to talk to him. Now that I'm not trying to work up the nerve, he's suddenly talking to me all the time."

"Poor guy. He looked brokenhearted."

Sandra snorted. "I doubt that. Come on. Let's get going."

When they got to the door to her apartment, Sandra turned to Joss and said, "You know, I've been thinking. Forgive me if I'm out of line, but maybe you don't want to be a full-time nanny anymore."

Joss laughed. "Well, I don't! Nothing out of line about that. But it's the only job I can think of that will give me room and board and a salary at the last minute like this."

Sandra frowned. "I've got an extra room, you know. If you want to apply for something else, you can stay here as long as you need to."

Joss was touched. "Gosh, I appreciate that, but I don't want to impose."

"Actually, I think I'd really like having you around. I've been alone in this cave for a long time." Sandra laughed. "On top of that, I have a vested interest in keeping you around for the shoe business. We need you to be available. You're the only one who can do any sort of Web design."

Joss felt her face grow warm. "I *would* like to pursue that. It's the opportunity of a lifetime."

"Then it's settled. You're staying here. Maybe you'll get some part-time work doing Web design around town, but the rest of your time is ours." She put out her hand. "Deal?"

Joss had never felt so happy in her life. "Deal." She shook Sandra's hand.

"And with that," Sandra said. "I have to go. I'm late. Wish me luck. I think tonight might be *the night* for Mike and me."

The night? Oh, no. "I really am in the way," Joss said. "I could go out, maybe to Lorna's when she gets home from work—"

Sandra put a hand up. "Don't worry about it. Mike's got a place. Just wish me luck."

Joss still worried that she was in Sandra's way, but she wasn't going to argue. "Good luck!"

✳

"Debbie's coming tonight," Mike said, watching Sandra over drinks at the Zebra Room later that evening.

He mentioned Debbie every single time they got together. Tonight he hadn't even waited three minutes. Was he trying to tell her something? She had to ask. The old Sandra would have been too timid, but the new Sandra was direct. To the point.

Confident. Sort of.

"Mike, I've been meaning to ask you about that."

"About Debbie?" He looked like he knew this was coming. Like he'd been waiting for it.

"Yes. I can't help but notice that you keep mentioning Debbie in a really pointed way. Are you trying to tell me something?"

His face fell into a puzzled expression. "I'm . . . not sure what you mean?"

Confident.

Bold.

Straightforward.

"Are you and Debbie involved?"

"Are we—?" He looked like he'd just missed the bottom step. "What do you mean are *we* involved?"

"I mean is she your girlfriend? Is that why you keep mentioning her this way?"

His face was positively closing in on itself at this point. If he wasn't careful, it might snap right off.

"No . . . Debbie's not my girlfriend." Then—this was the worst part—he added in what he must have thought was a reassuring voice, "I thought *you* might hit it off with her."

"*Me?*" Like a *Titanic* victim clawing at the last few feet of the boat before giving in to the reality of the cold water, Sandra half wondered if he meant he was just one of those guys who wanted to see his girlfriend with another woman.

But she knew he wasn't.

He was one of those guys who *didn't* want his *boyfriend* to be with another woman.

She was hopeful—even foolishly hopeful—but she wasn't *stupid*.

Mike's face colored. "You're not gay."

"And you are."

He nodded and put his hands over his face, groaning, "Sandy, I am *so sorry*."

"Why on earth did you think I was?" Her disappointment was scooting its chubby little butt over to make room for self-deprecation. "Am I that undesirable to men?"

"No, of course not! No, no, and even if you were," he added, "that wouldn't mean that you were automatically attractive to lesbians."

There was something that aggravated her about him, and now she could admit it. She hated how he always had to be so politically correct about things. He could never just let a generalization go.

"But that's not the point," he said quickly, redeeming at least a few sensitivity points.

"No, the point is all this time I've thought we were dating and you were trying to set me up with some *woman*." Sandra sniffed. "She's not even that attractive."

"Margo thinks she is."

"Margo? Margo is her girlfriend?"

"Well . . . no. Margo is . . . Margo's *my* girlfriend—"

"But I thought—"

"She used to be called Mark."

Sandra looked at him in silence for a moment, trying to remember if she had accidentally popped a pill that said EAT ME, which then led her to this bizarre world.

Then again, even if she *had* found one of Alice in Wonderland's EAT ME pills, she wouldn't have known exactly who it was addressing or what it meant. . . .

"Okay. I've got it." She didn't really. "You're saying that Debbie is a lesbian—"

"Correct."

"—and *you're* gay—"

"Undeniably."

"And Margo used to be a gay man, but now she's a heterosexual woman, and she's with you. Even though she's now technically a woman and you're a man."

"Y-yes." Mike nodded his assent. "I suppose you could look at it that way. Although actually, I just did that for a change, hoping it would work out so my mother would be more accepting. The truth is, I usually like my men way more butch."

"I do, too," Sandra said. Oh, God, she couldn't believe this. But she didn't want to insult Mike. After all, it wasn't *his* fault she'd willfully ignored who he was. Sandra splayed her arms and shrugged. "Sorry, I'm just trying to get it all straight."

Mike suppressed a smile. "I don't think that's going to happen with this group."

Sandra tried to resist, but she couldn't help smiling with him. "Okay, okay, but what I don't get is how you could be so incredibly wrong about me. I mean, I thought you and I—?"

He held up a hand. "I know, I know, I feel just awful about it. What can I say? The gaydar was off. I think when you said, years ago, that you were dating women, I assumed you meant that's what you do. I sat back on fifteen years of assumption instead of looking at what was right in front of me."

"When I said—*what?*" She couldn't believe this. Had Mike been thinking she was someone else all along? On top of not being in love with her—or even interested in her giving him a blow job—did he think she was LeeLee McCulsky or something?

"You said you were sick of men and you were going to try women for a while."

She looked at him, blank. "What the hell are you talking about, Mike?"

"That time after gym class. Eleventh grade? No, maybe it was twelfth. You were hoping Drew Terragno would ask you out, and he didn't, so you said you might as well go for Patty Reed."

Drew Terragno she remembered. And, yes, she *had* had a crush on him. Like a million years ago.

She joggled the facts in her mind. "Drew was dating Patty, right?"

"Yup."

"And I said . . ." She remembered all at once, though truth be told she *still* didn't remember that Mike had been there. "I said I might as well go after Patty—"

"That's right."

"—because that was the closest I'd get to Drew."

To his credit, Mike listened and comprehended. Then nodded. He got it. "Sarcasm," he said.

"A little bit."

"And I've spent all this time thinking we had so much in common."

"Apparently not enough to actually date *each other*."

He laughed and put his arm around her. "I had no idea that's what you wanted. I'm really flattered."

She scoffed.

"No, seriously," he said, looking completely earnest. "I mean it. A guy would be lucky to have a girl like you."

"Unless he wants a guy like Margo," she finished, then immediately regretted her bitterness.

Fortunately, Mike got her. Just like she had thought, all this time, he *got* her.

He just didn't *want* her.

"If I didn't want Margo, if I didn't want a guy like Margo, I'd want a girl like you," Mike said kindly, putting his hand up to caress Sandra's hair. "Honest."

And, for some reason, that helped her. No, it didn't make up for the entire heartache, but it made her feel a hell of a lot better. Maybe because it proved the fact that Mike's rejection wasn't about *her*, it was about *him*, and the fact that he wanted something that she could *never* give him.

Sandra had spent a long time with poor self-esteem, but she was wise enough to be realistic. If Straight Mike rejected her, there were about a million things she could point to by way of explanation.

But if Gay Mike rejected her . . . well, there was only one thing she could point to.

"All right, then." Sandra slapped her palms against her thighs in a *let's move on* gesture, and said, "So Margo is dating you and not Debbie. Is there anything else I should know?"

Mike nodded. "Debbie has gotten back together with Tiger," he said, very seriously.

And if he hadn't been quite so serious, Sandra would have given in to the impulse to laugh. Instead, she dug her fingernails into her palms privately and asked, "Tiger?"

Mike nodded. "Her ex-girlfriend. That's what I wanted to talk to you about. They're back together."

So . . . Debbie wasn't available either.

Sandra was *that* much of loser.

"Okay, let me get this straight," she said. "Let me get this absolutely straight. You were not only trying to set me up with a woman, but you were also planning to essentially put an end to that imagined relationship tonight because she's dating someone else." She couldn't believe this. She'd had some bad turns in her life—the time she'd hit a guy dressed as a taco and smashed the windshield of her brand-new VW Beetle as she was driving it out of the lot, came to mind—but this *really* sucked.

314 ★ Beth Harbison

She was being dumped by a woman she'd never dated and by a man she wanted to date except for the fact that it turned out he was gay.

Mike gave a gorgeous, humble, and ultimately homosexual nod of agreement. "I'm afraid that's the way it is."

And until he said it right to her, she hadn't entirely believed it. Like a fool, she had continued to hope her instincts were insanely wrong.

"Hey," he said. "We're just all trying to live, love, laugh, and get laid every once in a while. It's the only way to get through this life."

Chapter 22

"So he was trying to set you up with a lesbian," Lorna said, trying to sum up the incredible story Sandra had just told them.

"Yes. Yes, he was. Is it time to rinse my hair yet?"

Helene looked at her watch. "Five more minutes. I still think you should have gone to Denise."

Sandra shook her head. "As soon as I realized I looked like a green-haired lesbian, I couldn't spend one more moment out in public. Besides, it's been a few weeks. It's probably safe. And if it's not, how much worse can it be to have a crew cut? At least it won't be green." She shuddered. "God. I cannot believe this."

"You had *no idea* he was gay?" Lorna asked.

"Well, in retrospect, I suppose there were some pretty obvious signs. The eyebrow plucking. The exfoliation." She sighed. "The fact that he watched *Pride and Prejudice* with me three times."

Lorna raised an eyebrow. "Colin Firth, Matthew Macfadyen, or Laurence Olivier?"

"Firth."

Lorna sucked air in through her front teeth. "That's a flag. Men with good taste in other men is *always* a red flag."

"Cheer up," Joss said. "At least you have Carl."

Sandra blushed. "Though you've got to wonder what kind of guy *he* is if he wants a green-haired lesbian."

"But you're *not*!" Joss objected. "In ten minutes your hair will be Autumn Chestnut again."

There was expectant silence in the room.

"Oh! And you won't be a lesbian," Joss added with a giggle.

"You know, Sandra," Helene said, observing her. "You really seem to be okay. I would have thought you'd be devastated by this. I mean, almost anyone would be."

Sandra nodded. "I know. I don't know what's wrong with me. It's like . . . Okay, at first I was hit hard. It's disappointing when your dream guy isn't interested in you, but then again, if he's not interested in *any* women, that takes a little bit of the sting out of it."

"That's true," Lorna said. "You can't ask yourself what you could have done because, short of growing a penis, there isn't anything."

"Right." Sandra nodded enthusiastically. "This is one time I really and truly know it's not personal. But also, I don't know, I've changed. So much has changed for me recently, and gotten better, that I'm starting to trust that things *do* work out by themselves sometimes."

"Which leads us to this Carl guy," Lorna said. "Who is he? Are you holding out on us?"

"She's been totally holding out on us," Joss said excitedly. "Carl lives upstairs and he's really cute and he's crazy about Sandra. You can see it in his eyes."

"Has he asked you out?" Helene asked. Seeing the changes in Sandra's life and confidence was actually making Helene something of a believer in fate, too. She was eager to hear more good news.

"He asked her out the other day," Joss said.

Sandra shot her a good-humored look. "Am I going to be allowed to talk?"

"Sorry." Joss smiled, and added in a smaller voice, "But he really is cute."

"So he asked you out and you're going, right?" Lorna raised an eyebrow.

Sandra shot Joss a silencing look, then said, "He asked me out and I said no because I didn't want my gay boyfriend to get jealous."

"Ooh." Lorna clicked her tongue against her teeth. "Bad call."

"As it turns out," Sandra agreed.

"So tell him you made a mistake," Helene suggested. "Tell him you've been thinking about him and you really want to get to know him better."

Sandra looked at her with admiration. "That's good. That's really good."

"Do it!" Lorna urged. "To hell with your gay boyfriend."

"Amen. Which reminds me, I have something to show you all." Helene reached for her bag and started rummaging through it.

"You're like Mary Poppins there," Sandra remarked. "Are you going to pull out a lamp?"

"Better." Helene produced a photo of a dark-haired man. His bone structure was like something carved in marble, his eyes the deep bedroom brown of the luckiest Italians. He was beautiful. Absolutely beautiful. "This," she said triumphantly, "is Phillipe Carfagni."

A collective gasp sucked the air out of the room.

Then a bell dinged.

"Time to rinse," Lorna told Sandra, still staring at the picture.

"All right." Sandra got up and tightened her terry cloth robe around her as she stepped over Joss. "When you see me next I'll be—what was it?—some sort of chestnut." She disappeared into the back.

"Let me see that picture," Lorna said, and Helene handed it to her. "You know what we have to do, don't you?"

Helene nodded. "Get him in front of the public eye. I'm already on it. There's a huge dinner at the Willard next week. It always attracts the movie stars, which attracts the press, and I'm trying to get him to come to town for that."

"We need to send press releases out, maybe make up some cool story—" Lorna stopped. She had an idea. A great idea. "Wait a minute. There's nothing people like better than juicy gossip, right?"

Helene frowned. "What are you getting at?"

"Maybe we could leak a blind item in the *City Paper*? It's not the *Post*, but it's not bad."

Helene paled. "A blind item about what?"

For a moment, Lorna couldn't figure out what was upsetting Helene; then she remembered. "Oh, not about *you*," she assured her. "I mean we could say something about Phillipe. *What handsome young shoe designer is rumored to be coming to town for some grand event . . . .* That sort of thing. We'd have to come up with something better, but that sort of thing."

"I like it," Joss said.

"But how are you going to get someone to write it?"

Lorna gave a laugh. "Have you read that column? Sometimes it resorts to political *dogs*. Literally. They'd be glad to have some juicy real person tidbits." She'd just make some up if necessary.

"So we make him a romantic figure," Helene said.

Lorna gestured at his picture. "What else *could* he be? He's Romeo. Which"—she turned to Joss—"is where you come in."

"Me?" Joss put a hand to her chest. "Do you want me to pick him up at the airport or something?"

"Actually, that would be good." Helene laughed. "But what we need is for you to be his date for the dinner."

"Oh, come on, *me*?"

Lorna and Helene exchanged glances, and Lorna said, "What's the matter, Cinderella? Don't you want to go out with Prince Charming?"

Joss looked at the picture of the living god. "There is no way I can go out with a guy who looks like that. I would melt. Just melt. I'd be Jell-O in my cheap shoes." She shook her head. "No way."

"You'd be perfect," Helene said, then to Lorna, "Can you see it?"

Lorna nodded knowingly. "You two will look great together. The photographers are going to go nuts."

Joss's face went scarlet. "*Photographers!* Do you know who you're dealing with? Let me show you my driver's license picture."

"Don't bother, they're paid to make you look bad," Helene said, taking out her cell phone. "I'm getting you an emergency appointment with Denise. The sooner we get you out in front of people as our spokesperson, the better. Then, when Phillipe shows up." She snapped her fingers. "Magic."

✳

It *was* magic.

The moment Joss laid eyes on Phillipe Carfagni, she felt something she'd never felt before.

Lust.

She was standing outside in the main terminal of Dulles airport, holding a sign with his name on it and a big outline of a shoe—a touch Lorna had insisted upon—searching the crowd for his face.

When he emerged, she saw there was no reason to search. It was like looking for the moon in a starry sky. He was even more beautiful in person than his photo had been, and the crowd parted around him slightly, perhaps so they could get a better look.

When his eyes landed on Joss, he smiled, and approached her with a light, melodic laugh. "The shoe," he said, his thick accent evident even in those two small words. "Is nice. Good."

She smiled back. "Good."

"You is . . . Jocelyn. Yes?"

The way he said her name sent tingles down her skin. "Yes. Phillipe?"

He smiled. Dazzling. Dizzying. Did she hear music? "Phillipe Carfagni." He took her hand and raised it to his lips, holding her eyes with his own. He stepped back and looked her over, stopping, of course, at her feet. "You have thirty-eight feet?"

Her cheeks went hot. "No? No. Two." She shuffled her feet awkwardly and held up two fingers. "Two."

He smiled again, and raked a hand through that glossy dark hair that curled down over his collar. "No, no, *cara mia . . . misura.*" He lifted his foot and tapped it.

She didn't understand. "Misura?"

"*Scarpa.*" He held his hands up, like he was telling her the size of the fish he'd caught. "*Numero.*"

"Numero . . . Oh, *size!*" She slipped her shoe off and pointed to the 6 stamped on the bottom. "Size. Six. Not thirty-nine." Good lord, how big would a size thirty-nine foot *be*? Obviously he didn't really think that was her size. He was just making a joke. A weird joke.

So what? He was gorgeous.

He frowned, a small dent marring that otherwise-perfect forehead, and shrugged.

"It doesn't matter," Joss said. "Good shoes never fit me right anyway."

"Don't . . . fit?" he echoed, shaking his head.

She nodded and did the fish gesture, then made it bigger. "Too big." She remembered tenth-grade Spanish and took a chance that it would be close enough. "*Grande.*" She made a face and shook her head.

"*Grande?*" he laughed. "No, *bella*. My shoes . . . for you." He kissed his fingertips. "*Perfezione.*"

That, she understood.

And the fairy tale had gotten it right all along. When the shoe fits, you find Prince Charming.

Only in her case, she had to find Prince Charming in order for the shoe to fit.

*

By the time Helene headed back to town at lunchtime, it had already been a *long* day. So many emotions, so many questions, so much *business* . . . she was exhausted.

So she probably should have just gone straight home and gotten into bed, but she thought it was best to stop at Jim's office first and tell him exactly what was going on. If he knew what she was planning, businesswise, and she knew what *he* was planning, politically, maybe they could still work together to create a good enough façade to fool everyone a little longer.

It wasn't Helene's first choice, but now she had a child to consider, and maybe it was better for the child to have some semblance of a Mom–Dad household in the early years than to grow up in a Mom-only house.

That's what Helene was thinking before she got to Jim's office, anyway. *Façade.* That was good enough for now.

But when she got to his place of work the front office was completely empty. Anyone could have walked right in, laid a fistful of anthrax on the desk, and left.

Given the idiotic giggles that were coming from behind the executive office door, Helene wisely guessed that not quite everyone had left. She had a pretty good idea of who had not, too.

She expected rage—anyone would have—but it didn't come. Instead she felt a deadly calm. This answered all of her questions. She dismissed, entirely, the idea of creating a façade of a life with Jim.

The problem wasn't *just* that he was fooling around with his assistant, or Chiara, or whomever else he'd had along the way—that had ended the marriage, of course, but it wasn't the reason she was unwilling to even pretend.

No, it was the complete and total lack of respect that went into being this indiscreet that tipped her over the edge.

She burst into his office—unlocked, of course—and found him, pants around his ankles, leaning a girl who looked about eighteen up against his desk.

He looked so shocked to see her that Helene had to laugh. "I gather you weren't expecting me," Helene observed.

"*Shit!* Helene, what the hell are you doing here?"

Like it was her fault.

"The reason I came by doesn't really matter anymore," she said calmly. "This changes things."

He fumbled to pull his pants up.

"Oh, don't bother with that," Helene said. "This won't take long. Then again, as I recall, neither would *that*." She looked at the girl, one she'd never seen before. Probably a new intern. "Sorry, honey, but could you cover yourself and get the hell out for a moment while I talk to my husband?"

The girl nodded frantically and looked around for her clothes. She didn't even try to get dressed, she just held them against her and ran out of the office.

Helene turned her attention back to a decidedly withered Jim. "I want a divorce."

"*What*?" He looked at her, mouth agape.

"Surely you're not surprised!"

"Do you know what this could do to me politically?"

She clicked her tongue against her teeth. "Now, now, dear, don't worry, you'll learn to love again."

"This will ruin me."

"Oh, it will not," she said. "What you and your colleagues need to learn is that people understand normal human situations, like divorce and maybe even infidelity. It's the *lying* we hate."

"You knew there were others."

She raised her eyebrows. "Did I?"

"Don't fuck with me."

She gave a laugh. "It seems I'm about the only one who *isn't*. Now, here's the deal. I want a divorce, and I want the house free and clear. I also want a net settlement of two million, so you're going to have to pay the taxes on it before I get it."

He looked at her with open hostility. "You bitch."

She narrowed her eyes. "Oh, you ain't seen *nothin'* yet. Try and screw me over, and I'll take this public and you really won't have a future."

He twisted his lips into a smug smile. "You just said the public would forgive infidelity."

"I don't mean a political future. I mean a literal future—thanks to that detective you hired to follow me, I have some really excellent pictures of you and Chiara Mornini. In her red silk bed. You remember that, right?"

Jim paled three shades.

"I don't think Anthony would take the news nearly as well as I did." Helene stood up. "So I can expect you to agree to my terms, right?"

He glowered at her. "And I can expect you to be discreet, right?"

She nodded, as if they'd just agreed to a dinner date. "Absolutely. Lucky for you, I can be *far* more discreet than you." She turned to go and tossed over her shoulder, "Let me know where you'll be staying, so my lawyer can contact you."

She didn't listen for his answer. She didn't care anymore. She had the upper hand and she knew it.

She was leaving with her head held high.

And she was going straight to Ormond's to buy those Bruno Maglis.

Epilogue

One Year Later

I've got it!" Lorna called, hurrying into the newly expanded offices of SAA, Inc. She held up a copy of *Women in Business*, a national monthly that had profiled Lorna, Helene, Sandra, and Joss a couple of months ago for this, their October issue.

Sandra and Helene hurried over, Helene holding six-month-old Hope Sutton Zaharis on her hip, despite her two-thousand-dollar Armani suit.

"What did they call it?" Helene asked, hoisting the baby over to her other hip so she could move in and look over Lorna's shoulder.

Lorna flipped through the pages. "'Sole Distributor.'" She nodded approvingly. "Nice. Accurate."

"Where's Joss?" Helene asked. "She should hear this."

"With Phillipe, of course." Sandra laughed. Where *else* would she be?"

Joss and Phillipe had been spending a lot of time together and, as a

326 * Beth Harbison

result, not only was Joss aglow with infatuation, but her shoe taste had improved *enormously*. Phillipe had even named his latest creation, a gorgeous satin peep-toe pump with a stacked stiletto heel, the Jocelyn.

"They should just get married," Lorna said, scanning the article. "It would be great publicity. Oh! Oh! Look at this—'*record orders* from Nordstrom, Macy's, Bergdorf Goodman, Saks, et cetera, et cetera, et cetera.' Here we go. 'With the creative eye of former senate wife Helene Zaharis, and the consumer sense of former spendthrift Lorna Rafferty, the group has forged forward into the hearts and minds of shoe addicts everywhere.' I can't wait to show Holden that *Business-Week* finds my former spending ways to be an asset to the company."

"What about me?" Sandra teased. "Just because I don't sleep with power or overburden my credit cards, I don't get a mention?"

"Don't worry, here you are: 'Potomac native, Sandra Vanderslice, is credited with being the group's moral compass, keeping the company on environmentally high ground, and implementing fair trade initiatives.' How do you like that?" Lorna wiggled her eyebrows. "You are our moral compass!"

"Many of my former callers would agree with that."

Lorna laughed and read on. "'Jocelyn Bowen, armed only with an AA from Felling-Garver (VA) Community College, put together a business plan that excited so many investors that the IPO was completely snapped up within an hour of trading.' That was amazing," Lorna commented, then read on, "'She is now the steady amore of star designer Phillipe Carfagni, and he calls her his muse for his spring collection.' Aw. Isn't that so sweet?"

"She deserves it, too," Sandra said without a trace of envy. "At least one of us got the fairy tale without having to kiss all the frogs first."

"And she got the shoes, too," Lorna said wistfully. "All the perfectly fitted, beautiful Carfagnis she could ever want."

"So do you," Helene said, giving Lorna a nudge. "It's one of the big benefits of owning this company."

"You're right." Lorna laughed. "Free shoes for life. I guess it's a fairy tale come true for all of us. I guess your addictions can either kill you or make you rich."

"I'll take rich," Helene said.

"Hear, hear." Sandra agreed.

And they did.

Keep reading for a sneak peek at

Secrets of a Shoe Addict

coming in June 2008 from St. Martin's Press

Chapter 1

Loreen Murphy hadn't meant to hire a male prostitute in Las Vegas. It was all just a big, stupid, *expensive* misunderstanding.

The night had started out pretty normal. There was no visibly strange alignment of stars, no static electricity in the air, nothing to warn anyone that things were about to turn so weird.

She, along with other parents—mostly mothers—of the Tuckerman Elementary School band members from Travilah, Maryland, was in Las Vegas, where the kids were competing in a National Battle of the School Bands. Loreen, as the PTA treasurer, had been instrumental in working out a deal with the airline and several Las Vegas hotels so that parents and siblings could attend the contest.

And everything had gone fine, right up until they tucked in the little third-place-winning musicians and handed their trust over to a hotel babysitter who looked a little like Joan Crawford but was able to produce identification to prove she was employed by the hotel.

Loreen was ready to go out and have fun, but she wasn't letting go of her caution *entirely*. Jacob was still the most important thing in the world to her, and there was no way she was taking any kind of chance with his safety.

So, confident that their kids would be fine, Loreen and her fellow PTA officers—Abbey Walsh (vice president of the PTA and wife of the local Methodist minister) and Tiffany Dreyer (president of the PTA and one of Loreen's best friends since their kids were in first grade)—went down to the casino and spent a little time playing the nickel slots and sipping free margaritas from the hotel bar.

For Loreen, life began to veer off course with the idea of taking a break from an hour of slot machines and free drinks to get up and move around so she didn't get slot machine elbow or whatever you'd call a repetitive-motion injury from playing the one-armed bandit for too long.

Besides, she'd allocated twenty-five dollars to gambling, and according to the high-tech slip the machine had just spit out at her, she had only ten dollars left. When that money was gone, she'd decided, the evening was over for her.

"Are you sure you don't want to come look around with me?" she asked Tiffany, Loreen's friend since both their kids had eaten a container of paste in Mrs. Kelpy's first-grade classroom and thrown it up in the cafeteria line half an hour later.

"No way." Tiffany kept her baby blues fastened on the machine in front of her. "I've invested almost two hours in this machine. It's going to hit the jackpot. I can just *feel* it."

"This is how gambling addiction starts, you know."

Tiffany nodded and lifted her drink to the one Loreen was taking with her to the bar. "I think alcoholism starts this way, too."

"Touché."

Loreen made her way through the crowd—hundreds of people she'd never know. The feeling of freedom was exhilarating. Jacob was safely with the sitter upstairs, and Loreen, who was a month away from her final divorce decree, was a "bachelorette on the loose" for the first time in eleven years.

Robert, her soon-to-be ex, thought she was a control freak who focused too much on her child and not enough on her life. Well, she was going to change that tonight.

The lobby of the Gilded Palace was crowded with people, marble columns, and large potted palm trees. There was Muzak playing through some distant speakers, adding just enough vague ambience to make it feel like this was someone else's life and she was free to do whatever she pleased with it.

That's when the trouble started.

When Rod—that turned out to be his name, or at least the name he gave—first sat down and started talking to her, her first thought was that it must be on a dare from one of his drunk friends, who were undoubtedly hiding behind one of the gold Corinthian columns or enormous potted palms somewhere.

But if he had drunk friends with him, they were hiding for a really long time. And besides, Loreen wasn't unattractive enough to make a dare like that funny to a bunch of assholes. She was just . . . she looked like a mom.

Not a MILF, just a mom.

Her dark hair had lost some of the luster of youth and was cut in a sort of hopelessly plain brown variation of Prince Valiant. No matter where she went to get it styled, and no matter what pictures she took with her, she always seemed to leave with the same schlumpy mom look.

And the stylists' advice that, "You have a different face. I can't make you look like TV actress *X*, movie star *Y*, fill-in-the-blank, but this is the same basic haircut. . . ."

In other words, *You're never gonna be that hot, honey. Give it up.*

It was true, too. Loreen was also suffering a little from post-childbirth spread. Nine years post-childbirth. Her butt was considerably wider than it had been the last time she'd been single. Her high-waisted jeans kept everything sucked in pretty well—someone trying to identify her across the room wouldn't call her "that fat woman over there"—but she wasn't exactly what you'd call buff either. And there *was* a telltale balloon of flesh below the waistband that she just couldn't seem to get rid of. At least not without a steady diet of carrots, celery, and Pilates.

But Rod looked at her as if she had just stepped off the cover of the *Sports Illustrated* swimsuit edition.

Upon reflection, that in itself probably should have made her more suspicious.

"Margarita, huh?" He nodded at her glass and smiled. The way his mouth curved, showing white-white teeth, made him look like a real-life movie star. "Pretty lady like you deserves something more special than that."

It was such a lame line and she knew it, but she got a kick out of it anyway. "Well—" She swallowed a burp and hoped he didn't notice. "—they put a Grand Marnier floater on top."

"Ah. So it's got a touch of class, like you." He smiled again. "I'm Rod, by the way."

"Loreen Murphy." Not only was it nuts to give her last name to a total stranger, but she held out her hand like a total dork. "Nice to meet you."

He lifted her hand to his lips and kissed the back of it, keeping eye contact all along, just like Leonardo DiCaprio did with Kate Winslet in *Titanic*. "Where are you from, Loreen?"

"Is it that obvious I'm not from here?"

He laughed. "You look way too happy to be from here."

"I'm from Maryland."

"And what do you do in Maryland?"

"I'm a Realtor." And a PTA treasurer, and a mom, and a soon-to-be ex-wife and a whole lot of other easy-to-pigeonhole labels.

He looked impressed. "Keep your own hours and cream the top off every deal made. Good gig."

She shrugged. "It's feast or famine."

"What about tonight? Is it feast or famine tonight?"

"Feast." She smiled. It really was. This letting-go stuff was pretty good. Maybe Robert had been right. A little bit, anyway. "Tonight, it's all feast."

Rod chuckled charmingly and gave an approving nod. "Are you looking for company tonight, Loreen?"

For a crazy moment she was ten years younger, one impending divorce lighter, and free to be a flirt. It felt *awesome*. She took another sip of her drink. "Well, I don't know. Are you offering?"

"As a matter of fact, Loreen, yes. I am."

She could not *believe* this gorgeous hunk of man was coming on to her! This *never* happened at home!

Take that, Robert.

Just last week Jacob had told Loreen that Robert had a girlfriend who came over for dinner.

So, with that little piece of icky news in mind, what the hell? Rod was a gift from God as far as she was concerned. As for why he would be interested in her—well, why not? No, she wasn't a supermodel, but she wasn't a dog either. In her day, plenty of guys had come on to her. It hadn't happened for a while now, but maybe this was the first time she'd been relaxed enough—and anonymous enough—to put out an *available* vibe.

"Sounds good to me," she said with a laugh. Females all around them were looking on with clear envy, and Loreen liked it. "So you can tell all these other women you are *taken*."

A nod. "Consider it done."

She'd worried he wouldn't get the joke and would think she was seriously jealous already, so she was glad for his response. "Well, I'm honored."

Robert had moved on. So would she.

Even if it was for only a few minutes.

"The honor is mine." Rod lifted a perfect brow over one pale blue eye. Actually, his brows were so perfect that she concluded he had to wax them, which was a little troubling. But then again, one look at his whip of a smile and it didn't matter anymore. "Do you like champagne, Loreen?"

"Depends what you mean by champagne. I've never had the good stuff." It was true. Her experience was limited to the sort that tasted like melted Popsicles and could be used to sweeten coffee. But tonight she'd had enough tequila to lubricate her confidence and fuel her awkward flirting. "Does it come with the deal, Mr. Rod?"

"Of course, if you like. The menu is always à la carte." He signaled the bartended with one breezy motion and said to him, "Piper." Then he turned back to Loreen. "So you're a fine champagne virgin. And I get to break you in."

She smiled. In fact, she damn near trilled. "Be gentle with me."

"Whatever you like." He smiled, and the bartender set two tall phallic flutes on the bar and poured bubbling gold liquid in.

"Thank you, Piper," Loreen said to him.

Rod chuckled again. "You"—he clinked his glass to hers—"are adorable."

"So are you!" she gushed, a little too enthusiastically. Then, in a misplaced effort to regain the cool dignity she was going for, she said, "For someone so young, I mean." Oh, that was dumb. Really clumsy. And it didn't seem like she was going to be able to stop herself any time soon. "How old are you anyway?"

He looked at her very seriously. "About the same age as you, I'd guess. I'm twenty-four."

"Smooth, Rod. That was really smooth."

He looked at her guilelessly. "What do you mean?"

"I'm *not* twenty-four," she said, downing the rest of her champagne. "And you know it."

"Twenty-three?" he guessed, then furrowed his brow in mock consternation. "Younger? Tell me I didn't just buy a drink for an underage Lolita."

"You're good. You're really good." Loreen smiled and took a sip of the champagne. It was sort of blah as wine went. Like unsweetened ginger ale. But, hey, if this was the drink for celebrations, she'd go for it, because *this* was a celebration. "This is great."

He gave a nod and looked deeply into her eyes. "So what are we going to do next? Or should I ask *when*?"

It would have been the perfect opportunity to say something sophisticated and witty, but apparently Myrna Loy wasn't available for channeling right then. "I—I'm . . . not sure."

"Obviously we could use some privacy."

Mmmm. His voice could melt butter.

As a matter of fact, his voice—or maybe his long-lashed baby blues or perhaps that shiny mop of dark hair that her fingers were just *itching* to run through—*was* melting something deep in Loreen's long-chilly nether regions.

And he wanted to be *alone* with her!

This was a night she'd *never* forget.

"Privacy would be nice," she said, then giggled as the champagne bubbles actually tickled her nose, just like all the bimbos in old movies said it did.

"I have a room upstairs unless . . . you'd prefer your room?"

She pictured meeting the babysitter and all the kids at the door and laughed. "Let's go to your room."

"Of course." He held a hand out and helped her off her stool. "Send the bottle up, please," he said to the bartender.

"You and Piper seem to know each other."

He looked puzzled for a second, then smiled. "There you go again. Yeah, Roger and I have worked here for a long time."

"Ah." She hadn't realized Rod worked there, but she'd already said so many dumb things that she didn't want to add to it by asking what he did, just in case it was somehow obvious. "How long have you worked here?"

"The hotel or the town?"

"Um . . . I . . ." She didn't really care either way. "The hotel."

"Oh, about a year and a half now."

Only a twenty-four year old could think that was a long time. "You like it?"

"It allows me to meet beautiful women like *you.* How could I not love it?"

She could have gotten stuck on that plural—beautiful *women*—but since this wasn't a real relationship in any sense of the word, she let it slide and just took the compliment. "You're quite the flatterer."

"No, I mean it." He stopped her and looked her in the eye. "Sincerely."

She felt the heat climb into her cheeks. "Thanks."

He pushed the elevator button, and they glided upward to a suite on the top floor. One entire wall consisted of windows that overlooked the aurora borealis–like glow of the Las Vegas strip. It was enchanting.

Loreen was standing in front of the window, looking for the big guitar they always showed in movies, when Rod came up behind her and put his arms around her. "Like it?"

"I love it. I could look at this view every night for the rest of my life." As soon as she said the words, Loreen had the horrible feeling that maybe this handsome stranger was a serial killer who was about to murder her and, though he would be the only one to know, her final words would echo ironically through time.

There was a knock at the door, and Rod went to get it, murmured some things, and came back into the room with an ice bucket, a bottle, and two champagne flutes.

As he poured the champagne, Loreen noticed the label: piperheidsieck. Oh, shit. Rod hadn't been calling the *bartender* Piper; he'd been asking for the champagne.

But then, like an idiot, she'd proceeded to call the guy "Piper" and, worse, feel really clever doing so.

Fortunately, Rod seemed to think she was joking, and even said she was adorable. So . . . she'd go with that.

"That was nice of Piper to send up some more Piper," she said, knowing it was pathetic, but at the same time at a complete loss about what else to say.

Rod moved over to Loreen and smoothly took the glass from her hand and set it on the end table by the sofa. "I can't wait any longer to do this," he said, then lowered his mouth down onto hers.

He didn't give her time to work up some nervousness. He just went for it.

Never—*never*—had she been kissed like this. Everything in her tingled, from her head right down her spine and into the center of her being. Rod undressed her slowly, so slowly that even the fabric running across her skin felt like a caress.

He was an expert at touching a woman, pushing buttons she didn't even know she had, bringing her to the crest of ecstasy over and over again, then backing away just long enough to make her nearly scream with need.

By the time he finally got down to business, she wanted it more than she'd ever wanted anything in her life.

She couldn't say how long it lasted. Maybe an hour, maybe five, but the time Loreen spent with Rod was so intense that his abrupt withdrawal at the end of it came as a shock.

"Oh, shit."

It wasn't exactly the romantic conclusion she was expecting. "What's wrong?"

"The fucking rubber broke."

"What?"

"I said the *fucking—rubber—broke.*" Suddenly Rod sounded like a seven-year-old who'd struck out at bat.

So much for ol' Rico Suave.

But Loreen's first reaction was one of relief. The *"Oh, shit"* wasn't because he'd just realized what he'd done, with whom, and regretted it. "The rubber broke?" she echoed, trying to get a grasp on what he was *actually* saying.

"Yeah." He threw up his hands. "Fuck."

She swallowed the urge to say, *I believe we just did,* and instead asked, "Are you sure?"

He nodded. "I've done this enough to know when there's a problem, and *this* is a problem."

A moment of heavy silence dropped between them.

"Have you been tested?" Loreen asked, her former relief replaced rapidly by panic as she realized the implications. She'd just had sex with a stranger and the condom had broken, spilling all kinds of potential diseases and bacteria right into her most vulnerable parts. Short of slashing open her wrist and rubbing it on a petri dish, she couldn't do something more bacterially dangerous.

"I'm tested every month," Rod said. "What about you?"

"I haven't had sex in about a year."

He nodded like that was unsurprising. "Yeah. But have you been tested?"

That *yeah* was insulting. "My doctor did that test," she said, "along with every other medical test, last year when I couldn't shake the flu. It was negative."

His shoulders lowered slightly with relief.

She waited a moment, then, when he didn't volunteer the information, prompted him with, "And *your* tests?"

He waved the question away like it was silly. "Negative on all counts. We have a really good doctor here who checks us out really thoroughly."

"Heck of a medical plan you have."

"It's the law." He shrugged. "What about pregnancy? Are you on anything?"

For the past year? On the remote chance that she'd have sex with someone without taking the time to plan? Not likely. Good thing she couldn't have more kids. "After my son was born, I had my tubes tied," she lied. It was easier than explaining that she just wasn't able to get pregnant, that a couple of years of trying with Robert had proved that beyond a doubt, and that it made her hang on to her only son's childhood like it was a life raft in the ocean.

"Good thing." Rod gave a dry laugh. "I'm sure the last thing you need is a pregnancy."

"Right," she agreed, because she was polite. But . . . what did he mean by that? The last thing *she* needed? Even though it was true, what was it about his words that sounded distinctly detached? No, they didn't know each other and no, she *definitely* wasn't going to get pregnant from this, but still . . . What a dick.

Nah, she was probably reading way too much into this. She'd had a weird night—a one-night stand! The first time in her life! That was so unlike her. And she was still out even though it was—she looked for the green glow of the digital clock by the bedside—11:36 p.m.

Good Lord, she had to leave. Everyone was probably wondering where she'd disappeared to.

"I've got to run," she said, meaning it literally. She threw back the sheets and started running around the darkened room, collecting her clothes.

"Are you sure? I'm still available for a few hours. And I had a great time with you," Rod said, and back was the mellow sexy tone that had drawn her to him in the first place. Then he grabbed her wrist, pulled her to him, and kissed her deeply. If it weren't for the time, she would have fallen right back into bed with him.

"I did, too," she said, wishing she could come up with something more clever—more *memorable*—than mere agreement.

"Maybe next time, then." He ran his hands down her back, sending tingles along the trail of his touch.

"I don't come here often," she said to him as she pulled back. She had to get dressed and leave, no matter how great his hands felt on her.

"Well, if you do," Rod said, pulling up his jeans and turning to her with the button tantalizingly undone, "you know where you can find me."

She nodded and gave a laugh. "At the bar downstairs?" She was joking.

He nodded. He was not joking. "Unless I'm already working."

"Oh." Okay, so he hung out at the bar all the time? And he could say, absolutely, that he'd be there at some nebulous time in the future?

Something here wasn't adding up.

"You can just leave the money on the dresser, sweetheart." He was buttoning his shirt, and didn't have so much as a *hint* of a smile when he said it.

But Loreen laughed. Because . . . it had to be a joke.

"Shouldn't that be my line?" She was trying to keep the mood light, but still . . . *ew.* She didn't like this joke. It wasn't really funny, no matter who said it.

Rod looked at her, confused. "I'm sorry?"

"Oh, nothing, I was just kidding." *Too.*

Right?

He gave a vague smile and gestured with a hand that suddenly seemed a little limp. Something less masculine than it had seemed just a couple of hours before. "Yeah. So, the dresser is right over there." He gestured and went into the bathroom. "And tag on a hundred and forty for the champagne."

Oh, God. He wasn't kidding. He was . . . She'd just . . . Oh, God, she'd just hired a male prostitute. How the hell had this happened? She thought back over their conversation, trying to figure out just where the breakdown in communications had occurred.

Are you looking for company tonight, Loreen?

What had she said? Oh. *Are you offering?* An innocent question. Flirty. Not really a proposition.

Yes, as a matter of fact, I am.

What an *idiot*! How had she not seen this before?

"Loreen?"

She snapped back to attention. "Yes?"

"Is something wrong?"

"No!" She said it too quick. "I was just . . . I just realized we didn't discuss . . ."

He narrowed his eyes at her. Suddenly he didn't look so sexy. "We didn't discuss what, Loreen?"

"Price." It sounded like a question. From a tiny little person. She could barely eke the word out.

His brow relaxed fractionally. "Right. When you didn't ask, I thought you were a regular, and that for some reason I just didn't remember you."

Great. Not only had the whole flattery thing been a game, but he actually thought she seemed like someone who *regularly paid for sex.*

From *him.*

The guy actually thought he'd fucked her before—perhaps more than once—and forgotten. And he thought that didn't really matter. Like . . . her feelings wouldn't be hurt?

She felt sick. "No," she said coolly. So much for looking at her like she was a swimsuit model. But it was stupid to be upset with a prostitute for not telling little white lies to be polite. This was all so confusing.

She had to get out of here.

"It's one g." He put Rembrandt Extra Whitening on his toothbrush and started to brush vigorously, presumably to remove all DNA traces of Loreen so he'd be fresh and clean for the next pathetic loser who came along.

"I'm sorry, I don't . . . How much is that?"

He spit a foamy toothpaste mess into the sink, then swished water in his mouth and spit again. Less attractive by the second. "A thousand dollars," he said, taking the hand towel from the chrome rack and blotting his face. "Plus the champagne, like I said."

Her heart leapt into her throat. A *thousand* dollars.

He'd said these three hours were going to be *$333 an hour*. She hadn't had a therapeutic massage since Mother's Day six years ago because she couldn't pay the sixty bucks an hour. There was no way she was going to have to pay $333 an hour, times three, for having *sex* with this guy. Good lord, she'd even gone down on *him*.

He *had* to be kidding.

But this wasn't a guy who was into kidding around.

He was a businessman.

And somehow she had to come up with a thousand bucks *quick*.